Praise for *Second Shot*

"Sharp as an assassin's bullet, *Second Shot* by Cindy Dees is a must-read for every spy novel enthusiast out there! I couldn't put it down!"
—**Lisa Jackson,** *New York Times* **and** *USA Today* **bestselling author**

"A pitch-perfect adventure, filled with nuance and dire exploits. Take a breath, hang on, and enjoy the ride with this smart and clever heroine."
—**Steve Berry,** *New York Times* **bestselling author**

"A breathless thrill ride from the explosive opening scene, *Second Shot* delivers both high action and a twisted murder mystery. Helen Warwick is a refreshingly mature heroine who uses her extensive experience and sharp wits to turn the tables on all who come gunning for her. Definitely a series to watch!"
—**Sara Driscoll, author of the FBI K-9s series**

"CIA assassin Helen Warwick's hopes to ease into retirement are dashed when she's pulled back into the business. . . . This will mainly appeal to readers who like their thrillers light."
—***Publishers Weekly***

"What a fabulous start to a new series! Cindy Dees has created an exciting action-packed and suspenseful thriller with a more mature main character. This fantastic novel is shocking, emotionally charged, and pulse-pounding. Readers who enjoy action thrillers and espionage thrillers will likely enjoy this book."
—***Mystery & Suspense Magazine***

"You won't want to stop reading *Second Shot* once you start. It's heart-stopping, ironic, humorous, and entirely believable. . . . I can't wait for the next Helen Warwick thriller."
—***Criminal Element***

"Cindy Dees has crafted a highly entertaining tale that's part espionage thriller and part murder mystery with an incredibly deadly quinquagenarian woman at the center of it all. *Second Shot* is fascinating and irresistible!"
—**Steve Netter,** *Best Thriller Books*

The Helen Warwick Thrillers
by Cindy Dees

Second Shot

Double Tap

DOUBLE TAP

CINDY DEES

KENSINGTON
PUBLISHING CORP.

www.kensingtonbooks.com

KENSINGTON BOOKS are published by

Kensington Publishing Corp.
900 Third Avenue
New York, NY 10022

All Kensington titles, imprints, and distributed lines are available at special quantity discounts for bulk purchases for sales promotion, premiums, fundraising, educational, or institutional use.

Special book excerpts or customized printings can also be created to fit specific needs. For details, write or phone the office of the Kensington Special Sales Manager: Attn. Special Sales Department, Kensington Publishing Corp., 900 Third Ave., New York, NY 10022. Phone: 1-800-221-2647.

Library of Congress Card Catalogue Number: 2023952662

ISBN-13: 978-1-4967-3978-0

First Kensington Hardcover Edition: June 2024

ISBN-13: 978-1-4967-3979-7 (ebook)

10 9 8 7 6 5 4 3 2 1

Printed in the United States of America

DOUBLE
TAP

CHAPTER 1

HELEN WARWICK SQUINTED AGAINST THE GLARE OF SPOTLIGHTS pointing at the stage. She couldn't see a thing past them. Not the reporters she knew to be out there nor the friends and family here to lend support.

She viscerally hated standing in front of a crowd like this, on display like some prize cow. She craved the shadows. Invisibility. Seeing but not seen. Yet here she was.

Being exposed was bad enough, but being blind was even worse. It went against every fiber in her hunter's soul to be so exposed, so helpless to spot an incoming threat and protect herself.

Her son, Mitch, stood at a podium center stage with his wife, Nancy, at his right elbow. Her other two children—middle child Peter and his husband, Liang, and her youngest, Jayne—lined up behind Mitch. Her husband, Gray, the lucky dog, was in South America trying to save the rain forest and had dodged this miserable event.

On the other end of the line of family was her mother, Constance Stapleton. It was just as well that they were on opposite ends of the stage. Her indomitable mother, veteran of dozens of Henry Stapleton's runs for Congress, would've told her to stop fidgeting and smile for the cameras.

With a sigh, Helen pasted a fake smile on her face and suppressed an urge to tug at the collar of her silk blouse. She felt the caked-on stage makeup cracking on her skin and dialed down the smile a little. No need to add more wrinkles to her face than she already had.

Somebody on the other side of the spotlights called out a thirty-second warning before they went live on the local news. Mitch, acting district attorney for Washington, DC, after his boss had been gunned down three months ago, was announcing his candidacy today for the permanent DA job. Hence the command appearance by the whole Warwick clan in their Sunday best at his press conference.

The heat of the lights made Helen sweat under the makeup, and the odd jumpiness she'd been feeling ramped up even more. Pressure built in her chest until she could barely breathe. Every instinct in her screamed to get out of the light or die. To *move.* Now.

Mitch would kill her if she ruined his big moment. *Must. Stand. Still.*

A drop of perspiration rolled down her temple and slid down her cheek. She tried to breathe, but her entire chest felt paralyzed. Adrenaline surged through her, making her body feel hot and cold, weak and strong, coiled to spring. She trembled from the effort of forcing herself to stand still. She couldn't do this. She couldn't stand here exposed and unable to defend herself.

Stop it. Stand still. Do. Not. Panic.

Nope. The urge was too much to control. She'd spent too many years listening to her instincts, backing out of situations where she suddenly felt as if she were lined up in somebody's crosshairs, to ignore the warning screaming in her mind.

She eased to the left edge of the raised platform erected in the middle of a much larger stage and turned sideways. She slid to the forward-most edge of the dais where she could stand beside those blasted spotlights and not in front of them any longer.

Ah, better. It took most of the remaining TV countdown for the dancing spots in front of her eyes to clear. But as the stage manager held up his fingers and flashed three, two, one, she could see again.

Mitch had always been a handsome boy, and he was in his element now, glowing with pride and excitement. Even Nancy looked especially good today. Normally, the girl was so bland in temperament and appearance that Helen found her gaze sliding over her daughter-in-law and barely noticing her. But as Nancy stood dutifully at Mitch's right elbow, slender and elegant, Helen began to understand why Mitch always said she was the perfect political wife. She was attractive to look at but did nothing to pull the spotlight off him.

Mitch launched into his declaration speech, opening with a joke that made the reporters crowding the flat orchestra area below and in front of the stage chuckle. He flashed one last charming smile and started into the meat of his speech about what he planned to do to address crime and corruption as the new district attorney.

Helen tuned out. She'd heard her father deliver so many campaign speeches over the years that all stump talks blended together in her head—pretty oratory, catchy sound bites, and empty promises.

She tried to be subtle in searching for the source of her panic attack, gazing out across the theater with that stupid smile still pasted on her face. It was starting to make her cheeks ache.

Attached to a swanky hotel and built in the Gilded Age, this theater was pretty in a gaudy, self-important way. Not her taste. Way too many nooks, crannies, and columns for a sniper to hide behind. Not to mention a thousand sight lines to the middle of the stage, exactly where Mitch stood. Methodically, she catalogued where she would and wouldn't set up shop to take out a target.

There weren't really any good angles to target a person standing behind a podium from the floor of the theater. The VIP boxes lining the sides of the space above the orchestra level were too cliché. Although this wasn't the Ford Theatre, Lincoln's assassination was still a stain that this town's theaters bore with a certain shame. Plus there would only be a single narrow hallway to access the boxes or leave them in a hurry. Too much chance of getting trapped by hotel security.

Maybe the balcony stretching across the back of the space? She could lie on her stomach behind the last row of seats near an exit door. Use the seats for cover and shoot around the end of them. Egress would be a breeze. Out the exit and straight down a wide staircase into the usually crowded hotel lobby, where she could blend in and simply walk out the front door—

Something flickered at the edge of her vision, and her attention snapped back to Mitch. Or rather to the brilliantly lit space directly in front of him. The spotlights were so bright that individual motes of dust visibly floated in the beams of light.

There it was again. A flicker of lime green. If this were a warm summer evening, she would attribute it to a lightning bug looking for a mate.

But this was no backyard barbecue, and that flash of green no innocent insect.

Her gut shouted a warning even as her brain identified what she was seeing.

Surely not.

But a little voice in the back of her head began chanting fearfully, *No, no, no, no, no . . .*

Not here. Please, no. Not her family. Not her child . . .

She had to be wrong.

But what if she was right? What if that was a targeting beam from a laser gun sight? In the past few years, green and blue lasers had supplanted red ones as the preferred colors in daylight conditions.

She reached for her purse and the handgun she always kept inside, then swore under her breath as she recalled too late that Nancy and Constance had insisted she leave her purse with theirs on a table backstage. Frantically, she looked around the theater in search of the threat. She had no way to fight back. No way to protect her children.

That laser targeting beam had been slightly above Mitch's head. It was coming from the balcony, then. She looked up at the second-story protrusion and its dozen rows of upholstered seats. The whole balcony was dark, shrouded in shadows. No way to spot a shooter up there without specialized night optical equipment, even if she could make it to her own weapon in time to suppress the would-be killer's fire.

Her gaze snapped back to Mitch.

The laser beam flashed again, steadily this time. From her vantage point to the side of the stage, she saw the tiny green dot flash on his chest and then rise toward his face. Time stopped as she lurched forward.

Not Mitch.

Not my baby.

She bolted forward with speed born of a mother's terror, a special speed of pure panic. The green dot landed on the spot between Mitch's eyebrows. It wavered, then steadied as Helen launched herself airborne, leaping at her son with the intent to take the bullet for him.

Must get between my boy and that laser.

She slammed into her muscular son, who had multiple inches on her in height. Mitch staggered into Nancy, and all three of them went down in a pile just as a quiet, oh-so-familiar spit sounded beneath the exclamations of surprise from the crowd. The accompanying *whoosh* of disturbed air as a round flew past—close—made her blood freeze in her veins.

Time resumed its course, and more shocked cries erupted around them.

"Are you okay?" she asked Mitch urgently from a range of about six inches.

"What the hell, Mom?" he demanded.

"Someone tried to kill you," she grunted, winded by falling that hard. "You two stay behind the podium. I'm going after the shooter. *Stay down.*"

She rolled off Mitch, untangled her legs from Nancy's, and pushed clumsily to her feet. God, she hated tight skirts and high heels. She never wore them in the field for this exact reason. She ran awkwardly in the stupid stilettos to the far edge of the stage and the table with her purse. Her hair had come out of its carefully coifed granny bun and tangled around her face.

Someone tried to kill my son.

That truth roared through her like a wildfire and, where it passed through, left blackened certainty in her heart that this was somehow her fault.

She grabbed her bag and ran for the steps at the side of stage leading down to the floor of the theater, reaching inside the bag to grip her Ruger SR40c, a compact but powerful handgun. The shooter would race down the stairs to the lobby any second. She had to get there first. Spot the shooter and follow him or her. Take them out. Nobody shot at her boy and lived.

A strong hand grabbed her arm, spinning her partway around. "Have you *lost your mind?*" her mother hissed.

"A gunshot. At Mitch. Have to go—" She yanked her arm free from her mother's grip and bolted forward. Except as she emerged from behind the heavy velvet curtains onto the stage itself, she abruptly saw hundreds of eyes riveted on her in avid interest.

The press. All those video cameras. No way could she pull out a highly customized shooter's weapon and flash it in front of all these people. Even she wasn't that suicidal. Thirty years of iron discipline, of always—*always*—maintaining her cover, belatedly kicked in. Reluctantly, she let go of the pistol still in her purse and drew out her empty hand.

A rectangle of light up on the balcony flashed and then disappeared. The shooter was getting away. Swearing luridly under her breath, she skidded to a stop.

She wouldn't catch the shooter now if she tried. And if she sprinted out of here, it would no doubt make the evening news. Supremely frustrated, she glared at everyone and no one in particular.

"Someone just tried to shoot my son," she said grimly.

Except it was just as likely the shooter was her enemy and not his. Not that she dared to say those words to the press. Or to Mitch, for that matter.

An excited buzz went up. The more savvy reporters in the

bunch, likely the ones with combat experience, ducked away from the glare of the lights and looked over their shoulders warily.

A pair of hotel security guards aggressively stepped out of the wings of the stage, and one of them said, "Ma'am, nobody shot at your son."

Irrationally enraged, she glared at him. "Oh, yeah? Let's go look for the bullet I heard fly over our heads." She pointed at the other one. "You. Do your job and protect my family. Get my son and his wife under cover. *Now.*"

One of the men peeled off to where Mitch and Nancy crouched behind the podium.

Still furious, she stomped for the back of the stage, glaring the other security guard into following her. She glanced over her shoulder to track the rough trajectory of the bullet from balcony to podium to back here.

"Do you have a flashlight?" she asked the dubious guy following her.

He dug a small penlight out of his pocket and handed it to her.

It took a minute, and the hole was lower than she'd expected— the shooter must've rested his weapon on the back of the last row of seats in the balcony instead of shooting around them from the floor the way she would've—but she found the finger-sized round hole in a wood panel. She felt the hole, and sure enough, its margin was still warm to the touch.

Someone tried to kill my son.

This time, when the wildfire of panic passed, steely determination to find the shooter and take him out rolled through her. Nobody messed with her family and walked away from it alive.

The security guy's eyes widened as he, too, touched the hole and felt the heat. He pulled out a cell phone to talk urgently into it.

"The shooter's long gone," she told him in disgust. "Your people won't find him. But I would like to take a look at the security footage of the hotel lobby for the past few minutes."

"That's a job for the police, ma'am."

She rolled her eyes. Sometimes it purely sucked being a woman of a certain age. The worst part of getting older was that nobody took her seriously anymore. Most of the time it was the perfect cover. But now and then it was a huge pain in the butt.

"Do me a favor," she asked the guard. "Go out there and tell the press I'm not crazy."

"I've got to clear the room anyway," he said officiously. "We need to evacuate the theater."

"Maybe, instead of ushering my son out into the lobby where the shooter could be waiting to try again, you should keep him and everyone else inside the theater until you know the shooter has cleared out of the hotel?" she suggested gently.

The guy shot her an irritated look. Didn't like being told how to do his job, did he? Tough. She'd forgotten more about how assassins operated than he would ever dream of knowing.

The guard stepped forward to the podium and said into the microphone, "We've had a security incident and need all of you to stay here until we clear the hotel."

Skirting the back of the stage as far from the spotlights as she could go, she made her way across the stage to the other side where Mitch and Nancy were embracing tightly.

"Are you two okay?" Helen asked them. "I'm sorry I had to knock you down."

"Why?" Nancy demanded in a rare outburst of anger. "Why do you always ruin everything?"

Helen sighed. "I saw a laser gun sight trained on Mitch. I thought it might be a good idea to get between him and the shooter."

Mitch stared at her over his wife's head. "You were trying to jump in front of me?" he asked blankly. "Take a bullet for me?"

"Yes, dear. It's what mothers do."

"Not regular mothers," he snapped.

"Well, this one protects her children with her life," she snapped back. "And it might be nice if my children showed a little gratitude from time to time. I know I was a terrible mother when you kids were little, but I'm doing my best to make up for all the times I wasn't there for you."

"You didn't have to jump in front of me," he said more mildly.

"Yes, Mitchell, I did. You'll always be my baby boy. No one was shooting you on my watch."

"We don't even know there was a laser. Or a gun," Nancy said peevishly.

"Actually, the security guard and I found a bullet hole in the back of the stage just now. The wood around the edge of the hole was still warm. Someone did, indeed, take a shot at Mitch."

"Ohmigod!" Nancy gasped. But even in her distress, the girl kept her voice down and didn't draw attention or cause a scene. Helen didn't know who had trained her to be a political wife, but whoever had done it had been darned good at it.

Mitch blurted, "We need to get out of here—"

Helen cut him off. "We *need* to stay put. The shooter has undoubtedly fled by now. This is the one place he or she won't be. After the hotel is cleared, we'll have the security guards, and the police, who I expect are en route to the hotel, move you out to a car and get you home."

"At least it'll ensure that my announcement makes the evening news," Mitch said pragmatically.

"Really? Someone tries to kill you and all you're thinking about is the publicity it'll get you?" Helen demanded.

Mitch shrugged.

Politicians. They were all the same. Annoyed, she asked, "Who wants to kill you? Have you received any threats recently?"

"You do know what my job is, don't you?" he replied dryly. "I get threats every day, and I put criminals in jail all the time. The list of my enemies would fill a phone book."

She sighed. He was not wrong. "I'll speak with the police. Arrange full-time protection for you. And I know a few guys who've gone into private security. I'll give you the names of the very best—"

"I can take care of it, Mom. Don't you worry about it."

Lord, she hated that placating tone he took with her.

"I can help, Mitch—"

"I'll let you know when I need help." His voice was firm.

"Fine," she added, grumbling under her breath, "but if you die, it's on your head."

Even as she turned away in disgust, though, she knew that wasn't true. No way could she sit by and do nothing if someone was out to kill her child.

CHAPTER 2

*I*T TOOK LONGER FOR THE SECURITY TEAM TO CLEAR THE HOTEL than she'd expected, and Helen was antsy as she waited for the all clear. She wanted to take a look at the balcony for herself. Check out the shooter's nest. Get a feel for the style of shooter she was up against. Was he a pro? An angry amateur? Sloppy? Obsessively neat?

The press and guests at Mitch's announcement milled around on the floor of the theater, and Constance imperiously signaled Helen to come down from the stage and circulate among the potential supporters and donors.

Ugh. She knew how this game was played, but that didn't mean she had to like it. Now was the moment for damage control. Spinning the narrative away from "a DA so controversial that people were trying to kill him" to something like "courageous young attorney stands up to crime and is willing to risk his life to uphold the law."

She shook hands and answered lame questions, saying modestly that she'd had no intention of being a hero. She added breathlessly that when she'd seen that laser dot land on her son, she'd just jumped for Mitch, acting totally on instinct. It was a mom thing, apparently. She threw in a little hand wringing and pearl clutching for good measure and prayed they bought her act.

For the most part, the reporters seemed to swallow her line of bull. Which privately amused her. Seriously, how many middle-aged housewives knew on sight what a laser designator looked like? Thankfully, nobody thought to ask her that question.

She'd made one full circuit of the theater—thankfully, the positive spin on the shooting seemed to be taking hold—and was girding herself to make another circuit when a hand touched her elbow purposefully from behind.

A low male voice said from the shadows, "Don't turn around. I need you to follow me."

"Why?" she muttered, not moving her lips.

"Someone needs to speak with you. If you want to know what happened here, back up behind the curtain and slip through under the stage access door."

Oh, she bloody well did want to know what had happened. Somebody was going to pay for taking a shot at her kid.

The fingers fell away from her elbow, and the voice fell silent. Moving casually so as not to draw attention to herself, she turned around. Nobody was there. She peered behind the fall of heavy velvet hanging to the floor. Nobody was there. But the faint outline of a hidden door cut into the paneled and painted wall was visible behind the curtain.

Looking around to be sure nobody was watching her, she reached into her purse to grip the pistol inside, pushed on the door, ducked through its low opening, and slipped into the darkness. She shut the door and leaned her back against it, waiting tensely for her eyes to adapt to this inky blackness.

A flashlight lit a circle of grimy floor in front of her. "Follow me," the man murmured.

This was insanity. He could be leading her into a trap. Heck, he could be the shooter. But her instincts weren't sending her any more urgent warnings, and the guy turned away from her, giving her his back.

Worst case, she could shoot this guy through the leather of her purse. Although she hated the idea of destroying another beautiful designer purse so soon after she'd destroyed her last one.

The man pointed his flashlight at the floor behind him, lighting a path for her to pick her way over thick ropes, electrical cables, and a canvas tarp. If he was a would-be killer, he was a polite one.

A second low door opened in front of him, and her guide ducked out into a well-lit, full-height hallway. It looked like a service corridor for the hotel, with a tall rack of folded bath towels parked along a wall.

The man was muscular. Short hair. His suit fit well and was perfectly neat. She knew the type so very well. This guy was government all the way. It only remained to be seen which alphabet agency he worked for. His hair was short enough for the FBI, but the suit—it was expensive enough for the CIA.

He moved swiftly down the hall, and she had to hurry in her stupidly tight skirt and high heels to keep up with him. She would be twice damned if she complained about his speed, however. They reached a steel exit door, and he threw it open. Daylight flooded in. She smoothed her hair as best she could and stepped out into a rather grungy alley.

A sleek black town car was parked only a few feet away, and her escort was already reaching for the back door handle. He swept the door open and gestured for her to get in.

As if. She never got into an unidentified car with strangers.

She did, however, move cautiously out of reach of the big guy and bend down slightly to peer inside, all the while keeping her pistol inside her purse trained on the man holding the door. One aggressive move in her direction—a mere flinch to suggest he might try to shove her into the car—and she was turning him into Swiss cheese.

"Hello, Helen. Thanks for coming out to speak with me."

She straightened in exasperation. "Oh, for the love of Mike, James. Why didn't you just text me and ask me to come out here? Why all this secrecy and sneaking around? I nearly shot your thug here."

The thug in question scowled at her. "I didn't say or do anything threatening!"

"Other than covertly pull me out of a crowded room minutes after someone tried to shoot my son." Rolling her eyes, she turned sideways to slide into the Town Car. She prayed her skirt wouldn't twist so badly around her legs that she was paralyzed once inside.

It did. Irked that she couldn't politely lift up her rear end and yank the stupid thing back into place, she resigned herself to being immensely uncomfortable for the duration of this conversation.

James Wagner, the director of Central Intelligence, opened his mouth to speak, but she cut him off. "Did you order a hit on my son?"

His eyes popped wide open in what looked like genuine surprise. However, the man was a consummate actor. She wasn't about to believe him because of that wide-eyed look.

"Why on earth would I order your son sanctioned?" James blurted.

"I don't know. You tell me."

"No, Helen. I did not order a hit on Mitchell nor on any of your other children. I want you to come back to work for me, not go to war with me." He snorted to emphasize his point.

It was a good point. She would, indeed, go to war with anyone who messed with her family. And anyone who'd known her more than two minutes would be fully aware of that.

If not James and his merry band of murderers, then who? Who wanted to kill Mitch? Her mind raced with possibilities. She had to talk to her son—

James interrupted her train of thought with, "Don't make me ask you, Helen. You know why I'm here."

She leaned back, arms crossed. "You're the man who forced me out of the agency. Why would I come back to work for you?"

His gaze narrowed. "Because I need you."

She pursed her lips. After their last meeting, the one wherein he'd explained she was too old to be a hired gun for the CIA any longer, she'd said a few rather sharp things to him in return.

Sharp enough that she'd been fairly sure this day would never come.

"I'm retired, James. Retired. It means having left one's job and ceased to work."

He exhaled hard. That was the same sound her husband made when he was expressing long-suffering exasperation with her.

"As I recall," she drawled, "you made it clear the last time we spoke that you would work with me again on a cold day in hell."

James huffed again, this time in definite irritation.

Not her problem. She had no reason to make this conversation any easier for him than she cared to. And she didn't care one iota to help him.

"Fine," he bit out. "Hell has frozen over."

"Has it, now?" Against her will, a flicker of interest tickled her breastbone. No! She was not getting sucked back into that world! She'd been lucky to make it out alive in the first place, and she'd been doubly lucky to survive a gambit by past enemies to take her out after the CIA removed its mantle of protection from her last winter.

She was not going back. Ever. She'd promised herself that, and more to the point, she'd promised her husband she was done.

Wagner rolled his eyes. She hoped he was truly, deeply hating every moment of having to grovel like this.

"It's snowing in Hades as we speak, Helen. I need your help. I need to reactivate you."

She tilted her head to study him. "Or else what?"

"There's no 'or else.' I need you back. That's all."

"There's always an 'or else,' James."

Another theatrical huff that privately amused her. He must've been quite the drama queen as a child. "I didn't want to have to use it," he said earnestly. "But there is a file. On your son. The one running for DA."

Of course, there was. The bastards.

"Is it real?" she snapped. Lord knew, the agency had the resources to fake some terrible scandal in Mitch's past guaranteed to tank his political aspirations. It was exactly the sort of dirty trick the CIA excelled at.

Wagner looked her in the eye. "Yes, it's real."

Well, fudge. He didn't give her a single tell of a lie. He probably did have a file on Mitch. And whatever was in it was damaging enough that Wagner thought it would bring her to heel.

Of course, there was also the fact that the agency's nearly limitless resources could come in very handy as she hunted down whoever had taken that shot at Mitch.

"Please, Helen. Your country needs you," James pleaded.

Damn it. That was the other argument without blackmail to back it up that might sway her to come out of her well-earned retirement. She hadn't been raised by a US congressman for nothing. Service to country had always ranked above all else in her life.

"What's going on?" she asked tiredly.

"I can't tell you until you agree to come back."

"Then it's been lovely seeing you again, James. You might want to lay off the sweets and carbs a little. You're going a little thick around the middle, there."

He glared coldly at her, showing her a glimpse of the steel required of any DCI.

Tired of needling him, she said, "Seriously. I've been keeping secrets for you people for thirty years. You know I won't repeat anything you say. What's going on? Talk to me."

The rigidity about his shoulders collapsed, and profound exhaustion abruptly wreathed his features. Now that she looked more closely, a certain gray cast tinged his skin. "When's the last time you got a good night's sleep?" she blurted.

"Before I took this damned job."

She waited him out, and he finally said, "That guy you shot in the woods by the barn—you know the one."

She did indeed. She and Yosef had found a man artistically crucified inside the barn in question. It had been the most sickening thing she'd ever seen. And in her line of work, she'd seen things that would make most people quail in utter revulsion.

"You know how we all thought the guy you shot was Scorpius?" Wagner asked.

"What about it?" Alarm jumped in her belly.

"Turns out it wasn't him." Again, James's gaze didn't waver.

"What?" she cried out, horrified. No! She'd killed the mole in the CIA, the same mole who'd been named by the crucified man as his killer. The mole who'd nearly managed to kill her.

Crap. Was Scorpius behind the attempt on Mitch's life today?

"The only hit we got on the dead man's identity shows him to be a contract killer known to work out of Cartagena. Probably an American. Not only can we place the dead guy in Venezuela during the last known sighting of Scorpius, but Scorpius sent a message to Moscow this week. The bastard's definitely alive. Worse, he's still active inside the agency."

She leaned back hard against the plush cushions. Every fiber in her being protested that it couldn't be true. It just couldn't. If it was, her family was in grave danger. She was in danger. And yes, her country was in danger.

She had no choice but to accept Wagner's blackmail-shrouded offer now.

But that didn't mean she had to like it.

Reluctantly, she made eye contact with Wagner. "Let me make this clear, James. I wouldn't come back to help you. I would hunt Scorpius purely to protect my family. That's all."

Wagner sagged in relief. "That's good enough for me."

"So what dirt have you got on my son?" she asked lightly. "It had better be good. In this day and age, aspiring politicians can get away with practically anything and not be ruined by scandal."

Another shrug.

Not going to tell her what he was using to coerce her into going back to work at the agency, was he? *Jerk.* He owed her at least that much, simply as a courtesy. However, James did not seem to think they'd arrived at a quid pro quo that obliged him to return any favors.

She sighed. Lord, she hated office politics. "Any idea who took that shot at Mitchell just now?"

Wagner shrugged. "My money's on Scorpius. He'll come after your family to get to you."

As logical a deduction as that was, it didn't feel right when she heard it spoken aloud. Now why was that?

The obvious answer: Scorpius wouldn't have missed Mitch. He wouldn't have taken so long to line up the shot, and as soon as he'd seen her jump for her son, he'd have pulled the trigger.

Not to mention, if Scorpius wanted her dead, she'd been exposed on that stage and lit up like a deer in headlights, too. The laser designator would have been pointed at her, not Mitch.

She would also bet Scorpius planned to pull the trigger himself if and when he decided it was time for her to die. He wouldn't send a flunky to take her out. Not after she'd come so close to exposing him last winter. This thing between them was personal.

Today's shooter could've been hired by Scorpius. Except a mole like him was too good, too connected to the heavy hitters in the world of assassins, to have hired someone who would miss. Yes, she'd tackled Mitch at the moment of the shot, but a professional shooter would've taken a second shot, and a third if necessary, to finish off his or her target.

There'd been plenty of time after she'd scrambled off Mitch, as she'd run from the stage in one direction and Mitch and Nancy had fled in the other, for a trained assassin to have taken out Mitch. One thing she knew for sure about Scorpius. He was highly efficient. He wouldn't send an amateur to do a professional's job.

Wagner was speaking again. ". . . will have someone read you in on what the team hunting Scorpius has done so far."

The cold terror knotted in her gut exploded into hot anger again, but for a different reason this time. A few months ago, she would have dutifully let Wagner drive her back to Langley or to a safe house somewhere to brief her on her next mission. She would have left her family behind like a good little employee, flown halfway around the world, and quietly killed whoever her country needed her to eliminate.

But no more. She'd turned fifty-five, and the CIA—this man

specifically—had terminated her employment and summarily kicked her to the curb. She was done being a good little soldier.

Her gaze narrowed. "Darling, I'm afraid you've made a small miscalculation."

"What's that?"

"I haven't said yes. And here's the thing. You may need me. But I don't need you."

"What about the file on your son? If he wants to stay district attorney, you need me to keep it buried."

It was her turn to do a little bluffing. "For all I know, you don't have anything on Mitch. He's planned to go into politics ever since he was a child. He's kept his nose clean—or at least knew not to get caught—for a very long time. And here's the thing, my dear boy."

James Wagner was about her age, but he'd never worked in the field. A political appointee to run the CIA, he'd never been shot at. Never been alone in a hostile country on his own and on the run. He might know how to play politics, but he didn't know how to play chicken with people like her. He was a babe in the woods in her world.

"What?" he finally blurted when she didn't continue.

"Now that I know he's alive, I can hunt Scorpius without you. I'm also confident that with my . . . unique skill set . . . I can clean up any mess my son might have made in the past."

"Scorpius is bigger than you know."

Indeed? She absorbed that with interest. Was Scorpius possibly more than one person? Not that it changed her target. Cut the head off the beast, and the body still died. She didn't need to take out an entire Scorpius team, just the shadowy figure of a man she'd glimpsed once on a cold winter's night, wearing a wool coat and an old-fashioned fedora—moments before he'd killed the one man who could identify him to her.

It had been Scorpius who sent a hit team to kill her in her middle child Peter's home, and Scorpius who almost killed her longtime handler and dear friend, Yosef Mizrah. If she had anything to say about it, Scorpius was a dead man walking. She would find him, and she *would* take him out before he harmed anyone else she loved.

"Look, Helen. We have a mutual interest in seeing Scorpius eliminated, and I have all the resources you could ever need. Let me help you help your family."

Oh, now he was taking a conciliatory tone with her? After he'd threatened Mitch's career? Problem was, James knew where to find her entire family, and he'd just unsubtly reminded her of that fact.

Worse, he knew her loved ones were her Achilles' heel. If she didn't play ball with Wagner, he could undoubtedly ruin the lives of not only Mitch but her younger children, too, maybe even go after her husband. No matter how estranged she and Grayson might be, she was still fiercely protective of the father of her children.

At the end of the day, Wagner was no less dangerous than the Russian mole he wanted her to hunt. If going after her immediate family didn't make her toe the line, he wouldn't hesitate to turn on her mother or Yosef. One by one, he would dismantle the lives of everyone close to her.

The flip side of that coin was that Scorpius could just as easily go after everyone she loved and kill them. She truly had no interest in tangling with the Russian mole again. He'd come way too close to killing her last winter. Only a fool tempted fate twice.

She'd made it out alive once. She wasn't so sure she would make it out a second time. Like it or not, she wasn't as young as she'd once been. Her reflexes weren't quite as sharp, her fitness not quite as good, her body not quite as fast to recover. Not to mention, the technology of the trade was advancing so quickly nowadays that she didn't even try to keep up with it.

Truth be told, she was ready to retire. She might give Wagner hell over how he'd gone about forcing her out, but at the end of the day, she'd enjoyed the past few months of peace and quiet. She rather liked the idea of not having to look over her shoulder constantly. And she desperately wanted to reconnect with her family before it was too late.

"Why would I work with you? I have no reason to trust you, James."

"You have no reason to distrust me."

She answered lightly, sweetly even. "Other than getting unceremoniously tossed out of the agency because a day on a calendar came and went? Other than getting no support whatsoever from the agency after I retired and a sociopath tried to kill me? Other than the agency throwing me to Russian wolves without a second thought? Why no, I have no reason at all to distrust you."

"It's policy for field operators to retire at—" he started.

She made a sharp slashing gesture with her hand, cutting him off. "A policy that obviously can be overlooked given we're sitting here right now and you're trying to bring me back into the fold."

He sighed. "I made a mistake by sidelining you. Is that what you want to hear me say?"

"I want to hear you say you'll leave me and my family alone and never darken my doorstep again."

"I can't do that. You're the only person who can help me."

She leaned back against the leather upholstery, assessing him. That was quite an admission from him. He had the entire CIA to draw from and she was the *only* one he could turn to? "My, my. You must be in quite a pickle if I'm the *only* person who can help you. Do tell."

He hit the button on his armrest to raise the soundproof, bulletproof partition between them and the driver. Given that it was already fully raised, she judged his jabbing at the button to be a nervous tic. James Wagner was scared, huh? Fascinating.

He lowered his voice. "I can't give you the details here. But I have reason to believe Scorpius is highly enough placed to cover his tracks from *everybody*."

Whoa. Only a tiny handful of senior officers at the very top of the CIA could say that. No wonder the director was panicking.

Wagner continued, "I need someone from outside the agency, someone I *know* not to be Scorpius, to find him and take his ass out."

"Is it because I'm retired or because Scorpius tried to kill me that you're convinced I'm not him?" she asked dryly.

"Both. That and we know he's referred to as a man inside the Kremlin." He added in a rush, "Helen, there is no one else I can ask this of. Everyone—literally *everyone*—at the agency is a suspect."

"What about all the other competent female officers in the agency, which I know there are hundreds or even thousands of?"

"He may have recruited other officers in-house to work for him. My female employees can't be trusted either."

"Then why not bring in the FBI or the NSA to hunt your guy?"

"Because I don't know how wide Scorpius's reach is. How deeply he might've infiltrated other branches of government."

Okay, that was alarming. "Do you think Scorpius is running a spy ring? Or a conspiracy of some kind?"

"I'm hoping you'll tell me if he is." He paused, then added in a reluctant tone, "In the interest of full disclosure, I do expect him to make a run at you when he finds out you're hunting him."

Lovely. Studying him closely, she asked bluntly, "How bad is what you've got on Mitch?"

James answered equally bluntly, "There's no statute of limitations on murder."

Murder? Mitch? Not a chance.

Sure, she could kill without batting an eyelash. But Mitch? Was he that ruthlessly ambitious? Had someone gotten in his way? Pushed the wrong button? Did her eldest son have the same ability to set aside all emotion, all moral doubt, and kill like she did?

Oh, God. Had she passed on some sort of fatal genetic flaw to him? Had she unconsciously taught him to be just like her? Was this her fault?

Psychologists had assured her more than once that she was not the least bit sociopathic. That her ability to compartmentalize her emotions was a strength in her line of work. Of course, they'd also warned her it would cause problems in her personal relationships. They had not been wrong.

She had to talk to Mitch. Find out what had happened that had made it into Wagner's file. Fix it for her son before it derailed everything he'd worked so long and hard to achieve.

"I need to get back to my son's press conference," she told Wagner.

"Will you do it, Helen? Will you come back to the CIA and hunt Scorpius for me?"

CHAPTER 3

"MOM. WHERE DID YOU DISAPPEAR TO?" MITCH GROUND OUT from behind a fake smile. "You can't do that in the middle of a press conference. Not with all these cameras rolling."

"I'm sorry, sweetheart. Something came up. I had to handle it quietly."

"What could possibly be more important than me announcing my candidacy for elected office?"

"We'll talk about it later. Smile, darling. People are staring at us. We mustn't air family dirty laundry in public, must we?"

As the words crossed her lips, Helen shuddered. How many times had she hated it as a girl when her mother said the exact same thing to her? *Smile, Helen. Look happy, Helen. Support your father, Helen. His career is everything.*

It set her teeth on edge to even contemplate becoming her mother. Constance had been the ultimate politician's wife. So much so that Helen had often wondered why her mother hadn't run for office instead of her father. Sure, her father had enjoyed his thirty years in Congress. But that had been plenty for him. Constance had always wanted more. She'd aimed for the Oval Office itself.

Honestly, Helen never had understood why her dad didn't run for president. It would have been the perfect cap to a perfect career. He'd been getting ever more prestigious congressional leadership roles, amassing more favors owed. He'd even had a giant war chest of campaign funds built up. But he'd shocked both her and Constance to their toes by abruptly, and without warning, announcing his retirement. He'd just stopped. Walked away.

Constance had been so furious she'd barely spoken to him until his death, not long after he retired. Her mother had always said the life went out of him once he was no longer in office, doing the important work of the people. She still hadn't forgiven Henry for deciding to retire without giving her a chance to talk him out of it.

Helen gazed around the auditorium, where journalists gossiped and noshed on the snacks laid out for them. Her father would have been so proud of Mitch. He would've loved knowing that the family tradition of public service was being continued.

Henry had never known what she really did, had never had any idea just how uniquely she'd served her country. He'd always been disappointed that she'd taken a menial desk job better suited to what he'd termed "a lesser person." It had been hard to take the barbs and insults from Constance and the disapproving looks from her father. But they could never know she'd been no midlevel trade representative at the Department of State.

"Where did you run off to?" Constance whispered angrily from behind Helen, startling her. "We need all hands on deck to fix this mess you made."

"Don't sneak up on me like that, Mother. You know I hate it when anyone does that." And how was this her mess? She hadn't shot at the kids.

"Do you have any idea how bad it looks when the proud mother of the candidate *bails out* in the middle of his big day?"

Helen took a deep breath and released it slowly. "I'm sorry, Mother. But I didn't bail out. A problem came up, and I slipped away to deal with it. And before you ask, everything's under control. Weren't you always the one who said it was the wife's job to work behind the scenes to make sure everything goes smoothly for the politician?"

"Mitch has Nancy to do that," Constance snapped. "You're supposed to be the sweet, saintly mother."

A crack of laughter slipped out of her before Helen could bite it back. "Mom, I'm a lot of things, but I promise you, neither sweet nor saintly is one of them."

"Then you'd better be a good actress. Because your job is, for once in your life, to be motherly"—Constance's teeth clenched, and she bit out from behind them—"and a freaking saint."

The jab hit its mark, and the old guilt and remorse surged up in her belly. She'd always wanted to be there for her kids. She'd truly tried to be a good mom. But it had been hard with all the traveling her job had required of her.

She pasted on a plastic smile and turned away from her mother rather than throttle her. She walked blindly through the crowd until a voice startled her from nearby. "Helen, how lovely to see you!"

She turned toward her mother's oldest frenemy, June Veenstra, wife of a congressman who'd come to Washington about the same time Helen's father had. June was renowned as the biggest gossip inside the Beltway. Constance swore June knew things before they happened in this town.

"Mrs. Veenstra, thank you so much for being here today," Helen gushed insincerely.

The white-haired woman murmured, "I have to say. I'm impressed your family is going back into politics after the way your father's career ended. Your mother was so brave to stand beside Henry the way she did. I don't know if I could've taken the humiliation. Getting cut out of Washington society like that . . ." June shook her head mournfully.

So there *was* an old scandal related to her father's retirement. Helen had always wondered about that. "My mother seems to have made her way back into society's good graces," Helen replied lightly to the older woman. "My family always does find a way to land on its feet."

"Well, best of luck. I do hope the press doesn't dig up any old dirt." She leaned in close and whispered, "They won't hear about it from me."

"Thank you, Mrs. Veenstra. You always were the soul of discretion." Which was a total lie. But a little sucking up couldn't hurt if the old biddy really did know where the bodies were buried.

Helen glanced across the room at her mother, who was chatting up the host of an influential weekend political show. Surely Constance knew the real scoop on Henry's political demise. Why hadn't she said anything before Mitch announced his candidacy? Did Constance judge it a nonproblem? Or was she wrong? Was it bad enough to touch Mitch all these years later?

"Mrs. Warwick, care to comment on where you disappeared to midcrisis?"

She turned around to face a young male reporter who was shoving a microphone under her nose. Her innards quailed at the cameraman behind him, pointing a shoulder-held digital video camera at her. In her line of work, one never allowed one's face to be photographed. Ever.

Retired, Helen. You're retired. These vultures can film you whenever they'd like, and it's okay. But how to act with these guys? Her mother's angry words abruptly filled her mind. *Motherly. Sweet. Saintly.*

There was no way she could be saintly at anything, but she might be able to pull off being the folksy and slightly quirky mother of the candidate.

"Tell me, young man," she said warmly, "are you married?"

"Um, yes."

"Children?"

"No, ma'am."

"Ah, that explains it," she replied, nodding sagely.

"Explains what?"

"My dear boy, when a woman who's had several children reaches a certain age, let's just say her female musculature does not have the same structural integrity it once had."

"Huh? What does that mean?" The young reporter shot her a

blank look. But the cameraman, who looked to be in his fifties, grinned beside his camera lens.

"It means I had to pee"—she looked at the reporter's name-tag—"Michael Brown of the *Washington Gazette*."

"Oh. Um, okay." He turned away, red-faced, muttering to his cameraman, "Well, that was a bust."

The back of Helen's neck tingled a warning, and she looked around the theater for the source of the feeling.

Please let it just be a hot flash coming on.

Nope. The tingle persisted, traveling across her back until her shoulders hunched with tension.

She gazed intently around the room full of people. Was Scorpius here? Or was one of his people here, watching and waiting for an opportunity to kill her?

She sighed. File on Mitch aside, she had no choice but to accept Wagner's offer. Until Scorpius was eliminated, her family could be in serious danger. No way would she stand for that. And the agency could bring resources to bear that she couldn't begin to match on her own.

The only real question was when Scorpius would come after her. Probably as soon as he heard she was running the team to find and destroy him, if she had to guess. Not that she could blame the guy. She was determined to kill him the next time they met, too.

Surely he wouldn't choose this public a venue to take her out. There were too many cameras. Too many witnesses who could help the authorities piece together what had happened and who'd done it. Who, then, had shot at Mitch?

Was this the opening salvo from Scorpius, or did Mitch have another dangerous enemy out to kill him? She had to get up in that balcony and take a look around. Except that as she glanced up at where the hotel's security and a couple of police officers milled around above her, it was clear at a glance that any evidence the shooter had left behind had either been collected and removed already . . . or totally destroyed.

She sighed. Not many beat cops knew how to examine a shooter's nest and read the details of it the way she could. But it was not to be. The balcony was already cordoned off with yellow police tape, and Mitch—or Nancy—would kill her if she went up there and made a spectacle of herself.

If only she knew why Scorpius was so set on killing her. It might help her identify who he was. At least now she would have a whole team of CIA experts to help her answer that question.

I'm coming for you, Scorpius. You're never touching my family while I still live.

CHAPTER 4

"WHAT WERE YOU *THINKING*, TAKING A SHOT AT MITCHELL WAR-wick? I told you to see to it he gets elected, not kill him!"

Subject no. 15 winced as his boss raged at him. "You did tell me to get him elected, did you not?"

He watched cautiously as his employer, code-named Zero, pulled up short. "How does trying to kill him get him elected?"

"With all due respect, sir, if I had wanted him dead, he would be dead."

Zero frowned.

Fifteen knew his employer was not prone to outbursts or even raising his voice. He also knew his boss was absolutely vicious when he did get angry.

Being careful not to come across as whiny—which Zero de-spised with a fiery, burning passion—he added placatingly, "The shooting got Warwick's press conference covered on all the local news channels as the lead story, and it even made national news. Just like that, Warwick is a star. A young, handsome hero standing up against crime so forcefully that the bad guys want him dead. He couldn't have asked for a better kickoff to his campaign."

His boss said icily, "No more shots at Mitchell Warwick. Under-stood?"

"Yes, sir." A pause. "What about his wife?"

The boss thought about that one for a few moments. "If it's

necessary to get Warwick elected, I have no objection to that. The wife and the mother-in-law aren't close."

Huh. The mother-in-law had knocked down both her son and the wife in an impressive tackle that looked aimed at both of them. He didn't voice any disagreement to Zero, however.

"But don't kill the wife. I'm not about to let you or anyone else derail the plan by bringing down some huge murder investigation on this program. Not after all these years of hard work and preparation. I won't let anything or anyone stop me now."

Chills chattered down his spine. He knew what a man about to commit violence sounded like, and this was it. Zero was wound so tight he looked ready to explode.

Speaking carefully, soothingly, Fifteen asked, "I don't see how someone taking a potshot at a local political candidate derails the—"

Zero interrupted, "Warwick's mother. She could be a problem."

"The lady who threw herself at him?" he blurted in surprise.

"Her name is Helen Warwick. Don't underestimate her."

"Um, okay."

His boss bit out, "She'll go hunting for whoever shot at her boy."

"Hunting?" he echoed, startled. "Isn't that a rather extreme reaction?"

Zero glared. "It's what I would do if someone took a shot at my kid."

Fifteen gulped. He didn't doubt it. Over the years, he'd heard a few whispers among the other team members. Rumors about grisly things the boss had done to people who crossed him.

Zero was speaking again, ". . . she catches wind of you, that could lead her to me."

"There's nothing to catch wind of regarding me. My past is completely erased. I'm a nobody."

"That alone would catch her attention," his boss snapped. He added, "She is—was—a wet-work specialist. A good one. Smart. Retired from the CIA last year." He added more to himself than to Fifteen, "A worthy opponent."

Fifteen's jaw dropped. *That sweet-looking, middle-aged mom in the pink suit?*

"Sir, if I'm going to keep the son's campaign on track and keep the mother under surveillance, I could use some help—"

Zero cut him off. "I've got the mother covered for now. I have another asset close to her. You stay on the son. But don't let the mother spot you."

Sensing that he was dismissed, he turned for the door, but Zero barked behind him. "Don't go."

He turned back around slowly. Nonthreateningly. He knew that look in his boss's eyes. He got it when the need to kill was hard upon him, too.

"I need to go out tonight," Zero said in a voice completely devoid of any human emotion.

Needed to blow off a little steam, did he? The man did look in need of a good hunt. A bloody, violent one. "Shall I run overwatch for you, sir?"

Zero nodded tersely.

"My gear's in my car." He was never without a spotter's scope, a drone with infrared and night optical cameras, and of course, a high-powered rifle.

His boss smiled, and the expression chilled Fifteen to the bone. "We won't be needing your gear. I have something more . . . hands-on . . . in mind."

Sick pleasure unfurled in his gut. He'd heard stories—whispers, really—of the things Zero did to relieve his stress. Oh, this was going to be fun.

CHAPTER 5

"*I*'M HERE TO JOIN ANDREW MIZUKI FOR DINNER," HELEN SAID PO-
litely to the doll-like hostess dressed in a pink kimono. She'd gotten a text message earlier from James Wagner asking her to meet
his second-in-command here at this high-end Japanese restaurant. Apparently, Andrew was going to brief her on the details of
her mission.

The word *mission* alarmed her. There was no mission implied
in supervising a working group doing an internal investigation of
a possible mole in the agency. Unless, of course, they wanted her
to kill Scorpius after her team found him. As much as she hated
to admit it to herself, she was afraid of the Russian mole.

The young woman replied in soft, Japanese-accented English,
"You will follow me?" and led her to a low table separated from
the main dining room by sliding rice paper and wood panels.

Helen took off her shoes outside the private dining room and
left them beside the expensive pair of men's dress shoes already
there. She stepped up onto the tatami mat-covered platform and
sank down onto the unoccupied pillow in front of a low dining
table, immensely grateful she'd worn slacks to this meeting.

Wagner couldn't afford to have Helen seen coming and going
from his office regularly to give him updates. He'd texted her to
suggest that Andrew act as an intermediary between her and the
DCI's office. *Whatever*. She expected people in the agency kept an

eye on Andrew and who he met with, too. He was too close to the crown not to be spied upon.

Quiet Japanese instrumental music played in the background. Something stringed and twangy that she found oddly soothing.

"Thanks for coming tonight," Andrew said pleasantly.

He was a good-looking man of Asian descent, settling nicely into middle age. A touch of gray at his temples lent him an air of distinction. "Thanks for seeing me," she replied.

With a smile, he laid a device about the size of a handheld tape recorder on the table beside him and pushed a button. She recognized a signal scrambler. Anyone trying to eavesdrop on them electronically would only hear static. And as long as they kept their voices down, no one on the other side of the walls should hear them either.

"I took the liberty of ordering *ichiju-sansai* for us," Andrew told her.

"One soup, three sides?" she translated.

"It's the traditional way of eating in Japan. Many small, individual servings as opposed to one large plate of food."

"Perfect," she replied, smiling. "I gather, then, that you will be reading me in to what James expects of me?"

"First, let us enjoy the fine beverages."

She nodded, pleased to get a chance to relax a bit.

"Tea or sake?" he asked. "I ordered both."

"Maybe sake afterward," she replied. "But some tea now would be lovely."

He did the honors, pouring green tea into a delicate porcelain cup for her with great solemnity, then filling his own cup with sake. They both sipped in appreciative silence.

Eventually, as she cradled the nearly empty teacup between her palms and debated asking for a refill, he said quietly, "Thanks for helping us. James is freaked out."

"Why is the director so upset?"

"We have reason to believe your target has been ordered to eliminate someone high-ranking within the agency."

"Besides me?" she blurted. "Not that I'm now or ever was high-ranking."

"Besides you," Andrew confirmed solemnly.

"And you think Scorpius will pull off this hit personally?"

"Unlikely. We expect he has passed on the assignment to one of his flunkies."

She jolted. "Scorpius definitely has flunkies, then? Wagner hinted to me that Scorpius might be a group and not a lone individual."

Andrew leaned in closer. "We believe the individual in question runs a team of some kind. Whether it's commandos, spies, some sort of conspiracy, or a network of informants inside our government, we don't know."

"That's ominous," she murmured. If she were Scorpius, she would want fully trained field operatives working for her. The kind who could make dead drops, tail suspects, conduct surveillance, and kill the odd problem person. She would want to keep her hands as clean as possible and farm out the dirty work to others.

She asked Andrew, "Are Scorpius's guys agency employees or private mercenaries?"

"Unknown."

"You don't know if your own people are working for him?" she blurted.

Andrew shrugged. "The world you black ops types operate in can be . . . murky."

"I should hope so," she snapped. "I would hate to be right out in plain sight where anyone can see me and what I do—did—for *you* types."

He dipped his chin slightly to acknowledge her barb. "Your mission is to identify not only Scorpius but also his team."

"Do you have any information at all about where I should start looking for him and this team of his?"

"Sorry, no."

She snorted. *Some help they are.* Andrew poured her another cup of tea and refilled his sake, and she sipped thoughtfully.

If she were Scorpius, she would've collected a team slowly over the years. As she met people who earned her trust, she would build loyalty to her and bring them into the inner circle gradually. Maybe find their Achilles' heel—be it money or sex or power—and exploit it to put a leash on them.

Andrew said in a low voice, "We have reason to believe Scorpius's people may be gearing up to do something dramatic."

"Like what?" she demanded. "Are we talking some sort of attack on the country?"

"We've picked up rumors that assassinations may be involved."

"Assassinations, plural?" she blurted. "Why would they do something like that?"

"You tell me. You're the assassin," Andrew replied.

"Former assassin." She continued, "Once a team of operators goes on a flashy crime spree, the government will throw all its resources at catching them and destroying their network. They'll all be caught or forced to go to ground. Why would they do something so self-destructive?"

"You tell me why," he replied grimly.

She stared at him for a moment, working through the logic. "The only reason to blow up a whole network is if its end goal has been achieved or will be achieved in the act of blowing up the team."

"I concur with that assessment." A pause, then he added, "Which begs the question, what is the mole's end goal?"

"You tell me," she retorted.

He sighed. "I wish we knew. Why would a man who's been passing intelligence to the Russians for years, most likely for large sums of cash, up and turn off that cash flow?"

"Is he retiring? Maybe being recalled to Moscow? Is this thing he's planning a parting shot on his way out the door?" she suggested.

Andrew frowned. He opened his mouth to answer but said nothing as a quiet knock sounded on the door panel. Another Kewpie-doll young woman in a pink kimono minced to their table and deposited steaming bowls of rice, egg drop soup, a slaw-style salad, and various hibachi-fried meats, seafood, and vegetables.

The server left, and Andrew murmured, "The Russians would never pull their guy out as long as he's not compromised. He's too valuable an asset where he is."

"How do we know that?" she asked lightly.

"Because we are not without our own resources inside the halls of Russian power. We have some idea of the intelligence he has passed to them over the years."

She wasn't surprised. While the Cold War might have gone into half-time between the USSR and the United States when the Iron Curtain fell, resuming with the Ukraine War, it had never stopped for the two countries' respective intelligence agencies.

She reached for a bowl of rice and spooned steak, shrimp, and grilled vegetables over it. She sprinkled the whole with a savory soy-horseradish sauce and dug in, using the enameled chopsticks the table was set with.

Andrew ate in silence with her for a few minutes, then said, "I've let the Scorpius-hunting team know you'll be taking over."

"How do they feel about that?"

He shrugged. "They'll do what you tell them to if that's what you're asking."

"I didn't doubt that. I'm not the mother of three grown children for nothing. I can whip any group into shape. I'm just curious how hostile an environment you and James are throwing me into."

Andrew shrugged. "They're Richard Bell's people. They're no doubt disappointed he's been promoted away from them."

"Tell me about Bell," she said.

"He's one of the few people in the agency with both field and analytical bona fides. He's a cool customer, ultraorganized. Above all, he's smart. His recent promotion was well deserved."

That tracked with what she'd heard about him. Although the way she'd heard it, Bell wasn't cool. He was as ice-cold as they came. And she'd heard him called words like compulsive, OCD, and anal retentive from people who'd worked with him. The one thing everyone did seem to agree on was that the man was brilliant.

Andrew was speaking. ". . . your team, of all people, will understand there's no one else but you whom we can trust to run them."

"Why is that?" she asked curiously. "Why, in the whole agency and all its thousands of employees, is there nobody Wagner trusts?"

"We trust you," Andrew observed.

"James doesn't trust me," she retorted. "He just knows I can't be Scorpius."

Andrew shrugged.

They ate for several minutes in silence, which Helen appreciated. Silence was a lost art among the young these days. Eventually, she asked, "Do either of you have a guess as to who Scorpius is?"

Andrew frowned and tugged at his tie, loosening it a little. "No. But it has to be somebody high-ranking."

"Or merely with access to high-level materials," she pointed out. "The two are not necessarily the same. He could be an admin with access to someone's computer or files."

"True. But some of the information intercepted at the other end of the line leads us to believe he sees original intel reports, edits material out of them, and passes them to Moscow without ever passing the same information on to us."

"What makes you think that?" she asked curiously.

"Is it hot in here?" Andrew asked. He did look rather ruddy, now that he mentioned it.

"Hot flash?" she asked sympathetically. "They suck, don't they?"

He threw her a faintly annoyed look as he pressed both palms against the surface of the table as if to stabilize himself. *Feeling dizzy, maybe?*

He murmured, "I apologize, but I think I should go. I'm not feeling well all of a sudden."

"Is your driver here? Or a bodyguard?" she asked in concern.

He was starting to sweat, and his skin had taken on a faintly gray cast.

"Outside," he mumbled. He picked up a water glass to take a drink, and his hand shook badly.

Okay, she was starting to be alarmed now. His breath was developing a raspy quality that sounded like an asthma attack.

"Do you have any heart issues, Andrew? Or asthma, maybe?"

"No. I'm a runner," he panted.

"Why don't you lie down?" She rose from her seat quickly and went around the table, placing the pillow she'd been sitting on under his head as he practically fell backward. She loosened his tie even more and unbuttoned his collar. "I'm going to get you some help."

She opened the paper screen door, jammed her feet in her shoes, and rushed over to the first pink-kimonoed girl she saw, ordering her tersely, "Do you know if there's a doctor in the house?"

"I believe the gentleman at that table over there with his wife is a doctor."

"Fetch him. Discreetly. It's important that there be no fuss. Ask him to join me and my dinner companion in the private dining room. After that, I need you to call an ambulance."

The girl frowned but nodded.

Helen watched the young woman head for the table with the doctor. *Good.* The girl wasn't drawing attention to the unfolding problem. Helen headed back toward the closed rice-paper door.

A man said from behind her, "You asked for a doctor?"

"Come with me," Helen said tersely. She ushered him into the private dining room.

In the few moments she'd been gone, Andrew's condition had worsened considerably. He was now curled on his side in a fetal position, groaning, his hands laced across his middle. The doctor hurried forward and dropped to his knees beside Andrew.

"Have you had your appendix out?" the doctor asked him.

"Yes. Years ago."

The doctor pressed a hand to Andrew's neck, undoubtedly checking his pulse. "Get an ambulance," the man bit out.

"Already on the way," she replied. "I'm going to get his security team."

She paused in the doorway of the private dining room to gaze around the restaurant. Nobody was overtly watching her. Still. Her spidey sense was tingling a warning. There was a threat in here.

Ignoring her sudden jitters, she headed outside the restaurant and looked around for an armored car or SUV with a couple of big guys in or beside it. There it was. Down the street about a hundred feet. She ran for it, and the man leaning against the hood straightened aggressively.

She stopped far enough away that he couldn't grab her and asked tersely, "Are you Andrew Mizuki's guys?"

"Who are you?" the man responded shortly.

"He's having a medical emergency inside the restaurant. I've already had an ambulance called, and there's a doctor with him."

The guy took off running, and she yelled after him, "First private dining room on the right!"

She waited for the driver inside the vehicle to finish a quick phone call, no doubt asking for backup, then she sprinted back with him. As the second guard rushed inside and headed for the dining room, she hung back by the front door where she could watch the other patrons.

Unfortunately, two big dudes in suits running through the restaurant had drawn pretty much everyone's attention to the private dining room. She had no way to tell if anyone was taking a particularly alert interest in where she and Andrew had been meeting.

By the time she slipped inside the now crowded private dining room, Andrew was having a seizure of some kind. His whole body twitched and jerked while several diners the doctor must have recruited all but lay on top of him, holding him more or less still. When the seizure finally subsided, Andrew groaned every few seconds in what sounded like intense pain.

"What did you do to him?" the driver demanded beside her.

"Me? Nothing! He complained of being hot and was flushed.

Then he went pale and started to sweat. Said he wasn't feeling well. I suggested he lie down, and I went for help."

The doctor, kneeling on the floor beside his patient, said without looking up, "His respiration is shallow and elevated, pulse rapid and thready, fingernail beds blue. He's not getting enough oxygen for some reason. Also—" He broke off, swearing, as Andrew went limp.

"He's lost consciousness. Where's that ambulance?" the doctor said to no one in particular.

"We can get him to a hospital fast in our vehicle," the driver responded.

"He needs respiratory support sooner than that. The ambulance will have it," the doctor bit out. "When the ambulance gets here, tell them to bring in oxygen with the gurney."

Someone behind Helen said they would take care of it and ran toward the exit.

The doctor rolled Andrew onto his back and held his hand over Andrew's mouth, then felt for a pulse again. Swearing again, he started CPR.

What on earth? Andrew had been alert and talking with her just a few minutes ago. Another man stepped out of the crowd and identified himself as a former firefighter with CPR training. He knelt beside the doctor and took a turn at doing the strenuous chest compressions.

The bodyguard pushed the bystanders away to give them room to work. Helen found herself shuffled back into the main dining room with nothing to do. A hum of panic vibrated in her gut. What was happening? Did Scorpius do this? Was he here? When she made a kill, part of the job was sticking around long enough to confirm it if the circumstances allowed. Had Scorpius or his minion done the same?

She eased her cell phone out of her pocket and hit the button to record video, surreptitiously filming everyone in the dining room as she turned in a slow three-sixty. She tucked her phone back into her pocket. An urge to flee rolled through her. The only reason she didn't give in to it immediately was because she was safer in this crowd than she would be alone on a dark side-walk outside.

As the men worked to revive Andrew, she silently prayed for his recovery from whatever this was. A massive heart attack perhaps? Or an aneurysm? What else could lay low a healthy man so fast?

Although she didn't like the answer that came to mind, she did have to ask herself, what if this was something more sinister?

CHAPTER 6

AT LONG LAST, SHE HEARD A SIREN APPROACHING. SHE HELPED THE restaurant manager and other customers move people and tables back to give the paramedics a straight shot at Andrew. They came in fast, took over CPR, slapped some sort of pressurized oxygen mask over his face, and lifted him onto a stretcher. They ran for the door like he was dying, and Andrew's men ran beside them.

Just like that, the crisis was over. Andrew was gone. The people in the restaurant buzzed like a hive of disturbed bees, and she wasn't sure what to do with herself. A girl in a pink kimono silently cleared the table and cleaned up the bowl of rice Andrew must have knocked to the floor in his convulsions.

Her instinct that a threat remained nearby intensified abruptly. A need to flee so strong she couldn't possibly ignore it swept over her.

She retrieved her purse from the corner where someone must have kicked it aside and ducked into the kitchen. She spotted the restaurant manager coming toward her, frowning, and improvised, "Did my companion already pay for our meal, or should I settle the bill?"

"Good heavens, no. Go be with your husband and let us know when he's all right. Next meal for you two here is on the house."

She didn't bother to correct him.

Glancing back through the round window in the swinging kitchen door to see if anyone was moving this way, she spied a man

of medium height and lean build headed in this general direction. But he could also be heading for the restroom. She didn't
stick around to find out, as she gave in to her impulse to flee.

"*Deyguchi?*" she asked the kitchen staff in her rudimentary
Japanese. *Exit?*

A prep cook pointed his knife toward an unmarked door at the
back of the kitchen and went back to chopping vegetables. She
hurried to the door, passed quickly through a storeroom, and
slipped out the delivery door into an alley. She took off running,
grateful for having chosen sensible flat shoes tonight.

She found a doorway inset deeply into a wall, wreathed in thick
shadows, and ducked into it, breathing hard. From a hidden compartment in her purse, she pulled out a piece of magician's silk,
ultrathin and black. She draped it over her blond hair and across
her face, hiding her fair skin, leaving only her eyes exposed. She
took a deep breath and held it, listening intently. *Yep.* Those were
footsteps. Running ones.

She exhaled slowly, forcibly relaxing her body from her hair-
line to her toes. She pulled all her energy inward, pushing down
her stress until she was as calm and still as the cold steel door at
her back, her presence minimized to practically nothing.

People in her line of work had an uncanny sense of when other
people were nearby. Pulling in her chi—her emotions and energy—to hide her presence from detection was a trick she'd
learned long ago from a renowned Korean sniper.

In a few seconds, a dark shape barreled past her hiding spot.
She only caught a glimpse of his face, but it was enough. It was
the guy from inside the restaurant.

She briefly debated jumping him from behind, but he'd run
past like an athlete and she could do without having to fight for
her life, hand-to-hand.

Patience was perhaps the most important skill of all in her line
of work, and she employed it now. She held her position, listening to the guy's footsteps retreat. Silence fell in the alley beyond.

He must've rounded the corner into the street. She stayed put
long enough for the guy to figure out he'd lost her, circle back to

the alley entrance to check it one more time, and then to move off, perhaps in search of her car, or perhaps to return to the restaurant and a possible partner.

Finally, as the cool evening started to make her shiver, she eased forward. She peered left and right cautiously. The alley was deserted. She headed back toward the Japanese restaurant and moved past it stealthily, sticking to the shadows.

He came at her from a recessed doorway much like the one she'd hidden in, slamming into her, his momentum sending both of them crashing into the brick wall on the far side of the alley.

At the last moment, she relaxed her body, absorbing as much of the impact as she could with her arms, which were trapped between them.

Still, she let out a pained *oomph* as her head hit the wall. Using the bounce of her skull off brick to her advantage, she snapped her head forward, opening her mouth wide. Her teeth contacted his neck, and she bit down as hard as she could.

He yelped, and his arms fell away from her. She snapped up her right elbow, throwing a glancing blow against his jaw.

His head snapped to the side, and he jumped back, shaking his head to clear it. His gaze was cold. Flat. The gaze of a killer.

Aw, hell.

Rather than wait for him to settle into the fight, she attacked fast, jumping after him as he backed up. Her only hope was to stay well inside his reach, taking away his strength and advantage in arm and leg length. And then it all came down to being willing to take the pain, guarding her automatic lose-the-fight zones, and getting lucky enough to hit one of his fight-over zones.

To that end, she threw one punch at his nose and another at his throat. He got his forearm up in time to block the nose shot, but she got in a good punch at his throat. He staggered back, coughing.

As he did so, he threw a wild roundhouse kick.

It wasn't a bad idea, but it was thrown too high. Rather than block it, she dodged back, then jumped in to give the leg a good shove in the same direction it was traveling as his foot whipped past her. It knocked him to one side, and he took a big, unbalanced step that put his head about chest-high to her.

Grasping her purse, still hanging over her shoulder, she slammed it into the side of his head, end first. The leather was thick and stiff, backed by the weight of the pistol inside. He grunted as he spun away from her. As her own weight pitched forward, she rammed him in the back.

Lunging forward, staying right on top of him, she shoved her hand in her purse. Gripping her trusty Wilson Combat EDC X9, she yanked it free and swung it at the back of his neck. He dropped to his knees and started to roll, but she followed him down, finishing the blow.

The pistol, which weighed about three pounds loaded, smashed into the back of his skull. In the act of rolling with the intent to pop back to his feet, her assailant dropped flat and went still.

She backed away cautiously, training the pistol on him. It crossed her mind to pause and take a picture of him, but most knocked-out people don't tend to stay unconscious for more than a few seconds, and she really didn't want to go another round with him. She turned and ran.

When she reached the end of the alley, she paused to check the street. The guy behind her would rouse soon, and she needed to be gone by then. But she also didn't need to burst out into traffic wielding a pistol and cause a panic.

Putting her pistol back in her purse, she eased out of the alley just behind a couple walking in the same direction as her car. She peeled off to unlock its door and slip inside.

She pulled out into traffic and drove for a few minutes. No tails showed themselves.

Breathing a sigh of relief, she pulled into a public parking lot, dug out her phone, and called the one person she always called when she was in trouble or didn't know what to do. Yosef, her long-time handler and best friend in the whole world.

"Hello, Helen. To what do I owe this pleasant surprise?" he said into her ear.

"Andrew Mizuki just collapsed in front of me. They were doing CPR on him by the time the ambulance took him away."

"Heart attack?" Yosef asked doubtfully. "I thought he was some sort of triathlete."

"He said he was a runner when I asked him about his health."

"You were with him then?"

"Having dinner at a Japanese place. Called Koyabi."

"I know it. Good food." There was a pregnant pause, which she recognized as Yosef thinking. "Cheating on me, were you?" he teased lightly.

"Never," she replied stoutly. "I just . . . don't know what to do. Who to call. Should I call Director Wagner? Let him know?"

"I'll call him if you'd like."

"Thanks. You're a gem."

Yosef replied dryly, "I also have James Wagner's personal cell-phone number. I doubt you can say the same."

"True. Also, a guy followed me from the restaurant and jumped me. I think he was inside Koyabi, and I might have a video with him in it."

"Go home. Have a glass of wine. Take a hot bath. I'll let you know how Andrew is when I hear something. In the morning is soon enough to look at your video and find your follower."

Relief flowed over her. He was right. Tonight, she should take care of herself. Relax. Rest. She was getting too old for this game. "Thanks for taking care of me yet again."

"No problem. That's my job."

Now, why did he say that in the present tense? Did he know she'd been asked to go back to the agency to lead the hunt for Scorpius? Had he recommended her for the position, perhaps? She didn't get a chance to ask him, because he disconnected the call, no doubt to call Wagner and let him know his second-in-command was in the hospital.

She drummed her fingers on the steering wheel, fidgety. She was way too wired after that fight to go home and relax. Not to mention that she was only a few minutes from the hospital where the ambulance crew said they would be taking Andrew. She would sleep better if she checked on him before she headed home to an empty house to fret over who that guy in the alley had been.

Of course, she didn't go directly to the hospital. She made a series of last-second turns, ran a yellow light, and watched the whole time for any sign of a tail. She spotted nothing. If someone was back there, he was better than she was.

She parked in the garage beside the big hospital and walked quickly to the emergency room reception desk.

"I was with the man they brought in by ambulance a little while ago. Andrew Mizuki. He'd have had a pair of bodyguards with him."

"Are you his wife?" the nurse asked.

"No, ma'am."

"A relative, then?"

"No. A friend."

"Then I can't tell you anything."

"Will you please tell his bodyguards I'm here? The name's Helen Warwick."

The nurse pointed at the chairs in the waiting area as a phone rang on her desk. Helen sighed. This could be a long night.

But it was only a minute or so later when the man she recognized as Andrew's driver strode out to the waiting room. She stood up to greet him, but he grabbed her roughly by the arm, bodily dragging her toward the exit.

"I can walk under my own power," she ground out under her breath. She yanked her arm free as he glared at her. She glared back.

As soon as they cleared the hospital entrance, he turned and demanded aggressively, "What did you do to him?"

"You asked me that at the restaurant, and my answer stands. I didn't do anything to him. Is he going to be okay?"

"He's dead."

"What?" She stared at him, aghast.

"What did you give him?" the man growled.

"I beg your pardon?"

"You poisoned him."

"I most certainly did not!"

"You are an assassin, aren't you?"

She looked around in alarm, lest anyone overhear him. It was an old habit ingrained over many years of keeping her profession secret. She kept her voice low as she ground out, "I *was* one. Past tense. I'm retired, thank you very much. And I didn't kill Andrew. "

"Why were you with him?"

"Because Director Wagner told me to meet with him," she bit out.

"Why?"

"Above your pay grade to know, my dear boy. And if you don't step away from me and lower your hands to your sides, you and I are going to have a problem."

She might not be the spring chicken she once was, but she knew some seriously violent hapkido and Krav Maga moves and wasn't afraid to use them.

A car drove up just then, and a man rushed around to the passenger door to help out his hugely pregnant wife, who was struggling to stand up.

"Don't be an ass. Go help the woman in labor, for goodness' sake," she snapped at Andrew's driver.

He shot her one last murderous look and turned to help the couple. She took the opportunity to duck back into the hospital. As soon as she was inside, she took off running down a random corridor, away from the homicidal bodyguard who seemed convinced Andrew's death was her fault.

She ran most of the way across the sprawling hospital complex before she found an exit and headed for the parking garage, pulling out her phone as she walked.

"Hey, Yossi, it's me. I'm at Sibley Memorial."

"Any news on Andrew?"

"Yes. He's dead."

"What? How?" Yosef sounded as appalled at the news as she had been.

"Don't know. But his driver thinks I poisoned him."

"That was never your preferred method of killing," Yosef said scornfully. "You were a shooter. Always wanted to make a head shot and guarantee the kill."

"Exactly." She looked both ways and jaywalked across a street before ducking into the parking garage.

"Be careful, Helen. Something bad is going on."

"Ya think?" she muttered as she paused in the shadow of a concrete pillar to observe her car and her surroundings.

"Be on high alert," Yosef said grimly. "Expect someone to come after you."

"Why do you say that?" she blurted in surprise.

"You were at that meal, too. And food at Koyabi is served family style. You should've been poisoned, also."

"Why is everyone so sure Andrew was poisoned?"

"What else kills a perfectly healthy man in something like thirty minutes?" Yosef asked logically.

She huffed. "Fine. It did look like poison. The only thing he consumed that I didn't was the sake. But just because I was there doesn't mean I did it."

"I never said you did it, Helen."

"I'm sorry. I'm a little on edge. A man I was just having dinner with keeled over in front of me and died. Then his driver accused me of killing him."

"Be careful, will you?"

"Always."

Did this have to do with her assignment to lead the Scorpius team? That was what she and Andrew had been at that restaurant to discuss. Was James Wagner going to think the same thing Andrew's driver did? That she'd killed his number two? What in the world had she just stepped into the middle of?

CHAPTER 7

*D*ANIEL BELL JOLTED WHEN HIS CELL PHONE RANG LOUDLY AND leaped across his bedroom to his desk to silence it. *Crap.* His father hated it when anything woke him up. Especially this late at night, and even more so on weekends when he caught up on his sleep.

For the thousandth time, he told himself he should move out of the house and get his own place. But it sounded like so much work. And why not live on his parents' dime as long as they would let him? College was so much easier with a housekeeper picking up after him and doing his laundry and having three square meals a day prepared for him.

The now silenced phone continued to vibrate insistently.

Who could be calling him at this hour?

He picked it up to look at the caller ID. Shayna? His hot chemistry lab partner? He'd been trying to figure out how to ask her out ever since the school year began. And yeah, it was nearly spring break. He sucked with social interactions. So sue him.

The phone vibrated again, and with a start, he put it to his ear, speaking low so as not to further piss off Richard. "Hey, Shayna."

"Thank God, Danny," Shayna whispered frantically. "I'm in trouble, and I didn't know who else to call. No one's answering their phones."

He frowned. "What kind of trouble?"

"Karly—she's my roommate—brought me to a frat party. And now I can't find her, and I feel really weird. I think someone tried to roofie me. But I spilled my drink, and I didn't finish it. I feel dizzy and kind of sick. I can't find my purse, and somebody deleted my rideshare app off my phone. I can't figure out how to redownload the app, and I don't know how to get home . . . and Karly's gone. What if they roofied her, too? Should I go looking for her?"

"No!" he said sharply. "Are you in a public space?"

"Um, sort of. I mean, everyone's trashed, and there are couples making out all over the living room."

"What frat? Do you know the address?" He was already jamming his feet in tennis shoes.

"Um, Sigma Rho Alpha. I don't know the address."

He headed down the dark hall past his sister's room and ran down the curving staircase. "I'll find it. I'll be there in about twenty minutes." He ran for the kitchen and grabbed car keys out of a basket by the back door.

He bit out, "Don't go upstairs, and don't leave the living room. At all costs, stay where there are lots of people—and girls."

"All the girls are so drunk. I mean, some of them look practically passed out."

"Stay put," he ground out as he jumped in his father's stupidly fast Porsche.

The streets were deserted as he raced toward the campus just outside DC where the rich and powerful sent their kids to college. His tires screamed as he slid around a corner and onto Greek Row. Big old mansions, now converted to fraternities and sororities lined the street. *Sigma Rho Alpha, where are you?*

He'd heard of the frat. Among the exclusive social clubs on this prestigious campus, it was the most exclusive of all. The sons of politicians, industry captains, and the ridiculously rich got into SRA. Non-Greek kids on campus called the frat Stupid Rich Assholes, in fact.

There. He spotted a carved stone by the curb in front of the biggest, fanciest mansion of them all. Windows on all four floors of the huge Victorian spilled light out onto the perfectly mani-cured lawn. Clearly the party was still in full swing. He headed up the long driveway lined with sports cars more expensive than his. As he neared the front door, the cars blocked the entire driveway.

He swerved onto the lawn and pulled up as close as he could to the grand entrance. He jumped out of the Porsche, sprinted around a four-tiered concrete fountain, and ran up the wide front steps to the carved double doors, which stood wide open on this warm spring night.

He skidded to a stop in a marble-floored foyer. To each side were huge rooms full of couples engaging in sex and near sex. Okay, then. So this was an orgy.

Shayna was in here somewhere. He chose a room at random and strode into it, examining the faces of the women in various stages of getting screwed. Several of the frat boys told him in rude terms to scram. Most of the girls looked too drunk or stoned to notice him. *Jeez.* Were they all roofied? Alarm and the beginning of something else deep in his gut, something hard and cold, began to coalesce.

He headed for another room, practically running. He'd barely stepped inside when a fast-moving body crashed into him, star-tling him mightily. It was Shayna, trembling in fear.

"Thank God you came," she sobbed against his neck.

He wrapped an arm around her waist, enjoying greatly how her breasts smashed against his chest. Her tears were a huge turn-on, and he felt his body reacting powerfully.

"Let's get out of here," he choked out.

"We have to find Karly," Shayna said frantically.

He didn't want to find her stupid roommate. He wanted to get her out to his car and let her cry on his shoulder some more. Maybe make out with her if she'd let him.

"C'mon," she said urgently, stepping back from him, grabbing his hand. He let himself be dragged upstairs because honestly, he was enjoying her fear and the novel sensation of being cast in the role of knight in shining armor. Usually, his fantasies ran more to-ward bondage and dark mastery over fearful women.

But he liked the combination of fear and trust she displayed. He could do whatever he wanted to her, and she would let him. He could see it now. Her on her knees in front of him, begging him to do unspeakable things to her—

Shayna opened a door, and a male voice inside complained, telling her to get out.

"We can't run around barging into every room," he protested. Shayna wasn't listening. She seemed prepared to do that very thing.

About half the doors were locked, and in most cases rattling the knobs elicited complaints from a frat guy on the other side. A few doors caused multiple guys to call out something rude, and in a few cases, female giggles were audible.

"We're never going to find her!" Shayna wailed.

"Lemme see if I can find someone who'll help us," he suggested, growing bored of searching for the missing roommate.

At the next door he pushed aside Shayna's hand and turned the knob himself. Unlocked. He stuck his head inside, and a guy, sprawled naked on his back with a girl apparently passed out across his lower torso, looked up.

"Hey. I'm looking for a girl named Karly," he said casually. "What does she look like, Shay?"

"Long dark hair to her hips. Slender. Pretty. Wearing a red dress."

"Oh. Yeah. She checked out a while ago," the naked guy said.

Shayna swore behind him.

Danny replied, "Thanks, man. Uh, carry on."

The naked guy grinned. "I'm taking a break. I'll do her again before she wakes up."

Danny frowned. Where was the fun in having sex with an unconscious girl? Sure, a guy could do stuff she might otherwise object to, but then the guy wouldn't get to hear the protests and pleas, the tears, and finally, the submission—

"I can't believe she ditched me!" Shayna was saying angrily behind him.

"C'mon. Let's get out of here. I'll drive you back to your dorm."

He endured Shayna's tirade all the way back to his car, when she broke off, saying, "Wow. You tore the crap out of the lawn with your tires."

"I don't care. Do you?" he asked flippantly.

"No. These jerks deserve it. I think they roofied, like, all the girls. I can't believe they think they'll get away with a stunt like that."

"Looks to me like they already have gotten away with it. Every guy in the place, um . . . scored. The SRAs are rich and all, but the only way for every single guy at any party to score is to spike the drinks."

Shayna turned to face him in the passenger seat. "You're really smart, aren't you?"

"Yeah, I am," he answered factually as he started the car. "Shall we leave a donut or two in the lawn on our way out?"

"Yes!" she exclaimed joyfully. "Tear it to shreds!"

He obliged, gunning the engine and throwing the low-slung car into a series of three-sixties that tossed up great clods of sod and left black streaks of dirt all over the front yard.

He'd pretty much destroyed the entire lawn before someone finally came outside to investigate the noise and yelled at him. Danny stuck his left hand out his window, flipped off the guy, and gunned his car out the gate and onto the street.

"Slow down, will you?" Shayna asked nervously as he rode the adrenaline high of wrecking something expensive and raced across campus.

"Oh. Um, yeah." He slowed the car to a more sedate pace. *Dang.* Messing up that lawn had been better than sex. Well, better than vanilla sex.

He pulled up in front of Shayna's dorm, a high-rise building. She jumped out of the car before he could come around and open the door for her, and he frowned. That was the rule. Open doors for ladies. Discomfort at having broken a rule coursed through him.

"Want me to walk you inside?" he asked in an effort to get back on the proper etiquette track.

"No. I'm about to chew Karly's head off, and I don't need your help with that. She scared me half to death . . . and then she *left* me there alone! If I hadn't spilled that drink and not gotten the whole roofie, and if you hadn't come when I called—" She broke off and visibly shuddered. "Thanks again, Danny. You're a lifesaver. I owe you huge."

He merely nodded, unsure of how to respond to that. His first impulse was to suggest that she could repay her debt by dating him, but he'd studied social interactions long enough to suspect that wouldn't go over well with her.

He watched Shayna until she was safely inside the lobby and had turned around to wave to him. Then he threw the car into gear and pulled away from the dorm thoughtfully. He could definitely parlay this into her sleeping with him. But how soon?

He swore and stomped on the gas. If only he understood women better. Maybe he would be having sex right now.

CHAPTER 8

*H*ELEN SAT AT THE COMPUTER IN HER HUSBAND'S HOME OFFICE and plugged her cell phone into Gray's large monitor—the one he used for examining insects under the attached digital microscope.

It took watching her video of the restaurant a couple of times to finally spot the man who'd jumped her. He'd been standing near the back of the crowd, doing nothing to draw any attention to himself.

He had nondescript brown hair, ordinary features, and was of average height and slim in build. The only remarkable thing about him was the precise fit of his suit. The thing had looked painted onto his body.

Moving bit by bit through the video in stop-action mode, she isolated the best still image of him that she'd captured. Emailing a copy of it to herself, she printed off several color copies of the picture.

She would need to run the digital image through a program to clean up and sharpen its edges, and then she ought to be able to run it through a facial recognition program, both of which she could do in her new office at the CIA. If her attacker was in any database anywhere, she should get a name, and maybe a home address.

She started to forward the image to Yosef but, at the last moment before hitting the send button, deleted the email. Honestly, she wasn't sure why she did it. Just an instinct to keep the image to herself for now. Or maybe she didn't trust the internet. Either way, she swiped a USB drive from Gray's desk drawer and copied the image onto it. Pocketing the drive, she spent a few minutes erasing her user history and shutting down the computer before heading up to bed.

She tossed and turned half the night trying to figure out who might want to kill her and Andrew. She tossed and turned the other half of it wondering who wanted to kill Mitch.

One thing she knew for sure. Mitch's shooter was an amateur. No professional would miss at a range of less than fifty yards. She could put a round through a dime at two hundred yards without even trying hard.

Which ruled out Scorpius. At least she had the comfort of knowing he wasn't targeting her family. Yet.

The next morning, after she showered, dressed, and ate break-fast, she headed for the Patrick Henry Building. Two blocks north of the mall in downtown DC, it was where the offices of the DC district attorney were housed.

Knowing Mitch, he would be in his office on a Sunday, work-ing. In fact, he'd probably been there since the crack of dawn. Ideally, she would catch him alone so they could have a private conversation.

The parking lot was less empty than she'd expected on a week-end, but the halls of the government building were mostly de-serted. Folks must be catching up on work at their desks.

Stepping up to what looked like a central reception desk, she said to the young woman seated there, "I'm Helen Warwick. I'm here to see my son Mitchell, and no, I don't have an appoint-ment. But I only need a minute or two."

"Mr. Warwick is just finishing up a conference call, ma'am," the woman who looked and dressed like a newbie lawyer replied. "He should have a few minutes before his next meeting . . . if you'll take a seat . . . can I get you something to drink?"

"No, thank you." She sat on a deeply uncomfortable wooden chair in the waiting room and fidgeted impatiently.

"Mom. What brings you down here on a weekend?" her eldest asked from the doorway of his office.

She rose to her feet with alacrity and glared at the godawful chair. "Thank goodness. Another few seconds in that torture device and I would've spilled all my deepest darkest secrets to your intern. Do you have a moment for your old mom?"

He threw her a withering look. "Of course. And you're not old. Far from it."

"Bless you, Mitchell." She certainly felt old and creaky—and sore—after last night's fight.

She followed him into his office and closed the door behind herself. He sat down at his desk, a brow arched in apparent surprise that she pointedly wanted privacy.

"What's up, Mom?"

"I want to talk with you about what happened at the press conference."

"Nancy and Gran are both pretty steamed about you ditching my big announcement. They seemed to think you're due for a scolding over it."

"Tattletales," she muttered. "And you know that's not what I came here to talk about. Who's trying to kill you? Surely you have some idea."

"And yet I don't," he answered lightly.

She rolled her eyes at him. "Wanna try that again before I tell you how I've known since you were four when you're lying to me?"

He rolled his eyes back at her.

"You make too direct eye contact with the person you're lying to. That's your tell. You stare at me as if willing me to believe you. That's how I know you're lying."

For an instant Mitch looked chagrined, but then his expression smoothed out once more. "That's ridiculous."

"Which part? The way I know you're lying or the fact that you're lying to me now?"

"Both," he grumbled.

"Too bad. So tell me. Did the police find anything useful up in the balcony where the shooter was?"

"No. Nothing."

As she'd expected. The cops had no idea what to look for in a shooter's nest. She sighed, disappointed. "I'm guessing you've had your staff reviewing the files of everyone you've put in jail who's gotten out recently. You already have a list of names, and I want a copy of it."

"This is a *police* matter, Mom."

"I'm better than the police."

He blinked at her in surprise. *Whoops.* That might have been a wee bit too revealing. She backtracked quickly, explaining, "I can hire top-notch private investigators and work outside the boundaries of the law. It'll be faster and likely more effective at identifying who took that potshot at you."

"Leave it alone. The police can handle it."

She huffed. "Promise me this. If the police don't nail down the identity of the shooter in the next few days, you'll let me give it a go."

He gifted her with another roll of the eyes and didn't say yes. But he also didn't say no. She would take it.

"Tell me this, Mom. Where *did* you go when you ducked out of my press conference?"

He was deflecting, and they both knew it. She could call him out on it, but she knew him well enough to know he would stonewall her if she pushed too hard. Better to let him lead her away from the subject of who wanted him dead and circle back to it in a minute.

She took a deep breath, hating where this conversation had to go next. "An old acquaintance of mine, someone I worked with in the government from time to time, approached me discreetly and asked for a private conversation. That's where I went."

"And?" he prompted.

"And my friend suggested that anyone going into politics would be wise to clean out their closets first. All of them. Thoroughly."

Mitch just stared at her.

C'mon, Mitch. Don't be dense. You know what I'm suggesting. So talk already.

He continued to look at her steadily, giving away absolutely nothing. Why did he have to go and find a great poker face now of all times?

She sighed. "Is there anything you'd like to tell me? Any skeletons you need help cleaning out of your metaphorical closet? I'm here for you, you know. I'll do anything for you. Anything at all."

Still no response.

"Look, Mitch. I have a lot of contacts inside and outside the government. No matter what kind of problem you might have, I probably know someone who can take care of it."

"Like what?" he finally asked.

She glared at him, irritated that he was making this harder than it had to be. "The person who approached me suggested that you might be implicated in something in your past of a . . . damaging nature," she finished delicately.

If possible, he went even more still.

Ah. She knew that particular stillness. She did it when she sensed a threat nearby and wanted to focus all her senses on it. Her kids always did have good instincts—

"My past is squeaky clean, Mom. Granddad taught me that before I even ran for sixth-grade class president. Whoever this acquaintance of yours is, he or she is wrong. I have nothing to hide in any of my . . . closets."

She'd been afraid he would do this. Rebuff her and freeze her out. This was the problem with not telling her family what she'd been doing for all these years. Like everybody else on the planet, they vastly underestimated what she was capable of.

"Mitchell, may I invoke a moment of attorney-client privilege?"

"I'm not your attorney, so technically, no. But if you want to ask me to promise to keep something you want to say in complete confidence, I can do that."

"Will you? For me?"

He tossed a hand up in the air. "Sure. Why not? Confess away."

"Let's just say trade deals aren't always as boring and mundane as they sound. Sometimes they became highly contentious. And sometimes each side in the negotiation spends considerable effort trying to find out what the other side is thinking and planning. They want to know what cards we hold, and we want to know what cards they hold."

"Why are you talking to me about cards and trade deals?"

"Don't be obtuse, Mitchell. You know exactly what I'm saying. I know . . . people." She chose her next words delicately. "People who can do . . . things." Another pause. "If you ever need something handled quietly—you need something erased, or someone silenced—I can make it happen."

That earned her several owlish blinks of his eyes.

"I'm family, Mitch. I would do anything—*anything*—for you kids. And you know I can keep a secret. Who else can you trust to deal with stuff like this, if not your own mother?"

"I have no idea." Finally, he seemed to be taking this little talk in the spirit it was meant.

She leaned forward and said quietly, "If anyone else comes after you, if you hear anything about a smear campaign, if you get any inkling that someone is contemplating playing dirty against you in this campaign, you let me know. Okay? You keep your hands clean and let me handle it. I know how to get my hands dirty and tidy up after myself."

He stared at her. Hard. He was obviously measuring exactly what she'd just offered him. Finally, he blurted, "You're my mother. I can't ask you to do anything like that—"

"I'm volunteering, Mitch. I came to you. I offered. I'm one of a very few people whom you can trust absolutely with your reputation, your career—heck, your life. And I'm telling you. I'm the right person to ask if you have that sort of problem. You hear me?"

"I hear you. I'm just not sure I believe you."

She leaned back in her chair and smiled a little. "Trust me, darling."

He looked shocked. *Good.* They were both adults here. It was high time he realized she was not a normal mother who'd lived a normal life and done normal things. Even if she would never, ever tell any of her kids the specifics of what she'd done in her career.

"I'm going to ask you one more time, Mitch. Is there anything in your past that needs to be cleaned up before the public or your opponent digs it up?"

"I'm good. I promise."

She couldn't tell if he was lying or not. Her heart wanted to believe him. But hardheaded realism suggested that nobody made it to his or her midthirties without at least a few skeletons buried somewhere in their past. If he was convinced those skeletons were buried deep enough never to be found, she would have to take him at his word.

For now.

She clutched her purse and stood up. "I'll let you get to your work then. If anything comes up, I'm here for you, Mitchell."

"Um, thanks."

She sincerely wished her children would stop sounding so damned surprised every time she told them she was there for them. She meant every word of it. She *was* back in their lives now, and she wasn't going anywhere. She was here for all of them.

CHAPTER 9

*H*ELEN HAD JUST WALKED OUTSIDE AND TAKEN A CLEANSING breath of spring morning air when her phone rang. The caller ID said it was Angela Vincent, a lawyer whom she'd helped prove her clients hadn't committed a string of recent murders.

"Hey, Angie. How are you doing?"

"I'm fine, thank you."

Formal Angela. This was a work call then. "What can I do for you?"

"Is there any chance you could come downtown? My son could use your opinion on something rather . . . odd."

Helen frowned. Angela's son, George, was a police detective, newly promoted to the Homicide Division after being instrumental in solving the murder of the district attorney a few months back. With her help, of course. She'd fed him her knowledge of setting up an assassination by sniper rifle, and he'd parlayed that information into his promotion.

"How's George doing these days?" she asked.

"He's enjoying being in Homicide. But he's got a case he could use a little help with. The kind of help you can give him."

She'd never admitted to Angela or George that she'd been a professional sniper, but neither of them was slow on the uptake. They'd put two and two together when she'd popped off with technical knowledge of shooting that no amateur could possibly possess.

"Um, sure. Glad to help if I can," she replied. Cautiously.

"Could you meet him at the morgue? Today?"

"I'm actually downtown now. I suppose I could head over there and meet him if he's available."

"Great. I'll call him and let him know you're on your way," Angela said.

Helen thought she detected a certain caution in her friend's voice. "Is everything okay, Angie?"

"Yeah, sure. Why?"

"I don't know. You sound a little tense."

Angela laughed, but the sound was forced. Helen's spidey sense triggered. Angela wasn't telling her something. The lawyer said lightly, "I've got a big thing brewing. I'm in that 'figuring out what to do' stage where I turn into a bitch and obsessively clean house until I decide how to attack the problem."

That sounded honest, at any rate.

"Well, good luck with it. Call me if you need someone to bounce ideas off of."

"I may take you up on that. Thanks."

Lie. She had no intention of calling Helen to talk over her legal strategy. Now, why would Angela specifically want to keep her away from a case? She made a mental note to see if she could trick George into telling her what Angela was working on.

Helen couldn't help feeling twitchy as she walked into the Consolidated Forensics Laboratory on E Street downtown, a modern glass and steel building combining various crime labs and the Office of the Chief Medical Examiner for the Washington, DC, area.

Even on a Sunday morning, plenty of uniformed cops walked the halls. Her New Year's Eve run-in with local police had left her nervous around them. It had been awfully hard to explain to the police how a retired woman had shot and killed three armed intruders in her son's home in a pitched gun battle.

She took the elevator up to the fifth floor and the viewing room where George had texted her to meet him. There was stainless steel everywhere. Countertops, gurneys, even the door frames were dull silver.

The smell of the place was complex—a light odor of formalde-hyde and maybe a cleaning solution, with notes of blood and raw meat, both of which she was familiar with from her work and able to identify immediately. Beyond that, she thought she smelled feces, and burned . . . something. She didn't question what ex-actly might be burned in this place.

"Thanks for coming, Mrs. Warwick," a handsome black man in a suit said as she stepped inside what looked like a waiting room at a doctor's office.

"George! It's good to see you. And do call me Helen. Congrat-ulations on the promotion. Welcome back to the world of civilian clothes at work."

He snorted. "Nobody warned me what a decent suit costs these days, or that I sweat through them every time I have to testify in court. My God, the dry-cleaning bills."

She smiled in commiseration. Trying to put her at ease, was he? Okay. She would play along. "I can only imagine."

"If you don't mind my asking, ma'am, have you ever seen a dead body?"

She'd seen dozens of them, most dead by her hand. Aloud, she said, "You don't get to my age without experiencing at least a little death up close and personal."

He made a well-practiced sympathetic face and then said, "I've got a body I'd like you to take a look at. But I have to warn you, it's grisly. Can you handle that?"

She'd obliterated people's heads before. She could most cer-tainly handle a little gore. "If I can help you do your job, solve a murder perhaps, I'll do my best not to get the vapors."

"This way." He led her through a set of double doors into a large, brilliantly lit room. The smell of formaldehyde and blood was stronger in here. Ventilation fans hummed overhead, sucking air up and out of the room strongly enough she felt it moving against her skin. Several bulky stainless-steel tables took up the middle of the space.

George led her to a table holding a human-body-shaped object covered by a light blue sheet. "Let's start with the feet. That's less shocking. We'll work our way up to the worst of it."

The worst of what? Confused, she looked on as George folded the sheet back from a pair of human feet and lower legs. The top of the feet and calves, facing up, were bone white. The legs were covered with thick, dark hair. Probably male then.

The corpse's heels, backs of his ankles, and backs of his calves were dark purple. She recognized *livor mortis*, the pooling of blood after death. She looked more closely and was startled to see the man's toes were mostly black and had no nails.

"Where did his toenails go?" she blurted.

"We believe they were pulled out," George said evenly.

Pulled out? That sounds like torture.

George lifted the sheet higher, and she stared at a large, indented wound above the dead man's right knee.

"Do you mind if I look at that more closely?" she murmured.

"Be my guest."

She stepped up next to the corpse and studied the wound. It looked as if something the size of her finger had chewed its way deep into the man's thigh, possibly all the way to the bone. She couldn't be sure of that though, because the tissue around the sides of the hole had collapsed inward. It was a bad puncture wound and looked as if something like a piece of steel rebar had pierced the man's leg.

"Ready for more?" George asked grimly.

"Can we just get to what you brought me here to see?" she asked, feeling a little queasy in spite of herself.

He moved around to the far side of the table and lifted the sheet all the way off the corpse.

She gasped.

Took a staggering step back.

Swallowed the saliva pooling thickly in the back of her throat, preparatory to vomiting.

"Oh, my," she breathed in horror.

The body before her had been horrifically mutilated. But worse, she immediately recognized most of the injuries to be the result of torture.

There were burns, ligature marks, and more holes like the one in his leg. *Ah.* If torture had made that hole, she would lay odds a drill had been plunged into his leg. The ear facing her appeared to have been drilled into as well.

The dead man's fingers were all missing their nails, and there wasn't a single tooth left in his wide-open mouth. She thought his tongue might have been cut out based on the odd way the jaw was positioned, but she didn't lean over to check inside his mouth.

She noticed more details. The eyelids were strangely sunken in as if the eyeballs beneath had been removed. Along the rib cage facing her, there were a dozen or more thin cuts in his flesh that appeared to wrap from his back around to his side. Whether they came from a blade or a whip of some kind, she couldn't tell. The body was too discolored and the flesh too shredded for that.

She continued her examination, noting that the tips of his fingers were black and charred. She glanced back at his toes. Was the blackness in them from electrocution, then?

And that was when she noticed that the corpse's genitals were missing. "Dare I ask where his, um, private parts went?"

"They were found stuffed in his mouth," George answered without emotion.

"What in the bloody hell happened to this poor man?" she blurted.

"That's what I was hoping you could tell me."

"Where did you find him? Do you have a suspect? What does the medical examiner think happened?"

"Before I tell you anything, would you mind giving me your first impressions?" He added dryly, "I wouldn't want to bias you."

She glanced up at him, startled.

"Take your time. Tell me everything you see."

She took a deep breath and looked down at the corpse between them once more. Blocking out the humanity that this man had once had, she focused instead on individual wounds. One by one, she examined the ones she could see on this side of the table.

She moved around to the other side of the table and found identical injuries on the corpse's left side. Indeed, the injuries on his left almost exactly mirrored the ones on his right. But not quite.

As she examined this set of wounds more closely, she noticed something odd. She moved back to the corpse's right side to take another look, and then went back around to the left side.

"What do you see?" George asked.

She looked up at him. "The hole in the left hand is crooked. Whatever pierced the hand appears to have hit a bone and tipped the—" She broke off.

"Finish that sentence," George said quietly, his voice steely.

No. It would reveal too much about her to name the object that had made the holes all over the dead man's body.

She searched for bland words. Words that wouldn't get her in trouble. "I was going to say that whatever pierced the hand hit a bone and tipped the thing that made the hole on its side. That's why the wound elongates off to one side, at the surface."

"That wasn't what you were originally going to say."

Damn it. He was a cop and good at his job. He could smell a lie at twenty paces.

She turned away from the body sharply. She'd already said too much.

George came around the table swiftly to stand too close to her, crowding her. He ground out, "I need you to tell me what you see. Everything. No evasion. No hesitation. Just spit it out."

"I can't get involved. Can't testify. *Won't* testify," she mumbled. *Good Lord.* The questions her family would have for her if they found out what she knew about this man's injuries. The mere thought of it made her shudder.

"I see." He took a step back from her, and she let out a careful breath. He added, "If I swear not to subpoena you, not to take a statement from you, will you talk to me then?"

She shook her head.

"What's it going to take?" he asked practically.

If he was anything like his bulldog lawyer of a mother, no way was he going to let her walk out of here without spilling her guts. She answered reluctantly, "Complete anonymity. What do you call them? Confidential informants?"

He stared at her intently. "Okay. I can work with that. So, brand new CI of mine, what do you see when you look at this body?"

"You promise? On your word of honor? My name never comes up?"

"I swear. On my word of honor."

"Including your mother. You never speak of this to her."

He was slower to agree to that but eventually nodded in the affirmative.

She stared at him doubtfully, and he stared back at her. His gaze never wavered.

"Fine," she said in sudden decision. She turned back to the body. "You know as well as I do that these wounds were inflicted by various methods of torture. The wounds on the right side of the body, however, are cleaner—more professional, if you will—than the ones on the left side."

She pointed at the corpse's left hand. "Take this hole in the back of his hand. On the right hand, the hole is neat. Vertical. It goes between the bones cleanly. On this hand, the power drill was placed too near the wrist, where the hand bones are very close together. It should've been placed more toward the fingers, where the bones are farther apart. That's why the drill bit hit the bone and tilted, maybe skipped out of the hole and made this gash beside the drill hole."

"And how do you know a power drill made those holes?"

"No comment," she bit out.

"That's not the deal—"

"No questions about how I know what I know, or I'm out of here," she snapped.

George threw up his hands. "All right, already. So talk."

She continued, "If I didn't know better, I'd say someone was being trained to do torture on this man. An experienced pro did the things on this right side, and a newbie tried them on the left side. I expect the medical examiner was able to identify how all of these various wounds were made, so I won't go into detail, if you don't mind."

George nodded tersely.

She tilted her head, studying the corpse. "One thing confuses me, though."

"What's that?"

"When you pull out a fingernail, the bed of the nail bleeds. A lot. But there's no sign of blood on his fingers or toes. I mean, I get that the ME cleaned up the corpse. But there should still be raw flesh. This guy's nail beds hardly look disturbed . . ." She trailed off, unsure of what she was trying to say. Maybe it was a postmortem thing that the nail beds went back to looking more or less pristine.

"You're sure two different people did this . . . damage?" George asked.

She nodded. "Fairly sure. If I could see the wounds on his back, I could probably be more certain."

"Why his back?"

"Knife work, or whip work for that matter, is highly individualized. There would be two distinctively different patterns of wounds if two people made them."

"What if a person made one set with his right hand and one set with his left hand? Would that account for the difference?"

"I suppose. But most people are hopeless with their off hand if they try to carve something with a knife. Maybe if the torturer was ambidextrous, you might see two patterns. But still, there's an art to using a knife. Most people have a strong signature."

"I have so many questions in response to that," George declared.

She stared at him stubbornly, and he sighed. "I think I can pull up photographs of the corpse's back on the computer over here."

He signed into what looked like some sort of police database and, with a bit of fiddling, was able to pull up the pictures in question. Relieved to move away from the body, she took a look at the computer monitor.

"Oh, yeah. No question these were made by two different people. Look at how the set of cuts from the right come to sharp, straight ends. And then look here. The wounds starting from the left curve off a little and get shallow toward the end of the cut. Someone who wasn't very sure of himself made those."

She added, "They must've been interrupted before they finished with this guy."

"Why do you say that?" George blurted, sounding surprised.

"Because those are flaying cuts. You make two parallel cuts about an inch and a half apart, then you go back to the beginning and slip the blade of your knife under the skin sideways. Once you've got a flap started, you can peel back the strip of skin between the original cuts. But these guys never got to take this man's skin off."

"That is arguably the grossest thing I've ever heard."

She shrugged at George. "All torture is gross. Not only is it about pain, it's also about causing psychological horror. It's about breaking the victim's will to resist."

"Spoken like a professional torturer," he said tightly.

She responded quietly, "I will tell you this. I have never tortured anyone, George. But I have seen the aftermath of it."

She didn't add that she had been sent out to dispatch torture victims a few times. To put them out of their misery. They'd been shots she'd been glad to take. The victims she'd seen had been so broken, physically and mentally, they would've never recovered. Killing them with a quick bullet had been a mercy.

He sighed. "Anything else you can tell me?"

"Some of the techniques used on this man look . . ." She searched for a word. "Official."

"Meaning what?" George blurted.

She explained reluctantly, "Like someone trained by a government might have done this work."

"Our government?"

She shrugged. "A government. Not necessarily ours. Some governments are more brutal than others. For the record, ours isn't the worst of the lot." She added, "This is Washington, DC. There are people here from many governments all over the world."

George frowned thoughtfully at her.

"Your turn. I think I've earned hearing what you know about this poor man."

"Cause of death is a drug overdose. Heroin laced with Tranq."

"What's Tranq?"

"An animal tranquilizer called xylazine. It intensifies an opioid high. But, unlike heroin and fentanyl, Narcan can't reverse its effects. We're seeing a sharp spike in overdose deaths from it."

"This torture didn't kill him?" she exclaimed, surprised.

"He was dead before he was tortured," George said soberly. "There was little to no blood associated with any of the wounds."

"Could the torturers have cleaned up his body after the fact?" she asked.

George shook his head. "ME says there was no bleeding subcutaneously—below the skin. He was dead first."

Thank God. "So that's why his nail beds didn't look right," she commented. Then she asked in confusion, "Why torture someone after they're dead?"

"That's what I was hoping you could tell me."

She glanced back at the corpse. "Torture training, maybe?"

"Does that feel right to you?"

She shook her head. "Most torturers learn on animals. They already know what they're doing by the time they graduate to humans."

"Again. So gross."

She sighed. "You're the one asking the questions. I'm just trying to give you honest answers."

"And you're absolutely sure it's two people?" George asked.

"Positive. Why?"

"This." George moved to the corpse and lifted the man's rather long bangs carefully.

Helen gasped. There was a brown fingerprint in dried blood in the exact center of the man's forehead. It had a distinctive V-shaped scar slashing across the whorls.

"One signature on the body," George said tightly. "Not two."

"Have you identified the killer then?"

"Nope. The print doesn't show up in any database *anywhere*. And before you ask if we checked them all, we put the highest priority rush on it. When the FBI saw the body the print came from, they moved heaven and earth to run the print through every database in the US, Interpol, the foreign counterparts, you name it, in under forty-eight hours. It was a freaking miracle. Never seen 'em move so fast on a fingerprint."

What kind of person signed their tortured victim like that? She didn't like the possible answers that came to mind. They all pointed at a serious sicko.

George asked, "Tell me this. Why do two people find themselves a dead guy, torture his corpse, and then sign their work?"

She said reluctantly, "I doubt he was dead when they found him. He was probably stoned out of his mind but not dead. People who do stuff like this are predators. They're hunters first and foremost. They wouldn't scavenge a dead body to play with. They would hunt a live victim."

George nodded slowly. "Makes sense. Continue."

"Do you have a suspect in custody?" she asked.

"No. The perp—perps—left no evidence on the corpse besides that one intentional fingerprint. The body was definitely moved from wherever all this was done to it. There was no blood or tissue residue of any kind at the scene where the vic was found."

"No evidence at all?" she blurted. "No DNA, no hairs, no fibers, nothing? With everything they did to that poor man?"

"No. Nothing."

"Definitely a trained killer then," she declared. "Could be a cop, for that matter."

George scowled at that. "Whoever did this was a damned animal."

She shrugged. "Or a good, old-fashioned sociopath."

He shuddered and gave his shoulders a shake. "I've seen some messed-up stuff in my career, but this takes the cake."

"Go where the druggies get their fixes. Look for someone hanging around who acts and moves like a hunter. Someone quiet. Stealthy. Observant."

She could've added a half-dozen more adjectives to that list, like patient, unnoticeable, and unexpected. One of the keys to her success over the years had been her unassuming mom vibe. Who looked at a nice, middle-aged lady like her and saw a trained killer? Nobody.

"One more thing, George."

He looked up from the computer where he was backing out of the police database and shutting it down.

"This won't be the last body you find like this."

"Why the hell not?" he demanded.

"Because predators are never satisfied with just one kill."

CHAPTER 10

MONDAY MORNING, HELEN PARKED HER CAR INSIDE A TALL IRON fence in front of a warehouse in a big industrial complex on the outskirts of DC. The security guard at the gate had been pleasant enough and did a credible job of looking like a bored, middle-aged guy to whom life hadn't been kind. She didn't buy it for a second. He was an employee of the agency and fully as lethal as he didn't look.

She parked and glanced around carefully. She didn't spot any cameras, but surely they were out here. She did note a decided lack of flashy cars in the parking lot. But then, spies tended to shy away from that which called attention to them . . . bless James Bond's silly, fictional heart.

Here went nothing.

Inside the warehouse, a short hallway led to a caged office crammed with binders and piles of paperwork. A guy sat inside with his feet propped casually on the corner of a big metal desk.

"Can I help you?" the guy asked gruffly.

"I hope so. My name is Helen Warwick, and this is my first day of work—"

The guy's boots thudded to the floor as he swore under his breath. Caught him by surprise, had she? But then, she'd dressed in the most grandmotherly blouse and skirt she could find. She'd even sprayed gray highlights in her hair for the occasion. Her instinct was not to show all her cards with this bunch.

"Uh, welcome, Mrs. Warwick. We've been expecting you." He opened a drawer and pulled out a manila envelope.

She tore the tape off the envelope's flap and pulled out an ID badge on a black lanyard. She looped it around her neck. Onto the high counter, she dumped out a set of office keys, a magnetic swipe card, a small key by itself, and a sealed envelope with the word *passwords* neatly written on it. She stuffed all of it into her purse.

"Be careful crossing the warehouse," the man warned. "The forklift operators are supposed to beep every time they cross the yellow stripes into the pedestrian walkway, but sometimes they forget."

"Thanks for the warning. I'm not as spry as I used to be."

He said briskly, "Elevator's in the middle of the building. Hit the down button and enter S4 on the number pad."

"Thank you." Did that mean there were subfloors one through three, also?

"Welcome to the Box, ma'am."

An apt name. As she stepped through the door at the end of the hallway, a gigantic space, crisscrossed by dusty beams of sunlight, yawned in front of her. Loaded cargo pallets stood in numbered squares painted on the floor, and tall rows of metal shelving, towering twenty feet high, held crates of all sizes and shapes. A pair of yellow lines outlined a path about the width of a sidewalk leading forward. She followed it across an open area and between rows of the shelves to a square, floor-to-ceiling tower in the middle of the chaos.

The elevator took longer to descend than she expected. Was it just slow, or was this CIA remote site buried very deep? Brief claustrophobia swept over her at the thought.

The elevator doors slid open, and she stared in surprise.

Another cavernous space, this one as dark as night, stretched away in front of her. Her shoes scuffed on the concrete floor as she stepped into a space partitioned off from the greater whole by temporary walls. It was filled with desks, computers, monitors, clear glass writing boards, and a half-dozen people looking up at her in surprise.

A youngish woman with dark, curly hair stepped forward. "You must be Mrs. Warwick. Bill called down to say you were here."

Bill must be the guy in the cage. To the dark-eyed beauty in front of her, she said, "Please, call me Helen."

"I'm Ritika Singh. Junior analyst."

"Nice to meet you, Ritika."

An athletic man—thirties, clean-cut, decent suit, ambitious look in his eyes—stepped forward. "Jack Zellner. Acting office supervisor. I assume you've been briefed?"

"No. I haven't actually," she replied.

Odd. For a second there, she thought she saw satisfaction flit through his pale gaze.

"I'll be happy to bring you up to speed—"

"I'll do that, Jack," a strident female voice said from behind him. A woman who looked to be in her well-preserved forties, wearing a tight skirt and expensive silk blouse, was coming toward them from her desk at the far end of the cluster of workstations. Given how Jack fell silent and even took a small step back, here was the person actually running this operation.

"And who might you be?" Helen asked pleasantly, sizing up the woman as she approached. Total alpha female. Aggressive, smart, tough. A bitch. *Takes one to know one.*

"I'm Polina Semyonova. Yes, I'm native Russian. No, I'm not the mole."

The woman radiated hostility. *Okay, then.* She had probably wanted to be named team leader when Richard Bell had been promoted out of here. *Yippee. Nothing like a resentful employee to wreck a workplace atmosphere.*

Helen smiled pleasantly. "*Ochen priyatno,* Polina."

The woman shrugged, obviously not impressed that Helen knew a basic "pleased to meet you" in Russian. She didn't disabuse Polina of the notion that the new boss was showing off and didn't speak the tongue. It had been a while since Helen had drunkenly argued politics in Russian, but she still considered herself fluent enough for government work.

"Who else have we got here?" Helen asked no one in particular.

Jack jumped in to field the question, pointing at a desk to his right. "Mason Chunenko, IT guy and hacker. We call him Chunk."

A rail-thin guy with a beard, wearing a sloppy T-shirt and staring at a computer monitor intently, raised a hand over his head and went back to typing furiously on his keyboard without ever looking up at her.

"Interesting name," she murmured.

"He's Ukrainian," Jack supplied.

She could've guessed that from the -ko ending of Mason's surname, but she merely nodded.

Jack continued the rapid-fire introductions, pointing at the next desk down the row. "That's Greg Ford. Documents and photo analyst."

A balding man wearing thick glasses started to push to his feet, but Helen waved him back down to his chair.

Jack finished the personnel tour with the guy standing by the last desk on the end. "Benjamin Cabelo. Security."

A big guy with a hard gaze, he looked as if he could handle himself in a fight. He nodded tersely in her general direction and didn't look terribly interested in the goings-on around him. She knew the type. He wasn't missing a single thing about this introduction.

She pegged him for a Special Operations Group guy. Probably had gotten injured in the field or was due for a down-time rotation and had gotten stuck here babysitting these desk jockeys. He would be bored, condescending, and antisocial. She liked him already.

"Is there a desk for me, by any chance?" she asked the group at large.

"Right over there, Mrs. Warwick," Ritika answered helpfully, pointing at a glass-enclosed office off to one side. While it might offer audio privacy, that was all it offered. *Fine.* If they could watch her every move, she could also watch theirs.

She headed for the office and noted the conference room beside it, also glass-walled. What if she had to give a briefing above the classification of someone out here? Frowning, she asked, "Does the conference room have curtains?"

Ritika picked up a remote control lying on the front corner of Helen's desk. "The walls of your office and the conference room go opaque with a press of this button here."

Abruptly, the walls of her office went white, and the people and warehouse outside disappeared. Man, how she hated all these high-tech inventions nowadays. Give her a pistol and her wits, and she was at her most comfortable. But artificial intelligence, drones, self-targeting sniper rifles . . . the youngsters could have them.

"Can I get you something to drink, ma'am?" Ritika was asking.

"I don't know. Are you my assistant?" Helen asked.

"No, ma'am. Technically, that would be Jack."

"Then have him bring me a bottle of water and a cup of tea—Earl Grey, ideally, but any black tea will do—with one lump of sugar, the next time he has a minute."

A tiny smile creased Ritika's face and then disappeared. "Yes, ma'am."

"And Ritika. If we could keep the ma'aming down to, say, every third declarative statement or so, I'd be grateful."

"Yes, ma—All right."

Ritika must be the junior person on the team, based on how hard she was trying to please and how she'd been relegated to fetching drinks.

This group seemed very invested in their places in the pecking order around here. Sharp divisions of power and authority weren't her style, personally. She was more the "let's all pitch in and pull together to get the job done" type. Thank God she'd never had to work at a desk job in an environment like this. She would've lost her mind.

Helen sat down at the big desk she'd inherited from Richard Bell. At least as assistant director of Operations he would have an office with windows now. She pressed the button on the remote control, and her office walls went clear once more.

Everyone outside lurched into motion. Gossiping about the new boss, were they? Let them. As long as they helped her find Scorpius, they could think whatever they liked of her.

If she wasn't mistaken, those were computer server towers along the far wall of the cavernous space. Lights blinked continuously across the faces of the black cabinets. Polina walked over to the photo guy's desk—what was his name again? Right. Ford. Greg Ford—and the Russian woman dropped a folder in front of him. The bald man opened the folder and studied its contents. The hacker, Chunk, was still typing as if his life depended on it.

She pulled the envelope of passwords out of her purse and unfolded the single, typed sheet of paper on the desk in front of her.

"Got a minute?"

She looked up at Benjamin Cabelo, the security guy. "Sure." She turned the sheet of paper face down and leaned back in her chair to study him.

"I've heard of you," he said without preamble.

"What have you heard?" she asked evenly.

"Is it true you do wet work?"

"Did. Past tense."

His eyebrows sailed up, then slammed together in a frown. "You don't look the type."

"Why, thank you." Amused, she watched confusion pass across his face. She was happy to play granny if it kept this bunch off balance. After all, Wagner had been clear that *everyone* was under suspicion as she hunted for the CIA's mole.

Cabelo recovered with admirable speed. "If you need anything, let me know. Also, tell me if you think anyone is following you."

She debated for a moment telling him that someone had probably tried to poison her last night and attacked her behind the restaurant, but decided against it. Although her first instinct was to trust him, she didn't know him. "Have you had trouble with

team members being followed since this working group was
formed?"

"No. Just being cautious."

"Thank you, young man. I appreciate your conscientiousness."

His mouth twitched in response to being called a young man,
as if he was already in on the joke of her pretending to be
Granny Helen. She added perceptive to her mental list of attrib-
utes for him.

She asked, "Before you got stuck down here, who did you report to?"

"Kyle Colgate."

As she'd thought. Colgate was the head of the Special Activities
Center, where the agency's blackest operators were assigned. She
looked up to ask him how he'd gotten put here, but he'd already
left her office as silently as he'd arrived. Didn't want to tell her
anything more about himself or his career, did he? He didn't
trust her then. Noted.

The computer on her desk finished booting up, and a notice to
cease and desist using it under penalty of law if she did not have
the proper clearance to access it flashed on the screen. Well, that
was a cheery screensaver. First chance she got, she was uploading
the most adorable picture she had of her Golden Retriever grand-
pup, Biscuit. The six-month-old puppy was her son Peter and Li's
stand-in for a child at the moment.

Polina poked her head in. "I just uploaded the in-brief for you.
If you'd step into the conference room, I'll bring you up to
speed."

Helen didn't recall saying anything about being ready for an
in-briefing, but apparently, Polina felt free to dictate when it happened. Pursing her lips, she chose not to assert herself just yet.
Better to let these people show their true colors before she bared
her claws.

Good grief, she hated office politics. This was precisely why
she'd stayed in the field her whole career. It was so much easier to
hunt and kill people than it was to deal with the maneuvering and
the backstabbing that came with offices full of political climbers

and spies, whose natural tendency was to manipulate everyone and everything around them.

The rest of the team filed into the conference room as she moved to the head of the table and took a seat, refraining from pushing Polina's laptop to one side.

With a sniff, Polina picked up the laptop and carried it over to a lectern, where she plugged it in. The back wall of the conference room went white, and some sort of high-tech projector, maybe from behind the wall, showed a timeline.

Helen leaned forward with interest.

First known communication from Scorpius to the FSB occurred eleven years previously. "He or she's been active for more than a decade?" she exclaimed.

"Correct," Polina bit out, sounding annoyed at the interruption. "And we believe Scorpius to be a man based on references to him inside the FSB and Kremlin being in the masculine."

"Sorry. Continue," Helen said meekly.

Polina walked through a list of a dozen intercepts the CIA had made over the intervening decade, each encrypted, and each believed to originate from the mysterious Scorpius.

"How many of his messages have been successfully decrypted?" Helen asked.

The hacker, Chunk, fielded that one. "The early messages went out before 256-bit encryption and were cracked years ago. Although the intel was sensitive at the time, the contents of those first several messages do not remain damaging. Messages five and six were only cracked recently. Both contained top secret material, but the damage caused by their leaks has been contained. The last half-dozen messages remain encrypted."

"Why's that?" she asked curiously.

"Blockchain encryption. It's a bitch," Chunk answered.

"Is it decryptable at all?" she followed up.

"It's technically possible to brute-force a decryption if you throw enough supercomputing power at it, but in practical reality, no," he answered ruefully.

She was intrigued that the second most recent Scorpius intercept was only a few months old, right about the time the DaVinci
Killer had been terrorizing Washington, DC.

A sicko named Ryan Goetz had murdered people and then
staged their bodies to imitate great works of art, earning himself
the DaVinci moniker. She and everyone else had believed he was
Scorpius.

Except, with his dying breaths, Goetz had confessed he was a
copycat. He believed it was the original DaVinci Killer who had
crucified him in imitation of a Salvador Dali painting called *Christ
of Saint John on the Cross.*

That was right before a man had shot Goetz where he hung on
the cross. Goetz's last words had been to shout, "Scorpius! No!"

Helen had chased the shooter through a snowy forest, ultimately killing him. The man had worn the same wool coat and fedora she'd seen Scorpius wear the one time she'd gotten close to
him before.

But then, James Wagner had hijacked her in his limousine a
few days ago and told her the dead man in the woods was not, in
fact, the Russian mole.

And here she was. Standing in the middle of a snake den.
Metaphorically barefoot. And she *hated* snakes.

Polina had resumed the briefing. ". . . also have a file of intel
obtained from within various Russian agencies believed to have
originated with Scorpius. From that, we've built a list of possible
suspects."

A list of names flashed up on the screen. There had to be three
dozen of them. *Ugh.* She refrained from pointing out that it was
possible Scorpius was more than one person, which meant the actual suspect list could be *much* longer.

If this group was convinced Scorpius was one person, she was
willing to work with that premise for now. Even though DCI Wagner seemed convinced Scorpius might, in fact, be a team.

"Let me guess," she said dryly. "Exhaustive investigation of the
suspects on your list yielded no evidence that any of them could
be Scorpius."

"Correct," Polina snapped, sounding chagrined.

Grouchy much? Clearly the woman didn't like having her thunder stolen. Helen subsided, leaning back in her chair to let Polina finish her briefing without any further interruptions.

"We widened the scope of our investigation after the initial suspect group was eliminated. We identified subordinates, coworkers, and superiors of the original list who might plausibly have access to the Russian intel from Scorpius." Polina continued, "Again, our investigation yielded no evidence of a mole."

Obviously, or the task force wouldn't still be up and running.

"We then widened our scope to anyone who might've had access to the means and methods of contacting our Russian counterparts."

Helen stared in surprise. That had to encompass just about everyone in the agency. "And how did that go?"

"There was no way to narrow down the suspect list. We ultimately decided on a new approach: to wit, investigating high-level intel officers whom we felt could do the most damage to the agency if they turned out to be Scorpius."

An interesting tactic. Rather than hunt the guy, they would try to eliminate as suspects the people they most hoped weren't Scorpius.

Polina put another slide up on the projection wall showing a long list of names. Out of perhaps a hundred, only two were redacted and unreadable.

"Who are the redactions?" she asked.

"Two individuals we have ascertained cannot be Scorpius," Polina answered, visibly reluctant.

"Their names, dear. What are their names?"

"The first is Richard Bell. Given that he was in charge of hunting Scorpius and put this team together to help him hunt, he can't very well *be* Scorpius."

"And the second name?" she asked gently.

"Uh . . ." Polina didn't finish the sentence. In fact, the woman looked around at the others at the table in what looked like con-

sternation. The rest of the group stared back in similar consternation.

Finally, Ritika blurted, "You, ma'am. The other person is you."

Helen didn't react, not with any expression of surprise, nor
with any change whatsoever in her body language. When swim-
ming with sharks, one did well never to show fear. She remained
relaxed in her seat, studying the people staring back at her.

"Why did you eliminate me from consideration?" she asked.
Privately, she was pleased with how unconcerned her voice sounded.
She hadn't lost all her acting skills, by golly.

Ritika opened her mouth as if to answer, but then Polina
glared her into silence and fielded that one herself. "We followed
you extensively. Searched your home. Tagged and bugged your
car. But when Scorpius was linked to an attempt to kill you, it became obvious you couldn't be him."

Not to mention she was the wrong gender to be Scorpius and
she'd been retired when the last two messages from Scorpius had
been sent. They'd followed her, huh? And searched her home?
That was cheeky of them. She made a mental note to search her
car and home thoroughly for any lingering listening devices or
trackers.

Bits and pieces of the past few months started falling into
place. The woman jogger in the National Zoo that day last winter
when she'd killed the Russian sniper . . .

She never forgot a face.

In fact . . . Helen gazed down the table at Ritika. She mentally
dressed the young woman in a jogging suit and ski cap, pulled her
hair back in a ponytail, made her cheeks red with cold, and put a
cloud of condensed breath in front of her face. No doubt about
it. Ritika was the jogger from the zoo.

That night a couple of months ago when her house alarm had
triggered—that must've been this crew, too. Good to know. A relief, actually. She'd been convinced at the time it was Russians trying to kill her.

She asked, "Was it you guys who followed me away from Yosef

Mizrah's house late one evening in, let's see—that would've been early January?"

Everyone at the table exchanged loaded looks. Benjamin finally answered, "No, ma'am. That wasn't us."

Ritika blurted, "She doesn't like being called ma'am."

The group fell awkwardly silent. Helen shrugged. "Ritika is correct. Please call me Helen. And I'd appreciate it if you would all take a deep breath and relax. I've come out of retirement to head up this one investigation, and then I'll be going back to my knitting, baking, and spoiling my grand-dog. I'm not here to play political games or climb the corporate ladder. Once we catch Scorpius, I'm out. And you're sure it wasn't you at Yosef's house?"

Benjamin answered again, "Mr. Mizrah rarely goes out once he arrives at his residence. We send the surveillance team home as soon as he's tucked in for the night."

So they were watching Yosef, too? Was he a serious suspect to be Scorpius?

Benjamin was saying, ". . . don't have the manpower to keep teams sitting around watching people sleep."

Just how much manpower did they have? They couldn't very well watch every senior CIA officer in the entire agency. Or could they?

She didn't know whether to believe Benjamin or not when he denied having followed her from Yosef's house. Why would this bunch lie to her? Did they still think she might be Scorpius? Was there another suspect list that didn't have her name redacted from it? Or was it more about them having been Richard Bell's people and suspicious of some outsider? Either way, the tension within this group, and between it and her, was palpable.

"What's the status of the investigation now?" Helen asked to break the taut silence.

"The last victim of the DaVinci killings was a man named Ryan Goetz." Polina flashed up a grisly image of Goetz hanging, dead, from a large wooden cross suspended high in the air.

If Polina had thought to shock her, she could think again. Not only had Helen watched dozens of her targets' heads vaporize over the years, she'd also been in that barn with Goetz in the last minutes before he died.

The image in front of her didn't include the slow sound of Ryan's blood dripping to the tarp below, or the labored rasp of his breathing with lungs full of fluid and partially crushed by hanging on a cross. It didn't include the metallic smell of Ryan's blood, the stench of him having soiled himself, and it didn't show the desperation with which she and Yosef had searched for a way to get him down before he expired.

The picture on the wall also didn't include the deafening report of the gunshot from the doorway behind them as the man they'd thought was Scorpius killed Goetz where he hung.

Helen asked casually, "What does this poor young man have to do with a CIA mole?"

Everyone looked away in varying degrees of disappointment and confusion. Helen mentally snorted. As if every grandma in creation hadn't seen blood and gore aplenty by the time they'd lived for decades, particularly if they'd raised families. Women her age were a lot tougher than they looked, thank you very much.

Polina continued, "When the FBI searched Mr. Goetz's apartment, they found this." The woman paused dramatically before flashing up the collection of photographs, newspaper clippings, printed emails, and the like that Goetz had collected and pinned up on his bedroom wall in a macabre homage to the original DaVinci Killer.

It had been Helen, Yosef, and Angela Vincent, acting in her capacity as an attorney to witness their entry to Goetz's home, who'd found the collage in the first place.

Helen asked innocently, "Did you learn anything interesting from Mr. Goetz's collection?"

Greg piped up. "Goetz seemed to think the DaVinci Killer was a Russian spy calling himself Scorpius."

"Did Goetz have any evidence to link the two?" she asked.

"Not that I saw."

If she trusted this crew, she would share with them that when she and Yosef had first seen the collage, it had been clear that several key pieces of evidence had been removed from the wall. She and Yosef believed Scorpius had gotten to the apartment first and stolen anything that would identify him or positively link Scorpius to the original DaVinci Killer.

But she didn't trust this crew. So she said nothing.

She'd spent a lot of time wondering why a Russian mole would engage in serial killing as a hobby. After all, a mole's prime directive would be to draw no attention to himself. Not only had the DaVinci Killer run around murdering people, he'd done it in the flashiest possible way, posting artistic videos on thrill kill sites on the Dark Web. He'd been famous in certain underground circles.

A profiler would probably say Scorpius sought attention through his DaVinci kills. That keeping the secret of being the most successful mole in the world, and receiving no recognition for it, chafed at him. That Scorpius relished the fame and fear his DaVinci kills inspired.

Still, if the guy wanted to impress people, why choose murder as the means?

Her best guess was that Scorpius felt a need to blow off steam from time to time. That the stress of his double life got to him. And that committing violent acts somehow relieved his tension.

"Who's your current prime suspect to be Scorpius?" she asked the group.

Nobody answered.

"No harm, no foul, kids," Helen said lightly. "I'm asking for a guess. I won't report what you answer to anyone. I'm just trying to get a feel for where we are in the investigation."

Polina crossed her arms defensively, and Jack and Benjamin were only slightly less obvious in their dislike of the question.

Ritika looked over at Greg, who finally sighed heavily and leaned forward. He said, "Best guess right now is Lester Reinhold—"

Holy cow. The director of Operations for the entire agency? The man in charge of all field operations, all covert officers, all informants, all human intelligence operations?

"Or Yosef Mizrah," Greg finished.

Yossi? Her handler of some thirty years? They thought he was a Russian mole? An urge to burst out laughing nearly overcame her self-discipline. It was beyond ridiculous. She knew him better than she knew her own husband. No way.

And yet . . . the paranoid side of her brain that operated in suspicion and innuendo, that questioned everything and everyone, whispered, *But his wife is in the end stages of ALS. Her health care has to be costing a fortune. And Yosef would do anything for Ruth. Anything at all.*

Had he turned on his country to pay for making his wife's last days as comfortable as possible? When had Ruth gotten her diagnosis anyway? She tried to think back, to pinpoint a date.

It had to have been close to a decade ago. Yosef had talked about how glad they were she'd had an unusually long period of relative health before the disease had destroyed her quality of life and begun its long, terrible descent toward death.

Helen happened to know Ruth's doctors wanted her hospitalized now, but Yosef had chosen to bring in round-the-clock nurses and expensive medical equipment to honor her wish to die at home.

An ache started in the vicinity of her heart and spread outward through her chest. Surely not Yossi. He'd been her friend, her anchor, her stalwart defender inside the agency and outside.

He'd planned her missions with her, built emergency escape plans for her—he'd even talked her through using them when needed. He was solely responsible for bringing her home safely to her family more times than she could count.

He'd been her only emotional support out in the field, her bulwark against the creeping paranoia and paralyzing fear inspired by her work, for as long as she'd worked for the agency.

Her husband had only a vague idea of what she really did, and her children, mother, and friends had no idea whatsoever that she'd been an assassin. Only Yossi knew everything about her and loved her anyway.

Her breastbone felt as if it was slowly, agonizingly cracking in half.

Not Yossi. Please, God. Not Yossi.

CHAPTER 11

DANNY LOOKED AROUND THE CHEMISTRY LECTURE HALL, SEARCHING for Shayna. He didn't see her anywhere. *Weird. She never cuts class.*

He spotted one of her friends, a girl he thought lived in the same dorm, and stepped over a couple of guys to sit down beside her.

"Hey, Danny."

"Hey." He couldn't remember her name. "Where's Shayna?"

"Didn't you hear? Her roommate has gone missing. The police are searching for her and everything."

He stared at the girl in shock. "Did they search the frat Karly was last seen in?"

"They started there. No sign of her, though. Nobody there knew where she went. Apparently, there was some giant orgy at the frat the night before, and everybody got ragingly drunk and passed out. A whole bunch of girls were still there, and everybody was just waking up the next afternoon when the police arrived."

He said, "I heard the university is investigating the party."

The girl shrugged. "Sigma Rho Alpha is full of rich kids. Sons of politicians and businesspeople. Their daddies will roll in and get the university to drop the whole thing." She added bitterly, "You watch. In a few days, there won't be even a whisper of scandal. Just a missing scholarship girl nobody cares about."

"Where do you suppose Karly went?" he asked.

"Who knows? Her cell phone went dark. Her parents say she

would never run away. Her grades were great. Shayna says Karly was happy and not depressed or anything. Never talked about taking off or suicide."

"Is there a boyfriend?" he tried.

"No. She wasn't into dating, and guys weren't into her. She was pretty focused on her studies."

"Weird," he murmured as the chem professor stepped up to the lectern.

"I know. Right?" the girl murmured back.

What was Shayna saying to the police? Had she told them his name? How he'd given her a ride home from the party and torn up the lawn of the frat? Was he in trouble for wrecking all that stupid grass? His dad was gonna be pissed if he had to pay for replacing the whole front lawn of that stuck-up frat.

As the professor launched into today's lecture, he fantasized about what Karly's dead body might look like. Had she been buried? Would it be covered in dirt? Clothed or naked? Or maybe she'd drowned. Nah, he didn't like that scenario. She would bloat up like a balloon and be gross. Maybe she'd been raped. Left for dead somewhere. In a forest, maybe. With her long hair spread out around her. Better. He liked that image quite a lot.

He would bet insects had eaten her eyes out by now. He envisioned empty eye sockets staring up at the trees, the only witnesses to her end.

It was a great chemistry lecture.

CHAPTER 12

*A*FTER THE BRIEFING, HELEN RETURNED TO HER DESK AND PULLED another sheet of paper out of her purse. This one had the name of a classified website and Yosef's log-in information, which he'd given her yesterday over the phone.

A facial recognition program opened on her screen.

Surreptitiously eyeing her team and waiting until no one was looking her way, she plugged in her husband's thumb drive and loaded the image of the guy from behind the Japanese restaurant into the software. Yosef said she would either get a hit right away, or it would take hours.

She waited several minutes, but the hourglass icon on the screen continued to spin slowly. *Okay, then.* This was going to be a slow one.

She turned off the monitor but left her computer running as she left her desk. Walking out into the main room, she pulled up a spare desk chair and sat down beside Ritika. She kept her voice low. "Tell me about your coworkers. What are they like to work with?"

"Oh, uh, they're fine," the young woman said nervously.

Helen lowered her voice even more. "I can already tell Polina's quite the bitch. I gather she and Richard Bell were close. Is she mad he didn't take her with him to his new job?"

"She's furious she's still stuck down here," Ritika said quietly.

Ha. Polina *was* Bell's spy.

"And Benjamin? Is he one of Richard's guys?" Helen asked lightly.

Ritika looked startled. "He's a recent addition to the team. I think someone else muscled him into the Box. Jack is Richard Bell's guy, or at least he wants to be. Followed Mr. Bell around like an eager puppy waiting to perform a trick and be told he's a good boy."

"What about Greg?"

"He keeps to himself. Doesn't say much to anyone. He's smarter than he looks, though. Doesn't miss a thing that goes on around here."

"Is he loyal to Richard Bell?"

"No idea. He just comes in, looks at pictures, writes up reports, and goes home."

She highly doubted his life was that dull. But from Ritika's midtwenties perspective on life, that was probably all she saw in people of middle age.

"Can I help you with something?" Polina asked officiously from behind Helen.

Helen looked up. "You can give me a tour of the equipment and capabilities we have down here. Just don't get too technical with me. All this newfangled stuff gets a little overwhelming." She waved her hands helplessly.

She caught the look Polina and Jack exchanged over her head. *You two go right ahead and underestimate the old lady Wagner brought in to babysit you.*

She sensed Ritika's tension beside her, and now that the younger woman had mentioned it, she noticed that Greg was subtly keeping an eye on the conversation over here. What was his deal?

If she were Scorpius, she would definitely want someone loyal to her down here to report every lead the team found that might point at her. Was Greg that guy?

Helen noticed out of the corner of her eye that Jack was hovering just behind Polina. As far as she could tell, he had climbed up Polina's metaphorical ass and was firmly lodged there. Which meant he thought she was going places in the agency and could take him along for the ride. The guy probably wasn't wrong. Smart, ambitious people who could play ruthless political games usually did well around here.

Realizing she'd been silent a long time, she asked, "Do we have an ID on this hit man you think Scorpius hired to kill Goetz?" Which was to say, the hit man she'd chased after he shot Goetz and whom she'd eventually killed herself.

When nobody else answered her question, Greg piped up from his desk. "No ID. He's a John Doe. I've got a picture of him around here somewhere."

She stared at him in surprise as he fished around on his messy desk. "With access to basically every database anywhere, the agency hasn't been able to match any identification at all to him?"

"Nope. Guy's fingerprints were burned off. He had full dental implants and cosmetic surgery to alter his face. Medium height. Medium build. Medium everything. He was flying completely under the radar."

Exactly like a completely off-the-books assassin would if he was out to completely erase his identity. And someone like that had worked for Scorpius? She didn't like this, not one bit.

She knew firsthand that John Doe had been good. Very good. She'd been lucky to make it out of the woods alive. It had taken every ounce of her training and decades of experience to prevail that day. There had to be some way to figure out who he was.

"Here we go," Greg announced.

Helen stood up and went over to Greg's desk to stare down at a head shot of John Doe's corpse. Greg was not wrong about the guy being completely unmemorable. Which was a common trait among the best assassins in the world.

Frowning, she asked, "What about John Doe's weapon? What did he kill Goetz with?"

Greg fielded that one, too. He fished around in a pile on his desk and pulled out an eight-by-ten photo of a handgun, which he laid in front of her.

She identified it at a glance as a Remington XP100 but played dumb and asked him, "What's that?"

"It's a special pistol designed for long-range shooting. This one has a bunch of after-market modifications. Ben's been working on tracking down who made the mods, but he can't find anybody who recognizes this weapon. He thinks the dead guy made the mods himself."

"I gather then that every avenue this team has pursued has led to a dead end. In other words, Scorpius is as much a ghost today as he's ever been."

"Correct," Greg answered gravely.

Great. She was supposed to find and kill a man who'd successfully evaded the best surveillance on the planet. How in the heck was she supposed to do that? Worse, her family's lives might very well depend on her succeeding.

Helen returned to her own desk. The hourglass on her computer screen was still spinning. While she waited for the search to finish, she pulled out a pad of paper and a pen to take a few notes on possible new ways to hunt Scorpius. She slid a plastic clipboard behind the top sheet of paper to leave no impression from her writing on the sheets below and jotted down:

Better way to trace Scorpius messages?

ID important intel of interest to Russia—watch its handlers.

Reluctantly, she added to her list:

Continue surveillance on Yosef and Lester Reinhold.

She couldn't bring herself to write down the truly crazy idea, which would be to use herself as bait to draw out Scorpius. She liked that idea about as much as she liked playing office politics.

Of course, she had to accept the possibility that the facial recognition program wouldn't find anything on the guy from the restaurant and that she would be back to square zero on her hunt for Scorpius.

She stared at her list in frustration. There had to be another way to find Scorpius.

Without warning, her computer screen lit up. The facial recognition program had a result. Holding her breath in anticipation, she clicked on the button that said VIEW NOW.

Roger Skidmore. Age 42. Residence: Arlington, Virginia. She printed off a copy of his driver's license and laid it beside the printout she'd made at the hotel. She was startled to compare the two images. At a glance, the pictures looked nothing like each other. In fact, she had to stare hard at both to pick out the similarities in cheekbones, the set of the eyes, and the shape of the jaw.

In the driver's license picture, Skidmore had a beard that obscured his lower face. The man from the restaurant had brown hair and dark eyes. The guy in the driver's license had light hair and light eyes. She had to give him credit. He was quite the chameleon. But ultimately, he hadn't been able to fool a computer.

Who are you, Roger Skidmore? Which, of course, wasn't his real name.

She was going hunting, it seemed. To that end, she pulled up Skidmore's address on a map program and studied the neighborhood around the high-rise apartment building.

She was interrupted at memorizing egress routes from the area by her desk phone ringing. "Hello?" she said cautiously. Scratchy static filled her ear, and a green light illuminated on the phone's base unit. *Ah. A secure call.*

"Helen, it's Jim."

Jim? She didn't know any—oh, James Wagner. Glancing up, she noticed Polina watching her from her desk. Helen nodded pleasantly at her and then whited out her office walls in case Polina read lips.

"What the hell happened at that restaurant?" Wagner demanded.

"Andrew was fine one minute and feeling terrible the next—" she started.

"It was cyanide," Wagner interrupted. "He was poisoned."

She felt as if she'd just been punched in the stomach. "Oh, my God."

"How come you weren't poisoned?" he demanded.

"Gee, I love you, too." She took a breath to collect herself. "The sake. It was the only thing he consumed that I didn't."

"Our people went back to the restaurant, but the dishes had

been washed and the food disposed of. No way to trace it." Wagner sounded exasperated, as well he should.

"Quick question, sir. Did Richard Bell tell you his team has nothing at all on Scorpius?"

"I beg your pardon?"

Damn it. Wagner sounded surprised. If she told the DCI exactly how little Bell's team had accomplished, she would make an enemy of Bell. Sure, she was going back into retirement after this, but Bell was a senior CIA official and could go after her kids' careers. Mitch was running for office and Li, Peter's husband, worked at the NSA. Jaynie was still looking for a job, but she had faith Bell could find a way to mess with her life, too.

Of course, if she lied to Wagner and he found out, he could tank her kids' careers as easily as Bell could.

Helen said grimly, "I just got briefed. This team has nothing. No leads. Nada. Zilch. They've resorted to tailing people whom they think would be most damaging if they are Scorpius, in hopes of eliminating them from suspicion."

"Bell told me they'd narrowed down the suspect list considerably."

She snorted. "Yeah, and then they found nothing. They have no idea who Scorpius is."

She waited out a pregnant pause from the other end of the line. Then Wagner said, "Keep at it, Helen. We've got to find this mole. If he killed Andrew to cover his tracks, he could take out anyone else in the agency who gets close to his identity."

Yeah. Like me.

She pointed out, "Scorpius could've taken out Andrew because he was ordered to by Moscow."

He burst out, "They'd better *not* have ordered him—" He broke off and said more calmly, "I won't go to war with the FSB without proof that they ordered the hit on Andrew."

"Speaking of which, I may have a lead on who poisoned him."

"What is it?" he asked quickly.

"A guy jumped me as I was leaving the restaurant—"

"Jeez, Helen!"

She continued, "I'm fine. I have a face and a name. I'll send them to you—"

He cut her off sharply. "Don't send me anything. We have to assume every line of communication inside the agency is compromised."

"Even this call?" she blurted.

"I'm on a stupidly encrypted crisis phone and can't do this often—it draws too much attention. Questions get asked. I'm only supposed to use this line in a national emergency. If you find out who killed Andrew, tell me in person. Off campus."

Meaning away from CIA headquarters. "Understood, sir."

"If it's war the FSB wants, it's an effing war they'll get," he said grimly.

"Let's not start killing Russian agents just yet," she said in alarm.

"Find out who killed Andrew."

"Does that take priority over Scorpius?"

"I'm betting one will lead to the other. And hurry. We need to stop Scorpius before anyone else dies."

"You think Andrew wasn't the only target?" she blurted.

"I'm sending my new number two out of the country on an unscheduled vacation, one day after appointing him," he snapped.

Holy cow. He seriously thought Scorpius was going to take out more senior CIA officials? That would be a declaration of war indeed by the Russians.

Except . . .

She frowned, confused. Why would the Russians take a highly placed mole who'd been feeding Russia valuable information for years—and who could keep on doing so indefinitely—and turn him into an active killer? The Russians had to know the agency would turn itself inside out to find the killer and stop him. Did the Russians think Scorpius was about to get burned? Had they ordered him to eliminate as many high-ranking CIA officers as he could before he was caught?

"Maybe you should take a vacation, too," she suggested.

"Find Scorpius, Helen. And when you do, take the bastard out."

"I have an official sanction then?" she asked tersely.

"Yes. Kill him. Find anyone who works with him and kill them all."

Well, okay, then.

The line went dead.

She had to assume from Wagner's dramatic declaration that he was scared to death. After all, the CIA would undoubtedly prefer to interrogate Scorpius within an inch of his life before actually killing him.

Wagner clearly believed Andrew was not the only target. Which meant her boss also believed the CIA *was* about to go to war with the FSB. It hadn't happened often in the history of the two intelligence agencies, but when it had, dozens of operatives for both organizations had died all over the world. As for the CIA, it had taken years to rebuild some of the spy networks and informants it had lost.

She swore under her breath as she stared down at her notepad. Grimly, she wrote down:

Use self as bait.

It would be a last resort, but she could no longer rule it out.

CHAPTER 13

Angela Vincent looked up as her friend Helen stepped into her plain, old-fashioned law office. She kept this place the way it had been the day she first hung out her shingle. It reminded her of where she'd come from. No matter how rich or successful she got—and she was both—she'd come from nothing, educated herself, and had come home to serve the people she'd grown up with.

She pushed back from her desk and came around it to hug Helen.

"How are you holding up, Angie?" Helen asked in warm concern.

A knife of grief sliced across her middle. Her lover, Derek Cahill, the district attorney Helen's son was running to replace, had been murdered a few months back, leaving her devastated. Worse, because she was the other woman, people seemed to expect her to keep her grief as secret as her relationship with him had been.

She replied, "I'm not gonna lie. It's been hard. I've been trying to box up his things, but I can't bring myself to do it."

"Can I help? Let's go upstairs right now and take a look, shall we?" Helen said briskly.

Ugh. She wasn't happy at the prospect, but it did have to happen sometime. She marched up to the swanky crash pad she kept over her law office for late nights—and until recently, trysts with her boyfriend.

Embarrassed, she opened the door and stepped back as Helen entered the chic space.

Her friend gazed around impassively at the mess. Open cardboard boxes sat everywhere, half-packed. "Aw, honey," Helen said sympathetically. "Who is all this stuff supposed to be shipped to anyway?"

She sighed. "His wife wants his things back."

"Do you want to give it back?"

"The stuff here was ours, not his wife's."

"Then send her a box of his dirty laundry and call it good," Helen said practically.

Angela laughed. "And that's why I love you."

Helen headed for the bedroom, snagging an empty box on the way. She barged into the big walk-in closet and scooped up the laundry basket sitting on his side of the space beneath a row of expensive men's suits. "Is there anything in here you're attached to?" she asked, shoving the basket toward her.

Angela poked halfheartedly in the laundry. "I don't see anything . . ."

"Perfect." Helen dumped the contents in the box and closed the lid. "There. Mail that to his wife and tell her it's everything."

Angela dashed a few tears from her cheeks. If only she could pack up and mail this pain and loss to his widow instead. The way Derek had described the woman, she was an unfeeling bitch only interested in the perks his career had brought her.

Helen asked, "Have you opened the safe yet? Didn't you say once that he kept some of his files here at your place?"

"I haven't been able to bring myself to do it. Not to mention, I lost the combination. Derek wrote it down for me when he first had that thing installed. But I don't know what I did with it."

"If he had information on any ongoing prosecutions in the safe, the district attorney's office might need it."

"I know, I know. I'll do it soon, I promise."

"This is a rip-the-bandage-off situation," her friend advised. "Promise me you'll do it today."

"Fine. I promise."

"By the way, Angie. Is there any chance you know how I can get in touch with Clint? I've been trying to call him, and he hasn't picked up or returned my messages."

Clint was the private investigator she used when she needed that kind of help with a case. He was a military vet and a terrific PI when his PTSD wasn't flaring up.

"Clint? Have you got a problem? Anything I can help with?"

Helen sighed. "I'm not sure. I'll let you know if I need a lawyer's help."

Angela shrugged. "Clint disappears from time to time. Goes off the grid for a while. If I hear from him, I'll tell him you're trying to reach him."

"Thanks."

She walked Helen out and returned reluctantly to her apartment.

It took a lengthy search of her desk, but she finally found the index card with the scrawled safe combination on it. She dialed it into the lock and opened the thick metal door. The scent of Derek's cologne wafted out of the interior, and she dropped to her knees, sobbing.

They'd been convinced their opposing careers would cause trouble if they went public with their relationship, and of course, there'd been the problem of how much his wife would extort from him in return for a quiet divorce. He'd feared a messy one would have a negative impact on his career.

If only they'd known they would have so little time together. Maybe they would've thrown caution and their careers to the wind and been a couple for real.

If only. Oh, how she hated that phrase.

As the wave of grief passed through her and receded for the hundredth time, she reached woodenly into the safe and pulled out the tall stack of files. She carried it into the living room and flopped down on the couch with it.

She opened the first file. Inside were photographs of a rather prominent congressman . . . dressed in women's clothes. *What on earth?* She thumbed through the pictures, which became increasingly lurid, including pictures of the congressman kissing a young man and pictures of them in bed.

For all the world, these looked like blackmail pictures. Surely Derek hadn't been holding these over a United States congressman!

She set the file aside and picked up the next one. Inside was a lengthy legal document. This was more like it.

Except as she started to read the draft of a court filing, it accused the wife of an extremely powerful lobbyist of a hit-and-run accident where she'd drunkenly struck and killed a pedestrian.

Angela frowned. She didn't remember hearing about anything like that. It would've made the news, and surely Derek would've mentioned it to her. They'd discussed most of their cases with each other when there was no conflict of interest in doing so.

She fetched her laptop and typed the name of the lobbyist's wife into a search engine. Nothing about a car accident popped up. She got the date of the accident from the file and typed it in as well. Still nothing.

She sat back in dismay. Had Derek been paid off to bury charges against the woman? Surely he hadn't been crooked. He'd believed fiercely in the law. Been the staunchest defender of justice.

In disbelief, she picked up the next file. As she read through the pile, case after case that Derek—or someone—had squelched, was inside. The evidence was all here.

Some of the cases were fairly old. They must've dated back to Derek's earliest days in the DA's office. Had he been dirty his whole career? Had she known him *at all*?

Except, as she went through the files, she realized many of them were in areas of legal specialty that Derek wouldn't have prosecuted. How on earth had he ended up with all this information, then? Had he been collecting it for some purpose? Maybe to expose corruption in the DA's office?

She latched onto the idea hopefully. That sounded more like the man she'd known and loved.

She pulled out a pad of paper and started back through the files, going through them more carefully, listing the dates and what prosecutors had been involved with each case. Was there a pattern here? Someone—or several someones—in the DA's office who came up again and again in conjunction with suppressed or quietly dismissed cases?

She opened yet another file and started to read it. The son of a powerful government official had gotten in trouble. Something to do with a frat party that got a little too wild. A missing girl. But the investigation had been wiped off the books.

She glanced through the paperwork for the name of the attorneys involved. Except it wasn't the prosecutor's name that caught her eye. It was the name of the legal intern on the case.

Her jaw dropped.

Mitchell Warwick.

CHAPTER 14

AFTER A HOT BATH AND A CHANGE INTO FUZZY JAMMIES, HELEN SAT cross-legged on the worn-out sofa in the family room of her rambling farmhouse, sipping a cup of steaming tea. She would be darned if she would let anybody scare her away from her home. Not to mention that she had the best security system money and the tech geeks at the CIA could buy. And a handgun rested on the cushion beside her.

She picked up a legal pad and wrote down the names of the Scorpius hunting team and her initial impressions of each of them. She found that writing down her observations by hand helped clarify her thoughts.

Her cell phone rang. She smiled when she saw the caller ID. "Clint! Thanks for calling me back. How are you doing?"

He skipped the niceties and replied gruffly, "Why'd you call?"

"I could use your help."

"With what?"

Not long on words, this one. She answered, "I'd like you to do some oppositional research."

"You mean like digging up dirt on a political candidate?"

"Exactly," she replied.

"Who's the candidate?"

"Mitchell Warwick."

"Your kid?" he blurted.

"Can I rely on your complete discretion, Clint?"

"Isn't that why you called me?"

"That and you're very good," she allowed.

"And?" he prompted.

She sighed. It was a big risk to trust him. Particularly given that he had PTSD bad enough to trigger paranoid episodes. But he'd done good work for her when she'd needed him to track the Russian mobster who'd almost led her to Scorpius. And there was no one else she could call in this town whom she trusted to keep their mouth shut. Practically everyone and everything was for sale in DC if the price was high enough.

"You still there, Ms. Warwick?" Clint asked.

"I'm here. So here's the thing. An old acquaintance hinted to me there might be a scandal in my father's past, and that it might come back to bite my son as he runs for district attorney."

"Your father?"

"Congressman Henry Stapleton. His career ended abruptly about fifteen years ago. I need you to find out if something or someone forced him out of Congress and what or who it was."

"Old stuff like that can be hard to dig up."

"Price is no object, Clint. Bill me at whatever hourly rate you think is fair."

"Ain't about the money, ma'am. It's about the people in the know being dead. I'll do what I can, but I can't promise results."

"That would be an answer in and of itself. If you can't find anything, I'm confident nobody else can either."

"I'll be in touch."

"Call me if I can be of any help—" The line went dead in her ear.

He might not be long on manners, but she knew him to be a very good investigator. She picked up the empty plate from the coffee table and padded toward the kitchen.

Something was going on behind the scenes with Mitch's political campaign. She could feel it. She just couldn't see it yet. If only she and her mother were on speaking terms, she would ask Constance what she thought was going on. Her mother had the best political instincts of anyone she'd ever known.

But no way would Constance tell her squat. Especially if it besmirched Henry Stapleton's oh-so-pristine reputation. Constance treated his legacy like some kind of holy relic.

Her cell phone rang, her husband's personalized ringtone, and she dried off her hands hastily to answer it. "Hey, Gray. How's Brazil?"

"Bad. We're having no luck convincing local officials to enforce burn bans in the Amazon. But we'll keep at it. How are you?"

"Tired. My old boss asked me to come back to work for a few weeks on a trade deal I initiated before I retired. They're having trouble with it and need my corporate knowledge." Lord, the lies still slipped off her tongue like melted butter. It was alarming how easily the skill came back to her.

"Does it involve travel?" he asked in alarm.

"No, no. I couldn't travel right now anyway. Not with Mitch's campaign kicking off and the special election only a few months away. He needs the whole family to help him. Speaking of which, is there any chance you'll be coming home soon to campaign for him?"

Gray sighed. "Am I really a good optic for him?"

"Why? Because you're black? Anyone who doesn't vote for Mitch because of the amount of melanin in his father's skin isn't his voter. Mitch would love to have you out on the campaign trail for him. He could use you." She added, "Not to mention, I'll beat up anyone who says anything mean about you."

He laughed, the warm timbre of it reminding her of other times when they'd first met, working together in student government in college. She'd been drawn to his passion from the start and to his eloquence and vision of a better future.

It hadn't hurt that he was hot either, nor that his passion for causes had carried over to passion in other areas of his life. No matter how rocky their marriage had gotten over the years, there had always been fire in their relationship. Enough to see them through the worst of times and pull them back together eventually.

"I've never been any good at polite politics, Helen. You know that."

He was dodging coming home. And she was undoubtedly the

reason. He was probably as exhausted of fighting over her work and travel as she was. A sense of defeat settled heavily upon her. How was she supposed to fix her marriage if her husband wouldn't come home and interact with her? There was only so much they could talk out over the phone.

She sighed. "If you're so bad at politics, why are you in Brazil lobbying to protect the rain forest?"

"Because the Amazon is the lungs of the planet. If we don't protect it, humanity is in serious trouble. Also, politeness isn't required down here. I can say exactly what I think and not worry about who I offend."

Concern speared through her. "Be careful about that. There are some dangerous players in that part of the world. Logging companies could get violent to protect their profits. Drug lords who grow their crops in the jungle could come after you. Shining Path terrorists traffic out of Peru—"

"Honey, I'm sitting in a swanky hotel in Brasilia sipping an aged bourbon on the rocks."

As if criminals weren't rich and didn't hang out in hotels like that? "Grayson, I'm serious. Be careful who you tangle with. I'd hate to have to come down there to rescue you. It could get very messy."

He snorted. "There's no need to call in the cavalry on my account."

"Keep it that way, eh?"

"I will. And good luck with the new job."

"Old job. Hopefully a short one. And then I can go back to my peaceful retirement."

He snorted. "The same retirement that got the boys' house shot up?"

"I can't help it if I happened to be the one at Peter and Li's place when robbers broke in."

"The same way you can't help it that three of those *robbers*"—he leaned on the word heavily—"ended up dead?"

She shrugged. "I'm a good shot. What can I say?"

"Uh-huh. No more shenanigans like that out of you, okay? You're done. Retired."

"On that, we are in complete agreement. I'm ready to settle down and learn how to cook."

"God save us all."

"Hey, now!" She added sincerely, "Good luck with your lobbying."

"These people. They're so blinded by the size of the Amazon, they think it's okay to cut it down by the millions of acres and it'll just keep growing back—"

"You don't need to give that speech to me—" She broke off. "I'm sorry. I'm tired. Today was my first day of work, and I'd forgotten how much I hate office politics."

Silence fell between them. The same silence she'd never known how to fill and that had driven them apart over the years.

She took a deep breath and tried to bridge the gap. "Come home soon. I miss you."

He seemed surprised when he replied, "I've missed you, too."

Missed. Past tense. She sighed.

He cleared his throat awkwardly. "Right. I'll let you go to bed then. Just promise me. No travel. And no guns."

"I already said I wasn't going to travel."

"I'll hold you to that," he said direly.

"Good night, Gray."

"Good night, Helen."

Frustrated at his reluctance to come home and help with Mitch's campaign, as well as at being maneuvered into going back into the CIA at all, she put her dishes in the dishwasher, checked the house alarm, and headed upstairs to bed. Tomorrow would be another long day.

CHAPTER 15

*H*ELEN WALKED INTO THE BOX AT 9:00 AM THE NEXT MORNING and was surprised to see only Ritika and Greg there. She made a mental note to have a gentle word with the team about not abusing her casual approach to work hours.

As she headed for her office, Ritika sent her a significant look and infinitesimally jerked her head to indicate that Helen should join her. She changed course and strolled over to the young woman.

"Any progress with getting the Russia desk to share hot intel with us?" Helen asked her.

"They're stonewalling us. They say we don't have a need to know any special compartmentalized information."

"I was afraid of that." Helen pondered whether she could talk Yosef into unofficially sharing the most sensitive intelligence he had on Russia with her. It felt like an abuse of their friendship to ask it of him—

"But I have an idea," Ritika was saying.

"What's that?"

"What if we get the Russia desk to tag its intelligence reports somehow? Then all we would have to do is track the tags and not the actual information in the reports."

Helen rolled Chunk's chair over beside Ritika and sat down in it. "Interesting. What kind of tag could we use?"

"I expect the Russians are extremely careful with their super-mole and make sure nothing that comes from him is tagged in any of the usual ways. Like stripping any extraneous computer code out of emails or files he sends."

"Agreed."

Ritika continued, "If Scorpius is operating old school and making paper drops, the Russians will surely scan the heck out of anything he gives them for microdots or tracking fibers."

"What's a tracking fiber?" Helen asked.

"A thin filament of metal that can be embedded in anything—fabric or paper, for example. It's passive, meaning it doesn't send out a signal. But it can be tracked using a scanning device that picks up the magnetic signature specific to that filament."

Ritika must've caught Helen's frown, since she added, "Think of the filament like a strand of DNA. Magnetic information is stored at various points along its length and creates a unique code that a scanner can be programmed to look for."

Interesting. "Can information be coded onto the filament?"

"I suppose it could," Ritika answered, looking surprised. "I'm not an expert in that kind of tech, but I can ask."

"Not important. I'm sorry, I've sidetracked you. We were talking about tagging Russian intel reports."

"Right. Like I was saying, the Russians will check for any tracking devices, physical or electronic, on any reports Scorpius sends to them. But what if we go *super* old school and slip a code word of some kind into the reports themselves? We can ask the Russia desk to put a specific word into each report it generates that's not used in any other current intel reports. It could be a name or a very specific vocabulary word. Then we have the computers look for that one word in outgoing message traffic."

"A single word could generate thousands of hits in a search, couldn't it?" Helen asked.

Ritika shrugged. "What else have we got to do around here except sort through emails? And we know it would be highly classified message traffic, which would narrow it down considerably. Plus we can choose weird, old-fashioned words or maybe get the

Russia desk to use odd code names for a while. You know, like made-up words."

That she could see Yosef agreeing to. "I think I could get the senior Russia analysts to do that."

Ritika warmed to her topic. "Then they wouldn't have to share intel with us. They could just share a list of code words attached to the intel they think is likeliest to be stolen by Scorpius. We might only have to track a few dozen words instead of hundreds or thousands."

"Great idea. Well done. If you could write that up for me, maybe include a few examples, I'll hand deliver it and twist a few arms to get them to play along."

Helen put her hands on the desk to stand up, and Ritika did an odd thing. She reached forward casually and laid her hand on top of Helen's. As Helen felt something slip under her palm, it dawned on her that Ritika was using her body to block Greg from seeing the exchange.

Ritika leaned back and said a bit louder than necessary, "I'll get right on it, ma'am."

Helen smiled and stood, pushed Chunk's chair back to his desk, and headed for her office. She whited out the walls before she opened her hand. A rolled scrap of paper lay in her palm. She unrolled it and read a message handwritten on it.

P. and Ch. cloned ur computer.

Ur? Ah. Shorthand for *your.* Polina and Chunk, huh? Was this a legitimate warning? Or was it some sort of gambit by Richard Bell's people to make her paranoid and throw her off balance?

It was Tradecraft 101 to take nothing at face value, of course, to assume everyone had an ulterior motive for everything they did. What was Ritika's motive in passing her this note? And why would Polina and Chunk clone her computer?

First order of business, she needed to find out who Ritika worked for. Was the young woman loyal to her and trying to help by passing this note, or was she in the Richard Bell camp, too?

Helen thought back to everything she'd done on her office desktop computer. The one real thing she'd done on it was the facial recognition search for Roger Skidmore. Given that she'd told no one where she'd seen him or why she'd searched for him, she doubted Polina and Chunk would make anything of it.

So much for gathering information on Richard Bell from her desk, though. For that matter, she probably couldn't use any of the agency computers safely to look for information on a man like him.

She sat down at her desk and wrote up a progress report to James Wagner rambling on about getting settled into her office and getting up to speed with where her team was at with their investigation. She said exactly nothing of significance. But she might as well keep Polina and Chunk fed with fake information for Bell.

For that matter, she would lay odds someone on Scorpius's payroll worked down here and was reporting to him, too.

Now, how do I go about actually hunting for Scorpius under everyone's noses?

CHAPTER 16

*H*ELEN MADE A POINT OF SITTING AT A TABLE COMPLETELY OUT OF view of the restaurant's windows. The last time she'd met Yosef for a drink, he'd been shot through the front window of the pub and nearly died.

She let her gaze wander across the crowd of diners and staff, looking for any movement out of the ordinary, any surreptitious glance her way, any indication of awareness of her presence. She also looked for people whose backs were turned but whose phones were pointed in her direction, anyone seated where they could see a reflection of her in a window or the mirror behind the bar. It had taken her an hour to be reasonably certain no one had followed her from her home, and the last thing she wanted to do was lead Scorpius or some killer he'd hired to Yosef again.

Yossi can't be Scorpius. He just can't.

At their last meeting, Yosef had passed her an encrypted document sent by Scorpius to someone who worked for him. Surely Yosef wouldn't have done that and then had someone shoot him in the middle of the chest in what should have been a fatal attack, just to hide his tracks if he *were* Scorpius.

Speaking of Yosef, she spied his silhouette in the doorway and watched him make his way toward her, noting with sadness that he was moving like an old man these days. He was still recovering from his gunshot wound. Of course, Ruth's impending death also had to be taking a toll on him.

"Helen, it's so good to see you."

She rose to embrace him, and they traded kisses on both cheeks, European-style. "You're looking well, Yossi."

"That's a lie, but a kind one. Thank you."

A waitress came and they ordered bottles of spring water and the lunch special—a sandwich, soup, and salad combination. The young woman took their menus and disappeared, leaving the two of them alone.

"So how've you been?" he asked, casting his voice low under the din around them.

She spoke in the same tone, careful not to move her mouth enough for a lip reader to figure out what she was saying. "Did you hear Wagner brought me back to run the hunt for Scorpius?"

"I did. Lester Reinhold mentioned it to me."

She shook her head. "My team has zero idea who Scorpius is. Which leaves them with nothing but ambition and the knives they're busy stabbing in one another's backs."

"Sounds like the sort of group Richard Bell would assemble," Yosef commented.

"Meaning what?"

"Meaning Bell has a reputation for enjoying watching his underlings engage in blood sport for his entertainment."

She sighed. "A couple of them seem okay."

"They're the ones to watch the most closely, of course," Yosef replied dryly.

"I know." A pause, then she blurted, "I just hate the posturing and politics."

"Lucky for you, I took care of all that during your career."

"A fact for which I become more grateful every day," she said fervently.

"I gather you didn't ask me to meet you for lunch so you could gripe about your coworkers?" he asked.

She tensed. She couldn't help it. The next words she had to say tasted like bitter gall on her tongue. "Did you know the Scorpius hunters have been investigating you?"

He leaned back in his chair. Studied her in silence for a long time, his expression inscrutable. Which was saying something.

She'd known him for thirty years and could usually read even the most subtle nuance of his body language.

Why, oh, why had he chosen this moment to shut down on her? What was she supposed to think? Was the team right? Was he Scorpius? Agony tore through her. *Not dear Yosef. Please not him.*

Finally, he said blandly, "It makes sense to look at me."

Exactly the sort of thing he would say if he wanted to convince her he wasn't Scorpius. But what if he wasn't Scorpius and was legitimately trying to be helpful?

Gah. Her head hurt from the circles inside circles of logic she was spinning in.

"Why you?" she asked.

"Because I'm one of the highest-level people on the Russia desk. I have access to the kind of information the Russian government would be most interested in. Frankly, I would be disappointed if your team didn't investigate me."

"You're far from the only person on the list," she said lightly.

"Well, now I don't feel special," he teased.

The waitress came with their food, and Helen changed the subject. "How's Ruth?"

"The end is near. She has a feeding tube now and has to be on oxygen all the time. ALS is fully as horrific as we were told it would be. I can see in her eyes that she wants to die. I'm tempted some nights to put a pillow over her face and end it for her. But . . ."—he was silent for a moment and then shrugged—"she's my Ruth. I couldn't live with myself if I ended her life, no matter how compassionate the reason."

Helen reached over and gave his hand a supportive squeeze. "If there's anything I can do, anything at all, you know you only have to ask."

His gaze snapped to hers, and the expression in them shocked her into complete stillness. He'd contemplated asking her to kill Ruth, had he? She'd had no idea he was so desperate.

"Why didn't you tell me it was so bad, Yossi?" she asked softly.

"Because nobody wants to hear about the dying. It reminds us all of our mortality. And God knows, nobody wants to go the way

Ruth has had to. Besides, she would hate being the object of any-one's pity."

"You have gone above and beyond to preserve her dignity, and she knows it. You must see that she's grateful for all you've done and how you've stood beside her."

"She would've done the same for me," he replied sadly.

"Indeed, she would've. She loved—loves—you with all her heart. And I know you've always felt the same about her." Helen admitted, "I was jealous more than once of how happy the two of you were in your marriage. Not all of us are blessed to find our soulmate."

"I don't know. You and Gray seem like a pretty good fit for each other."

She shrugged. "To the extent we've tolerated each other pur-suing careers that took us far from home for extended periods of time, I suppose we are a good fit. But it has not been without its challenges."

"Now that you're done traveling and the two of you can spend more time together, you'll get back into sync and remember why you fell in love," he said wisely.

"I hope so. I really do." It was her greatest fear in life to lose Gray and the kids. She prayed every day that they would forgive her for all her long absences, all the missed holidays and birth-days, all the times they'd needed a wife or a mom and she hadn't been there.

They ate in silence, and throughout the meal she debated whether or not she trusted him. Finally, she arrived at a decision. If she couldn't trust him, she couldn't trust anybody in her life.

She laid down her napkin and reached into her purse, pulling out a plain, white letter envelope with Ritika's plan for tagging Russian intelligence inside it. "Take a look at this when you get back to work and let me know what you think of it. It's an idea one of my people had for tracking our friend."

"You're not using your work computer?" he murmured.

"Nor my office phone," she replied.

Yosef nodded without comment and slipped the envelope into

a pocket inside his suit coat. The waitress brought them coffee, and they sipped it in companionable silence.

"So," Yosef asked as he drained his cup and set it down, "was the main reason you invited me to lunch to watch my reaction when you told me I was being investigated?"

She smiled a little at him. "Actually, I was hoping to get some advice on how to handle my fractious and unproductive team."

He leaned back, studying her intently—as if he didn't believe her. At length, he said, "You're a parent. If they act like teenagers, treat them like teenagers."

She sighed. "Gray and my mother handled the kids when they got unruly in their teens. As you'll recall, I was rather busy during that period." She sighed. "I never was any good at keeping my cool while herding cats."

"I'm sorry about all the travel I asked you to do. You were at the top of your game, and we had a lot of terrorists on kill lists at the time."

"No apologies required. I served my country when it needed me."

"Mm. But at what cost to your family?" Yosef mused.

She tried not to think about that too often lest guilt overwhelm her. Her family, too, had served its country. In a way, they'd been like a military family that sent a loved one off to a war zone and had to stay home, waiting and wondering when she would return, without having any real idea what she was doing or going through.

Gray knew she came home from some trips frazzled and exhausted, but he never commented on why a trade negotiator's work would be so stressful. They had a silent understanding that he wouldn't ask and she wouldn't tell what else she did when she was overseas working on behalf of Uncle Sam.

She was fairly sure he thought she was a spy. But she was also fairly sure he had no idea she'd been an assassin. It was a weird double life to live. She had to pretend to keep a fake secret to hide the real one.

Yosef leaned in close and lowered his voice. "Honestly, my best advice is not to trust anyone on your team. Richard Bell is a snake, and anyone he chose to work for him is probably just as bad."

"A snake how?"

Yosef shook his head. "I don't know. Call it a gut feeling. I've heard he was involved in a few really dark programs over the years."

"Dark as in grim or dark as in ridiculously secret?"

"Both."

"Like what?" she asked curiously.

Yosef didn't answer. Instead, his gaze roamed, taking in the people sitting around them. Bell had been into stuff too classified to risk even hinting at in a public space then. Not surprising. The CIA was clandestine for good reason. It did some of the nation's dirtiest work.

"If you want to understand your staff, understand Bell," Yosef muttered.

Was he trying to tell her subtly that he thought Richard Bell was Scorpius? The guy who'd built and run the team to hunt for that very mole? Surely not. But it would be a diabolically clever way to cover his tracks if Bell actually *was* Scorpius.

Yosef glanced at his watch and said in a normal speaking voice, "I've got to run. Meeting back at the office."

"Of course. It was good to see you and give my love to Ruth."

Understand Bell, huh? Who was he anyway? What did he do for the agency before he'd been promoted to assistant director of operations? And what constituted "really dark" to a man like Yosef, who'd run some pretty dark ops himself?

CHAPTER 17

DANNY SEARCHED THE HOUSE AS SOON AS HE GOT HOME FROM chem lab to make sure he was alone. He fetched a pair of latex gloves from a box hidden in his closet and pulled them on as he headed back downstairs.

Shayna had been a mess today, but she'd hugged him when he offered to find out what the police knew about her missing room-mate. Who knew what she would do if he was able to follow through on that promise?

Erotic possibilities swirling in his mind, he slipped into his father's office—a space that was and always had been off limits to him, Christine, and even their mom—and closed the door.

He sat down at Richard's desk and laid his palms on the leather desk pad on either side of his father's personal laptop. He exhaled hard, and a surge of pleasure at breaking the rules like this rolled through him. *Screw the bastard and his rules.*

He opened Richard's laptop and typed in his father's user name and password. All the computers in the house were on the same secured network, but from here, he should be able to access the CIA's computer system. He couldn't get into the really good CIA stuff from here—he knew; he'd tried before—but he could get into a system classified enough to include police reports and unpublished intelligence reports.

A window popped up on the screen saying that access to the requested network was being blocked by the house's encryption and security protocol. It requested a password he didn't know to bypass it. Irritated, he turned off the protection program altogether and tried again to log in to the CIA system.

Yes. A government sign-in screen with a dire warning about ceasing and desisting if he was not authorized to use the system popped up on his screen. Ignoring it, he typed in his father's credentials.

Now to find out what the police knew. He typed in the fraternity's name and the name Karly. He didn't even get to her last name before a search engine popped up two reports. He scanned them quickly.

The cops didn't know much. A missing person report had been filed, and the case had been transferred from the campus cops to the local police department. But the second report was more interesting. It was a private email addressed to Richard Bell. What the hell?

Danny read on. Apparently, this wasn't the first time a girl had disappeared from one of Sigma Rho Alpha's parties. Somebody had sent Richard an email asking him to take care of this mess the same way he had the last one.

What last one? Had his father taken care of another missing girl? God knew, Danny didn't have any trouble believing that. His father was the coldest SOB he'd ever met. But how had his father taken care of her? Had he killed her? Hid the body? Or had he just cleaned up the media mess and made it go away? He'd heard his father talk on the phone with someone once about killing a news story. He'd gotten the impression Richard had dirt on the journalist and had threatened to expose it. Was that what he was being asked to do in this email, too?

Danny didn't recognize the name of the sender, Marcus Bickford.

He sat back, frustrated. Shayna wasn't going to sleep with him if he told her the police had nothing and his father was covering up whatever had happened. Maybe he should go have a little chat with the guys at the frat. See if he could get them to talk to him.

After all, he wasn't his father's son for nothing. He knew a few things about getting people to spill their guts.

He jolted as he heard the garage door opening. *Shit.* Nobody was supposed to be home now!

He closed out the CIA database fast, slammed the lid of the laptop shut, and sprinted out of Richard's office. He raced upstairs to his room and sat down at his own computer hurriedly. He heard footsteps coming upstairs and realized belatedly he still had on the latex gloves. Swearing, he tore them off and stuffed them into his desk drawer.

"Hey, Danny," his sister said from behind him.

He looked over his shoulder nervously, praying she hadn't seen him hiding the gloves. "Hey, Pristine." His sister hated being called that. But it wasn't his fault if she was annoyingly perfect.

She scowled and stepped into his room, closing the door behind her. "I heard you go out late last Saturday. Where'd you go?"

He scowled. "You're not my keeper."

"No, but Dad is. Today at breakfast, he mentioned he'd found grass in the wheel wells and bumpers of the Porsche. He didn't want to be late for his flight, so he didn't wake you up to ask you about it."

"What flight?"

She shrugged. "Business trip."

Richard didn't take those as often as he used to, but it was by no means unusual for his old man to disappear for a few days or even a few weeks. He never told where he went, and his family never asked.

"So where'd you get grass and mud on the Porsche, Danny Boy?"

He wasn't a boy, damn it. He snapped, "So what? Now you're checking up on me?"

She shrugged. "You know the rules as well as I do. I'm just trying to look out for you. Make sure you didn't do anything stupid."

He said defensively, "I didn't kill that missing girl if that's what you're asking."

"What missing girl?"

She didn't know about Karly What's-her-name? He swore. He

hated it when he outed himself by accident. But he always had been more impulsive than his sister.

"What missing girl?" Christine asked ominously.

He huffed. "A girl on campus went missing last weekend. Shayna—she's my chem lab partner—called me late Saturday night because her roommate ditched her at a frat party. Shayna needed a ride home. The driveway of the frat she was at was full, and the only way to get out of there was to drive on the grass."

"Where's the roommate now?"

He looked his sister in the eye. "I don't know. She's the missing girl."

"Did you have anything to do with her disappearance?"

"No!"

"You don't have to lie to me. I'll cover for you with Dad if you need me to."

Yeah, but at what cost? Nothing was ever free with Christine. She was like their father that way. Always calculating, always stacking up favors owed, always looking out for her own interests first.

But then, he was no different. He just wasn't as good at playing the game as she was.

"I'm serious, Danny. If you did something bad—you know, real bad—to break the rules, I want to help you."

For that he was grateful. Breaking one of their father's ten commandments of civilized behavior inevitably resulted in the kinds of punishments that would give even the most hardened criminal pause. Sometimes they were incredibly painful. Other times they were so twisted, so diabolical, that they left a person emotionally scarred. He knew that all too well.

Christine, on the other hand, followed the family rules scrupulously. To his knowledge, she'd never run afoul of any of Richard's rules. Not a single one. Lucky bitch.

He glanced down at the neat row of faint circular scars on the inside of his forearm. That had been the result of getting caught smoking behind his middle school with some older kids. He'd screamed but good that night.

Christine came over to where he sat and laid her hand lightly on his shoulder. "It's us against the world, Danny. We're family. If you've done something bad, let me help you. Let's make sure you don't get caught, okay?"

His insides quailed at the thought of what their father would do to him if he actually had kidnapped that girl and done any of the things he'd fantasized about doing to her. He would be lucky if all Richard did was kill him.

"I swear, Christine. I had nothing to do with Karly's disappearance. Shayna and I searched the frat as best we could, and we didn't find her. When I dropped Shayna off at her dorm, she was headed upstairs to read Karly the Riot Act for leaving the party without her."

"Okay, Danny. That's good. Very good." She patted his shoulder a couple of times before her hand fell away.

Wait a minute. Had Richard sicced her on him to question him? To get him to admit to kidnapping the missing roommate or worse?

God, he hated his father.

But he feared the man more. Much more.

And that was why he followed the rules.

Mostly.

CHAPTER 18

*H*ELEN HAD A PHONE CALL TO MAKE. ON THE ASSUMPTION THAT Polina and Chunk had bugged the phone on her desk as well, she picked up her purse and headed up to the surface where her cell phone would work. She signed out of the facility and headed for her car.

Sitting in it, she dialed her son-in-law. "Hi, Li. It's Helen. I have a small favor to ask of you."

"This one isn't illegal, is it?" he asked cautiously.

Last winter, she'd asked Liang to decrypt the memo Yosef had given her that he'd believed came from Scorpius. Indeed, once he'd decrypted it over at NSA, it turned out to be a message from Scorpius to someone he was assigning a mission to. Liang had refused to share the details of the mission itself with her, citing that it was classified.

She couldn't very well admit to him that, in her day, she'd probably had a higher security clearance than he had. And so, she'd never learned exactly what the mission was. But it had been enough back then to know Scorpius definitely worked inside the CIA.

To her son-in-law she said, "No, dear. It's not illegal. Far from it. I just need two personnel records pulled."

"Why?"

"Because someone has cloned my computer and I don't want that person to know I'm checking personnel records."

"Why are you checking personnel records? I thought you were retired."

She sighed. "I was asked to come out of retirement temporarily. My boss needed help on a project I was involved with before I retired. They're having trouble getting it across the finish line."

"Why was your computer cloned?" Li asked.

"I'm sure I have no idea."

"How did you find out it was tampered with?"

"A coworker told me."

"And you believed him?" Liang asked.

She had to smile at his suspicion. The man definitely worked in the intelligence field. She cast her voice in the most innocent tone she could, "Why would someone lie about something like that?"

He sighed. "Who do you want records on?"

"The names are Ritika Singh and Richard Bell." She spelled Ritika's name for him. "I'm trying to figure out who's loyal to whom and who might have hidden agendas."

"Office politics, huh?" Liang said sympathetically.

"I hate it," she replied fervently.

"I'll see what I can find for you."

"Thank you, dear. I owe you one."

"I think you owe me several if we're keeping score."

She laughed lightly. "Fair. Maybe I should bake you and Peter another apple pie."

"Please, no!" he replied in quick alarm. The last time she'd brought them a pie, their house had been shot to smithereens by a hit squad out to kill her. "I'll call you when I get the files."

She looked forward to retiring for real and settling down to the business of spoiling her children and future grandchildren. First, Scorpius. Then retirement.

CHAPTER 19

ANATOLY TARMYENKIN, *REZIDYENT* AT THE RUSSIAN EMBASSY IN Washington, DC, stared at the young man standing before his desk. Arrogant pup. Just because Nikko Yezhov was the Russian prime minister's special intelligence envoy didn't make him lord and master of everyone in this whole embassy.

As *rezidyent,* he was the Russian equivalent of a CIA station chief, the ranking spymaster in the United States, thank you very much. He'd been in the espionage business since before this asshole was born.

Anatoly asked sharply, "And why exactly should I open up a direct communication channel to my most valuable American asset for you?"

Nikko scowled. "Because I said so."

"I'm going to need more than that."

Nikko huffed. "My office has received independently verified intelligence from an impeccable source that Helen Warwick has been reactivated. Furthermore, she's leading a kill team hunting your precious Scorpius."

Anatoly winced. He'd encountered the Warwick woman before, and she was not an operative to be trifled with.

Nikko continued officiously, "She must be stopped. I am authorizing any means or methods. This mission has the highest priority."

Anatoly snapped, "I control the operatives in this country, and I authorize all sanctions my people execute."

"Then you're authorizing this one. The Warwick woman must die."

"Easier said than done, *comrade*." He hated that his government had reverted to using the old socialist title. But he was a small cog in a large machine and such decisions were above his pay grade.

"How do I speak with Scorpius?" Nikko demanded.

This was such a bad idea. Some bears were best left sleeping, and some should never be poked with sticks. Helen Warwick was both. He sighed. "We'll need to go for a walk."

"I don't understand."

"You will. Come with me."

Deeply unhappy with what it was likely to cost him in assets to kill the Warwick woman, he stood up and moved around his desk.

As he and Nikko passed through the embassy's tall security gate on foot and headed down Wisconsin Avenue, Nikko muttered, "Won't we be tailed by American spies if we walk?"

"Of course, we will. The CIA keeps junior agents parked outside the embassy at all times."

Nikko looked around in alarm, amusing Anatoly mightily. *Amateur.* Yezhov might be the prime minister's boy wonder, but he knew nothing about tradecraft. *Welcome to the big leagues, kid.*

"Not to worry. The locals won't stop us from achieving our objective," Anatoly replied, unconcerned. "Unlike in Moscow, they won't randomly pick us up and throw us in a black site for interrogation and torture. This is a civilized country that follows the rule of law."

He smirked when Nikko scowled at the dig. As well he should. It was Nikko's own Federal Security Service that was notorious for such snatch-and-grab operations inside Russia.

It was lunchtime, and the streets were crowded. He walked briskly, enjoying getting outside. Keeping up with him and Nikko would give the Americans a good workout today.

He led his companion into a deli owned by a friend of his country, nodded at the proprietor, and headed quickly for the restrooms. The short hallway was empty and out of view of the street, and using his key, he ducked through a door marked EMPLOYEES ONLY. Nikko followed him obediently.

He jogged up the staircase in the back of the storeroom and paused at the top to catch his breath. He really should cut back on the cigarettes. At least he'd shifted to smoking filtered American brands.

With one last cough, he led Nikko down the hallway to an unmarked door, a more complicated lock this time, and a small, bare office with no window. Nikko looked around curiously. "Will Scorpius meet us here?"

Anatoly laughed heartily. "You think I would let you meet my asset? You are a very funny boy."

Nikko bristled. Probably didn't like being called a boy.

"You asked for direct communication, not a face-to-face meeting," Anatoly pointed out as he sat down at the plain wooden table against the far wall. He logged onto the computer sitting on it. Almost a minute passed while the encryption, VPN, and other security measures kicked in, but eventually the message app he and Scorpius used popped open.

"How will Scorpius know to meet us in this chat room?" Nikko asked.

Anatoly shrugged. "He won't. Sometimes he happens to be at his computer and responds immediately. Sometimes I just leave a message for him."

"I was told I could speak with him," Nikko snapped.

"You get what you get. He's in deep cover. I'm not about to ask him to break it because you're starstruck and want to meet the great man in person."

"I'm not—" Nikko broke off, looking irritated that Anatoly had gotten a rise out of him. Again.

His mouth twitching with humor, Anatoly placed his hands over the keyboard. "What message would you like me to send to my asset?" Emphasis on *my*.

"Tell him what I told you. That we have verified intel Helen Warwick has been activated and assigned to hunt him."

Anatoly typed in the message and sent it.

"Now what?" Nikko asked.

Impatient child. "Now we wait. If Scorpius is at his computer, he'll respond. I usually give him about five minutes. If there's no answer, we go back downstairs, collect our sandwiches, and head back to my office."

An incoming message bubble popped up on his screen.

"We're in luck," he commented. Nikko leaned over his shoulder eagerly as the decryption program morphed random symbols into understandable words. He snorted with laughter as the message became readable:

Who do you think reported the hunt for me to Moscow?

Scorpius himself was the impeccable source? Why hadn't Nikko told him that? Now he looked like a fool to his own mole.

Nikko said eagerly, "Tell him we need him to take out the Warwick woman."

Anatoly looked back over his shoulder sharply. "That's not his job. He's in place to feed us information, not run black operations for us."

Nikko snapped, "I'm told we have no assets in place that can reliably eliminate her. My superiors think Scorpius can take care of it more readily than we can."

Cursing under his breath, Anatoly typed back, **We have no assets in place who can take out HW. HQ wants you to do it.**

He hit the encryption button and watched his message turn into gobbledygook. When it was finished, he hit send.

Scorpius's reply was immediate and succinct. **Get some. And get rid of her. She's good at her job.**

Anatoly jumped as Nikko slapped his open palm on the table with a loud crack of sound.

"Do you not have control of your asset, comrade?" Nikko hissed.

Anatoly leaned back in his chair and crossed his arms, staring up at Nikko's red face. "You do understand that Scorpius is a high-ranking CIA officer in his own right. He could burn us as quickly as we could burn him. We have an understanding. A partnership, if you will. But we don't own him."

Nikko cursed long and fluently, and Anatoly waited out the tantrum. When Nikko finally wound down, he asked, "What do you want me to tell Scorpius?"

"Can we get the assets we need to take out the Warwick woman?"

A complicated question. Of course, he could bring enough force to bear to overwhelm even Helen Warwick. But at what cost to himself and his network of spies in the US?

Not to mention that doing such a thing could very well cause retaliation by the Americans, which could lead to retaliation by men like Nikko, and even more retaliation by the CIA. The last thing he wanted was to start a war with the Americans.

In reality, Scorpius probably was better positioned to take out Helen Warwick than the Russians were. The way he heard it, his mole had a number of his own assets working directly for him. But if Scorpius didn't want to do it, there wasn't a blessed thing he could do to force the man into taking the sanction.

He'd learned over the years that Scorpius was nothing if not obstinate. When the man dug in his heels, no power on earth would move him. Sometimes he really hated the arrogant bastard. If only Scorpius wasn't such a spectacular source of high-level intel.

He looked up at his companion and answered reluctantly, "Yes. I can get the assets to take her out. But they'll have to be very careful not to start a war."

"No need to be dramatic," Nikko snapped.

Anatoly shrugged. "If you're taking responsibility for the fall-out of this sanction, that's fine by me. Let the record show I object to it and want no responsibility for it."

Nikko's eyes narrowed. "Fine. Then you'll get no credit for it either. The only fallout of this operation is going to be my swift promotion. And I'll remember you tried to get in my way."

Oh. So that's how it's going to be, is it? Anatoly sighed. He was getting too old for this crap. But if Boy Wonder wanted all the glory, he could take all the blame, too.

Anatoly typed back to Scorpius, **Very well. We'll handle her. Be careful until it is done**.

He hit send before the folly of warning Scorpius to be careful occurred to him. Embarrassment coursed through him. The man was the soul of caution. It was how he'd survived in place for two decades. Undoubtedly, at the other end of this conversation, Scorpius had just made a sound of disgust and muttered something to the effect of *Duh.*

No more messages popped up.

"Any reply from Scorpius?" Nikko asked eagerly.

"What? You expect him to kiss your ass for doing your job and protecting him?" Anatoly snapped. If he'd already made an enemy of the kid, there was no need to pretend to be polite to him anymore.

Nikko sent him a blistering glare, and Anatoly shrugged, unimpressed. He was not without resources of his own, after all. Worst case, he could quietly disappear into the emergency identity he'd set up years ago and retire to his fishing cabin in Canada.

Anatoly and Nikko retraced their steps downstairs, grabbed the sub sandwiches the proprietor passed over the counter to them, and strolled back to the Russian Embassy.

Nikko entertained himself trying to pick out their CIA tails while Anatoly lost himself deep in thought.

Who to send after the redoubtable Mrs. Warwick? A Spetsnaz team would be far too heavy-handed and likely to start exactly the kind of war he was hoping to avoid. An individual assassin then. It had to be someone good. Very good, indeed.

Like it or not, this was going to require him to call in some very expensive favors.

CHAPTER 20

*A*S SHE TOOK A CIRCUITOUS ROUTE HOME, HELEN WATCHED THE cars behind her as best she could. It was hard at night to spot a tail, particularly on the busy Beltway, but she was confident she wasn't being followed as she approached home.

Which was why it was a shock to see a strange pickup truck parked in her driveway. *What the heck?*

She drove on past, her pulse pounding. Who was at her house? It was nearly 10:00 PM. Whoever it was, it was no social call.

She proceeded to the next corner, turned right, and turned right again onto a narrow dirt road. Turning off her headlights, she drove slowly in the thick darkness under heavy tree cover. She followed the faint, pale strip of gravel to the ramshackle barn on the property directly behind her house. She secretly owned this lot, too, although she'd bought it under the name of a business entity hidden behind multiple nesting corporations that eventually led to a numbered bank account in the Cayman Islands.

Parking inside the barn, she got out of her car and headed for the stash of gear she kept here for just this purpose.

She stripped out of her business clothes and pulled on dark slacks and a black turtleneck. Some quick grease paint in vertical stripes down her face, a black stocking cap over her hair, and a pair of black tennis shoes, and she was ready to go.

She checked the load in her pistol and stuck it in the holster sewn into the back waistband of her pants. She pocketed a spare magazine of ammunition and headed out.

She knew the hill leading down to her house as well as she knew her own hand, and she made fast time in the dark, picking her way around boulders and bushes as much by memory as by sight.

She eased around the end of the farmhouse, overcome by a sense of unreality. This was her home. The place she'd raised her kids, for crying out loud. She wasn't supposed to be armed and sneaking around it, ambushing a bad guy.

Ducking behind the shrubs beside the garage, which she noted absently were in need of a trim, she made her way in an uncomfortable crouch. Long before she reached the truck, her thighs were screaming in discomfort. She was supposed to be finished with shenanigans like this.

Irritated, she paused just shy of the driveway to watch the truck. There was definitely someone sitting in the driver's seat. But his posture was weird. It took her a moment to figure out that whoever it was had his or her head tilted back against the rear window and appeared to be asleep.

Or dead, her work mind added pragmatically.

Some bad guy this was . . . napping on the job. He even had a baseball cap pulled down over his eyes. The bill hid his face from view. Disgust at the younger generation's lack of tradecraft and discipline coursed through her. Moving slow and staying low, she eased out onto the lawn, circling around the back of the truck to the sleeping driver's seven o'clock position, using the truck's natural blind spot to make her approach.

Crouching below the driver's side window, she contemplated the odds that the rusty, decades-old truck had bullet-resistant glass. She judged them to be extremely low. So, instead of throwing open the door dramatically, she stood up slowly, rising specter-like until she was staring into the vehicle.

Using the tip of her pistol's barrel, she tapped the glass.

The figure inside jolted awake and sat up, yanking off the baseball cap and staring down the barrel of her weapon at her.

She swore and lowered the weapon, stepping back as Clint opened his door and put his hands in the air.

"Don't make an old lady have to sneak up on you," she snapped.

He grinned, drawling, "No old lady could get the jump on me like that."

"You were snoring," she said scornfully.

"Didn't think being parked in your driveway was a high threat environment."

"It is if I don't know who you are," she retorted.

"Duly noted. You got a second to talk?"

"At this hour? I've got all night."

He glanced at the house. "You home alone?"

"You know I am, or you wouldn't be sitting in my driveway waiting for me."

He merely shrugged.

She sighed. "Come in. I want a cup of tea to calm my nerves after you scared me half to death."

He laughed at that. "Lady, the way I hear it, you have nerves of tempered steel."

It was her turn to shrug. She jogged up the front steps and unlocked the front door. Clint waited behind her as she disabled the house alarm and waved him inside. Smart man. She'd also installed several defensive upgrades to her home security system after someone—she now knew it to be the Scorpius team—had broken into the house a few months back.

The new pressure sensors under the hallway floor were wired to a pair of needle guns embedded in the foyer's walls. They were programmed to fire after a delay of a few seconds built in to let her disarm the security system. The flechettes they fired were coated in a neurotoxin that would rapidly disable anyone they even scratched.

She led Clint through the house to the big, modern kitchen in the back of the home. He sat down on one of the barstools at the island while she washed her face, made herself a quick sandwich, and brewed a cup of tea. He declined a drink but accepted her offer of food, and she threw together two turkey sandwiches on rye with all the fixings.

She shoved one sandwich on a plate across the big island to him and stood beside the sink to eat her belated supper. After they'd finished, she picked up her tea and carried it to the kitchen table. Clint joined her.

"So what brings you here, Clint? Have you found something on Mitch or my father?"

"Sort of."

"What does that mean?"

He sighed. "As I expected, there's not much of a paper trail on either of them. But I was able to dig up a few rumors."

She groaned. "Rumors are worse than actual scandals to fight off in a political campaign. There are no facts to disprove them."

"Which rumor do you want first?" he asked grimly.

"Mitch's," she replied promptly. Any rumors concerning him would be newer, more immediate, and of more interest to voters.

"Rumor has it your son was real tight with the last DA."

"I can confirm that to be true," she replied.

"Here's the thing. Derek Cahill was rumored to be dirty."

"What?" she exclaimed. "No way."

"I'm just telling you what I heard."

"Go on," she said, bracing herself.

"The DA is thought to have kept files on certain cases, on certain powerful people he helped out here and there."

An image of that safe in Angela's closet, the one she'd recently encouraged her friend to open and read all the files inside of, flashed across her mind's eye. "Cahill helped them out how?" she demanded.

"He looked the other way on some cases. Told the cops there wasn't enough evidence to prosecute on others. Quietly buried charges and arrests."

"In return for what?"

Clint shrugged. "No idea. Favors owed, certainly. Influence, probably. Did money change hands? Campaign contributions get made? That I couldn't tell you."

"And you think Mitch is doing the same thing?"

"I don't think anything. I'm just reporting what I was told. But my contact at the DA's office is convinced Mitch helped Cahill bury some stuff, and furthermore, Mitch has been doing the same thing since the DA was murdered. He's the go-to guy for the rich and powerful in this town when they need to make something criminal disappear."

Helen closed her eyes for a moment, disappointed that Mitch could be on the take.

"How likely is your source to be right?"

Clint shrugged.

"For what it's worth," he said, "my contact said it's the way business has always been done in that office."

"That doesn't make it right," she replied heavily.

"You're worried about right and wrong? With what you do for a living?"

"Did. Past tense." It was becoming a tired refrain, but she stuck by it, darn it. She was done killing people—with the exception of Scorpius, of course. And she'd only killed targets assigned to her by the US government for the good of her country.

Clint frowned. "I did hear something about a buried scandal at your son's fraternity when he was in college, but my source was vague. Didn't know anything more. I did some digging, but I couldn't find anything on it. I don't think it'll be a problem."

She supposed he was right. After all, it was no secret that there were booze, girls, and wild parties at frat houses. And if Mitch was telling her the truth, he'd been careful to steer clear of scandals even back then. Besides, he'd dated Nancy most of the way through college and law school. And her character was as pure as driven snow.

Helen asked, "Just out of curiosity, did you hear any of the rumors about the DA's office from Angela?"

Clint looked up at her sharply. He looked startled. "No. Why?"

Helen shrugged. "She hasn't been in a good place since Derek died. They were very close."

"I know."

"I'm worried about her. She's holding in all her grief and not letting it go. I would love to see her sink her teeth into some big new case that takes all her attention."

Clint shrugged. "Something will come her way eventually."

Hmm. Angela had hinted that she was dealing with something big. But if Clint wasn't researching anything for her, it must be mostly a technical, legal case. What then? Angela had been very evasive about it.

Helen's suspicion congealed into certainty. Angela *did* have Derek's old blackmail files.

Was Mitch implicated in any of them? Damn it, what had her son gotten himself into?

"As for your father . . ." Clint trailed off.

Her gaze snapped to him, and she took a deep breath. "Lay it on me."

"I assume you're aware he served on the House Intelligence Committee."

"I am."

He looked as if he was trying to find the right words to say next.

"Just spit it out, Clint. I won't take offense. After all, I'm the one who asked you to dig for dirt. And my father has been dead a long time."

Clint leaned forward. "I don't have much. Just a whiff of something. Old whispers. It's more of a gut feeling on my part than anything concrete. But something happened to end your father's career. Somebody—possibly several somebodies—died in some sort of operation the Intelligence Committee approved. There was a cover-up, and your father was involved in it somehow. The intel community got away with burying whatever happened, but it cost him his seat in Congress."

"Have you got anything more than that?"

"I'm lucky to have that much," Clint retorted. "Whatever happened, it's buried *real* deep."

"Do you infer, then, that it's something so bad it would damage Mitch's career?"

"Maybe kill it. Now that Mitch is running for office, people will dig into his past. His family's past. Your father was a politician, too. Investigators will certainly take a look at his career again. I get the impression some powerful people are still around who don't want whatever happened to your father to come out."

She studied the private investigator thoughtfully. "Are they powerful enough to keep it buried?"

He shrugged. "Secrets have a way of surfacing eventually, no matter how hard folks try to keep them hidden. And the bigger the secret, the harder the universe seems to want to expose it."

"Who would try to expose my family's secrets?"

"Real talk?" Clint asked cautiously.

"Give it to me straight," she said firmly.

"Some of your father's worst enemies are still around. They could come after your family. Your son has a few powerful enemies of his own. And then there's whoever you've pissed off over the course of your career."

"What do you know about my career?" she demanded.

"Sorry. I know a guy in the CIA Special Operations Group. He used to talk about this badass grandma who shot circles around the younger guys. She was the go-to shooter in some pretty high-profile sanctions. It didn't take a rocket scientist to connect the dots when you strolled into Angela's office and told her how the Canyon shootings had to be happening." He added quickly, "But don't worry. I won't tell. I figure you've already collected enough dirt on me to get me in a heap of trouble, too."

She smiled tightly. "Mutual self-assured destruction is an effective neutralizer, is it not?"

"It is." He gazed steadily at her for a moment and then dipped his chin slightly. She dipped hers back. They had a deal. He would keep her secrets, and she would keep his.

Thank goodness there was still a modicum of honor among thieves.

CHAPTER 21

MITCH WAS IN A HURRY TO GET OUT OF THE OFFICE; HE HAD CAM-paign events lined up for the *entire* weekend. The first one was a fundraising dinner in a half hour, and it was a forty-minute drive to the hotel where it was being held. Nancy, his mother, and his grandmother could handle the guests for a bit, and he could spin being late as him being diligent at his job, but that was only a good excuse up to a point. The donors wanted direct access to him in return for their money.

He grabbed his briefcase, threw open his office door—and jolted to a stop. The man in front of him holding up his fist to knock wasn't one of his bodyguards.

"Hey, Mitch. You got a second?"

It was Walt Kingston, one of his old fraternity brothers. Walt had recently taken over running his old man's hedge fund and was worth a cool billion dollars these days. Which made him a po-tentially important donor.

"Can we walk and talk?" Mitch suggested. "I'm late to a fund-raiser. You can come if you'd like. I'm sure we can find an extra seat for you."

Walt scowled. "I got a call from Marcus today. Somebody's been poking around about the incident."

Mitch didn't have to ask which incident. They'd all been se-niors at Sigma Rho Alpha when the bacchanalia had gone so ter-ribly wrong. "Poking around how?"

"Marcus has some sort of alert set for when anyone searches it on government sites or in police databases."

"Well, with that girl missing on campus this week, and her last being seen at this year's SRA bacchanalia, it makes sense that reporters are checking to see if there've ever been similar incidents. I wouldn't be too concerned about it."

"Yeah, but—"

He cut off his frat brother. "Marcus is in the computer security business. I'm sure he has deleted any old news stories he missed before that might've popped up now. And the police reports are completely buried. I saw to that."

"They'd better be. I'm not going down for something that happened all those years ago."

"A girl died, Walt. Maybe get your head out of your ass long enough to have a little sympathy for her and her family?"

"Yeah, well, this new missing girl had better not lead anyone to ours."

"It won't. Nobody knows where to find the bodies."

"There had better not be any bodies left to find!" Walt exclaimed.

"It was a figure of speech, dude. Chill out. I'm the acting DA. I'll take care of anything that comes across my desk. As long as I win this election, we're golden." He fell silent as the night bodyguard fell in beside him in the hallway.

Mitch glanced sidelong at Walt. "Speaking of winning, can I hit you up for a campaign donation, you rich asshole?"

Laughing, they stepped into the elevator, and the bodyguard pushed the down button. But a frisson of alarm chattered down Mitch's spine. The timing of that girl going missing over on campus could not have been worse. Maybe he should take his mother up on her offer.

Nah. Walt always had been a nervous Nellie. Everything would be fine. Gramps had buried the fallout of that night so deep it would never see the light of day.

CHAPTER 22

*T*HE BOX WAS IN AN UPROAR WHEN HELEN WALKED IN MONDAY morning. Everyone was clustered around Chunk's desk talking over one another.

"Let me guess," she said as she neared the buzzing group. "Sasquatch killed the Easter Bunny, and aliens have kidnapped Santa Claus."

Ritika said eagerly, "We caught a message from Scorpius, and he didn't use blockchain encryption on it."

"How did *that* happen?" she exclaimed.

Ritika answered, "Scorpius made a mistake. Whatever encryption system he normally uses wasn't activated properly when he sent this message."

"Can we decrypt it eventually?"

"Chunk already broke it. He's got the text."

"Well, let's hear it."

"The first part appears to be him telling Moscow that he was the person who told them about the hunt for him. In the second part, he tells them to get rid of a woman they're discussing."

Her heart dropped to her feet, and she felt the blood draining from her face in spite of herself. *She* was the person hunting Scorpius. So the Russians were going to come after her. Again.

Lovely. Their military might be in a shambles, but their intelligence services were not. They had any number of highly skilled wet-work specialists in their employ. Skilled enough to kill her.

"Did we catch Moscow's response?" she choked out.

"No." Ritika replied. "But we have to assume they'll protect their asset. He's too important for them not to take care of him."

"When was the message sent?" Helen asked heavily.

"We got it yesterday. But it could have gone out any time in the past week. The Echelon array had to catch the transmission and send it to England, then the Brits had to sort it out of the traffic, flag it, and send it back to us."

Helen rolled her eyes. It was illegal for the US government to spy on its own people, so it farmed the job out to the UK. She expected the US returned the favor to the British government.

Polina said tersely, "We need to tell Richard. After all, he's the person who initiated the hunt for Scorpius."

James Wagner had initiated the hunt, but Helen didn't correct her. It did make her wonder, though, why Richard had represented the hunt to his team as his idea. *Ego, much?*

Who was Richard Bell, really? Yosef neither liked nor trusted him. But then, Yosef disliked and distrusted most people.

Of course, she'd also told Yosef last week that he was being investigated. He'd had plenty of time since then to notify Moscow and ask them to eliminate her—

No. Yosef wasn't Scorpius. She'd trusted him with her life more times than she could count. It had to be someone else.

Who else knew about this team and that she'd been put in charge of it? Richard Bell knew. Of course, he was so obvious a suspect to be Scorpius she hesitated to believe it. Next time she spoke with Wagner, though, she made a mental note to ask him how and why Bell had been chosen to lead the Scorpius search team.

Andrew Mizuki had been high-ranking enough to be Scorpius and had known about her posting to this job, but he was dead.

Which left Yosef, James Wagner, and Richard Bell as known suspects. Oh, and Lester Reinhold. Lester was Yosef's and Richard's boss and reported directly to Wagner. It made sense that he was in the loop about the Scorpius hunt.

Was one of them Scorpius? They were four of the most highly placed officials in the entire agency. She didn't even want to think about the potential damage to national security if one of them was the mole.

Did she dare ask her team to start new investigations of all four men? Odds were that at least a couple of her team members were reporting on the sly to one or more of those men. But who? Which of her team members could she trust?

She reluctantly concluded that she could trust none of them. She was on her own. It was her against Scorpius and whatever network of spies, informants, and operatives worked for him. She felt vastly outmanned and outgunned. And suddenly she understood why Wagner had come to her to do this job. There was no one else he could trust either.

At least there was one bit of good news in all of this: by asking the Russians to kill her, Scorpius had, in effect, declined to kill her himself.

Which was odd. According to Wagner, Scorpius potentially had black assets under his control. Why wouldn't he use them to take her out? Was he afraid his people would get caught or killed? Or worse, were his assets otherwise occupied right now? Which raised the question . . . occupied doing *what?*

What are you up to, Scorpius? Are you lying low because of my team, or are you planning something big?

How did Roger Skidmore figure into all of this? Was he one of Bell's guys? A contract killer? A Russian operative? Or was he the creature of one of the other men on her suspect list?

Gah. Everywhere she turned there were no answers, only questions and more questions.

All four of her main suspects had access to high-level intelligence and controlled field officers fully capable of killing. If those were the main criteria for being Scorpius, she should probably add the head of the Special Activities Center, Kyle Colgate, to her suspect list, too.

Colgate had been in the Special Operations Group, which was part of the Special Activities Center, for much of her career, not that their paths had ever really crossed. She'd been a solo operator, and he'd specialized in leading teams of operators. Word inside SOG had it that Colgate was a squared-away guy. Steady. Smart. The right man for the job.

She headed for her office and hadn't quite reached it when Chunk exclaimed, "Scorpius sent the message from a private laptop!"

She turned around with interest.

"And?" Polina demanded tersely.

He shrugged. "Given a little time, I should be able to track down the specific computer and maybe its location. This was just the slip-up we've been waiting for."

Helen frowned, her gut shouting a warning at her. Men like Scorpius never slipped up. Was this a trap?

CHAPTER 23

*C*HUNK WORKED THROUGH THE DAY BUT HADN'T LOCATED SCOR-
pius's laptop when quitting time came. Helen left the Box with
the team and dawdled in her car until her people had all driven
away.

Then she pulled out her phone. "Li, darling, it's Helen. Any
chance you've made headway on the projects I asked you for help
with?"

"Yes, actually. I was going to call you in a bit. I've got both."

"Any problems getting them?"

"Not with one. The other was more of a challenge. Pete has an
auction tonight. Maybe we could meet, say, for cocktails?"

"I surely owe you a drink for your help."

He rattled off a bar and an address close to the condo he and
Peter were renting while their house was renovated again, and
she told him she could be there in a half hour.

After she met with Li, she needed to go home and catch a nap.
She wasn't twenty-five anymore, capable of sailing through all-
nighters unscathed, and she had a late night planned.

Stepping into the dark pub Li had chosen for their meeting,
she had to smile. She could see why the boys liked this place. It
was a traditional English pub, complete with Union Jack flags,
dart boards, and Premier League Football on the tellies.

Li waved from a table in the corner, and she made her way to him, dodging a dart game in progress. She kissed his cheek before sliding onto a tall bar stool beside him.

"I took the liberty of ordering you a glass of white wine," he said, indicating a glass in front of her.

"You're too thoughtful." She sipped the crisp, sweet vintage that had to be German. "Mm. Nice." She set the glass down. "So what did you find?"

He propped his elbows on the table and notably did not produce any printed documents. Instead, he said, "The young woman. Ms. Singh. Pretty straightforward career. Came in as a junior East Asia analyst. Shifted over to communications. Worked her way onto the congressional briefing team. Competent. Nothing too outstanding."

"Has she ever worked for Richard Bell?" Helen asked.

"Not that I found."

Helen frowned.

"What?" Li asked quickly.

"I'm wondering who put her on my team, then. If she's not one of Bell's flunkies, who is she loyal to?"

"Maybe Lester Reinhold. He ran the East Asia desk when she first joined the agency. Or she could be attached to James Wagner. Her job when he first became DCI was to act as his congressional liaison."

"Lord, I hope you're right. It would be nice to have one ally in my corner."

"I wasn't aware you'd gone to work for the CIA?" Li blurted.

Her gaze jerked up to his. "I haven't. But they get involved in trade deals from time to time. They are known to feed us helpful information on whoever we're negotiating against."

"And you feed them information from time to time?" he asked dryly.

Her eyebrows twitched into a frown. "I work on whatever trade deal I'm assigned to. I don't control which branches of government put which people on my team."

"Ah."

She had no idea what he inferred from that, and she didn't ask. "What about Bell?" she murmured.

"How do you know this guy?" Li asked rather more tensely than she would've expected.

"I've met him in passing a time or two over the years, but I wouldn't say I know him. I do, however, believe he placed someone on my team. I'm trying to find out what his angle is."

Li, who had as good a poker face as she'd ever seen, pulled out his best inscrutable expression now. Which, frankly, told her more than any big frown or expression of disapproval would have. He'd found something big on Bell. Now to get him to share it with her in spite of his rigidly upright ethics.

She said, "I think his person on my team is some sort of covert operative. I need to know how dangerous the person I'm being forced to work with is. Are the people I'm negotiating against at risk? Am I at risk?"

"He's certainly capable of being dangerous. Bell's early career was in . . . operations."

She gathered from that pregnant pause Li meant black operations, specifically. She replied, "From what little I know of the CIA, I understand there are operations, and then there are *operations*. Which was he?"

"The latter."

Her gaze snapped to Li's in alarm. "Am I in danger?"

"If you cross him, absolutely."

"How do you know that?" she blurted.

"Let's just say people who get in his way have a strange tendency to die accidentally or disappear without a trace."

"Really?" she asked in genuine surprise. Could he be the one who'd ordered Andrew Mizuki poisoned? "Who might he be involved with making disappear?"

"I'm not at liberty to say."

Damn it, why did Li have to be so by-the-book all the time?

"What can you tell me?" she asked in resignation.

"His entire career has been a series of compartmentalized operations. Even the names are all ridiculously classified." He added, his voice dropping even lower, "But there is one name I thought you might recognize. Operation Whitehorse."

"And why did you think I would know it?" she asked lightly, hoping she wasn't giving away that this was the first she'd ever heard of it.

"Your father was on the House Intelligence Committee when it was funded. I thought he might've talked about his work at home, maybe dropped a name here and there."

Her father had been scrupulous about not talking about his work on the House Intelligence Committee. But she wasn't about to tell Li that. Instead, she shrugged. "Dad might've mentioned it. My mother would have a better recollection of his work than me. I was young and involved in my own life back then. But I can ask her what she remembers about that name in particular."

Li leaned back in satisfaction. "You do that."

"Do you know the details of it?" she asked curiously.

His eyelids fluttered slightly. So he did know what this Operation Whitehorse was. She leaned forward and laid her hand on top of his in a show of nervousness that wasn't entirely faked. "How bad is it? Should I be scared?"

"Let me know what your mother says," he replied low.

"Will you fill in the gaps if she doesn't remember much?" Helen pressed. "I need to know if I should watch my back."

"Take my word for it. Watch your back," he said grimly.

He leaned away from her and took a long pull from his pitcher of beer. He was obviously done sharing. Operation Whitehorse, huh? Now what was that all about? *What did you get yourself mixed up in, Richard?*

Li seemed to think this operation was the key to Richard Bell's career.

Change of plans. She had two jobs to do tonight instead of one. Which meant no nap for her, darn it.

CHAPTER 24

*E*VEN THOUGH SHE WAS AT HOME ALONE, POLINA CAUGHT HERSELF looking around furtively before dialing her phone. Such was the fear that Richard Bell inspired in her. She'd never met a colder or more calculating human being. He was brilliant and headed for great things, which she fully planned to get a piece of. But in the meantime, he was one scary bastard.

She texted a random set of numbers to his cell phone to signal that she had information for him. The numbers themselves didn't matter. It was the act of sending them that would trigger a phone call when he was free to talk.

She started as her cell phone vibrated with an incoming call. *Whoa.* That was fast.

She took a deep breath and answered it.

"What?" Bell asked curtly.

"I'm sorry to bother you, sir, but there's been a development in the Scorpius hunt."

"Which is . . . ?" he prompted.

"This morning, we intercepted message traffic between Scorpius and someone, probably his Russian handler."

"Intercepted it?" he bit out. "How?"

"Large radio array transmitters picked up the wireless signal along with all the other electronic emissions on the East Coast. Our supercomputers picked it out of the signals it was sorting through, sent it to the UK, and the MI6 sent it back to us."

"Yes, but *how?* Everything Scorpius sends is heavily encrypted and wouldn't ping as message traffic of interest."

"Chunk thinks Scorpius turned off the encryption he usually uses."

"Turned it off?" he squawked.

Aware of how stupid that sounded, she said quickly, "There was discussion that it might be a trap of some kind. It's a big mistake and completely out of character for Scorpius. Ritika suggested Scorpius might have intentionally decrypted the message because he objects to killing American assets and is warning Helen Warwick that the Russians are coming for her and her team."

Richard snorted in obvious derision at that theory.

"Anything else?" he asked.

"The signal was sent from a laptop somewhere in the Washington, DC, area. Chunk is trying to find out where the laptop is located and who owns it. We thought you might want to be the one to bring this news to Wagner instead of the Warwick woman."

"Indeed. Tell Chunk he doesn't need to keep looking for the laptop. The second Scorpius figured out he left the encryption protocol for communications turned off, he'll have destroyed that computer."

"I'll pass the message along to him, sir."

"Is that all?"

"There's one more thing," she said reluctantly. She squeezed her eyes tightly shut and took a deep breath for courage. "We cloned Mrs. Warwick's desktop computer like you ordered. She ran a facial recognition search on it."

"Of whom?" Richard asked when she didn't continue.

"I don't know where she got a picture of him, but she ran facial rec on Roger Skidmore."

Bell sucked in a sharp breath. "Did she get his name?"

"And a home address."

"And you're just telling me now?"

"I didn't think it was a big deal. I don't know how or where she got a picture of him, or why she was interested in him. But there's no reason for her to associate him with you."

There was a protracted silence at that. "You know what you have to do."

Richard's priorities were ironclad. The security of his team mattered above all else. *All* else. It was understood that she and the others were expected to kill one another or even kill themselves to protect the team.

"I understand, sir."

"Let me know when it's taken care of."

"Yes, sir. Good night, sir."

Richard didn't bother to say good night back. The line went dead in her ear.

Helen sat in her car across the street from Roger Skidmore's apartment building in the dark. She'd followed him all day today, and he'd done absolutely nothing out of the ordinary. He apparently worked some sort of job in an office building on the north side of DC when he wasn't poisoning senior CIA officials and trying to kill her. Not that she was certain he'd poisoned Andrew. Not yet.

She'd spent the past few hours considering ways to approach Skidmore and ask him outright if he'd poisoned Andrew. She hadn't come up with anything that would get him to talk without trying to kill her first. She still had bruises from their first fight. She didn't relish tangling with him again.

And it wasn't as if she could come right out and ask him if he'd been hired by some spy calling himself Scorpius. No contract killer worth his salt would name a client. Not if he ever wanted to get another job.

She'd taken a chance when he'd sat down to dine alone in the restaurant that he would return home directly afterward. After all, it was a Thursday and a work night. She'd driven to his place ahead of him to set up surveillance shop here. It was one of the risks of working solo—having to disengage from the target from time to time.

Bingo. On cue, she spotted his car turning into the parking garage beneath his building. She counted about two minutes from when Skidmore had entered the garage and started watching for lights to go on in a window.

There. Third floor. An apartment on the west end of the building.

Maybe she should come back tomorrow during the day and have a look around his place—

Helen started as a woman with a large messenger bag slung over her shoulder walked toward her car. When the woman was about thirty feet from Helen, she abruptly crossed the street to head into Skidmore's building.

That was Polina! What was *she* doing here?

She must be checking up on the man she'd found on Helen's computer in the facial recognition search. Was the Russian woman planning some sort of direct approach to the guy? A bold move. Not one Helen would've made in the same situation. But to each their own.

Rather than stick around here and risk Polina spotting her when she left the building, she elected to leave while Polina was inside.

Several times during her drive across town to her second job, Helen stopped and snapped pictures of random people on the street. She would run them through the facial recognition program at her desk tomorrow. It would serve Polina right for snooping in her computer to send the woman on a bunch of wild goose chases.

CHAPTER 25

*H*ELEN SAT IN HER CAR IN THE DARK, STARING AT HER MOTHER'S stately Georgian home in an old, prestigious neighborhood on the north side of DC. Never in her life would she have guessed she would end up running a breaking and entering operation on the house she'd grown up in.

As a kid, she'd shimmied up and down the rose arbor just outside her bedroom window more times than she could count. But she wasn't a spring chicken anymore and had little interest in attempting the trellis if she could avoid it. Not to mention that the climbing roses on it were old and thorny now.

She'd arrived at her mom's place a little before 10:00 PM, so she got comfortable and settled in to wait out Constance's bedtime routine.

Sure enough, at the stroke of ten, the lights in the living room went dark. Moments later, a light went on in an upstairs hallway. Her mother was nothing if not a creature of habit. It would take another thirty minutes or so for Constance to do her nighttime moisturizing, brush her teeth, read a Bible chapter or two, and settle down to sleep. Then Helen could move in.

She waited patiently until the last light blinked out. She would give her mother a half hour or so to get to sleep, and then she would go.

To bring along a sidearm or not? Thing was, if her mother

caught her, she could probably lie her way out of being inside the house. But not if she was wielding a weapon. Plus she would hate to have her mother freak out and reach for the gun if they stumbled into each other in the dark. She slipped her pistol out of her purse and locked it in the glove compartment.

She walked down the familiar sidewalk toward the home she'd grown up in. She couldn't count all the times she'd walked down this street, to and from school and friends' houses, and all the times she'd come out here to escape the oppressive atmosphere of being the only child of parents with exceptionally high expectations of their offspring. She'd walked out here in all seasons, all weather, all times of day and night. She knew every nuance of the shadows—she even recognized individual cracks in the sidewalk where tree roots had forced the concrete to bulge upward.

Turning down the driveway, she took care to walk gently in her soft-soled shoes. In the backyard, she jogged up the wide brick steps to the sprawling back porch. *Huh.* Constance had replaced the outdoor furniture with a sleek new set with deep cushions. It looked nice.

One by one, she lifted the geranium pots in the row that lined the back wall of the house under the dining room windows. Under the fifth one, she spotted the metallic glint of a key and shook her head. She had to convince her mother to quit leaving a spare key in such an obvious location.

Quietly, she unlocked the kitchen door and slipped inside. She paused to wipe her feet carefully on the doormat. Her mother practically had X-ray vision when it came to spotting dirt on her immaculate floors.

She eased through the kitchen and into the front hallway. The house was silent, and flashes of all the times she'd snuck around in it like this came back to her. Memory of trips to the kitchen for late night snacks and letting in her high school boyfriend for make-out sessions in the front living room made her smile a little as she headed for her father's office.

She slipped inside, closed the door silently, and locked it before she turned to face her father's sanctum, unchanged since her childhood. It still had the same heavy, dark furniture, the tall bookshelves of intimidating law books, and—her imagination must be playing tricks on her—she fancied she still smelled the faint odor of his pipe tobacco. Its pristine, almost museum-like state gave her hope that her mother hadn't gotten rid of her father's meticulous notes from his decades in Congress.

Constance kept threatening to hire someone to write her father's memoir, which also gave Helen hope that his files would be intact.

She moved to the twin windows and pulled down the blinds before heading over to his massive desk. She trailed her fingertips along the edge of the highly polished mahogany. *Okay, Dad. Where would you have hidden your deepest, darkest secrets?*

She spent the next hour thumbing through the filing cabinet drawers built into the bookshelves to no avail. Everything in here was from his early days as a family law attorney—mostly wills, divorces, trust funds, and adoption papers.

She sat down at his desk and opened the pair of filing drawers beside each of her knees. In here were congressional records—research and notes on the dozens of bills he'd sponsored and cosponsored over the years. She glanced through the folders, and the contents all looked like dry, legal stuff.

It was possible the scandal that had ended his career was buried in one of these, but her gut feeling was that he would've kept something that damaging somewhere more secure. There was no sign of anything pertaining to an Operation Whitehorse. If it was as highly classified as Li said it was, she doubted her dad would've left notes on it just lying around in unlocked drawers.

She gazed around the office speculatively. Where would she hide if she were highly sensitive information?

She'd never heard either of her parents mention a safe in this room. The only safe she knew of in the house was upstairs in the main bedroom, and Constance kept her jewelry and a handgun in it. Would her father have kept his secrets there?

Nah. It had been a huge bone of contention between them that he didn't share everything with Constance about his work. He wouldn't have left anything he didn't want her to see where she could find it. His wife was nothing if not a snoop.

Helen smiled a little. A trait that ran in the family.

She stood up and carefully started removing books from shelves to peer at the walls behind them. She was about halfway around the room when she spotted a flat metal panel in the wall behind the bookshelves where everywhere else it had been wood paneling.

Working quietly, she took a cell phone picture of the shelf of books, then lifted out about three feet of law books and laid them on the floor in order so she could return them to their former positions later. The safe was wide but not tall, and she only had to clear out the one row of books to uncover the low steel door.

She stared at the combination lock in consternation. She was no lock picker. She tried her father's birthday and then her mother's. No joy. She tried her parents' anniversary. Still no luck. Frowning, she dialed in her own birth date and pushed down on the handle. It opened with a click.

Aw, Dad. It was sweet of him to use her birthday, but it was truly terrible op sec.

She pointed her flashlight at the opened safe and saw two piles of manila folders filling the space.

The scent of her father's pipe tobacco was stronger in here, and a wave of nostalgia rolled over her. She'd never been close to her father; he'd always been busy with work or the latest campaign. But she'd loved him dearly and spent her youth trying to make him proud enough to notice her. Although infrequent, his hugs had been the best.

She blinked away a few tears and pulled out the stacks of folders.

She carried them to the desk, considering the pile they formed. It approached a foot tall. It would take her all night, possibly longer, to read all of these. Better to take them home and go through them at her leisure.

Did her mother know about the safe? Would she open it and realize the files were missing? Helen decided to risk it. Her mother hadn't been on a tear to get her father's memoirs written recently. She couldn't imagine Constance checking his hidden safe, assuming she even knew about it, to see if a bunch of decades-old files were still there.

She closed the safe and replaced the books on their shelf, comparing their placement to the picture from her phone. Thankfully, her mother kept her house spotless and there were no dust disturbances to worry about.

Carrying the folders with her, she retraced her steps through the house to the kitchen. Opening the pantry door, she pulled a plastic grocery bag from the recycling bin. She slid the folders in it and tied the top shut.

Continuing to retrace her steps, she headed back outside and replaced the spare key under the geranium pot.

Maybe because it was old habit to be stealthy when sneaking out of her parents' house, she headed down the driveway quietly, hugging the tall hedge between their drive and the next-door neighbor's, pausing at the end of it by the sidewalk the way she always had. Which was why she spotted the movement in the shadows beside her car down the street.

Alarm surged through her as she stared at the shadow behind the huge old oak tree beside her car. The shadow was approximately six feet tall and all black. Not some neighborhood kid then. A hostile.

She considered her options quickly. Had she already been seen?

Without moving a muscle, she gazed up and down the street, searching for other shadows that didn't belong here.

She thought she spotted a particularly dark shadow on this side of the street, across from her car, as if someone might be crouched behind one of Mrs. Hinkelman's prized rhododendrons.

If there were two people out here, she would bet there were more. The last time someone sent a kill team after her, it had been four assassins strong. But where were the others? Perhaps down the street in the other direction? She dared not turn her head to look.

Frozen like a deer caught in headlights, she held her position, hardly daring to breathe as she considered her options. She really didn't want to get into a hand-to-hand fight with two or more killers. Kicking herself for leaving her handgun in her car, she resolved that retreat was her best option.

Moving at the speed of a glacier, she eased one foot backward. Inch by inch, she backed away from the street. As she eased along the hedge, she slowly turned her head until she could check the street in the other direction. Two men were walking down the sidewalks on each side of the street, coming toward her fast.

Crap.

CHAPTER 26

SUBJECT NO. 26 CROUCHED BEHIND A LINE OF SITKA SPRUCES, TOWering nearly a hundred feet above him in the night. The northern lights shimmered overhead, lime green with swirls of pink writhing in a slow, sinuous dance across the heavens. Up here in northern Alaska, far from even a hint of human civilization, the stars were thick and impossibly bright.

He preferred more complete darkness for his work, but it was what it was.

Pleasure surged through his veins, as close to lust as he was capable of feeling. Ah, how he enjoyed the hunt. It was the only time he truly felt alive, all the strange, incomprehensible pieces of him connected.

He eased forward, creeping across the gravel beach at a snail's pace, being careful to walk with no discernible rhythm as he approached the float plane moored to a short dock at this most rugged of fishing camps.

Three old-fashioned canvas tents were pitched side by side perhaps a hundred feet down the shore. At the moment, they were dark and still, their occupants peacefully asleep.

One of those occupants knew better—or should. As the director of Operations for the CIA, Lester Reinhold ought to have learned that nowhere was safe, not even this remote lake in the literal middle of nowhere. Reinhold should've accepted the offer of a security team to accompany him and his two teenaged sons on this Alaskan fishing trip.

Yet his brief for this mission had been clear: the Reinholds and their pilot were up here alone.

Reaching the dock, Subject no. 26 moved down it swiftly. He stepped onto the nearside pontoon of the Cessna 310, out of sight of the tents. He went to work, laboriously unscrewing by hand a panel on the underside of the wing near where it joined the fuselage.

He pulled the prewired block of C-4 out of his backpack, taped it to the wing spar—the backbone of the wing—and activated the remote detonation mechanism. No dramatic flashing light blinked red. That stuff was only for television consumption. He didn't need any lights potentially alerting anyone that this device was hidden inside the wing.

He screwed the panel back into place and pulled out a tiny bottle of white paint with a nail-polish-style brush to touch up the rivets where his wrench had chipped off bits of paint. When he'd finished daubing the rivets, he stowed the paint and tried the door to the right-side pilot's seat.

Unlocked.

Sloppy op sec, Lester.

Although failure to lock the doors was probably the bush pilot's fault. Still.

Sitting in the copilot's seat, Subject no. 26 detached the ADS-B from its clip mounting on the dashboard. The white, palm-sized radio transmitted to the Automatic Dependent Surveillance-Broadcast system, determining an aircraft's position via satellite and broadcasting it periodically, allowing it to be tracked even in a place this remote.

Working quickly, he pried open the ADS-B, lifted out the motherboard, and scraped the back of it with his pocketknife, destroying many of the soldered connections that made it work. Carefully, he replaced the motherboard and closed the case. He tried to power it up, and its display screen remained dark, inoperative.

A motion in front of the airplane made him freeze. Someone

had emerged from one of the tents and was walking down to the lake. He eased down to his side, lying across the left seat of the tiny aircraft until he could just peek above the dashboard.

Whoever it was stopped at the edge of the lake, dropped his sweatpants, and urinated in the lake. Subject no. 26 watched the person stroll back to the tent and disappear inside.

Time to go.

He slid out of the plane, latching the door behind himself quietly. Another crawl under the belly of the aircraft, a sprint down the dock, and a slow, arrhythmic retreat across the crunchy gravel beach.

He reached the woods and moved swiftly through the trees to his own tiny camp. Working efficiently, he took down his tent, stowed it and his gear in his backpack, and started the arduous hike around the lake to where it emptied into a local creek. He had about a mile to travel, but in the dark, in terrain this rough with no trail whatsoever to follow, it was going to take him a couple of hours. Might as well get it out of the way now.

He pulled a set of night optical devices down over his eyes, and the forest lit up in lime green almost the exact color of the aurora borealis now fading into ghostly wisps overhead.

He moved slowly, taking his time and following the old adage that slow was smooth and smooth was fast. Not to mention, a guy like Reinhold wasn't likely to get up at the crack of dawn. Not on the last day of his vacation.

A motion ahead of him caught his eye, and he crouched, waiting for a big grizzly bear to cross from left to right in front of him, heading up the slope away from the lake. When he was sure the bear was gone, he headed out once more.

Dawn was breaking by the time he reached the kayak he'd hidden beside the creek flowing out of the lake. He stowed his gear in the belly of the shallow-bottomed craft and headed for the lakeshore. He found a decent-sized boulder to lie down behind. Covering himself with camo cloth, he got comfortable peering through a small telescope.

Now the waiting began.

CHAPTER 27

HELEN SWORE AND TOOK OFF RUNNING BACK UP THE DRIVEWAY. She spied both men breaking into a run. As she sprinted beside the house, she tossed the bag of files under the hedge and thought fast. Unarmed, she dared not try to run around out here dodging a kill team, particularly since they would undoubtedly be equipped with night optical gear.

She needed cover and a weapon. Both were available inside her mother's house.

No way would she have time to fumble for that stupid key, unlock the door, and get inside before they were upon her, though.

She sprinted across the lawn and took a running leap for the rose trellis, praying the wood hadn't rotted over the years and would hold her weight.

Getting scratched all to heck as she scrambled up the rose arbor, she was shocked as old muscle memory kicked in and she raced from foothold to foothold, never missing a handhold above her. Please God, let her mother not have repaired the old lock on her window. She'd loosened it as a kid so she could slip a flat metal strip under the windowsill to unlock it from this side.

Panting, she hauled herself up until her nose was level with the windowsill. She fumbled in the dark for the old slit between the bricks where she used to hide the metal jimmy stick. Her fingers felt its edge. She had to pry it out with her fingernails. It must've rusted in place. But finally, it slid free.

She jammed it under the window and jerked to the right, hard. *Praise the Lord.* The lock opened. She dropped the metal strip and shoved with all her strength on the window. It slid up about six inches. She had to climb the trellis a few more feet before she could wedge her shoulder under the window and give it a frantic push.

Those men should be here any second.

The window finally gave way, and she tumbled through the opening, landing on the floor in a heap. She also made an audible thud.

Crap. Constance was a light sleeper.

She scrambled to her knees, pulled the window closed, and peered down at the backyard. One man was moving around the perimeter of the yard, and the other was peering in the kitchen windows, cupping his hands around some sort of night vision goggles as he stared inside.

She eased back from the window, breathing hard. Would they come inside? She and her mother had their problems, but she didn't want to bring killers into this house and put Constance in mortal danger.

As much as she hated to let her mother know she'd been here, she had no choice. Pulling out her cell phone, she texted 911, reporting armed intruders trying to break into a home, and giving her mother's address.

She hit send and then raced out of her bedroom and down the hall to her mother's room. Oh, this was going to suck.

Wincing, she opened the door to the main bedroom, slipped inside, and locked the door behind her. She raced over to the bed and pressed her hand over her mother's mouth.

Constance's eyes flew open, and she flailed her arms, hitting Helen about the head and shoulders.

Talking low and urgently, she said, "Mom, it's me. Helen."

Her mother tried to say something against her hand, and Helen talked over her. "There are some bad guys trying to break into the house. I need you to get your gun out of the safe and come with me. And don't make a sound. Do you understand?"

Constance nodded, her eyes wide.

Helen lifted her hand away cautiously.

"What on earth—"

She slapped her hand over her mother's mouth again. "Not. A. Sound. Your life depends on it. Silence, Mom."

Constance nodded and this time merely sat up and swung her feet out of bed when Helen lifted away her hand. She followed her mother over to the hinged painting that hid the safe, listening hard for movement downstairs as Constance fumbled at the combination and had to start over.

A scrape came from the vicinity of the kitchen. The hostiles were inside. *C'mon, police. Come in sirens wailing.*

Her mother reached inside the safe and pulled out an antiquated six-shooter revolver. Her hands were shaking so badly Helen doubted Constance could've pulled the trigger if she had to. She lifted the weapon out of her mother's hands as much for her own safety as her mother's.

"Extra ammo?" she whispered.

Her mother took out a box of rounds and shoved it at her.

She gestured for her mother to head into the bathroom. She followed Constance into the spacious main bathroom and looked around for a good hiding space. It had been redone recently and was bright white from top to bottom, all glass and mirrors.

Helen breathed, "Lock yourself in the toilet room, Mom, and don't come out until I tell you to."

Constance demanded under her breath. "Hide with me."

"No. I'm taking cover in the bathtub and shooting anyone who comes through the bathroom door."

"Honey, do you think that's a good idea?"

"I think it's an outstanding idea. Move, Mom. And not a peep out of you, no matter what you hear out here, even if there are gunshots and screaming. You hear me? *No matter what.* Your life depends on *nobody* knowing you're in there."

Thankfully, Constance didn't argue any further and disappeared into the tiny toilet room. A lock clicked on the other side of the door.

Oh, Lord. Was she ever going to have a lot of explaining to do when this was all over.

Helen climbed into the snazzy, freestanding bathtub and stretched out, bracing her feet against one end and resting her shoulder against the other end of the tub. She checked to make sure the weapon was fully loaded, which it was, then propped the barrel of the revolver on the edge of the tub and peered over it at the door. She hesitated to think of how badly this thing's sights were adjusted. Praying the factory settings, which would be reasonably accurate, were still in place, she lined up the spot just above the doorknob.

And then she went through her shooting routine. She cleared all thought from her mind. It was just her, the gun, and the target. She breathed in slowly and did her best to relax her entire body, muscle by muscle. The truth was it was always stressful to shoot a live target. But she had long years of practice managing that stress. She calmed her mind until she was one with her weapon, and it was one with her.

The doorknob in the outer bedroom rattled.

Surely the intruders had already tried it more stealthily than that and knew it was locked. Which meant the noise they were making was for intimidation purposes. They would kick it open right about—

Bang.

She jumped involuntarily. They'd shot open the lock. Not the most subtle of entries.

She heard a faint squeak from the toilet that cut off abruptly. Constance must've slapped a hand over her mouth.

But all of that registered distantly, not really disturbing her zen state of readiness.

At the very edge of her hearing, she thought she caught the faint wail of a siren. It wouldn't be here in time.

The bathroom door's knob moved slightly. Testing it to see if it was locked. She braced herself for the explosion. Inhaled and held her breath. Her finger tightened on the trigger—

A large shape exploded through the door, and she aimed throat-high, double-tapping two shots into him.

Bang. Bang.

Before his knees had barely buckled, a second black shape leaped into the room, moving sideways fast.

His weapon was ready in front of him, but he hadn't acquired her yet. Tracking his movement with the tip of her barrel, she aimed at his center of mass and fired.

She must've hit body armor, for he jolted backward, but his weapon came up swiftly.

As a muzzle flash from his weapon blinded her and chips of porcelain bathtub flew everywhere, she fired again, more by feel than sight. The revolver, which was now an extension of her hand, sent two rounds in his direction as fast as she could fire it.

Bang. Bang.

The weapon kicked up hard, and she brute-forced it back down into a firing position. Seeing little but blinding afterimages, she aimed purely by instinct and fired her last round.

The hostile's weapon fired up at the ceiling, and plaster rained down in front of the toilet room. She ducked down in the tub. Rapidly ejecting the spent shells from the revolver, she slammed in two more rounds and chambered them by feel, squeezing her eyes shut hard to clear her vision.

She raised the revolver barrel over the edge of the tub. When there wasn't immediate return fire, she risked peeking over the edge of the tub. The second man was on his back in front of the shower, rolling over onto his side to face her.

But she could see him now.

She took aim and put both rounds into his face. A spray of black covered the lower half of the glass shower door.

Once more she ducked down and reloaded, six rounds this time. She peered cautiously over the edge of the tub. Neither hostile was moving. The only motion at all was black liquid rolling lazily down the shower door.

She held her position. Were the other two men in the house somewhere?

The sirens were louder now, but still a block or more away.

Without warning, the window behind her exploded inward with an almighty crash of breaking glass. She jolted, rolling onto her back as a black shape smashed down on top of her, trapping her weapon between them.

Struggling with all her strength, she tried to angle the barrel of the revolver toward him. She pulled the trigger.

The bang was muffled between their bodies as his goggled, featureless face froze momentarily, just inches from hers. She yanked her arm one more time for all she was worth and managed to free her right arm. She jammed the revolver against his ear and pulled the trigger.

Hot blood and brain matter sprayed all over her face, and he went limp on top of her. He was *really* heavy, and she struggled desperately to wriggle out from underneath him. She made it halfway out from under him and pushed up, her head and right arm clearing the edge of the tub.

A fourth figure stood across the room, pointing an assault weapon at her. She whipped her revolver toward the figure, but as she started to duck below the level of the tub, she registered that the assault weapon was waving around wildly.

At the last instant before her weapon fired, she jerked it up toward the ceiling, sending a harmless round well over her mother's head.

"I told you to stay in the toilet," she grunted, shoving at the dead man sharing the tub with her.

"You're my baby. Anyone who wants to kill you is going to have to go through me."

Well, she and her mother had that in common, at least.

"Thanks, Mom." She crawled out from under the dead man and rolled out of the tub onto the floor. She pushed to her feet and moved over to her mom through the broken glass covering the floor. Man, it had hurt when that guy landed on her in the hard tub.

"How about we trade weapons?" she said gently to her mother as the assault weapon continued to waver all over the place in her mother's horrifically unsafe grip. She lifted it out of her mom's hands and replaced it with the much smaller and lighter .38 revolver. "There are three rounds left in the gun. And maybe don't point it in my direction. Okay?"

"Um, okay."

"Count how many times you shoot so you know when it's empty. Can you do that?'

"Uh-huh."

Constance was going into shock.

"Look at me, Mom. Breathe with me. In. Out. Good. Keep breathing. I don't need you to faint on me."

"Now what?" Constance asked in a small voice.

Surprise registered on Helen. It was the first time she could ever remember her mother sounding well and truly scared. Constance had always had the heart of a tiger and icy self-control in a crisis.

In a gentler voice, she said, "The police will be here any second. Any bad guys who are left will run away or be caught by the cops. We're going to sit tight in here until the police come for us."

"Is this what it felt like the night those robbers broke into Peter and Li's house and you were all alone?"

That had been more of a running firefight, and she'd been more pissed off than scared. But she answered, "Yes, Mom. It was a lot like this."

Of course, by the time she'd locked herself in the boys' upstairs bathroom, she'd been fairly sure she'd killed all the hostiles in the house. Hiding in the bathroom had been a performance for the benefit of the police. To convince them she was an innocent victim of a home invasion.

"I'm so sorry, sweetheart. I had no idea."

"It's fine, Mom. Why don't you take a seat on the toilet lid? It'll be a few minutes before the police clear the house. I'm going to call 911 and let them know where we are."

While she waited for the police, Helen moved over to the sink, laid down her phone, and wetted a washcloth. She used it to wipe the blood and gunk off her face. *Better.*

Picking up her cell phone, she used its flashlight to have a look at the dead men. Military gear. Russian night vision equipment and weapons. Bad teeth. Reaching out gingerly, she unbuttoned the first man's chest pocket where his body armor had slipped to one side. She found a pack of Russian Prima cigarettes inside.

She snapped pictures of the man's face, gear, and cigarettes, being careful to disturb the body as little as possible. Picking her way around the various pools of blood, she took pictures of the other two corpses and then joined her mother in the tiny throne room.

It took about five minutes for the police to clear the rest of the house and enter the bedroom. As soon as she heard them calling back and forth to one another, she called out, "We're in the bathroom, officers! Two women and three, um . . . dead men! We're going to lay down our weapons now!"

"Put your hands on the back of your head," an officer called back tersely.

Helen did as ordered. "You, too, Mom. Everyone's adrenaline is running high, and they don't want to take any chances. Lay the revolver down on the floor and then lock your fingers behind your neck like this."

"It's safe to come in, gentlemen," Helen called.

Two police officers stepped into the bathroom and turned on the lights. They stared in shock. As well they should. In the sudden brightness, Helen's first impression was that there was blood *everywhere.*

Constance gasped beside her, and her knees started to buckle. Helen jumped and caught her mother, wedging her shoulder beneath her mother's armpit.

A cop stepped forward and took over supporting Constance, while the other one stared hard at Helen. "You two did this?"

Constance answered tartly, "If you mean did we defend ourselves from a home invasion, officer, we most certainly did. We Stapleton women don't take threats to our family lying down."

Helen shrugged a little at the incredulous cop. "What she said." She added, "Any chance my mother and I could sit down? Perhaps on the edge of the bed? I'm also feeling a bit faint."

It was a total lie, but it did the trick. It shook the officers out of their rampant disbelief that two old ladies had shot and killed three armed intruders. She and her mother were duly deposited on the edge of the bed to sit, ordered not to move until they gave statements.

Armed police officers came and went for the next several minutes in a flurry of activity, making the weapons in the bathroom safe, taking initial crime scene pictures, and declaring the house and street secured.

Crud. The fourth guy must've gotten away. Had there been more bad guys out there? Who *were* they? Was this hit team the one sent to protect Scorpius? If so, how had they found her here? How had they followed her?

And then the moment she'd been dreading arrived. Constance frowned suddenly, looked over at her, and asked, "What were you doing in my house?"

CHAPTER 28

WHAT WERE THE ODDS SHE COULD LIE TO HER MOTHER AND GET away with it? She'd never been able to as a kid. But Constance was pretty shaken after the shooting.

Still. Better not risk it. She didn't need the police to hear her mother accuse her of lying and decide to ask her more pointed questions.

Beneath the din of people moving around the house, shouting back and forth, she said, "Someone told me there might be a problem in Dad's political past that could harm Mitch's chances of getting elected. I had to work late tonight, and by the time I got over here to ask you about it, all the lights were off. Rather than wake you up, I grabbed the spare key on the back porch— Mom, you've *got* to hide the key somewhere less obvious—and let myself in. I checked Dad's files in his desk, and I didn't find anything. I think Mitch is fine."

"What sort of thing in your father's past?" Constance asked sharply.

"No idea. The person telling me didn't know. They just heard a rumor. Something about supporting a controversial bill. Maybe about immigration."

Constance visibly relaxed the moment Helen threw out the immigration red herring.

Well, hell. There *was* something bad in her father's past career, and Constance knew what it was.

Helen said lightly, "The person said something about an Operation Whitehorse. Do you remember Dad talking about anything called that?"

The sound of a crash in the kitchen made both of them jump. Constance surged to her feet. "I'm not letting these hooligans destroy my house. It's not my fault those robbers broke in."

"Mom. Focus," she hissed under her breath. "Have you ever heard of Operation Whitehorse?"

"No."

"You're sure?"

"Positive," her mother snapped. "I have a memory like a steel trap, thank you very much."

Helen threw up her hands placatingly.

Constance looked over at the police detective standing guard at the bathroom door and said loudly, "I'm just so glad you were here . . . and so brave, sweetheart. What a good idea it was to hide in the tub. I had no idea you could shoot like that—"

Vividly aware of the cop listening to every word they said, she cut her mother off quickly. "It was at very close range. I probably couldn't hit the side of a barn if I had to shoot at a target for real. But those men were only a few feet away. All I had to do was point in their general direction, close my eyes, and pull the trigger-thing." She added breathlessly, "It was so loud. I had no idea guns were that deafening."

"Me neither," her mother declared. "Awful things, guns."

"Awful," Helen agreed fervently. Her mother met her gaze and nodded slightly in approval.

God bless her mother. Constance had totally orchestrated that exchange for the policeman's benefit. Her mom might be a manipulative bitch, but tonight—for once—she'd been a manipulative bitch on her daughter's behalf.

The detective turned back to the crime scene as if he'd lost interest in their conversation. Helen prayed he had. She remained seated on the bed while her mother headed downstairs to defend her house from harm. Knowing Constance, she would be feeding the whole crew in no time. That and talking earnestly to all of them about how they needed to vote for her smart, accomplished grandson.

Helen endured a long round of questioning by a pair of detectives about how the shooting had gone down. The only question that surprised her was their very last one.

"Ma'am, how do you suppose that last guy—the one who jumped through the window—got up onto the second-floor balcony?"

She couldn't help but smile a little. "When I was a rebellious teenager, I always climbed the rose trellis."

That seemed to do the trick. Both detectives relaxed and closed their notebooks. "Would you mind coming down to the station in the morning to make a full statement? We'll need you to write down everything you just told us."

"Is it possible for you to tape-record it?" she asked anxiously. "I have arthritis in my hands, and writing much is hard for me. And after I shot that awful gun, my wrists are *so* sore. How do you gentlemen do it?"

They rolled their eyes a little. The lead detective answered, "You can make a verbal statement if you'd like. And you might want to soak your hands in some hot water and Epsom salts. Always helps with my shooter's cramps."

She nodded, wide-eyed. "That's a good idea. Thank you so much, captain." Might as well give the guy a promotion in rank while she was buttering him up.

"I'm just a detective, ma'am."

"I'm so impressed. Your mother must be so proud of you . . ."

CHAPTER 29

*B*RIGHT, LATE MORNING SUNSHINE CREPT AROUND THE EDGES OF the motel's dark-out curtains when Helen woke up. Last night had taken more out of her than she'd realized.

A hot shower gave her a chance to work out the worst of the kinks in her muscles and wash the last of the blood and gore out of her hair. While she was showering, she handwashed her black turtleneck, scrubbing out the blood from where Window Guy had bled all over it. She blow-dried her hair and the turtleneck, used the complimentary toothbrush and toothpaste, and finally felt marginally human once more.

She ate a granola bar she had in her purse, made herself a cup of truly terrible coffee using the tiny coffee pot in her room, and sat down to look at her father's secret files, which she'd had a chance to fish out of the bushes at nearly dawn.

She opened the first manila folder. It was a report to the House Intelligence Committee regarding a program run in Africa to assassinate various terrorist leaders and destroy their networks for making money. As someone who'd worked in that field for a long time, she could read between the lines to spot outstanding work by operators like her in a truly dangerous part of the world.

She opened another file. It detailed a military operation that had gone wrong and some SEALs had died. The next file outlined an operation to destabilize a hostile foreign government.

She picked up the fourth file with a single initial scrawled on the label. *W.* Could this be it? Whitehorse?

Opening the file, she stared down at the cover page of a stapled sheaf of papers: *Briefing to the House Intelligence Committee on Operation Whitehorse, a CIA training program classified at Top Secret SCI.*

SCI stood for Sensitive Compartmented Information, which meant only people with a direct need to know anything about this program were allowed to read on.

How did her father get this file out of the SCIF—Secure Classified Information Facility—where it would have been briefed to the congressional committee? She turned the page. *Ah.* That was how he had this report. It was the redacted version. Large sections of the page were covered in black ink, covering sensitive information from the briefing.

Behind the thick report was a yellow sheet torn from a legal pad, covered in her father's cramped handwriting. As she read his notes, it became clear he must've been jotting down information from memory:

—*11 test subjects to date. 5 fails. 6 graduates.*

Graduates of what? Were operatives being trained to do something specific? Of course, knowing the CIA a few decades ago, the subjects could be graduates of LSD trips.

She read on:

—*5-year Funding: 20 M.*

Twenty million dollars? That was a lot of money for what appeared to be just some sort of training program. Especially a couple of decades ago.

Her father had added a note to that figure:—*up for renewal this year.*

—*Training facility: classified above us.* Her father had added a pithy comment to that in boldly slashed capital letters: *WTF?*

—*Program Director: R. Bell.*

Well, well, well. Hello, Richard.

She continued reading her father's notes:

—*Ready to go operational.*

Doing what?

—Committee split on whether or not to approve. Those opposed fear it could spin out of control.

He added one last, ominous comment at the end of that note: *If so, God save us all.*

She dug into the heavily redacted pages of the official report, trying to piece together anything from the unredacted fragments of text about what this Operation Whitehorse actually did.

As best she could tell, Richard Bell had recruited his test subjects out of the military. He'd moved them somewhere to train them to do something. She gathered he'd trained the first group himself.

One unredacted sentence stopped her in her tracks. It was innocuous, buried in the middle of a paragraph talking about using various military resources as needed. It read, *Military transport delivered the remains of failed trainees to their homes of record.*

Remains? As in their *bodies*? They'd died?

Holy cow. No wonder Li had been adamant that Richard Bell was dangerous.

Any information on how five of his trainees had died was redacted or not included in the briefing. Frankly, she was shocked he hadn't lost his job over it. Nobody was supposed to die in training, for heaven's sake. And five deaths? How had *one* death not gotten him tossed out on his ear or put in jail?

The summary at the end of the briefing suggested using one or two of the six successful graduates to train future participants while the other four were deployed into the field. The summary also indicated that the program director was asking for five years' more funding for the program to the tune of twenty million dollars. It concluded with the program director's belief that the program had proved itself to be both viable and successful.

She laid down the stapled sheaf of documents and picked up the last papers in the file: a record of who'd voted to extend the program and who'd voted to shut it down. The first vote was a tie: eight members voted to approve, eight voted to disapprove. She glanced down and noted that her father had voted to disapprove the program.

She turned to the second page of vote tallies. The first thing she noticed was that this second vote was taken nearly a month after the first one. In her recollection of hearing her father talk about his career, that was a *very* long time for a congressional committee to sit on a tie vote and not find a way to break the stalemate.

This time the vote came out with eight in favor, and seven opposed. She glanced down the list of voters and stared in dismay. Her father wasn't even listed as a committee member. She looked at the dates of the votes again. The first Operation Whitehorse vote had been taken in early March. The second one had come in mid-April.

She didn't remember the exact date her father had retired, but it had been right before the wildly awkward Easter dinner where her mother hadn't been speaking to her father. At all. So he must've retired in late March or early April.

He'd died less than two months later. His burial had been on Memorial Day, in fact. She vividly remembered the long rows of little flags on every grave at Arlington National Cemetery.

Had someone been holding off the vote until he left the committee? Who was the committee chairman anyway? *Huh.* Charles Veenstra. And he'd voted in favor of funding the program both times.

She frowned, perplexed. Her father had retired abruptly, apparently without telling *anyone* he was planning to do it. She remembered clearly how livid her mother had been when he'd called a press conference and announced it without saying a single word to her about it.

Had Veenstra known her dad was leaving Congress? Was that why he'd delayed the vote? What were the odds that now-Senator Veenstra would tell her the truth if she asked him about it? More to the point, would he tell her what Operation Whitehorse had been?

She put the papers back in their file folder thoughtfully.

Did Richard Bell know she was the daughter of one of the men who'd tried to terminate this training program of his? Was he the kind of guy to hold a grudge over something like that? Yosef certainly thought so. But it had been fifteen years since then. Surely, if Bell had wanted to get even with her, he would've done it long before now.

She'd only met Bell a few times in passing and mostly in large meetings where they'd barely exchanged a hello. They'd certainly never chatted or worked together directly. But he'd never shown her any particular animosity.

On the missions she'd led that he'd been involved with supervising, Yosef had always run interference, dealing with Bell himself and relaying any instructions from Bell to her.

At the very back of the Whitehorse file, she found a torn piece of paper, a scrap really, with three names scrawled on it in her father's handwriting, haphazardly tucked behind the vote tallies:

Marcus Bickford
Brandon McQuistion
Walt Kingston

She took a picture of the paper with her cell phone. Were these the names of operatives Bell had trained? Maybe congressional staffers who knew something about Operation Whitehorse? Or were they totally unrelated? When she got home, she would research them on the internet and see what she could find.

Speaking of which, she debated whether or not to risk returning to her house. The fourth attacker from last night had gotten away and could be lying in wait for her there. Or he could've already left the country after his mission failed and his teammates died.

She could use a change of clean clothes. And if nothing else, she would love to grab her emergency go-bag. It had not only clothing and toiletries to fit pretty much any situation, but it also had survival gear, surveillance gear, emergency weapons, and ammo.

It was broad daylight now, and she did have the handgun she'd left in her glove compartment last night. She really did need her emergency kit.

But first, she needed to make two phone calls.

On the first call, she had to drop her father's name and suggest she'd found something in his old files that could damage Senator Veenstra to get an appointment with him, but he could see her for five minutes after he got back from a lunch meeting today. She assured the aide that would be plenty of time for what she needed to discuss with him.

Her second call was to Yosef.

"Hi, Helen. What can I do for you?"

"I always do ask you for something, don't I?" she replied rue-fully.

"That's all right. It's my job to take care of you."

"For which I am eternally grateful."

"What's up?"

She filled him in quickly on the hit squad that had tried to take her out last night and her belief that they were a Russian team. She finished with, "What are the odds the FSB sent them after me to protect Scorpius?"

"High, I should think." He sighed. "I wish I knew who Scorpius was. But I'm as clueless as you and your team, I'm afraid."

"The reason I called you is I want to talk with Anatoly Tarmy-enkin. Face-to-face."

"Why?" Yosef asked in alarm.

"To ask him if he ordered the hit on me. I need to see his reaction in person."

"What for?"

"It'll tell me if he's Scorpius's handler or not," she replied.

"Ah. Interesting."

"Can you arrange it?" she asked.

"I can try." A pause. "But Helen, my dear, if the Russians are trying to kill you, a meeting with their highest-ranking spy in this country could walk you right into a trap."

"I'm aware of that. I'll take precautions."

"You're not invincible—"

She cut him off. "I'm well aware of my mortality, thank you."

He sighed. "I'll make the call. I can't promise he'll agree to meet with you."

"Thank you, Yosef. I owe you yet again. What am I up to? A hundred favors I owe you?"

"More like two hundred," he replied, a shade sourly.

"You're my hero," she said lightly.

An irritated huff was the last thing she heard before he disconnected the call.

CHAPTER 30

SUBJECT NO. 26 ENJOYED THE SKY TURNING PINK AND THEN ORANGE behind the snowcapped mountains at the far end of the lake. This was a beautiful spot, for sure. He particularly liked the idea of being the only human being for miles around. If anything, he resented Reinhold, his sons, and their pilot for intruding upon the perfection of this spot at the end of nowhere.

Unreasoning rage surged through him at their presence. He wanted this place for himself. Taking deep, calming breaths, he consoled himself with the fact that, in a few hours, this lake would be his alone.

The sun rose, and alpine birds began to go about their morning business, singing as they hunted the copious insect population. The mosquitoes up here were larger than any he'd ever seen in his life—and he'd been some places that grew the biting pests huge. The undiluted DEET he'd doused his clothing in did the trick, though, and the insects didn't bother him. Or maybe he was just too mean to bite.

Amused at the notion, he smiled a little and lifted his binoculars to gaze across the lake at Reinhold's camp. *Finally. Movement.* He'd begun to think they were going to sleep till noon. He had places to go and things to do.

He watched as the four figures in the distance struck camp and packed their gear in the back of the Cessna. At long last, they all climbed in the airplane.

Right about now, the pilot would be banging on the ADS-B, try-ing to get it to work.

Good luck with that, buddy.

It wasn't required equipment for flight, and the pilot would take off without it. Reinhold would register vague discomfort at something out of the ordinary but then would discount it because nobody on earth knew where he and his boys were right now.

Wrong-o, Lester.

The Cessna engine sputtered to life. The pilot jumped out of the plane and onto the dock, where he cast off the mooring lines and threw them in the back of the aircraft. Subject no. 26 watched carefully as the guy climbed back into the plane.

The airplane pulled away from the dock, and Subject no. 26 lifted his hand to feel the breeze. It was coming from behind him, which meant the plane would taxi down to the far end of the long, narrow lake, and take off coming back toward him.

Perfect.

If the pilot was any good, he would go all the way down to the end of the lake, almost a mile from this end of it. Safety dictated always putting as much landing zone as possible in front of one's plane and never wasting landing zone behind oneself.

The Cessna became a red and white speck in the distance. He had to use his binoculars to see it make a 180-degree turn and face its propellor directly at him.

Come and get me.

He fingered the black box in his palm but kept his thumb well away from the button mounted on its face.

The faint sound of an engine revving up to full power and the deep, beating noise of a propellor cutting through the air drifted to him. *Here they come.*

The plane popped into the air within a few thousand feet and gained altitude quickly, in anticipation of having to clear the mountain peaks behind him.

As it reached the deepest part of the lake—some four hundred feet deep—the plane was nearly a thousand feet in the air. He held up the detonator and mashed the button.

It wasn't a particularly exciting explosion. Just a flash of bright light under the right wing. But then the right wing tore free from the fuselage, and the plane flipped over on its right side and spiraled down toward the water.

It hit the water with a mighty splash. It bobbed once, then sank rapidly. The detached wing fluttered down and splatted on the water like a leaf. In less than a minute, the surface of the lake had gone still once more.

He swore to himself. His orders were to leave no evidence of the accident. He was gonna be pissed if he had to paddle out there and retrieve that wing—

Nope. There it went. All at once, one end of it dipped down while the other tipped up a few feet in the air. It slid beneath the water as well, disappearing completely.

He scanned the lake through his binoculars for any other debris. Only the iridescent shine of an oil slick was visible in the water. With the breeze kicking up as it was, though, that would dissipate soon enough. Long before anyone thought to come up here searching for a missing government official.

He stood up and took one last look around his lake, memorizing how grand it felt to be the only human alive in this place.

With a sigh, he turned his back on paradise and jogged to his kayak, hidden in the brush. He dragged it over to the creek and stepped into it. He had a long paddle ahead of him, with a couple of portages and a couple of class three rapids to traverse before it joined a larger river that would carry him downstream to where his Jeep was parked by the Dalton Highway. It would take nearly a week to drive back to civilization and home. His work finished, he figured he would take his time and do a little sightseeing along the way.

Yep. It was a good day. He enjoyed the sun on his shoulders as he dipped his paddle in the water and headed out.

CHAPTER 31

AFTER A QUICK STOP AT THE BANK TO DEPOSIT HER FATHER'S FILES in her safe deposit box, Helen turned her car toward home.

Regardless of her alarm system showing no threats, she came in fast, punching the garage door opener at the last second so it was barely clear of her car roof when she screeched into the garage and punched the opener again to close the door. She spun out of her car low and fast, pistol extended in front of her in case anyone tried to slip into the garage with her.

The garage door thunked against the concrete floor.

Wasting no time, she rushed into the house, coming in hot. She moved swiftly from room to room, clearing each, checking every spot where a human could hide—behind the family room sofa, crouched behind the kitchen island, on the front stairs.

When the kids had left home and Gray started spending most of his time abroad researching rain-forest ecosystems, she'd re-arranged the house to minimize hiding places for any hostile.

She ran upstairs and, puffing with exertion, cleared the up-stairs quickly.

Her search ended in the main bedroom's walk-in closet. She activated the hidden panel behind her shelf of purses and slipped into her secret armory and gear locker. The small space was undisturbed.

Being surrounded by the tools of her trade like this made her feel safe for a change. If the Russians thought she would be an easy kill, they had a big surprise in store. With all of this gear and her decades of experience, she could take on a small army if she had to.

Not that she wanted to, though. She recalled a time when she'd been eager to go head-to-head against the Russians to prove she was the best. Now she was just happy to come out of any situation alive.

She pulled out a large black duffel bag, already packed with most of the supplies she needed to go to ground. To it, she added a compact assault weapon, a hefty handgun—one of her beloved Wilson Combat EDC X9 pistols—and an extra box of ammunition for the sniper rifle already packed in the go-bag.

For good measure, she tossed in a couple of manila envelopes holding fake identities, two extra wigs, a handful of burner phones, and an extra wad of cash.

Her phone vibrated. She pulled it out of her pocket. *Well, hell.* Her home security system app was sending her a warning that there had been a power interruption to the home alarm system. The same system that had its own internal battery good for several days and a backup battery in case that failed.

Someone was trying to breach the house. She swore under her breath. Three guesses who it was, and the first two didn't count.

Time to get out of here.

On her phone, she pulled up the feed to the house's external security cameras, each of which had its own internal battery backup. She spied a big man dressed in dark clothing easing open the kitchen door and slipping inside. Good Lord willing, it was the lone survivor of last night's fiasco and he was working by himself today.

Temptation to go downstairs and kill him coursed through her. But she hated the idea of killing someone inside her home. Also, she would risk a neighbor hearing the shot and calling the police.

She'd shot not one but two sets of home intruders recently. Too many more of those, and the police were going to start asking her some very pointed questions. That, and she hated the idea of having to clean up a huge puddle of blood from her beloved hardwood floors.

She rolled back the small rug in the middle of the floor and pulled up the hidden trap door, about two-by-two feet, built into the floor of her hidden storeroom. She sat down on the edge of the hole, lowering her bulky duffel bag into the hole in front of her, hanging onto it with one hand.

Using her other hand, she grabbed the hatch, pulling it up beside her. As she shoved off the edge onto the steep slide that ran along the false wall built into her house, she pulled the hatch shut over her head and let go.

It was a tight fit as she whooshed down the slide. The duffel bag hit the hinged hatch at the other end and popped outside.

She landed with a muffled grunt on top of her duffel bag full of hard, sharp gear. *Ow.* Branches from a bush poked at her face. She shoved them aside as she rolled to her hands and knees.

Rising to a crouch that kept her below the level of the living-room window over her head, she hefted the straps of the duffel over her shoulders and ran awkwardly for the woods.

The woods came within about thirty feet of the house at this point, and she'd made a point over the years of planting bushes this side of the tree line, big ones full of thick foliage. She slipped behind one of them and paused to catch her breath. Why did guns have to be so darned heavy?

More to the point, why did she have to get old and lose the effortless strength of her youth? She made a mental note to start lifting weights if she lived through the current mess.

Using trees and bushes for cover, she made her way up the hill behind the house deeper into the woods. Crouching, she peeked out from behind a tree to watch her home.

Finally, the big man in black eased out the back door, closing it behind him.

Why hadn't any of the security alarms peppered throughout the house triggered a warning on her phone? He must've managed to disable power to the entire security system and to deactivate the backup battery. She made another mental note to have

the system rewired on multiple, separate electrical panels—a few
of which were hidden inside the house.

The intruder moved quickly and smoothly—like a special operator—and disappeared around the corner of the house. *Must be
heading toward the road.* He'd probably hidden a car somewhere
along it.

When she was positive her intruder wasn't going to circle back
and follow her out here, she finally rose to her feet.

Oh, Lord. Her legs screamed with pain as blood flow returned
to them. She bent over, gasping, as she rubbed her cramping
muscles vigorously until they finally uncramped. Giving her legs a
last shake, she headed for the barn on the property behind hers.

She kept her backup car in here, a crappy compact sedan that
had seen better days, but which was fully armored, had run-flat
tires, and hid a powerful engine under its dented hood.

Stowing the duffel in the trunk, she headed out. As traffic increased approaching DC, she drove like a maniac for several minutes, watching her rearview mirror for anyone matching her
insane driving, if only for a few seconds. Even a five- or six-car surveillance team would have to show itself briefly as they tried to
keep her in sight before passing her off to the next car.

Nope. Nobody was being an idiot behind her. *Praise the Lord
and pass the potatoes.*

She slowed to a normal speed and headed across the north
side of Washington to a random Metro stop. No way was she
going to try to park downtown in the middle of a workday with
Congress in session.

After her close miss with that intruder, she felt naked without
her pistol in her purse, but she wouldn't be allowed to take it into
a government building. She locked it in her car and headed out.

She got off the Metro train at Union Station and walked the
half mile or so south to the Russell Senate Office Building. It was
a sprawling, white limestone affair, four stories tall and built in
the same Federalist style as most of the government buildings
along the Mall.

No surprise, Senator Veenstra was late getting back from lunch, and she had to cool her heels in the outer office. Eventually, the staffer manning the desk told her, "The senator won't have time to see you today. He's due for a vote on the floor of the Senate shortly. Even if he returns now, he'll have to leave right away."

She smiled pleasantly. "We're old family friends. He'll make time for me."

The intern tried to argue, but she cut him off slightly less pleasantly. "I'm not leaving until I see Charles. And as I told you before, this will only take a few moments."

Finally, she heard Senator Veenstra's voice in the inner office. She walked purposefully past the aide's desk. "I'll see myself in."

"You can't just go—"

She opened the door and stepped inside. "Hello, Senator Veenstra. I'm Helen Warwick. Henry Stapleton's daughter."

"Helen! So good to see you again!"

She smiled archly at the young man who'd rushed after her and closed the door in his face.

She turned to face Veenstra. "I'll make this quick because I know you have a vote to race off to. I need to ask you a question about my father."

"Of course."

"Did you know he was going to retire before he announced it?"

Veenstra looked mildly startled. "No, I didn't. Nobody knew. He sprang it on us out of the blue. Caused quite a ruckus, what with the vacuum in leadership he left behind. Why do you ask?"

"I'm going through his old files, and I came across one from his time on the House Intelligence Committee that you chaired. I noticed you delayed a second, tiebreak vote on Operation White-horse until after Dad retired. How did you know to hold off the vote if you didn't know he was going to retire?"

Veenstra paled. Sat down heavily in his big, leather desk chair.

"Where did you hear that name?" he finally spluttered.

"I told you. My father's files. Why did you delay the vote?"

"I can't possibly remember one vote that many years ago."

"Senator Veenstra," she said gently. "You are famously able to remember what you ate for breakfast on any given day fifty years ago. I should add that my father made extensive notes about the Whitehorse program. I would hate to have those fall into the wrong hands . . . say, those of a journalist?"

"You wouldn't," he gasped. "That was a highly classified program—"

She interrupted. "And five people died in it. I'm sure their families would be fascinated to hear the details of how they died on your watch. The lawsuit they could bring against the government would be sensational. My goodness, the publicity—"

Veenstra raised a hand to stop her. "What do you want?"

She answered candidly, "I don't want to ruin you, nor do I want to expose Operation Whitehorse. But I do need you to tell me why you delayed that vote."

"Just between us?" he mumbled. "It goes no further?"

"Of course."

"Swear to it," he surprised her by demanding.

"My word of honor," she replied, startled.

He looked furtively at his office door and lowered his voice. "The man running Whitehorse. He told me to hold the vote. That he would take care of breaking the tie."

She froze, shocked. Richard Bell had taken care of breaking the tie by forcing her father to retire? *How? What did he have on her father?*

"And you did what he asked why?"

The senator threw her a withering look that suggested she should know the answer to that already.

Ah. Richard Bell had dirt on him, too. She blurted, "Was it just you Bell had dirt on or more than one person on the committee?"

Veenstra spit out, "The way I hear it, that man has files on everyone in this town." He stood. "If that's all . . ."

"What was Operation Whitehorse?" she blurted. "What was it training those ex-military people to do?"

"I can't tell you that."

"Fine. Then I guess my next stop is the office of a major newspaper."

"You said one question," he snapped.

"What did Whitehorse do?" she snapped back.

He stared at her defiantly, and she returned the stare, never breaking eye contact.

Veenstra deflated all at once. "It was a program to train black ops boys."

"The CIA has the Farm for that."

"Not for the sort of stuff those boys did."

The Farm trained all kinds of operators in all kinds of clandestine and illegal activities, including wet-work specialists like herself. What was so black and so secret it had to have its own training program?

There was a knock on the door behind her, and a voice called through it, "The vote has started, sir."

Veenstra looked almost ill with relief. "I've got to go. Are we square?"

"What were they being trained to do?" she ground out.

"Look in the paper files. Which, I might add, your father broke all kinds of laws by having."

She rolled her eyes. Henry had been dead for a long time.

As he swept past her, he growled, "Don't visit me again."

"Good Lord willing, I won't have to," she replied dryly.

CHAPTER 32

*D*ANNY PADDED DOWNSTAIRS BAREFOOT, WEARING A GRUNGY PAIR OF sweatpants and a T-shirt. The old man was out of the house by now, and his mom never said boo to a mouse, let alone criticized what he wore around the house.

He'd skipped his English class this morning because he'd been up until almost dawn playing a video game. Who cared about *Lord of the Flies* anyway? They were a bunch of savage kids on an island who couldn't obey rules. He looked down at the row of scars on his forearm. He would've ended up in control of all the other boys on that island in the book because he knew how to enforce a rule, by God.

He rounded the corner into the kitchen. It was all about the proper application of pain and fear—

"Dad! What are you still doing . . . I mean, I didn't realize you would still be home this late."

"Aren't you supposed to be in class?" his father asked mildly. Too mildly.

Danny swore under his breath, and a sudden urge to piss himself came over him. He clenched his bladder and sank into a chair on the other side of the table from his father. Cautiously, he reached for the cereal box sitting between them.

"I didn't sleep well last night," he explained. That sounded lame. Perilously close to whining, which was Family Rule Number

Ten—no whining. He added hastily, "I'm acing English, and I'm already done writing my essay on *Lord of the Flies*. It's not due until Friday."

"What is your essay about?" his father asked pleasantly.

Oh, God. He knew that silky tone of voice. He was in huge trouble. But over what? Surely not for skipping one lousy lecture. He'd done it before. As long as he kept his grades up, Richard hadn't seemed to care about it.

Right. What the essay was about. "Um, it's about the rules I would've made for the boys stranded on the island and how I would've enforced them. You know. To maintain order."

Richard tipped some cream into a cup of coffee and stirred it idly. "Your mother and I have always taught you and your sister that rules of behavior are necessary."

Danny nodded too eagerly, but he couldn't help himself. He was scared. "The family rules keep Christine and me safe. Out of trouble. We follow them for our own good."

"And your mother and I enforce them for your own good."

As if his mother had the gumption to enforce anything. She was as much a slave to the house rules as he and his sister were. He'd heard her cry out in pain a few times from his parents' bedroom, as if she was being punished for something, too.

As a little boy, he'd been afraid that she got punished when he was bad. But he'd eventually figured out his father was fair, if harsh. Each member of the Bell family paid for their own sins.

He'd also figured out long ago that it usually went easier on him if he got out in front of Family Rule Number Three, which declared that family never lied to family. He would happily confess now to whatever he'd done wrong if he only knew what it was. Where was Christine when he needed her? She had an uncanny ability to read their father and tell exactly what was upsetting him without Richard having to spell it out for her.

Danny poured milk into the bowl of cereal while he frantically reviewed everything he'd done recently that could get him into trouble. Had Christine narced on him after all and told the old man about the grass and mud on the Porsche?

He picked up his spoon. Laid it down again. "While you were out of town last week, I borrowed the Porsche."

Richard looked up from his cell phone that lay beside his coffee cup. "Why?"

"My chem lab partner got in trouble at a party and called to ask me to get her and take her home."

"In trouble how?"

"She got drunk. Maybe got roofied a little. Lost her roommate. She was pretty freaked out. That's why I took the Porsche. It could get to her fast."

"And the grass in the wheel wells and front bumper?" Richard asked evenly enough.

"The driveway of the frat house was full of cars. Only way to get up to the house was across the lawn."

"What frat?"

"Sigma Rho Alpha."

Richard's cup clattered onto its saucer.

Danny looked up from his bowl of cereal in quick alarm. "I didn't have anything to do with the girl who disappeared!"

"What girl?"

"Shayna's roommate, Karly. Shayna's my lab partner. Her roommate disappeared from the party. I swear, I didn't have anything to do with it." He repeated in desperation, "*I swear.*"

"I believe you. I taught you better than to pick up girls from places with that many witnesses around."

"Yes, sir."

Profound relief washed through him, a warm bath after a terrible chill. He picked up his spoon and took a bite of cereal.

"I also taught you never to touch my computer."

His gaze snapped to his father. "I would never touch anything of yours, including your computer." He added earnestly, "I would never go into your office without permission."

His father leaned forward, planting an elbow on the table, a breach of etiquette that made Danny gulp.

Richard asked, "Then perhaps you can explain to me how the house computer security system got turned off a few days ago?"

Oh, shit. His father had figured out he'd gotten into the CIA system to look for information on Shayna's missing roommate. "I, um, was trying to help Shayna find her roommate. I wanted to see if the police or newspapers were saying anything about a missing girl."

"And you had to turn off the computer security protocol to do that?" Richard's voice had taken on a distinctly more ominous tone.

He gulped. *Do not lie. Do not lie. Do not compound the crime.* "Well, yes. It wouldn't let me access the databases I needed to check."

Richard's eyes had gone flat. Expressionless.

Not good, not good, not good. Panic clawed at the back of Danny's neck. An urge to get up and run was so overpowering he had to hang onto the edge of the table with both hands to keep himself from bolting.

His father's voice was as cold and expressionless as his eyes. "And why didn't you turn it back on after you were done with your search?"

He'd forgotten to turn it back on? He could feel the blood draining from his face. His skin went cold and clammy, first on his face, then on his hands and feet, and then across his whole body. "Surely I turned it back on . . . ," he mumbled.

He'd heard the garage door opening. Panicked. Slammed his father's laptop shut.

Oh no. A little voice wailed in terror in the back of his head.

"You didn't. I'm going to have to destroy my computer because I sent a work message out on it. A message I believed to be properly encrypted and secured." Richard planted his other elbow on the table. "And it was neither encrypted nor secured."

"I'm *so* sorry," he gasped. "I should've remembered. It won't happen again—"

"Do you understand what you could've cost me?" His father's voice was rising in anger now.

"Your job?" Danny answered in a small voice.

"My job? Try my *life!*" his father bit out furiously.

The little voice in his head commenced screaming in raw terror. He'd never seen his father this angry before. *Never.*

"What can I do to make it up to you? How can I make amends?

I'll get rid of my computer. Get rid of my phone. Never go online in the house again." He was babbling, but he didn't know how to stop himself. He couldn't imagine the pain his father had in store for him.

"You threatened the safety of this family," his father ground out from between clenched teeth.

Oh, God. Panicked, he began reciting aloud, "Family Rule Number Four: You will obey Father in all things. Rule Number Five: Family takes care of family. Rule Number Eight: You will not draw negative attention to family." *Crap. What else?* He added frantically, "Rule Number Two: You will not get caught."

His father picked up a knife and stared at it contemplatively. He looked up at Danny and very slowly drew the blade of the knife across his own palm. A thin red streak of blood sprouted on his father's palm. *Holy Mother of God.* Richard was going to kill him.

"Please, Dad. I'll do anything to make it up to you," he whispered past the constriction in his throat that he was barely able to breathe past.

Richard stared at him.

Laid down the knife.

Picked up his napkin and pressed it against his palm.

Closed his fist around the napkin.

"*Please,*" Danny gasped. It was all he could get out. He was so panicked he had no air left for speech.

"I'll tell you what," Richard said calmly. "Prove to me that you're worth letting live."

"How? I'll do anything. Tell me what to do," Danny said quickly.

"You're not a child anymore. You figure out what will convince me you should live."

Danny stared in a combination of relief and horror as his father stood up, went over to the sink, and washed off the blood. Richard dried his hand and left the room without ever looking back at him.

What was he supposed to do now? How did anyone prove they were worth letting live?

Christine. She would know what he should do. She knew Richard better than anyone.

Except she wouldn't be home from the university for hours. Did he have that long to live before Richard decided he'd failed this test?

He stood up, his legs almost too shaky to hold his weight. He looked down, and realized he'd pissed himself after all. A sick feeling settled in the pit of his stomach that this wasn't going to end well.

CHAPTER 33

HELEN WOKE SLOWLY, HER BACK ACHING, AND PEERED AROUND IN confusion in the morning light. *Right.* She'd slept in her car somewhere in rural Maryland . . . or maybe Delaware. She wasn't sure how far east she'd driven last night.

She'd laid the back seat of her car down and stretched out into the trunk in a sleeping bag, wadding a coat under her head as a pillow. It had been tremendously uncomfortable, but she'd been off the grid all night, parked on a dirt road in the middle of nowhere that was more path than actual road.

She crawled out of the sleeping bag, half-fell out the door, and straightened creakily, groaning. With a few basic yoga moves, she did her best to stretch out the kinks. It didn't work. She felt like a board with a bad case of arthritis.

Digging into her emergency bag, she pulled out a bottle of water and a protein bar. Leaning against her car, she ate and drank. Pocketing the wrapper, she pulled out a burner phone and turned it on.

She called Clint's cell phone and got sent to voicemail. She said, "Can you look into a man named Roger Skidmore? I'm trying to find out what he does and who he works for. Also, where does he hang out when he's not home or at work? I'll text you his home address and a photo."

She ended the call, turned on her personal phone just long

enough to send the picture of Skidmore and his address to Clint, and then quickly turned it off.

Now what? Mitch wasn't talking to her, and the police were allegedly investigating who'd shot at him. She was no closer to identifying Scorpius than she had been yesterday. And last but not least, she had yet to find *somebody* who knew the whole story of Operation Whitehorse. Maybe someone inside the agency . . .

Frowning, she pulled out a small address book she kept in her purse and found a phone number she'd never used before. She dialed it on the burner phone.

A male voice on the other end said merely, "Go ahead."

"Hello, it's Helen Warwick. Can we meet somewhere and talk? As soon as possible. Where? An hour? I'll be there."

Helen jogged along the pretty, tree-lined path not far from the Virginia Valley College campus where Grayson taught biology classes when he wasn't on a research trip or lobbying foreign governments to protect precious ecosystems. It was a crisp morning with a bright blue sky visible through the fresh green leaves overhead.

It felt good to move like this. The soreness from sleeping in her car and that guy crashing on top of her in her mother's bathtub receded as she ran along the asphalt path.

Kyle Colgate was somewhere along this path today, allegedly jogging toward her. He'd been the one to suggest this public park for their meeting. It figured a guy like him would be a workout freak. She'd heard he was a SEAL and then a Delta operator before coming over to the agency.

The path rounded the curve of a hill and straightened into a long, flat section that traversed a slope about halfway up a shallow valley. But as she rounded the bend, she noticed a crowd of people well ahead of her beside the path and spilling onto it. None of them were doing calisthenics.

Her steps slowed to a walk as she approached a cluster of reporters and bystanders looking off the path and down the hill. She spied a large circle of yellow police tape below and craned to see what was contained within it. But the brush and foliage were too thick for her to make out anything.

"What's going on?" she asked a young woman who looked about twenty and wore a Virginia Valley College sweatshirt.

"They found the missing girl. She's dead."

"What missing girl?" Helen asked.

"The one who was last seen at that big frat party Saturday night. You know. Sigma Rho Alpha. Its annual bacchanalia blowout."

A buzz of disquiet erupted in Helen's gut. That was the fraternity Mitch had belonged to at the small, prestigious college. Of course, he'd graduated many years ago. It was undoubtedly just a coincidence that the dead girl had attended a party there.

"There you are," a male voice said to her left. "What's going on here?"

She looked at the muscular man with a short, graying crew cut who'd stopped beside her. Quickly, she relayed what the female bystander had told her.

Kyle said grimly, "Too bad. Her name was Karly Shaan. A missing person report on her came across my desk."

"So young," Helen murmured. "Her poor family."

"Spoken like the mother of a college-aged daughter," Kyle commented.

She looked up at him sharply. He knew her daughter's age? Or that she even had a daughter? A shade defensively, she replied, "Thankfully, my kids are all out of college now."

Kyle went still, staring alertly at something all of a sudden, and her nostrils flared in response. What threat did he sense? She, too, glanced around covertly. It didn't take a rocket scientist to spot the problem. A news crew complete with a camera guy was setting up shop and using the crowd of bystanders as a backdrop. A big, shoulder-mounted video recorder was pointing right at them.

Helen turned away at almost the same instant Kyle did. No surprise—he was as camera shy as she was.

"Shall we run?" he muttered.

She glanced sidelong at him. "Only if you'll take it easy on me."

He smirked briefly. "The way I hear it, you run circles around most of the younger kids."

She snorted. "Whoever told you that lied."

He led her back in the direction she'd come from. Thankfully, he set a leisurely jogging pace she would be able to talk through, albeit with a little panting. They ran side by side for a minute or two in silence, their steps falling into sync as he shortened his stride to match hers.

Helen said, "Thanks for seeing me."

"What's up? I thought you were out of the game."

"I was. Wagner reactivated me to do some oversight work inside the agency."

"No kidding? How's that going?"

It was hard to sigh and pant simultaneously, but she managed it. Aware that Kyle might be Scorpius, she chose her words with care. "It's not going great. I'm mostly bogged down in bureaucracy and paperwork."

"Bummer."

Hoping to surprise him, she asked abruptly, "Have you ever heard of Operation Whitehorse?"

Kyle swerved slightly away from her before righting his course and coming back to her side. He glanced at her in open surprise. "Where did you hear about that?"

"That's a yes, then?" she replied. "What is it?"

"Wow. I haven't heard that name in a long time."

"I have *all* the security clearances and permission from Wagner to dig anywhere I need to."

"Wagner mentioned he'd brought you in to take a look at something, but he didn't tell me what specifically. Is *that* what you're investigating?"

"What can you tell me about it?" she pressed.

"I don't know the details. It was a test program to take guys out of the military and train them to work for us."

"For the agency or for the Special Operations Group specifically?"

"I don't know if the program ever turned out any operational

intelligence officers. But if it did, they didn't come to work for
SOG. That I am sure of."

"Why not just run them through the Farm? Why a special training program? What's different about it?" she asked.

"No idea." Frowning heavily, he ran in silence beside her. She
got the impression he was debating whether or not to say any
more. And so she merely jogged beside him, letting him work it
out. In her experience, people like him—and her for that matter—tended to get stubborn when pushed to do anything.

They ran perhaps a quarter mile in silence. Without warning,
he said, "The way I heard it, the training methods were controversial. Some guys died."

"What kind of controversial training methods?"

"I never heard any details."

"Do you know anybody who might know more?" she tried.

He jogged thoughtfully for a while. "Have you tried the agency's
paper archives? You'd be amazed at some of the stuff that's pre-
served down there. It's a pain in the butt to find what you're looking for because, well, it's all on paper. But maybe you could find
something on it there."

That was exactly what Veenstra had suggested. He'd told her to
read the paper files. She'd assumed he was talking about her father's notes. But maybe he'd been referring to the CIA's private
archives.

"Good suggestion," she murmured.

She sensed no special reaction or relief from him that she didn't
seem to think he was the Russian mole. As Director of the Special
Activities Center, Kyle had access to the kind of intel Scorpius had
been sending to Russia, but he wouldn't have had that kind of access a decade ago when he was a regular SOG operator. Her gut
said to scratch him off her Scorpius suspect list.

The parking lot came into sight ahead of them.

"One last thing," she said quietly. "I don't know what's being
said about Andrew Mizuki's death, but I have reason to believe
other senior people in the agency like yourself might be in danger, too."

Kyle came to a full and abrupt stop in the middle of the jogging path. Startled, she took a few more steps before stopping and turning to face him.

"What happened to Andrew?" Kyle demanded.

"He was murdered."

"Murdered?" he echoed incredulously. "They're saying it was a heart attack."

"It was cyanide poisoning. I was with him when it happened," she replied grimly. "And no, I didn't do it."

Kyle swore under his breath. "I couldn't believe it when I heard his ticker went. I used to run with him. The guy was a beast."

"Just be careful, eh?"

"You, too."

"Will do," she replied. "And thanks for the information."

"Call me if you need anything. I know we never worked together, but we're family in our line of work."

It was one of the things she'd missed most when she'd been forced out of the agency—the sense of common purpose among like-minded individuals. There were not too many people in the world like Kyle and her. She greatly enjoyed getting to hang out with her own kind from time to time.

Without another word, Kyle turned and headed back the way they'd come, at a considerably faster pace.

She walked back toward her car, catching her breath. A hum of dread vibrated low in her belly. What would she find in the agency's archives when she went digging? She suspected it was going to be bad. Very bad.

CHAPTER 34

AFTER SHE SHOWERED AND CHANGED CLOTHES IN THE CAMPUS STAFF locker room—compliments of a copy of Gray's passkey that he didn't know she had—Helen drove out to the CIA's remote archival site in rural Virginia.

It never failed to surprise her how fast the Washington, DC, suburbs shifted from urban sprawl to bucolic farm country. She drove through rolling green countryside to an unmarked road off another unmarked road. It deteriorated to little more than a one-lane asphalt drive through thick trees, and then a tall, iron gate abruptly blocked the entire road.

A tall hurricane fence stretched in either direction. Helen knew it to be electrified and heavily monitored by hidden cameras. She'd been here once with Yosef, shortly before she'd retired, to deposit the files of her various missions.

A bored-looking guy stepped out of the guard shack beside the gate, and she passed her CIA credentials to him.

"Got an appointment?" he asked.

"Sorry, no. Something came up that I need to research right away."

The guy disappeared inside the booth and typed on a laptop computer. It took about a minute, but he stepped out, handing her both ID card and a clip-on pass with a big red letter *V* on it. "Go on in."

She closed her window and waited while the gate slid back slowly, then drove through with a wave to the guard. The road continued on through the trees, ending at a small parking lot with only three cars parked in it.

The building was nothing to write home about—a one-story cinder-block affair with no windows, perhaps twenty by forty feet wide and long.

She walked to the lone door and pressed the old-fashioned doorbell button beside it. She waited a long time without pressing it again. She knew the guard inside would be running a biometric scan and matching her and her credentials to her identification records.

Eventually, the door buzzed, and she pushed it open.

The room looked like a small-town police precinct, with a high counter in front of her and a dozen desks in rows behind it. A man sat at the desk in the far corner in front of a bank of video monitors, each showing a length of hurricane fence and a bunch of trees.

Ancient desktop computer monitors sat on each of the other desks. She could research scanned records from one of those monitors. But she expected that, given how classified and buried Operation Whitehorse was, none of its records would be available up here. She was going to have to go down into the stacks and dig for them. Literally.

A gray-haired woman spoke from behind the counter. "Can I help you find something?"

"I'm looking for anything you've got on Operation White-horse."

"Have you got a time frame on it?"

"It would've started around twenty years ago."

"It should be in the file stacks, then. Come with me."

Helen followed the woman to an elevator next to the restroom against the far wall. They stepped into the conveyance together. A biometric scanner read the woman's eyes, and only then did the door close. The woman pressed an unmarked button on the elevator panel full of unmarked buttons, and the car lurched into motion.

When it opened again, a room opened away from them, filled

with rows of old-fashioned card catalogs. The archivist stepped over to one, opened a long drawer about chest-high, and began riffling through the typed index cards inside.

Helen couldn't believe the most classified documents the US government had were stored in this primitive and archaic fashion. But that was the point, she supposed. They were nowhere online where an enterprising hacker or foreign intelligence agency had any chance of gaining access to them.

"Aha!" the woman exclaimed, startling Helen.

The woman copied down something from the card catalog into a small notebook she pulled out of a pocket in her cardigan sweater. Somehow, Helen wasn't surprised when the woman used a stubby, number two lead pencil to write the information.

"Follow me," the woman said, heading for an unmarked door in the far wall of the room.

The woman unlocked what turned out to be a steel door using a key hanging from a thin chain around her neck. Helen held the heavy door for the older woman while the archivist fumbled at the wall and turned on the lights. Helen squinted at the bright white, fluorescent light and pulled the door shut behind them. The lock clicked loudly in the utter silence down here.

A long, tiled hallway stretched away in front of them. Closed doors with biometric devices and small plaques beside each, bearing merely a number designation, lined the hallway.

They walked for a dozen yards, and a crossing hallway intersected the first one. Helen had been down here once before and knew that this facility stretched out like a huge spiderweb. For all she knew, it had multiple levels as well.

The archivist finally stopped at a door. More scanning, this time of both palm and face, and the archivist opened the door, gesturing Helen inside.

"Your file should be in this row," the woman said, heading for a bank of filing cabinets among a dozen identical-looking rows.

"Do you know where the operation ran?" the archivist asked.

"I believe it was in the United States."

"Well. That narrows it down considerably."

Helen frowned. Was the woman being sarcastic? But then it dawned on her most CIA operations would've run overseas. She added, "It was some sort of training program."

"Also helpful," the woman murmured, opening the top drawer in a filing cabinet.

Helen stood by, feeling useless as the woman thumbed through perhaps fifty manila folders. The woman closed the drawer and opened the next one down.

"Can I help?" Helen asked.

The woman glanced up. "No. These are Eyes Only."

"Director Wagner authorized me to look at anything I need to for the project I'm working on."

The archivist pursed her lips. "I saw that notation. But you asked about Whitehorse. That's all I can show you without you placing another specific request."

Fine. Whatever. She was just trying to be helpful. If this woman wanted to search all these hundreds of files by herself, so be it.

Helen's legs were tired, and her back was getting sore from standing around before the archivist abruptly exclaimed, "Aha!"

"Did you find it?" Helen asked eagerly.

"I found the funding file. That's good news."

"Why?"

"Because it'll reference the operational files." Indeed, the archivist glanced at the inside cover of the rather thin file, then took off down the row of filing cabinets confidently. This time, when she opened the bottom drawer in yet another cabinet, she quickly found and pulled out a thick manila folder and handed it to Helen.

Helen started to open it before the woman snapped, "Not here. Wait until we're back upstairs. We wouldn't want you to drop it and send papers all over the place where they might get lost."

Helen refrained from pointing out there was nowhere for papers to go except the narrow strip of floor between walls of cabinets. The archivist turned to the other side of the aisle, opening another drawer. She pulled out another file and handed it to Helen.

In all, the archivist pulled out six files and passed them to Helen before announcing, "That's it. Let's go."

Sheesh. This was as bad as being back in grade school and doing detention with the school secretary after that time she'd incited a spit-wad fight in seventh-grade English. Rolling her eyes behind the woman's back, Helen dutifully followed the archivist to the elevator and rode up to the surface in silence.

When they arrived back in the main room, Helen's escort merely pointed at an empty desk and then returned to the front counter, where she resumed typing on an actual typewriter. Helen guessed she was making more of those index cards for the card catalog.

Helen sat down at the desk with her back to the security guard and opened the top file, the one outlining the funding. She glanced through rows of dollar amounts annotated beside numeric accounting codes that meant nothing to her. She set aside that file and opened the next one.

Scope of Program: recruit candidates interested in military sniper training to cross-train into the CIA. If successful, activate them to operate as covert intelligence officers overseas.

She frowned. That sounded innocuous enough. What would've been so controversial about that? Thing was, all shooters usually went to Camp Peary, the main CIA training facility in rural Virginia nicknamed the Farm. She'd done all her training there, including advanced tactics, unconventional weaponry, ingress-egress training, makeup and disguise, the works.

Why create a whole separate training program? What was so different about how these shooters had been trained from how she'd been trained?

She turned the page and was startled to see not CIA paperwork but US Army paperwork, a psych eval of a candidate for sniper school. Her eyebrows shot up as she scanned a report indicating that the person was deemed unfit to undergo sniper training due to an antisocial personality disorder. *Holy crap.* ASPD was a fancy name for being a sociopath.

She certainly hoped the sniper candidate had been rejected for that. The last thing the government wanted to do was train someone with the capacity to become a cold-blooded murderer in how to kill effectively and not get caught.

She flipped the page and stared in shock. It was a photocopy of a letter inviting the same guy evaluated on the previous page to enter a government training program . . . to become a sniper!

Why would the CIA train guys whom the military had already classified as too unstable to train?

The next sheet in the file was the original of a handwritten letter accepting the offer. Dismayed, she turned the page. Meticulous notes, typed carbon copies, annotated the training of the guy, called Subject no. 1.

She recognized some of the training regimens—she'd been through them herself. Exercises in setting up a shooter's nest and how to ingress, hide, egress, evade, and escape were all pretty standard fare for snipers. Subject no. 1 was an excellent shooter to begin with and improved steadily over the course of his training.

And then Helen read a sentence that made her gape.

Subject no. 1 is ready for his violent tendencies to be triggered. The way she understood it, not all sociopaths were violent. Far from it. But all full-blown sociopaths had within them the capacity to become violent if properly provoked.

She read on grimly.

Apparently, a female prostitute was hired and instructed to come on to Subject no. 1. But when he responded sexually to her, she was to humiliate and reject him. Helen turned the page, reading on in apprehension.

The annotation was simple: *Subject no. 1 killed female prostitute by manual strangulation.*

She sat back in shock. Operation Whitehorse was about taking sociopaths, training them to kill, and then triggering them into violence? To what end? And Richard Bell had been in charge of this operation? No wonder Yosef said the guy had been involved in some dark programs.

In no small trepidation, she turned the page. *Subject no. 1 unable to control his violent urges. Subject no. 1 terminated.*

Urgently, she went back to the psych eval and wrote down the guy's name on the back of a grocery receipt she pulled out of her purse. The minute she got back to the Box, she was going to track down the cover story used to explain his death.

The next three subjects' notes listed changes that were made to the training regimen employed with the first subject. Also, each subject was activated to violence in a different way, apparently custom-tailored to fit their particular hang-ups and traumas. But they all ended up killing someone in a fit of rage. In all cases, the subjects were also terminated eventually. Helen wrote down each of their names on the grocery receipt.

It wasn't until Subject no. 5 that the program apparently succeeded in its end goal—whatever that was. The notes on this subject—a woman—said that imposition of strict rules of behavior seemed to have controlled the subject's more violent tendencies after she murdered a man who tried to rape her.

Apparently, the penalty for breaking a rule in Operation Whitehorse was death, and . . . *ohmigod* . . . Subject no. 5 witnessing the death of Subject no. 4 for breaking a rule apparently had driven that point home.

Her jaw sagged. What kind of sick and twisted outfit had Richard Bell run? Those subjects were American citizens. Soldiers. Volunteers for a CIA training program. And they'd been murdered in cold blood by their trainer.

The first file ended, and Helen opened the second one. It seemed that Operation Whitehorse's training regimen, once refined, resulted in a better pass rate for the next group of subjects. By the end of the second file, five more subjects had passed the training course and only one had been terminated. Furthermore, they'd been given new identities, new appearances, new jobs, and located in various major cities around the world, including two in Washington, DC.

Great. These cold-blooded, efficient killers could be anybody, anywhere.

Who in the bloody hell did they report to? Who controlled them now?

The third file followed six more trainees, of which only three passed the training. A note in the back of the file complained about the lack of true sociopaths applying for and being rejected from military sniper schools. The author of the note went on to speculate about the chances of finding civilian sociopaths and training them into Whitehorse.

A note near the end of the file gave her yet another shock. In it Bell described how only two characteristics were consistent across all of his sociopathic subjects. First, they did not want to die. And second, they feared pain. He'd used the second successfully to keep his trainees in line by . . .

Her mind went blank as it rejected the words on the page before her. She had to read that paragraph again, slowly, to let it sink in.

By putting a third party under duress in the presence of a Whitehorse subject, the reality of the pain I will subject them to if they break one of my rules seems to be driven home most effectively. It takes a reminder session approximately once every other year to keep the lesson front and center in their minds and my leash upon each of them firmly in place.

Under duress? That was nice-people-speak for torture. Particularly in conjunction with him demonstrating "the reality of the pain" to which he could subject his trainees.

How on earth had he gotten away with torturing "third parties" in an officially funded and approved CIA program? No way did the House Intelligence Committee, or the CIA leadership for that matter, allow such a thing on their watches.

And Richard Bell apparently did it casually and often as a training tool.

He was a *monster*.

Beyond appalled, she closed the third file.

The fourth file tracked six civilian sociopaths who entered the program. All were terminated within a matter of days. Apparently, they lacked the self-discipline to abide by any set of rules, let alone the stringent ones that would have been applied later.

The fifth file bitterly annotated the end of Operation Whitehorse as it lost its government funding a little over eleven years ago.

Eleven? Wasn't that about when Scorpius started sending information to the Russians? Coincidence or not? Was Richard Bell Scorpius? Or had Scorpius made contact with him when Whitehorse was terminated, maybe offered to keep funding his twisted school of torture and murder? She shuddered to imagine a Russian mole involved in creating unstable killers for some unknown end.

Which led to more questions, like where were the graduates of Operation Whitehorse now? Did anyone still monitor them? Keep them in line? And perhaps most disturbing of all, why had Richard Bell created this cadre of trained killers? Did he have a specific plan for them? Or God help everyone, what was Scorpius doing with them?

Interested to see what could be left to write about in a sixth file, she opened it curiously. And stared at a dozen pages of what looked like encoded information. Typical encryption files were clusters of numbers and/or letters in same-sized groupings, usually five to seven symbols each, separated by spaces. Such groupings covered every page in this file.

Glancing over at the archivist, who was staring intently at her computer monitor, Helen snuck out her cell phone and snapped a picture of the top encoded page. The librarian moved, and Helen held up the jacket of the manila file with one hand and used her other hand to photograph the remaining pages, hiding her phone behind the file jacket. She prayed the pictures were decent, but she didn't dare take any backup shots.

Dropping her phone into her purse, she closed the files and stacked them neatly in order.

"Find what you were looking for?" the gray-haired archivist asked from her desk.

"Yes. Thank you for your help."

The woman nodded. "Leave the files on that table. I'll put them back once I let you out."

As they walked toward the door, Helen asked, "How long have you been working here?"

"Twenty-six years."

Whew. Longer than Operation Whitehorse had been around.

This rather antisocial woman couldn't be one of Bell's test subjects. "Impressive," Helen murmured. "Thank you for your service."

For the first time, the woman's expression softened. "It's been a good job. Can't say as I like people much."

You don't say. Helen barely managed not to snort.

She stepped outside, disoriented by the sun's greatly shifted position. It had been midmorning when she entered the facility, and the sun hung low in the west now.

As soon as she left the shadow of the building, her phone dinged a bunch of incoming texts.

Of course. The building must have electronic shielding.

She sat in her car and scrolled through her messages, mostly unimportant. But there was a text from Clint. **Need to talk. Urgent.**

She texted him back. **Tonight. Tell me when and where.**

He sent back GPS coordinates that the map program on her phone placed in an uninhabited area north of DC. *Great.* Nothing he wanted to talk about in the middle of nowhere could be good news.

CHAPTER 35

*D*ANNY PACED IN CHRISTINE'S BEDROOM FOR HOURS, LIKE ALL DAY, waiting for her to come home. He was a nervous wreck and with every passing minute more certain he was going to die. Horribly.

She stopped in her doorway and demanded, "What are you doing in here? You know I don't let you come in my room."

"Dad's gonna kill me, Chrissy. Like for real. He effing sliced his own hand at the breakfast table he was so mad this morning."

"What did you do?" She gasped.

He shoved a hand through his disordered hair. "I messed up bad. I turned off the house computer security system and forgot to turn it back on. Dad sent some kind of message unencrypted, and he said it could've gotten him killed. He destroyed his laptop this morning. I saw him chopping it to bits with a hatchet in the garage."

Christine shook her head slowly. "You are so screwed. Did he say what he's going to do to punish you?"

"He said I have to prove to him that he should let me live. Then he'll decide what to do."

"Holy crap," she breathed.

"You gotta help me. I've been trying all day to come up with a way to prove I should live, but I've got nothing. You know him better than me. What should I do?"

Christine set her backpack down and perched on the edge of

her bed. Danny was silent, letting her think. She was a lot like Dad in that she didn't like to be disturbed when she was pondering something.

At length, she said, "You have to fix a problem for him. Something big that's bugging him."

"How should I know what's bothering him? He barely gives me the time of day, let alone talks to me about his problems."

Christine frowned. "This is bad, Daniel. Really bad."

"You're telling me! I've spent the past hour wondering if I could leave the country and hide overseas for the rest of my life without him finding me."

"You couldn't. He would sic the whole CIA on you. They'd find you."

Danny shuddered. "I'm dead. Maybe I should just kill myself and get it over with before he can torture me."

"That may be necessary if you can't figure out what to do to redeem yourself," she said solemnly.

He stared at her in shock. It was one thing to think it himself. It was another to hear his ever-so-logical sister say it out loud. Fear wasn't an emotion he experienced often, but he felt it now, all the way down to his bones. He was going to *die* if they didn't figure something out for him to do.

"Please, Christine. If not for me, help me for Mom's sake."

She stared at him hard for several seconds. "Fine. But you are to *swear* not to tell Dad I helped you or to tell him anything I did to help you, Family Rule Number Three notwithstanding."

He was so panicked it took him a second to recall what stupid Rule Number Three was. Oh, yeah. Never lie to family.

"I swear. On my life," he replied fervently.

"Well, that is what's at stake here," she replied dryly.

She locked her bedroom door, then pulled her laptop out of her backpack. Carrying it to her desk, she sat down in front of it and opened it up. He didn't see what she did, but in a few seconds, a long list of files started scrolling down her screen.

As in *long*. There were *hundreds* of files scrolling past too fast for him to read the titles.

She stopped scrolling near the bottom of the list, and he leaned over her shoulder to read the titles. He lurched back in shock. "Did you hack Dad's computer?"

"Let's just say I find it useful to know what he's up to."

"What *is* he up to?"

Christine did an odd thing. She frowned and looked . . . worried? He was no good at reading other people's emotions. She definitely sounded scared, though, as she lowered her voice. "You wouldn't believe me if I told you. He's planning something huge. Like *huge*."

"Oh, yeah? What?" he asked eagerly.

She shook her head sharply, as if she'd already said too much. "I'll just say this. If he ever comes for me the way he's coming for you, I have plenty on him to back him off for good."

Whoa. "Like blackmail?" he breathed. "That's brilliant."

"Oh, I'm not giving anything I've got on Dad to you. You're too impulsive to keep it to yourself. I'm taking a big chance even letting you know I have copies of his private files."

He scowled at her, but he couldn't honestly say she was wrong. Self-control always had been his Achilles' heel. "Mum's the word," he mumbled.

"It better be, or I'll kill you myself."

She said that so casually he couldn't tell if she meant it or not. She'd never had a taste for violence the way he had. But in pretty much everything else, she was a carbon copy of the old man—smart, calculating, tightly self-controlled.

She started opening files to glance at the contents. She was obviously familiar with them and going too fast for him to read much, but he was able to ascertain that these were, indeed, files of Richard's from the CIA. How much of this stuff was stupidly classified? Probably all of it. His gut quickened with excitement.

One file in particular caught his attention as it flashed up on the screen. All it contained was a short series of two-digit numbers separated by dashes. That looked a whole lot like a combination to a lock . . . or maybe to Dad's safe.

Quickly, he repeated the numbers to himself silently a half-dozen times until he was sure he had them memorized.

Christine was near the end of the list when she finally murmured in triumph, "There you are."

"What? What have you got?" he asked impatiently.

"This might do it. Even better, it's something you might actually stand a chance of dealing with successfully."

He made a face at her. He hated it when she called him stupid, even if obliquely.

"Dad took care of a problem for someone, like fifteen years ago. A congressman called him. Asked him to silence some woman who was making trouble for him—"

He interrupted. "What kind of trouble?"

"Her sister had died, and she wanted the FBI to investigate it."

"How did the sister die?" he asked with interest.

Christine rolled her eyes at him.

Okay, so he'd sounded a little too eager when he'd asked for the details there.

"Did Dad kill the woman who was making trouble?" Danny blurted. Damn it, that sounded too eager as well.

Christine scowled at him. "If you don't get yourself under control—and fast—I'm going to tell Dad to knock you off myself."

"It's not every day Dad threatens to kill his own kid. I've got a right to be freaked out," he declared.

"Fine." She looked back at her computer. "Of course, Dad took her out. I don't know why, but Dad opened this file last week and then wrote a search program to scrape newspapers for the names of both sisters. I think he may be worried their deaths might surface for some reason. Maybe he heard a reporter or podcaster is investigating it, maybe digging it up again. If you were to shut up that person, Dad might be grateful."

"That could work," he said doubtfully. Not that he had the first idea how to go about squashing a news story. But his gut said it wasn't a grand enough gesture. Christine hadn't seen the look in his father's eyes this morning.

She shut down her computer and closed the top. "Don't let the door hit you in the butt on the way out."

"Love you, too," he said sarcastically.

"As if," she muttered behind him.

She knew him too well. He wasn't sure he had any idea what love felt like. He operated in the realm of what felt good and what entertained him, but not really in the realm of big emotions like love. The only big emotion he'd had in a long time was the visceral terror coursing through him now.

At least she'd pointed him in the right direction. Take care of a problem for the old man. Now he just had to find the right problem to solve.

He walked down the hallway toward his bedroom and was surprised to see his parents' bedroom door cracked open. Doors were usually closed in this house. He heard his father's voice, and it sounded angry.

In Christine's clever spirit of spying on the old man, he crept up to the door, being sure to stay out of sight of anyone inside.

His father was saying, ". . . telling you. I saw Colgate and the Warwick woman on TV this morning. They were in some park together. Where the police found the body of that missing girl."

Body? Is Karly dead then? He wondered how she'd died. Had it been grisly—

He jerked his attention back to what his father was saying.

". . . can't afford to have those two get chummy. Colgate was stationed at the first military base I recruited guys at for Whitehorse. It's possible he's heard of it. I can't take even the slightest chance of him having said something about it to Helen Warwick. I'm not about to let that woman derail my life's work. Not when I'm so close to achieving everything I've worked so long for. I need you to move up the timetable on Colgate. Do it now."

Do what now? Danny leaned in a little closer.

Richard murmured, "Same as Skidmore. Make it look like she did it."

That sounded like his father had just ordered a hit and was planning to frame someone. Maybe the Warwick woman, whoever she was?

Richard responded to whatever the person on the other end of the call had said with, "What about her? I can't divert resources from the main plan right now to deal with Warwick. I'm not going after her in a half-assed way. She's too sharp for that. We'll have to deal with her later." A pause. "Yes, I know she could be a big problem. But it has taken me decades to put all the pieces in place, and the plan is already in motion."

This Helen Warwick person was a problem for his old man! A big one, from Richard's tone of voice. *Holy crap. Could it really be that easy? Take out this Warwick person and I'll be in the clear?* He could totally do that.

Danny crept away from the door thoughtfully. He'd never shot a human before, but how different could it be from shooting a deer? Or maybe he would bash in her skull like they did when they killed fish they'd caught. Or maybe he would burn her alive like he had that stray cat a while back.

CHAPTER 36

*H*ELEN PARKED AT THE SIDE OF A DESERTED COUNTRY ROAD BEHIND Clint's pickup truck. The dark was so thick she could barely make out the silhouette of the vehicle.

Grabbing the bag of cheeseburgers and fries she'd picked up at a fast-food place on the way, she climbed out and walked toward the man slouched in the shadows beside his truck. His army jacket seemed to be hanging more loosely on him than usual. Although he always looked a bit underfed when she saw him.

As she drew close, he climbed in his truck, gesturing for her to join him. She opened the passenger side door and wasn't surprised to see the interior of the truck was immaculate. She would bet there was a big engine tuned to peak performance under the hood, too. They were a lot alike, the two of them.

"What's up?" she asked, holding out the bag of food to him.

He took it, looked inside, and pulled out a burger. Unwrapping the paper around it, he proceeded to wolf down the sandwich.

Only when he'd downed another burger, pulled out the bag of fries, and commenced munching on them did he look at her. "You've got a problem. A big one."

"Tell me about it."

"That guy? Roger Skidmore? He's dead."

"Dead?" she exclaimed. "How did that happen?"

"Hard to tell, what with all the injuries he suffered from the torture, but I'm gonna guess the garrote around his neck killed him."

Helen's jaw dropped. "He was murdered?"

"Oh, yeah. No doubt about it."

She sat back in shock, staring across the dark cab of the truck at him. "Where did you find him?"

"In his apartment."

"When?"

"Right before I called you."

Late this afternoon, then. "Did you call the authorities?" she asked.

"No. Because you've got a bigger problem than him being dead," Clint said heavily.

"Which is?"

"There's security video of you exiting the vic's condo, and there's video of you leaving the building."

"Me? I've never been in his building!"

"You sure of that?" he bit out.

Her brows came together. "Yes, Clint, I'm sure. I've killed plenty of people in my day, but I've never tortured any of them, and they were all sanctioned by the US government."

He exhaled heavily. "I wasn't able to take the security tape. The guard came back from making the rounds, and I had to bug out of his office. But for all the world, the person who walked out looked just like you."

"It was a woman?" she blurted.

"Or a man with a hella nice pair of legs."

"Aw, thanks."

He shrugged. "If you were twenty years younger or I was twenty years older, I'd make a run at you, lady."

She smiled warmly. "If I were single, I might make a run at you, our age difference be damned."

He grinned briefly and raised a french fry to her in salute. His smile faded, and he said, "I got pics of Skidmore's body. I gotta warn you, though. They're nasty."

"Send them to me," she said grimly.

He pulled out his cell phone and clicked on a bunch of pictures. She felt her phone vibrate in her pants pocket.

"Any way you can go back there and liberate the security tape?" she asked him.

He shook his head. "I'm burned. The day shift guard saw me come in, and the night shift guy was just coming on duty when I left the security office. I think he saw me."

She sighed. "Fine. I'll take care of it."

She added stealing the tape to her mental list of crises to deal with. She hardly had time to keep up with everything she was trying to juggle.

"They burn the security video onto a CD-ROM in the laptop sitting on the guard's desk in front of the monitors. They change the CD once a week. You've got till tomorrow night to grab it."

She moved the CD higher up on her list of crises.

"Have you got anything else for me?" she asked him wearily.

"Ever heard of a bacchanalia?"

"You mean the Roman festival for Bacchus? Which is to say the annual toga orgy in Rome?" she replied.

"I meant the one at Virginia Valley College. Specifically at the Sigma Rho Alpha fraternity."

She frowned. Mitch was an SRA. She already didn't like where this was going. "Tell me about it."

"Annual party. Goes for an entire weekend. Free booze for all, lots of drugs, wild behavior encouraged, drunken sex games. All the usual stuff. Except it has a history of getting out of hand. Every now and then, the party goes off the rails and somebody gets hurt. OD's. Or worse."

"As in someone dies?"

"Yep."

She heard an echo of James Wagner's voice in her head. *There's no statute of limitations on murder.* She winced. "And you're mentioning this to me why?"

"Because Mitch's senior year of college, the bacchanalia went badly. A girl died, and the girl's sister committed suicide a few weeks later. In her suicide note, she said she couldn't live with what had been done to her sister at the bacchanalia."

She studied him intently. What wasn't he telling her?

"Your son was president of the frat that year."

"That doesn't mean he had anything to do with it," she replied quickly. "He swore to me he has nothing in his past that can hurt him."

Clint grunted in patent disbelief. "Everybody's got something in their past that can hurt them."

"I pushed him on it. He promised me," she retorted.

"He lied."

"How do you know?" she demanded.

"I can't tell you. Confidential source."

Ten to one his source was Angela. "What does the source plan to do with this information?"

He sighed. "I'm no politician. I don't play these Washington power games. But I don't think my source plans to do anything with what they know. Not now anyway."

Meaning the source planned to hang on to this damaging information until he or she needed a favor from the district attorney. She noted Clint's lack of a he/she pronoun to identify the source. The source was *so* Angela.

"Side note," he murmured. "A girl from VVC was found dead not far from the campus this morning."

"I know. I was out jogging and went past the crime scene. There was a big crowd around it."

"This year's bacchanalia was last weekend. And the dead girl was last seen at it."

"You think she died at the party and someone dumped her body off campus?" Helen asked quickly.

"I think her death is going to raise a lot of questions, and reporters may dig up information on the last time a girl died at that party."

It was Helen's turn to wince. This was bad for Mitch. Very bad. Even if he had nothing to do with those girls' deaths years ago. Clint was not wrong. Involved or not in the incident, Mitch had been president of the frat. The girls had died on his watch.

"Are there any existing news stories that tie Mitch to the old deaths?" she blurted.

"Not that I've found. But there are people who know. His frat brothers, for example."

"What about the family of the dead girls? Did they make a stink?"

"Nope. They were totally silent."

Helen frowned. "Odd. If one of my kids died and another was traumatized into suicide, I would be out for blood."

Who'd silenced the family? And how? Had Mitch been involved in that somehow?

Oh, Mitch, what have you done?

CHAPTER 37

S UBJECT NO. 5 STARED DOWN AND ACROSS THE STREET AT HER TAR-
get in a condo building in Silver Springs, Maryland, a suburb on
the north side of Washington, DC, just outside the Beltway.

A light came on in the target's condo, but the closed curtains
made visual contact impossible. No matter. She opened the laptop beside her. It was attached to a Camero XLR80, a look-
through-walls camera. She'd had it modified, boosting its usual
one-hundred-foot range to over two hundred feet. Which was a
good thing. She was about that far from his place. As it was, her
target was going in and out of view as he moved around his
condo.

He walked toward her and sat down on a sofa in front of a television that stood at a ninety-degree angle to her, looking like no
more than a thin line of metal emanating a bit of heat from the
side facing the target. She gathered he was eating from the way
his hand was moving down to his lap and up to his mouth.

She debated taking the shot now. The target was giving her the
side of his head. With the .50BMG round currently loaded in her
TAC-50C sniper rifle, she would probably blow his head to bits.
But she would have to put the shot through his ear, and she was
shooting downward at an oblique angle that would make dropping the round into his ear a bit tricky. Not impossible, but tricky.

With this target, she had to make the kill on shot one, or she was screwed. He was fully capable of shooting back at her and taking her out, and that big steel block in his bedroom was undoubtedly a gun safe.

Not to mention, this was a quiet neighborhood. When she took her shot, she would need to make a hasty egress before people started looking out their windows and calling the police. Worst case, she figured she had sixty seconds to get off the roof and another sixty to get out of the area before security guards stepped out of the condo buildings lining this street to look around.

The target moved from time to time, shifting weight, leaning forward to pick up a drink sitting on the coffee table in front of him. Better to wait until he went to bed and presented a perfectly still target.

The breeze buffeting her from time to time gradually stilled as the temperature dropped and the street below emptied of cars. Eleven o'clock came and went.

And then the target moved, lying down on the sofa with his feet toward her. He lay on his side, which didn't give her crap for a kill shot. Irritated, she waited him out.

It took about fifteen minutes, but he finally rolled onto his back. His right arm flopped to the side, lying partially on the coffee table. He went still.

If she put a shot in his torso, the downward trajectory from here should send the round through his spine. A .50 caliber round was a half inch in diameter and a bit over two and a half inches long, and from this weapon it would travel around three thousand feet per second.

The round itself would cause severe lacerations to the target's flesh. The weight and speed of the round would deliver a massive burst of energy to the surrounding tissue as it traveled, explosively pushing muscle and organs aside and creating an empty cavity as it passed through him. Then that cavitation would collapse violently, causing even more injury as everything slammed back. And then there would be the shock wave, powerful enough to all but liquify flesh.

Last but not least, if the round hit a bone, any bone, the

round's kinetic energy would literally blow it up, sending shards every which way at the velocity of low-speed bullets themselves, ripping through any body part that still happened to be intact.

God help the target if the shot hit both his sternum and spine. A pair of bones that large fragmenting explosively would literally tear him apart from the inside out.

She dialed in her gravity corrections and lined up the shot carefully. The fold-down bipod on the barrel made it an easy matter to hold the weapon perfectly steady. She engaged the infrared scope and pointed it at her target. Through the scope, her target was only an elongated blob. But based on the laptop image beside her, she targeted the top half of the blob.

She touched the record button on the camera and rested her face against the cheek piece. Her feet sprawled wide behind her, the rifle stock tight against her shoulder, she went perfectly still.

Inhaling slowly, she reached the dead space in her breath cycle and squeezed through the trigger. At this range, her breath shouldn't affect the shot. But she was a perfectionist.

The TAC50 had a smooth trigger pull naturally, and she'd honed and polished the trigger mechanism even more until it moved like silk under her finger.

Bang!

She grunted under her breath as the recoil slammed against her shoulder pad.

Reaching over to the laptop, she hit the rewind button, backing up about five seconds. She hit play and watched as red heat flares exploded outward from the target's chest in a spherical chrysanthemum, like a giant firework. The image stilled, and where there used to be a chest, a dark, gaping hole now appeared.

Kill confirmed.

Time to go.

She pushed up to her knees, slammed the laptop shut, and shoved it into her backpack, which she flung over her shoulders. Grabbing the thirty-pound rifle, she slung it over her right shoulder as she took off running across the roof.

Grit and dirt made the surface slippery, but she scrambled across it as fast as she dared. As she neared the far edge of the roof, she passed under the steel cable stretching from the top of a commercial air conditioning unit out into the darkness beyond the roof.

Using both hands, she reached up and grabbed the horizontal hand bar mounted to a zip-line pulley, then ran for the edge of the roof.

She flew out into space as the building dropped away from her. Metal zinged on metal as the pulley flew down the inclined wire toward the parking garage in front of her. She barely had time to yank up her feet enough to clear the concrete wall around the top deck of the parking structure.

The light pole her zip line was secured to came at her fast. Swearing, she let go of the hand bar and tumbled head over heels in two full somersaults before slamming into the pole.

Ow. That was going to leave a hell of a bruise on her left arm.

She pushed to her feet and picked up the heavy cable cutters she'd left propped beside the light pole. The cutters were three feet long and weighed as much as her rifle, but they snipped through the zip line like butter. It whipped away into the darkness, making a slithering sound as it fell off the parking structure to hang down the side of the building across the street.

She was already running again, heading for her car on the other side of the light pole. She threw the bolt cutters into the back seat, followed by her rifle and backpack. She jumped into the front seat and started the car, guiding it toward the exit.

She made a point of pausing under the light pole by the exit ramp, highlighting the short blond wig she wore. She reached up to adjust the rearview mirror, making sure the black leather of her jacket was also visible. It had taken her hours to get the prosthetics just right and to put makeup over them, so she might as well show them off. She turned her face to the left and stayed there for two full seconds, giving the surveillance camera a great look at the face of Helen Warwick.

Then she wound her way down through the garage. Using the

stolen access card that had come with her target package, she let herself out of the exit gate. She turned onto the street, leaving her window down.

Still no sound of sirens. If she was lucky, the locals had mistaken the shot for a truck backfire and no police had responded to the shot.

She drove to the southeast side of DC to park her car behind a crappy strip club that had gone out of business months ago. She wiped down the car for prints even though she was wearing latex gloves, and she used a hand vacuum to pick up any stray hair or fibers.

Then she pulled out a small envelope from her backpack and carefully peeled the plastic film off an index card. Leaning into the vehicle, she pressed the film hard around the steering wheel at the two o'clock position, where a person's right hand would typically grasp it.

Collecting Helen's fingerprints had been a breeze—she'd lifted them from the Warwick woman's computer keyboard. The hard part had been assembling them to look like a single handprint. But that was why she was a professional and got paid the big bucks. Subject no. 5 backed out of the car, being careful to touch nothing.

Lastly, she pulled out a screwdriver and took the license plates off the vehicle. She shoved them into her backpack and stepped back to have one last look at the car. After all, Team Rule Number Nine was, "Leave no evidence behind."

It was clean.

She transferred her gear to her own car and tossed the keys on the front seat of the car she was abandoning. Lastly, she changed out of the wig, pulled off the prosthetics, scrubbed off the makeup with wet wipes, and shrugged out of the leather coat.

Quickly, she forwarded the kill video from her laptop to her boss along with a text saying the evidence had been planted. She headed for home, well satisfied with the night's work.

CHAPTER 38

*H*ELEN LOOKED AT CLINT, WATCHING HIS REACTION AS SHE ASKED, "When you were in the military, did you ever hear of a program that recruited wannabe snipers who failed their psych evals?"

"Who says I was in the military?"

She sent him a withering look. "I see how you move. How you carry yourself. I know your type."

He didn't respond to that. Instead, he said, "Why would anyone recruit guys who failed psych evals? Those aren't exactly rocket science to pass."

"They are if you're a sociopath."

He stared at her. "Who would recruit them for anything? They're inherently unstable."

"So you've never heard of any program like that?"

He frowned. "Never."

"Can you ask around? Particularly your old buddies who were on active duty fifteen or twenty years ago. Maybe in Ranger units or the Navy's Surface Warfare School?"

"I'll ask," he replied doubtfully.

"Be careful, though. Don't make a big deal of it," she warned.

His frown deepened. "What are you poking around in?"

"I'm not sure. Let me know what you find out."

"Yeah, sure."

She reached down between her feet to pick up her purse, and

as she did so, the windshield shattered into a spiderweb with a sharp sound of glass cracking.

Clint dived across the bench seat, his hand grabbing the back of her head and holding her down. Not that she was about to lurch upright to have a look.

"You armed?" he bit out.

She withdrew her pistol and a spare clip from her purse. "Are you?" she retorted.

He reached under the driver's seat and pulled out a .45 revolver. "How do you want to play this?" he asked.

"Can you back your truck up beside my car so I can get into it?"

"Yeah. Why?"

"My car has bullet resistant windows and body armor."

He snorted. "Of course, it does." He reached for the ignition. "Hang on."

She braced her elbow against the dashboard and hung on to the door handle as he hit the gas. The vehicle jumped as he threw it into reverse. He sat up just enough to peer over the back of the seat as he swerved to the left.

Another bullet hit the truck with a ping of metal. A sniper then, standing off to one side and taking individual shots. A Spetsnaz team would've opened up with automatic weapons and put several hundred rounds through the truck already.

Clint hit the brakes, and she grunted as she was thrown against the dashboard.

"Go," he bit out, rolling down the window fast. As she threw her door open, Clint stuck his arm up and pointed his revolver out the window, shooting randomly.

Under his covering fire, she half-fell out of her side of the truck and landed in a crouch between the vehicles. She jumped into her car and slammed the door shut, locking it for good measure.

Two more shots rang out from the woods. Clint, bless him, kept his truck beside hers, providing cover and taking both bullets. No time to call him and ask if he was okay. She threw her car into reverse and stepped on the gas pedal. Her car tires spun on the gravel at the side of the road and then caught, throwing her backward.

She'd barely cleared Clint's truck when she jammed the gear into drive and threw the steering wheel hard left. When she was broadside to the road, she felt more than heard a round hit the passenger door and embed itself in the metal plating there.

She threw the car into reverse once more and then slammed the gear into drive, completing an aggressive Y-turn on the narrow road. As she accelerated rapidly, she looked in her rearview mirror.

She ground out, "C'mon, Clint. Follow me. Lemme see some headlights. Don't make me go back for you."

Finally, his truck barreled around the curve behind her. *Thank God.*

Clint's more powerful engine closed the gap between their cars with impressive speed. She approached an intersection and slammed on her brakes at the last second. She careened around the corner to the right. No surprise, Clint turned left. That way they left tire marks in both directions, and the shooter would have to choose which one of them to follow.

As she raced along the black strip of asphalt illuminated by her headlights, she replayed the shooting in her head. No doubt about it, the center of the spiderweb had been on her side of the truck. That attack had been meant for her. She had to get somewhere safe and inspect her car. She was positive nobody had followed her to the meeting with Clint. Which meant there was a tracker on her vehicle.

It also meant the shooter could take his sweet time following her back to Washington, certain of his ability to find her in an hour or two.

She drove as fast as she dared back to civilization and even then kept the speed up. The Beltway wasn't busy this late in the evening, and it wasn't unheard of to see a car pushing ninety miles per hour along it.

She veered off at an exit that had a car park by a Metro station and drove into the parking garage. The concrete might obfuscate the signal just enough to buy her the extra few minutes she needed.

She jumped out of the car and inspected it fast, running her hands along the wheel wells and under the bumpers. She finally had to lie down on her back and shimmy under the car to find it. The magnetic box, about the size of her palm, was attached to the undercarriage. She detached it, being careful not to deactivate it. She walked over to the Metro exit and waited impatiently for the next train to arrive.

A tired-looking guy in a suit exited and headed toward the parking lot. Helen followed him. As he unlocked his car door, she made a production of dropping her car keys behind his car. With a mumbled curse, she bent down to pick them up and pressed the tracker inside his rear wheel well. She held up her keys with a rueful smile at the guy and continued on.

She waited until the tagged car pulled out of the parking lot to circle back to her vehicle. She still had to ditch her car. It might not have a snazzy tracker on it anymore, but the shooter knew what it looked like and what the license plate number was.

It was late, and the aftermath of a big scare left her tired, but she drove across DC to a car repair shop in a rough part of town. The front was a legit shop, but she drove around back. A thick dude in a security guard's uniform at the locked gate looked at her skeptically as she pulled up beside him.

"I need to trade in my car," she told him. "Tell Manny that Grandma Helen is here."

The guy pulled out his cell phone and muttered into it. His eyebrows lifted in surprise, but he unlocked the gate and pushed it open for her.

She drove into what looked like a junkyard and wound through it to the back, where a bunch of cars were parked haphazardly. Chop shops like this one were busiest at this time of night when car thieves were most likely to bring in cars to dispose of. To her knowledge, Manny wasn't a thief himself. But he wasn't opposed to stripping stolen vehicles of valuable parts.

"What brings you here at this hour?" her host, Manny, asked. "You need an emergency modification on my baby here?" He stroked the hood of her car affectionately.

"I need a new car. With body armor and bulletproof glass. This one is hot."

He tsked. "What's a nice lady like you doing getting into so much trouble?"

"Believe me. I don't go looking for it. Trouble has a way of finding me."

"I only got one armored job on the lot right now. And it's conspicuous. You wanna wait for my guys to finish up something boring in a few days or you wanna take what I got?"

"I need wheels now. Go ahead and fix up something for me, though. The usual security package. A midsize sedan. Something a grandmother would drive. Nothing too flashy or new."

"I gotcha. Gonna take three, maybe four days if I put a rush on it."

"Put a rush on it, my friend," she replied.

He tsked again, and she followed him to a grungy little office with a pegboard on the wall, covered in keys. He pulled a set off the wall. "Come with me."

He led her to a white 1970 Cadillac Eldorado with a red velour interior that looked straight up like a gigolo-mobile. Helen laughed. "You weren't kidding when you said it's conspicuous. I'll have every cop in DC tailing me, waiting for me to commit a crime."

"Yeah, but you won't get shot in her."

"Speaking of which," she said, "I took a round in my passenger door tonight. Any chance you could dig out the slug for me?"

"Yeah, sure." Manny walked over to her car and pulled out a pocketknife. He widened the bullet hole in the exterior door panel and used a pair of pliers that emerged from his back pocket to pull back the edges. Frowning, he shone a flashlight into the hole. She was surprised when he opened the door to examine it from the inside and then turned to examine the car seat.

He got down on his knees to reach under the passenger seat and used the tip of his knife to dig in the side of the gear shift assembly. Finally, he emerged with a badly deformed slug in his hand. He handed it to her, saying, "Lotta lead. Big round. Hadda be a big gun to pierce that armor."

She picked up the round and examined it closely. Manny was correct that it had come from a long-range rifle. It looked like a 10.3 mm round. Maybe a .408 CheyTac. Which meant a no-kidding sniper had been out in those woods.

Good thing she and Clint hadn't stuck around to trade fire with the guy. She would guess the shooter had been wielding an SVLK-14, commonly called a Sumrak. It was a high-end Russian sniper weapon. Not the sort of weapon regular Spetsnaz troops could afford or regularly used.

What the heck? Was this Scorpius's work? Or the work of someone he'd hired? Or was this a killer the Russian government had sent in to take her out so Scorpius would be protected? Either way, it wasn't good news for her.

The Sumrak wasn't as big or powerful as some sniper rifles, but it was a highly accurate weapon plenty capable of killing at a thousand yards. Worse, it could put a round through several inches of steel. Even in the pimpmobile, she wasn't necessarily safe.

She looked up at Manny grimly. "I'll need that modified sedan fast."

He studied her car for a moment. "You know. I could just paint this car and put new tags on it. Patch up the door. Wouldn't take more than a day."

"Do it," she bit out. "Call me when it's ready, and charge the usual account."

"Pleasure doing business with you, Miss Helen. You be careful now, y'hear?"

"Always, Manny."

Except as she drove out of the yard in the obnoxious car, she felt exposed. Hunted. And worried.

CHAPTER 39

SHE WAS EN ROUTE TO A CAMPAIGN EVENT FOR MITCH IN THE JIGGI-lac, as she'd dubbed the Eldorado, when Yosef called her.

"Hey, Yossi."

"Meet's on with Anatoly. Tonight. Black tie affair at the Hirsh-horn Museum. It's a private fundraiser, but I've got us an invita-tion. There'll be heavy security, so no weapons, eh?"

"It's not that kind of meeting," she commented. "At least I hope not."

"It starts at seven. Say we meet at eight on the front steps?"

"Wow. My first date with the great Yosef Mizrah, and he's too cheap to pick me up," she teased.

He snorted. "I'll see you tonight."

"You, too."

She pulled up under the covered entry drive of a swanky coun-try club and was amused at the shock on the valet's face as she climbed out of the Jiggilac.

"Take good care of my baby," she told the kid as she handed him the keys. "And park her close. I may need to make a fast get-away."

The kid's eyebrows climbed even higher, and she smiled to her-self as she walked into the luncheon. Whether she would be fleeing the scene out of sheer boredom or because she'd spectacularly stuck her foot in her mouth remained to be seen.

She paused outside the main dining room to tug on her stuffy old lady suit. She adjusted her pearls, took a deep breath, and pasted a smile on her face as she stepped inside.

Thankfully, she'd timed her arrival so she only had to make nice with rich campaign donors for a few minutes before lunch was served. She found her place card at a round-top table near the front of the room and slid into her seat. The salad was limp, the chicken overcooked to the consistency of rubber, and the risotto undercooked to a gritty texture.

She gave up eating and stuck to sipping iced tea.

The elderly woman beside her was more deaf than not and possibly not all there mentally, which was a blessing. Instead of having to make polite conversation, Helen spent the meal merely smiling and nodding at the woman.

Dessert and coffee had been served, and it looked as if Mitch, at the head table, was getting ready to start his speech when Helen caught a snippet of conversation from across the table.

". . . you hear Brandon and Sydney McQuistion are getting divorced?"

Brandon McQuistion was one of the names from that scrap of paper in her father's files! She piped up, "Excuse me, did you say the McQuistions are divorcing? What a shame."

The woman who'd said it rolled her eyes at Helen. "The way I hear it, he's still a serial cheater. Good riddance, I say."

The woman beside her commented, "I swear. He would sleep with anything that moved in college. All the SRA boys were bad, but he was the worst!"

Helen lurched. Brandon McQuistion had been in Sigma Rho Alpha? She leaned forward. "Was Brandon at SRA the same time as Mitch?"

The second woman answered, "They were in the same pledge class."

Helen smiled and nodded. "I thought I remembered Mitch talking about him. And let's see. A Walt Kingston and a Marcus Somebody. Bickham, Bicker . . ."

"Bickford. Marcus Bickford. They were all in the same year," the woman replied helpfully.

As the two women devolved into speculation about whether or

not the McQuistions had a prenup and how much soon-to-be ex-Mrs. McQuistion stood to walk away with, Helen leaned back in her seat thoughtfully.

She glanced over at the podium where Mitch was taking his place. Why did her father stash the names of Mitch's frat brothers in his secret files? Was it a simple oversight—a scrap of paper that got stuck between files by accident? Or was there more to it?

She and her son were going to have a serious conversation. And soon.

Mitch started his speech with a mildly funny joke that got a polite smattering of laughter, then he proceeded to recognize the richest potential donors in the crowd by name. Bored, her gaze strayed, taking in the large room. It dripped of old money, with dark wood paneling, thick carpeting, and leather upholstered chairs for the diners.

Two stories tall, a second-floor balcony bar ringed the space. Round, narrow tables lined the balcony, and the walls were covered with golf memorabilia, autographed photographs of notable members and guests, and a dozen trophy cases.

Circular staircases in the corners led to the bar, and she watched a waiter nimbly descend the stairs balancing a tray of drinks. She would fall flat on her face if she tried that.

Mitch was just getting into the meat of his speech when, without warning, she heard an odd spit of sound. Nancy squeaked in her seat beside the podium, and Helen's gaze snapped to her.

Her daughter-in-law was looking down at her front. Nancy half-rose to her feet and then fell back into her chair.

But it was enough. Helen spotted the spreading stain of red on Nancy's right side.

Helen jumped to her feet, shouting, "Gun! Get down!"

The crowd predictably surged to its feet, screaming, running. *Idiots. A shooter could pick them off like fish in a barrel.* They needed to take cover under the heavy oak tables.

Thankfully, Mitch followed her directions, although he dived toward Nancy. The two of them disappeared behind the linen-covered head table.

Helen raced forward, yanking her pistol out of her purse and leaping behind the podium. She peered around it, checking both sides of the room, paying particular attention to the bar area.

"Honey, talk to me. Are you all right? Where are you hit?" Mitch was saying urgently to her right.

"Can you move, Nancy?" Helen said over her son.

"I don't know," Nancy gasped. "It hurts."

"Of course, it hurts. It's going to hurt more when Mitch puts pressure on the wound . . . which you should do now, Mitchell," Helen bit out as she finished scanning the room. If the shooter was still here, he was better hidden than she could pull off. She didn't see any potential hiding places at an angle that would give a sniper a shot at Nancy.

"I think the shooter's gone," she reported. "Mitch, pick up Nancy and carry her outside. I'll cover you. We can bring my car around out front and get her to the hospital faster than waiting for an ambulance."

Mitch nodded and scooped his arms under his wife. Helen went in front. They rushed out of the mostly empty dining room, and she brandished her pistol in both hands at shoulder-level, pointing it at every potential threat as she moved swiftly toward the exit.

A security guard ran for her as they burst out of the dining room, fumbling for his own pistol.

She called out sharply, "I'm Mitchell Warwick's mother, and his wife has been shot! Go clear the upstairs bar. It's where the shot came from. We're heading for the parking lot."

The guard looked startled but obeyed her command and ran past her into the dining room.

Mitch was pulling ahead of her, and she sprinted after him, cursing her kitten heels. At least they weren't three-inch stilettos. She made it to the front door ahead of Mitch and held out her arm to stop him.

"Stay here," she warned. "Let me clear the area. I'll let you know when it's safe to come out."

She spun out the door low and fast, taking up a position behind a huge concrete planter. She scanned the parking lot quickly. A hundred or more people were running between the cars, a few still screaming, but they were all moving away from her, escaping.

Nobody was standing still or coming this way. She ran down the steps toward the Jiggilac, which the valet had indeed parked only a few steps from the front door.

She jumped into the driver's seat and peeled out of the parking space, heading for the front portico. She lay across the big front seat and threw open the long, heavy passenger door, shouting, "Let's go, Mitch!"

He hurried down the front steps and climbed into the front seat of the car, cradling Nancy in his lap. He hadn't finished closing the door before she hit the gas.

She turned on her emergency flashers and drove like a bat out of hell for the nearest hospital, which thankfully wasn't far away.

"Keep pressure on the wound, Mitch. Push hard."

Nancy moaned as he did so.

"Where did the round enter?" she asked tersely.

Nancy mumbled, "By my belly button."

"Which side of it?" Helen snapped.

"Right. I think it came out my right side," Nancy gasped.

"Get pressure on the exit wound, too," Helen ordered Mitch. "It'll be bleeding worse than the entry wound."

She spared a glance for Mitch, and her son looked about ready to pass out himself.

"Breathe, Mitch. Nancy needs you."

"Right," he panted.

Driving with one hand, she fished in her purse for her cell phone and dialed 911. She told the operator to let the hospital know she would be coming in fast with a gunshot wound victim and to have a gurney waiting outside and a trauma team waiting inside.

In under ten minutes, she careened to a stop in front of the emergency room. Someone opened the door, lifted Nancy out of Mitch's arms, and deposited her on a wheeled bed. Whoever'd met them raced inside with Mitch running alongside.

The doors shut, and Helen sagged in her seat.

What the *hell* was going on with Mitch and Nancy? It was bad enough that a shooter had missed them from a range of a few hundred feet at his first speech. But how had a shooter missed Mitch from a range of as little as thirty or forty feet? A blind person could point a gun and hit a target from that range.

She opened her eyes and looked around.

Aw, hell. There was a news van turning into the hospital parking lot. She pulled away from the emergency room entrance and headed for the back of the parking lot. She found a heavy-duty pickup truck and parked beside it, hoping it would shield the Jiggilac from being spotted right away.

Quickly, she locked her gun in the glove compartment and hurried for the emergency room. She barely made it inside before the news crew caught up with her. Hustling over to the nurse's station, she identified herself as Helen Warwick and was shown into the back.

She had a word with the floor supervisor about keeping the press out of this area at all costs, and then she headed for a triage room to check on Nancy. As long as the round hadn't hit a major artery, the wound shouldn't be life-threatening.

Mitch sat in the tiny room alone, his head buried in his hands. She put her hand on his shoulder gently. When he looked up, his eyes were red-rimmed.

"She's going to be fine, Mitch. The bullet hit her in one of the few places on the human body where a bullet can't do much serious damage. As long as they clean up the wound well and get all the bleeding stopped, she's not only going to be fine, but she'll be fine very quickly."

"It's not her I'm worried about," he replied, sounding ravaged. "She's pregnant."

"Oh, Mitch. That's wonderful!" She thought fast, reviewing her extensive knowledge of human anatomy. Nancy couldn't be very pregnant, because she wasn't showing at all, which meant the baby and uterus were still small and low in the pelvis.

She said reassuringly, "The shot was high enough on her side that the baby shouldn't be affected."

"What about blood loss? Shock? I don't know . . ." Mitch ground out.

"Babies are resilient little creatures. He or she will be fine. And Nancy's a fighter. She'll keep that baby."

Mitch surged to his feet. "If I killed our child—"

She cut him off sharply. "Stop. If something happens to this baby, whoever took that shot did it. Not you."

"Nobody would've shot at Nancy if I weren't running for office. If I hadn't put her in harm's way."

She had no answer to that. But she could do something about whoever was trying to kill him. "Where was your security team today? Why didn't they vet everyone who went into the country club?"

"I can't have thugs looming over me everywhere I go, Mom. God knows, I can't have them patting down donors like criminals. It would make me look like a Mafia boss. Terrible optics."

She sent him a withering look. "Never send away your security team again. Promise me, Mitchell."

He huffed. "You think I haven't already beat myself up over that?"

"Promise."

"Of course," he snapped.

"I can't believe I'm saying this, because I hate everything about being in the public eye. But there are reporters outside. Do you want me to take care of them?"

"God, no!" he exclaimed sharply.

"Hey! I grew up around politics. I know how to handle myself."

"Yeah. Right up until the part where you'd threaten to kill whoever shot Nancy."

Well, there was that.

Mitch continued, "I'll have my campaign manager draft up a statement and give it to the press."

Speaking of the devil, Mitch's campaign manager, a sharp young woman and quite the go-getter, swept into the room just then. Helen stepped back as she and Mitch discussed what should go into the press release.

While they were engrossed, she slipped out of the room. She wanted to go back to the country club and have a look at the shooter's hide. Real police would've responded to the 911 calls and were not likely to have destroyed it this time.

She asked an orderly for another way out of the hospital that would avoid the circus outside the emergency room, then exited via a service entrance. Donning sunglasses, taking off her suit jacket to reveal a plain white blouse, and covering her hair with the black emergency scarf she kept in her purse, she made her way around the edge of the parking lot to her car. As she rounded the pickup truck beside it, she pulled up short. A man was sitting on the Jiggilac's front hood. Rumpled shirt, cynical demeanor, sharp eyes. A reporter, then.

"Nice wheels," he commented wryly, sliding to his feet.

"It's a loaner car." She reached for the door lock with her key.

"A loaner from who? Mobsters 'R' Us?" the guy replied humorously.

"I've got somewhere to be," she tried. "If you wouldn't mind stepping back . . ."

"Who's trying to kill your son, Mrs. Warwick?"

"How on earth should I know?"

He shrugged. "You strike me as a smart cookie, no matter how many granny suits you wear and how vacuously you've been instructed to smile."

She added observant to this guy's list of traits.

"Why aren't you across the parking lot with your compatriots? I believe Mitch's campaign manager is about to make a statement."

He shrugged. "We all know what it'll say. I'm curious about why somebody seems so determined to kill your boy and yet seems so unable to shoot a gun."

"You've been a war correspondent, have you?" she asked dryly.

A moment's surprise showed in his eyes. "Yes."

"Tell you what, Mr. . . . ."

"Jenrette. Tyler Jenrette."

She pulled open the heavy car door with its interior armor plating and stood behind it. "Mr. Jenrette. If you figure out why someone's shooting at Mitch and let me know before you publish the story, I'll see to it you get an exclusive interview with my son."

"How about an exclusive interview with you here?"

"Nobody's interested in me, Mr. Jenrette. And I really do have someplace to be right now."

"You'd be surprised, Mrs. Warwick. I think plenty of people would be interested in hearing more about how you shot dead three home invaders last winter and how you saved your son in the nick of time from the first assassination attempt. And then there's the rumor running around the metro police about a robbery at Connie Stapleton's house gone sideways . . ."

Crap. There was something in his eyes, a glint of suspicion, maybe of knowing more than he was saying about her. Clearly, he had a source in the police. Did he also have one in the Russian Embassy? Or heaven forbid, inside the CIA?

She put on her best innocent expression. "All moms are protective of their kids. Ask any mother on the planet, and she'll tell you that."

He snorted in open skepticism.

She put one foot inside the car. "My offer stands. If you find out who's trying to kill Mitch, let me know and I'll hook you up with an exclusive."

She slid the rest of the way into the Jiggilac and pulled the door shut. Jenrette shoved away from the car and watched her thoughtfully as she backed out of the parking space.

She drove with one hand and texted Yosef awkwardly with her other hand. **Who is Tyler Jenrette? Says he's a reporter.**

Yosef's answer was prompt. **He is a reporter. A sharp one. Be careful around him.**

The drive back to the country club took longer than she expected. She must've been hauling butt when she drove to the hospital.

She went inside and turned immediately to head up the wide staircase to the second floor. Police were plentiful and thankfully hadn't cordoned off this area yet. But as she approached the entrance to the balcony bar, a guy in cargo pants and a polo shirt stopped her.

"Are you the officer in charge of the crime scene?" she asked him.

"Yes, ma'am."

"Good. Then you can accompany me. I need to take a quick look at the shooter's nest. I know the protocols. I won't touch or disturb anything, and I won't contaminate your crime scene."

"And you are . . . ?"

"Helen Warwick. The target's mother. I'm here on his behalf."

"You can't—"

She cut him off. "Where's the crime scene entry log? I'm in a hurry. The district attorney asked me specifically to come over and take a look. He's mighty pissed off that someone shot his wife."

"How's she doing?" the cop asked.

"No official word, but the round hit her in the right side. Through-and-through shot. I'm confident she'll be fine."

The cop's eyebrows lifted. "I shouldn't—"

"And yet you're going to. Two minutes. I won't touch a thing."

He scowled and gestured at a clipboard sitting on a useless little table in the hallway holding a silk flower arrangement.

She signed the entry log, noting her arrival time.

The cop led her down the hall and into the narrow bar ringing the dining room below. A photographer was working downstairs, taking shots of the crime scene.

"Have you got a trajectory angle on the round?" she asked as he led her past a half-dozen tall bar tables.

"Preliminary. It places the shooter about here." He stopped beside a waist-high trophy case.

"Any casings?" she asked, examining the spot carefully.

"No, ma'am."

She squatted down and looked at the carpeted spot from an oblique angle. Faint vacuum marks were still visible. Surely the shooter didn't stick around long enough to fix those before he fled.

She stood up and looked over the railing. "Have you recovered the round?"

"Yes, ma'am."

"And?" she snapped.

"Slug looks like a .38 round at a glance. But it was badly de-formed."

She frowned. If it passed through Nancy's flesh and then hit soft drywall, it shouldn't have deformed all that much. Unless . . .

"If the round clipped Nancy's rib, that would explain the de-formation. Which also would have deflected the round some-what." She moved around to the other side of the trophy case and squatted again.

Bingo. There were very faint shoe impressions in the unworn carpet beside the case.

"Shooter stood here," she commented.

She looked around quickly. No fingerprints on the glass top of the trophy case. No shell casings. No visible powder residue on the wood spindles of the balcony. No indents to indicate the shooter took a knee. Not a speck of trash. It was clean. Profes-sional.

Frowning, she stepped over to the railing a few feet away from where the shooter would've knelt or lain, so as not to disturb any forensic evidence.

From here, it was about forty-five feet to the podium where Mitchell had been standing. The shooter would have been at Mitch's ten o'clock position. It would've been a simple matter to send a round into the side of her son's head. It wouldn't have been an elegant kill, but it would've done the job.

She glanced at Nancy's chair, still tipped over on its back from where Mitch had kicked it as he scooped up his wife to rush her out. Helen frowned again.

She called downstairs to the photographer who was currently shooting that very chair, "Can you point out the bullet hole on the wall to me?"

The guy glanced up at her. He reached out a latex gloved hand and pointed at a small spot low on the wall. She crouched behind the banister and held out her index finger in a fake handgun, lin-ing it up with the hole. She adjusted a bit higher and left to ac-count for the deflection of the round off Nancy's rib.

Neither the podium nor the spot Mitch would've been standing were even close to the line of fire between her finger and the photographer's.

Horrified, she stood up. She managed to say calmly to the officer behind her, "Thank you. I've seen enough. I'll get out of your hair now."

"What did you see?"

"Nothing much. I'll let you get back to your investigation, officer. Thank you for indulging me. I'll sign myself out on the entry log."

She retraced her steps, noted her exit time on the log, and left the country club swiftly. Why had the shooter targeted Nancy and not Mitch? And why had the shot passed harmlessly through Nancy's side? Even the most amateur of marksmen should've been able to hit Nancy's head, or at least the center of her chest, from that range.

At the first shooting, the one at the hotel, the line from the shooter's position to the hole in the back of the stage had definitely lined up with Mitch's center of mass. So one shot at Mitch, and now another at Nancy. Both had been easy shots. And both had missed a kill zone.

Was it possible? Had Mitch hired someone to take potshots at him to enhance his chances of winning the election?

She reached for her phone to text him but shoved the device back into her purse. She had to ask him in person. Watch his reaction. She would know if he was lying. She always did.

CHAPTER 40

STEALING THE CD-ROM FROM ROGER SKIDMORE'S BUILDING TURNED out to be ridiculously easy. The security guard was just leaving his office to take a walk around the building when she arrived. She waited until he disappeared outside, picked the stupidly simple lock to his office, and slipped inside. It took under thirty seconds to eject the current CD, insert a blank one in the laptop, and slip out.

As much as she would love to take a look at the alleged image of herself on the disc now, she needed to head back to the hospital to check on Nancy—and have a chat with Mitch.

She was sitting at a stoplight about halfway back to the hospital when her phone rang. Hopeful that it was news on Nancy, she answered it.

"Mrs. Warwick. It's George Vincent."

"What can I do for you?"

"Since you're my confidential informant now, I need you to come down to the morgue. I've got another torture victim."

"I'm a bit busy—"

"Now."

Well, hell. She didn't dare let him tell Mitch what she knew about torture. Squeezing her eyes shut for a moment, she acquiesced. "Okay. I can be there in twenty minutes if traffic isn't bad."

"See you then." George disconnected the call.

He sounded tense. Must be a bad one. Although she had a hard time imagining anyone tortured too much worse than that John Doe—

She jolted as it hit her. *Crap. The police must've found Roger Skidmore's body.* She had the pictures of Skidmore's corpse in her phone that Clint had sent her last night. She hadn't had time to take a look at those either. She fervently hoped Clint hadn't left any forensic evidence of his entry into Skidmore's place.

At least she was going to get a look at Skidmore's body in person.

Except, when George pulled back the sheet to reveal the new, tortured body, it was a female. She recoiled, both in surprise that it wasn't who she'd expected and at the gruesome condition of the corpse.

It had been neatly and completely skinned, with the notable exception of her face.

Helen blurted, "Please, God, tell me this was done to her postmortem."

"Nope. Not this time."

She looked up at George in horror. He met her gaze grimly as she murmured, "I'm thinking we have another sicko serial killer on our hands."

Reluctantly, she looked back at the female body denuded of skin. The muscle and flesh were the dark, kidney color of dried meat. Her forehead, too, was marked with a neat fingerprint in dried blood.

"Same print as before?" she asked in distaste.

"Yep. Same V-shaped scar."

A line from the Whitehorse file popped into her mind. *By putting a third party under duress in the presence of a Whitehorse subject, the reality of the pain I will subject them to if they break one of my rules seems to be driven home most effectively.*

What were the odds that Operation Whitehorse was still active in the DC area and that this victim was a demonstration to one of Bell's killers? Her gut told her the odds were low but not zero.

Surely not. But she couldn't rule it out as a possibility.

"Have other tortured murder victims been found in or around DC before?" she asked George.

"Not that I'm aware of, but I can run a search when I get back to my desk. You think this has been going on for a while?"

She shrugged. "Just asking."

"What makes you think these two vics aren't the first ones?" he asked shrewdly.

"Like I said," she snapped, "I was just asking."

With a shudder, Helen stepped closer and leaned down to examine the young woman.

A series of faint, parallel cut marks ran down her arms and legs. The rows of lines ran across her stomach at even intervals.

Gagging a little, Helen straightened. "When the medical examiner measured the cut marks, are they the same width apart all over her body?"

George, who stood by the computer, scrolled through what looked like a preliminary autopsy report. "Yep. Varied by no more than an eighth of an inch. All right around 1.5 inches apart."

She murmured, "As I compare cuts from one side of the body to the other, they appear pretty much identical. One torturer this time, then."

George commented, "The ME agrees with you. He was fascinated when I pointed out why you thought two people worked over the last vic. Wanted to bring you in and talk with you more about what you know about these types of injuries."

Alarmed, she blurted, "No way—"

"Never fear," George cut her off. "I told him that not only are you a confidential informant, you're a *very* confidential one."

Helen nodded, relieved. "Why am I looking at this poor girl?"

"How did he do it?"

She smiled a little. "I must point out that a woman could've done this. We're capable of violence and depravity, too."

George snorted. "I'm vividly aware of that. I figure this killer is a man, though, because both bodies were moved from wherever they were . . . worked on . . . to where they were found. They're heavy. First body could've been moved by two people. But if one person killed and skinned this girl, she weighed"—he looked down at the laptop—"one hundred fifty-four pounds. That's a lot for a woman to lift."

"It's not just the lifting," Helen commented. "The killer would have to be strong enough to maneuver the body. Maybe through a doorway, maybe into the trunk of a car. Lifting it out of the trunk would require bending over and still being able to lift that weight. That would take a lot of upper body strength. Okay. I'm convinced. The killer is probably a man."

George nodded. "Talk me through this killing."

"I have no idea—"

"Guess," George snapped.

She frowned at him. Looked down at the body. "You say this wasn't postmortem?"

"No. There was too much blood in the surface tissues. She bled before she died."

"Then where are the ligature marks? Particularly on her wrists and ankles?" Helen demanded.

"I beg your pardon?"

"Something like this would've been excruciating. She would've flailed all over the place. Even tightly restrained, she would've fought." She added distastefully, "Or at least thrashed around in agony."

She bent down to examine the body more closely. "There should be bruises. Rope or belt or handcuff marks. Maybe dislocated wrists or ankles as she tried to free herself. Humans will fight like animals when they're being killed slowly. She shows none of those sorts of injuries. Not to mention, nobody could make all those cuts so perfect and even on anyone moving around or fighting like that."

George merely said, "Go on."

"He must've drugged her. Or maybe like the last guy, she OD'd. Maybe she was already unconscious. Either way, she was knocked out when he skinned her."

"Anything else?"

"Her face. There's no rictus of agony. If she felt any of this, her mouth would be wide open. She'd have died screaming. Her jaw wouldn't be in this relaxed position."

"Maybe the killer posed her before rigor mortis set in," George pointed out.

"What position was the corpse found in? Did he lay her out? Fold her arms? Straighten her legs?"

George grimaced. "She was found in a heap. Beside a dumpster."

Helen winced. Her own daughter, Jayne, was about the same age as this young woman. *Her poor, poor family.* She took a steadying breath and forced herself to focus on the task at hand—helping George catch her killer and bring him to justice. And giving this girl's family a little closure. "Are drug screens back on her?"

"Preliminary testing shows opiates in her system."

"What else do you know?" she asked.

"Not much. Another drug user tortured, moved, and dumped."

"Are there similar drop-off points for both victims? Maybe they hung out in the same area? Shared a dealer? Anything in common?"

George looked frustrated. "Nothing we've found."

"A smart killer then. Organized. Careful. Covering his tracks. Definitely a sociopath."

"Why do you say that?"

Helen tilted her head. "Do you have any reason to believe either of these victims was tortured for a specific purpose? To extract information of some kind?"

"Like what?" he challenged.

She got the feeling he knew the answer but this was a test. "Like they have gang or mob connections. Or both victims were drug dealers or prostitutes. For that matter, they could've come from rich families. Have a powerful relative. Maybe they're, I don't know, foreign nationals who could've been spies. Is there *anything* like that in either of their profiles?"

"Nothing. They were both average junkies. No family close by. A few druggie friends. Hustled money for dope. The male victim mowed lawns for cash. We don't know how the girl supported herself yet."

Helen nodded thoughtfully. "Skinning someone—particularly so meticulously—would take a while. In my experience, rage dissipates quickly. Long before the two hours or more it would take to do this. It's possible the killer is OCD. Once he started the job, he felt compelled to finish it. And the work is extremely neat."

George grimaced again. "Anything else?"

"Yeah. Find this guy and stop him."

CHAPTER 41

*L*IFTING THE HEM OF HER EVENING GOWN, HELEN GOT OUT OF THE Town Car she'd hired to bring her to the Hirshhorn Museum. It was a warm evening, and she'd skipped a coat in favor of a silk wrap. As she looked around, she spotted Yosef coming toward her.

"Don't you look dashing in a tuxedo," she said warmly.

"You clean up pretty well yourself." He held out his forearm to her.

She looped her hand around his elbow, and they headed inside. They passed through the metal detectors that made this a good neutral ground for tonight's meeting. The fundraiser was already underway, and the main lobby and circular courtyard around which the museum rose were crowded. It appeared the party spilled into the outdoor sculpture garden beyond as well.

"Did Anatoly say when and where he would meet us?" she murmured.

"He just said to find him."

"And make it look like an accidental meeting, I assume?"

Yosef glanced at her. "Of course."

They found the Russian spymaster in the sculpture garden studying Rodin's *Crouching Woman*. As its name indicated, the bronze statue depicted a woman squatting on her heels, her right hand grasping her left ankle and her right cheek resting on her right knee.

"Good evening, Anatoly. What a pleasant surprise," Yosef murmured in Russian.

Tarmyenkin answered in English. "Yosef. You're looking well after your recent misfortune. I was distressed to hear you'd been shot."

"Anatoly. I believe you know Helen Warwick."

"Mrs. Warwick," he said stiffly.

She nodded coldly at him. "Comrade Tarmyenkin."

Anatoly turned back to the statue. "I think Rodin, he had a Russian soul. So erotic, this piece."

Helen frowned. She'd always thought it looked unnatural. Tortured. "As I recall, it's based on a figure from another Rodin sculpture, *The Gates of Hell.* Just because her lady parts are exposed doesn't make it erotic." She flashed back briefly to the corpse of the young woman she'd seen earlier.

"This is how we differ, we Russians from you Americans. We see beauty even in the midst of tragedy. We are romantics at heart. You . . . are not."

"In other words, you see what you want to see while we perceive the world as it is?" she replied lightly.

Anatoly bit out, "You misunderstand me."

Yosef said pleasantly, "We don't have long before we'll draw attention, standing here conversing with the enemy. Ask your questions, Helen."

Anatoly looked expectantly at her.

"First, did your people shoot at my son and then at my daughter-in-law?"

"Absolutely not." No hesitation. No shifting gaze. No over-direct eye contact. Okay, Tarmyenkin was telling the truth.

"Next question. Did you send a hit squad to my mother's house to kill me?"

His gaze was momentarily surprised and then chagrined.

Now why would he show chagrin? Was he embarrassed at being caught running a hit team? Or was it something else?

"I would never do such a thing. One's family—particularly

one's elderly, widowed mother—should be left out of our business affairs. No, no. It was not me."

"But you know who it was." She stated it as a fact and not a question.

He shrugged.

Several guests strolled past them, and Helen smiled pleasantly at Anatoly. When the party had retreated out of earshot, her smile evaporated. "Who was it?"

"I do not know. And in anticipation of your next question, we've had this conversation before, Mrs. Warwick. I told you then that I wish to retire in peace to my dacha and my grandchildren. I expect you wish to do the same. If I let you do so, you let me do so, no?"

"That is the way it works," she replied tartly. "Why, then, is a Russian hit squad trying to kill me?"

"One must remain retired for the quid pro quo to stand," Anatoly snapped.

She inhaled sharply. So Anatoly had been informed of Scorpius's demand that the Russians eliminate her and stop her investigation of him. "Are you his handler?" she demanded.

"I'm sure I don't know what you mean—"

"Can it, Anatoly. It's me you're talking to. We can do this here, or next time I'll invite myself into your home and bring a weapon."

He scowled, clearly not appreciating the reference to her break-in at his lake house several months ago, when she had indeed questioned him at gunpoint.

He was surly when he replied, "I am not at liberty to reveal my sources and methods any more than you and Yosef are."

"You know something about the attack at my mother's," she stated baldly. "Tell me now or tell me later."

Yosef intervened, perhaps sensing the standoff becoming hostile. "Anatoly, as you no doubt know, a high-ranking CIA official died under suspicious circumstances a few days ago."

"She killed three of ours two nights ago," Anatoly retorted, lifting his chin angrily at Helen.

Ha. So they had been Russian! She *knew* it.

"She defended her elderly, widowed mother inside Mrs. Stapleton's home," Yosef said a little less pleasantly.

"They came in hot," Helen added. "I didn't shoot first."

Anatoly looked unhappy.

Yosef said quietly, "I received word just before I arrived here that a second high-level agency official has died, again under suspicious circumstances."

Helen's gaze snapped to him. He hadn't said anything about it to her.

Yosef continued, his gaze never leaving Tarmyenkin, "I expect you don't want a war between our employers any more than I do."

"Is this true?" Anatoly blurted.

Yosef nodded solemnly.

Anatoly puffed out his cheeks and exhaled. He was thinking so hard Helen could practically hear the wheels turning in the Russian's head. Eventually he said, "I will need to confirm this through my sources."

Yosef shrugged. "Of course."

Tarmyenkin said earnestly, "My agency does not seek war with yours. This I know."

"Then you need to answer Helen's question, I'm afraid. Who sent in that hit team?"

"I am not certain. I will have to ask around."

"But you have a guess," Yosef said shrewdly.

Anatoly smiled without humor—a little sadly, even. "I always have a guess."

He knew who was behind that hit. She was sure of it. Which meant it hadn't been him, but it had been Russians. *Damn it.* Whoever had gotten that message from Scorpius was acting on it. And one of the guys from her mom's house was still alive and probably still active on the hit.

Yosef was talking. ". . . you get confirmation of the latest CIA death, contact me. I will tell you this. Wagner is out for blood. This will spin out of control very quickly unless we move fast to stop it now."

The light was poor, but she thought Anatoly paled as he looked over both of their shoulders. Helen was dying to turn around and look for whoever he'd just seen.

The Russian spoke quickly under his breath. "The same person who ordered that hit team may have operators here right now."

Helen swore under hers. And she didn't have even a throwing knife with her, let alone a proper firearm.

"You brought protection?" Yosef asked sharply. "You specifically said you would not bring backup if I didn't. We agreed."

"I didn't bring my protection detail," Anatoly said urgently. "It's another team. His team."

"His who?" Helen hissed, grabbing Anatoly's arm as he started to step around her.

Anatoly looked over their arms at her.

"Scorpius's team?" she pressed.

"No. My boss."

She asked the Russian urgently, "Do you need protection to make it out of here? Is your boss coming after you?"

The Russian looked startled at her offer to protect him. "No. He's coming for you."

"At Scorpius's request." Again, not a question.

"Correct," Anatoly bit out.

"We need to go," Yosef said tightly. He pulled at her free arm.

She told the Russian sharply, "Call your boss off, or I'll take out everyone he sends for me."

"I already told him that," Anatoly replied wryly.

Yosef paused in the act of dragging her away long enough to say, "Call it *all* off, Anatoly. The hit on Helen, the contracts on other agency officials, all of it. Or you *will* have a war with the CIA on your hands."

Tarmyenkin gave his arm a yank, but she hung on grimly. He met her gaze one last time. "I don't know who's killing your senior officers."

She growled, "Tell Scorpius I'm coming for him. And tell him if he's a man at all, he'll quit sending flunkies and come for me himself."

Anatoly's eyebrows shot up. "You seriously want me to tell him this?"

Yosef pulled hard on her other arm, dragging her away from Anatoly. She called back over her shoulder. "You tell him! I'm coming for him!"

Yosef tried to head deeper into the garden, away from the lights and crowds of people, but she resisted him. "No. This way."

She headed back toward the museum.

"The civilians," he hissed.

"The cover of a crowd," she replied sharply. "Can you go faster?"

Yosef nodded and picked up the pace. He was nowhere near recovered from his gunshot wound and was breathing heavily by the time they made it inside.

"How did you get here?" she asked him as she looked around for options.

"My car. Valet parked it."

"Head outside with a group of people. Stay with them until your car is brought around," she instructed him.

"I know my tradecraft," he retorted.

"Use it." She added more gently, "I can't lose you, Yossi."

He smiled a little. "What are you going to do?"

"Lead them away from you."

"You're not armed, Helen."

"I'm aware of that." And it was a big problem. If a hit squad was here, they'd undoubtedly circumvented the metal detectors and were armed.

"Come with me," he urged her.

"Go." She gave him a little shove and took off, weaving through the crowd toward the shallow, spiral ramp that circled the outer wall of the museum, winding upward for three stories.

It was a delicate balancing act, moving fast enough to put distance behind her and whoever'd made Anatoly pale in the garden but not so fast as to draw undue attention to herself. She kicked off her high heels, not to go faster but to make herself shorter. Harder to see.

She started up the ramp. Just before she rounded the gradual bend and lost sight of the lobby, she spied a beefy man in a tux moving purposefully toward the ramp. While that in and of itself wouldn't have been a red flag, the way he was reaching inside his jacket toward his armpit was.

As soon as she dared, she took off running. The incline of the gallery might be gradual, but it was deceptively tiring to race up it. Panting, she reached the gallery on the third floor and looked around frantically.

She took off running around the perimeter and spied a door marked EMERGENCY EXIT. She opened it and slipped inside fast, looking up and down the stairs in indecision. Surely a bad guy would be parked at the bottom of it. She headed up the last flight of stairs. The door at the top was locked. She fumbled in her purse, pulling out her lock picks.

She worked as fast as she could, but she could feel the kill team closing in on her. They no doubt had the bottom of the ramp covered as well, which meant they could take their time and search each floor methodically, herding her ever higher.

Finally, the last tumbler clicked. She pushed down on the bar opener and slipped onto the fourth and highest floor of the museum. It was dark up here, with only the EMERGENCY EXIT sign casting a dim glow.

Office doors lined the hallway. She took off down the hall, testing doorknobs, looking for an office to hide in. Nothing. It was hard to tell how far she'd gone because of the curving hallway, but she thought about halfway around the building. She spied a gray door that didn't look like an office. Maybe a storeroom? She could work with that.

She picked the lock, which thankfully went faster than the first one. It was a utility and janitorial room. Using the high-powered penlight on her keychain, she looked around.

She spotted a concrete stairway off to her left and jogged up it. Thankfully, the door at the top wasn't locked. She pushed it open and stepped into a boiler room about thirty feet square. This must be on the roof.

There was no way to lock the door from this side. She looked around for something to wedge against it but found nothing. Industrial heating and cooling units filled the space. Steel pipes and square air ducts snaked overhead and down the walls. She picked her way through the space, moving cautiously.

A noise behind her chilled her blood. The access door had just opened.

A beam of light slashed through the darkness, and she flattened herself against an air conditioning unit. She had to find a weapon—a pipe, a wrench, anything. Her silk wrap was probably strong enough to strangle someone with, but that took time. And whoever had opened that door wouldn't be alone.

Still, it was all she had. The wrap was made up of one long, continuous strip of silk folded back on itself a dozen times in an accordion pattern, the edges sewn together until the strip formed a rectangle about two feet wide and about six feet long. Working fast, she bit through the thread holding an edge strip to the next strip in. She yanked at the end of the two-inch wide length of fabric, tearing it free from the long side of the wrap.

She wrapped the strip of cloth around her fists until her hands were about two feet apart. The rest of the wrap hung below her right fist. She gave the silk a sharp tug. *Yep. It would hold to strangle a man.*

She heard a sound from her left and sidled right. Peeking around the side of the air conditioner—all clear—she eased around it. And that was when she spied another door. It must lead out to the roof.

Behind her, three flashlights crisscrossed the darkness. She moved forward fast and silent in her stockinged feet. She ducked sharply as a flashlight came her way. She'd almost reached the door when a man behind her yelled in Russian, "Vot ona!" *There she is!*

A flashlight lit her up, and she bolted the last few yards toward the door, running in a half crouch.

Gunshots exploded behind her. She ducked as sparks flew from rounds ricocheting off steel. She threw herself against the door, praying it was not locked. It opened, and she fell through it, landing in a heap.

She rolled and gained her feet, looking around frantically. A metal wedge that looked like a log splitter lay on the ground just beside the door. Probably was meant to prop it open. She jammed it under the door and kicked at it with her bare foot, suppressing a yelp of pain.

The door rattled in her face as someone slammed his weight against it. The wedge slid a millimeter. It wouldn't hold for long.

She took off across the roof at top speed. There was a waist-high wall all the way around it, and she ran along it frantically. Behind her, she heard bodies slamming against the door over and over while the men swore and shouted in Russian at her through the slowly widening gap.

As she ran, she tore at her wrap, continuing to pull the strip free into a longer and longer piece of silk. There. A steel pipe sticking out of the roof and bending over in an inverted *U*. Probably some sort of exhaust vent. It wasn't very thick, and she had no idea how it was anchored below the roof. But she was out of time. She looked back, and the door was nearly a foot open. A few more good hits against it, and the killers could slip through the opening.

She knelt by the pipe and knotted one end of the silk around the pipe. Her hands shook as she doubled the square knot and gave it a hard tug. That was all she had time for. The door was opening across the roof.

Grimly, she threw her partially unraveled wrap over the wall. She did the same with one leg and, lying flat on the top edge, grabbed the silk strip tightly in both hands. She rolled out into the yawning darkness and let her other leg slide off the wall.

As her hands took her body weight, her knuckles scraped painfully against the rough concrete. *Ouch.* She wriggled to turn and face the wall. She pushed off with both feet and let the silk slide through her fists. It heated up painfully as she swung back toward the wall, rappelling downward.

She pushed off the wall again. Although alarmed at how much speed she was picking up, there wasn't anything she could do about it. Her palms burned as the silk slipped through them.

Crap. She was coming to the end of the silk that she'd unraveled. As the edge of her fist hit the stitches holding the strip to the rest of the wrap, the thread ripped like a zipper under the force of her body weight.

Faster and faster she slid downward.

She heard a shout above her and looked up. One of the assassins was leaning over the wall, peering at her and pointing a handgun at her.

Her feet hit the wall, and she flung herself to the side, pushing off hard. She swung out into space and spun around. He shot twice at her, but she was moving fast, and a human body from the top was a small target.

She slammed into the wall with her back hard enough to propel her away from the wall a little. She contorted her body, trying to turn back around to face the wall. She hit again, this time with her left shoulder. She almost lost her grip but managed to hang on. Down and down she slid.

She risked a glimpse and saw the ground coming up fast.

And then her hands were suddenly empty. The end of the silk strip had just slipped through her fingers.

She dropped the last dozen feet and landed in a clump of tall, thick grass of some kind, smashing through it. She twisted into a parachute landing fall, rolling clear of the now flattened grass.

The momentum of the impact rolled her over a second time and then onto her hands and knees. She pushed up and took off running past the ornamental grass that had broken her fall and probably saved her life.

She was startled by how close to the street she was. She popped out onto a sidewalk, and everyone nearby stopped to stare at her. She must look like hell. Her hands and knees were dirty and scraped, she was barefoot, her stockings were shredded, and she had dead grass in the hair flying across her face.

A line of taxis had formed down the street, no doubt to pick up fares from the fundraiser. She sprinted for the cabs. Gunshots rang out behind her, and she pressed on grimly as screams erupted around her and people ran for cover. She reached the first cab and jumped inside.

"Drive!" she yelled.

CHAPTER 42

T HE CAB DRIVER, WHO WAS LYING DOWN IN THE FRONT SEAT, LOOKED up at her in terror.

"Go!" she shouted at him.

He nodded fearfully and sat up, starting the car and throwing it into gear. He peeled out into traffic, and there were screeching tires and honks behind them. He raced along the Mall to the Capitol building while she watched out the rear window for any cars pursuing them.

"You can slow down now," she finally told the panicked driver. "We're safe."

"What the hell happened back there? Are you hurt?" The guy devolved into mumbling and swearing.

"I think someone started shooting inside the Hirshhorn," she answered breathlessly. It was a breathlessness she didn't have to fake. That had been *way* too close a call. She'd lost her purse somewhere in her mad flight, which meant she didn't have a cell phone or her wallet either.

Closing her eyes for a moment, she opened them and smiled at the driver in the rearview mirror. "If you could take me home, I've got cash there. I'm afraid I dropped my purse in my panic to get away from the gunman."

The driver nodded, and she gave him her home address. She hated giving out her real address to anyone, but she had no choice.

She sat back in the seat and leaned her head back, letting the adrenaline wash through her and slowly drain away. It left her limp and feeling every year of her age.

As the cab neared her house, she gathered herself. Time to get her head back in the game. She took stock of her hands. Her knuckles were pretty scraped up, but her palms weren't in as bad a shape as she'd expected. The silk hadn't ripped them up, and she only had red marks across them instead of the serious burns she'd thought she'd gotten. *God bless silk.*

She took a chance and popped into the kitchen quickly in the dark to grab some cash without clearing the rest of the house. She got the taxi on the road and out of harm's way before climbing into the back seat of the Jiggilac, parked in the garage, and digging in her gear bag.

She called her cell phone, which had been in her missing purse, and sent it a command to wipe itself clean and destroy all the data on it. Then she dialed Yosef.

It had barely rung once before he answered tersely, "Helen? Is that you?"

Aw. He sounded so worried, bless him. "Yes," she replied, "I'm fine. You made it out safely?"

"Yes, I'm home. I heard on my car radio that shots were fired."

"It got a little hairy. But all's well that ends well." She blurted, "Who died at the agency?"

"Kyle Colgate."

She gasped. "I saw him just a few days ago! How did he die?"

"Shot dead in his apartment."

"Tell me about the shot," she bit out.

"Short range. Came from across the street. Large caliber, high velocity round through the window," Yosef answered.

"Surely Kyle didn't leave his curtains open," she responded, startled.

"Curtains were closed."

"A professional with high-tech gear then. Any security video or visuals on the shooter?"

"About that. Where were you last night?" he asked soberly.

"Why? What's going on?" she blurted.

"Just answer, and then I'll tell you."

"I met with a private investigator at about 10:00 PM. We got shot at by a lone sniper, probably Russian, possibly the survivor from my mom's house, and the PI and I fled the scene. I drove across town to pick up an armored car from a friend, and then I lay low in a motel."

"Can you verify all of that?" Yosef asked.

"Yes. What's going on?"

"A woman matching your description—exactly—was filmed driving out of the parking structure across the street from Colgate's condo last night at about midnight."

"At midnight I was with my car guy. He can vouch for me, as can his crew. I imagine he has hidden security cameras galore in his chop shop. As for a woman matching my description leaving the scene of a murder, this is the second time that has happened in as many days."

"What?" Yosef squawked. "Why didn't you tell me about the first time?"

"Because it's possible you're Scorpius, darling."

"Helen, this is me you're talking to. I'm not Scorpius."

A wave of relief so profound she felt an urge to sob pass over her. *Thank God.* Hearing him say the words so plainly, so matter-of-factly, was exactly what she'd needed to dispel her lingering doubts about him. And she really needed someone she could trust right about now.

"Is someone trying to set you up?" he asked sharply.

"I haven't really had time to think about it—things have been a little crazy—but I guess so."

"Talk to me about this other murder," he said with a compassion that intensified her need to cry. Apparently, she was more stressed out than she'd realized.

"Who was it?" he pressed.

"A guy followed me out of the restaurant the night Andrew Mizuki was poisoned. I got a picture of him. Ran it through facial rec and got a hit. Name was Roger Skidmore. I went to his place to do a little surveillance and spotted Polina Semyonova—she's on my—"

"I know who she is. Continue."

"I saw her walking into his building. I bugged out before she could spot me."

"Is it possible she killed Skidmore and disguised herself as you before walking out?"

Helen thought back. "I suppose so. She was carrying a purse large enough to contain a change of clothes." *And a garrote and torture tools, for that matter.* "But why would she set me up?"

"Because she works for Scorpius, perhaps?"

"But Polina's slavishly loyal to—" Helen broke off, horrified. *Richard Bell.* Was it true, then? Was Bell Scorpius? Had he really been in charge of the team hunting himself? It all made a certain sick kind of sense. Her mind galloped ahead to the next possibility. Was Polina a graduate of Operation Whitehorse? Was she one of Bell's killers—

Oh, Lord. Make that *Scorpius's* killers. Had a Russian mole trained himself a private army of sociopathic assassins? For what purpose?

"How did this person who looked like you get spotted?" Yosef asked, interrupting her train of thought.

"Security video from Skidmore's building." She added, "I've already taken care of that."

"Well, that's good at least. What are the police saying?"

"No one has reported the body to them yet," she replied.

"Good. Then we can get out ahead of this. Send me the address and I'll call in a cleanup crew."

She frowned. The only person it made sense to believe could be trying to frame her for Skidmore and Colgate's murders was Scorpius. And there had been a woman graduate of Operation Whitehorse. Subject no. 5. Was Polina Subject no. 5?

"Yosef, do me a favor, will you?"

"What's that?"

"Move Ruth out of your house. Take her somewhere safe, like a nursing home. I'm worried about you. Whoever's running around killing senior CIA officials could be coming for you next. If Scorpius is behind Andrew and Kyle's deaths, you could be in grave danger."

"It's kind of you to worry about us, but Ruth and I will be fine," Yosef said mildly.

Damn it, he wasn't taking her seriously! "I mean it, Yossi. If Scorpius is killing off senior CIA officers to cover his tracks, you could be next. You're senior on the Russia desk, and he's stealing intel to pass to Russia."

"I hear you, and I thank you for your concern," he said implacably. "And while we're on the subject, you should take extra security measures yourself. What possessed you to call out Scorpius like that to Anatoly?"

"We've got to find him before he kills everyone at the top of the agency. I'm using myself as bait."

"That's insane and—"

"I know. I know. And it's reckless and stupid," she replied.

"I was going to say suicidal," he added dryly. "Where are you now?"

"Home."

"Helen! You know better than to go there! It's the first place Scorpius will look for you."

"I had to pay the cabbie, and I'm only here long enough to grab my long-range shooting rig. I need more firepower if I'm going to take on Scorpius."

As she said the words, cold dread came over her. It probably *had* been insane to challenge Scorpius and however many trained killers he had working for him in Operation Whitehorse.

But it was too late to back out now.

Fetching her pistol from the glove compartment, she headed inside to arm herself for war against Scorpius and his team of killers.

Without her cell phone, she couldn't remotely check the alarm system, so she tapped the tablet mounted in the kitchen. It showed the alarm system to be in good working order and registering no threats.

Limping through the house barefoot, she headed for the stairs.

And heard a noise.

From upstairs.

Her body tingled as her pulse shot up. Quickly she tied the skirt of her gown in a knot above her knees. Pistol at the ready, she moved swiftly and silently up the stairs in the dark. Pausing on the top landing, she listened intently.

A door closed to her left. That came from the primary bedroom. The intruder must not realize he was no longer alone in the house. Had he searched the walk-in closet? Found the hidden door to her supply cache?

She eased the bedroom door open a few inches. No reaction. Crouching low on the side of the door away from the knob, she nudged the door a few more inches. Still no reaction. The slice of the bedroom she could see was empty. *Still.*

Taking a deep breath, she shoved the door open and surged inside low and fast, sweeping her pistol in an arc that took in the entire room. Empty.

The intruder must be searching the en-suite bathroom or Gray's walk-in closet that opened off it. She moved over beside the bathroom door and plastered herself against the wall, listening.

Without warning, the door beside her opened, and a big, dark shape stepped into the bedroom. She let the intruder take two steps, putting her behind him, and then she jumped him. Wrapping her left arm around his throat, she pressed the barrel of her pistol against the right side of his neck, just below his ear.

At the same time, she snarled, "Who are you?" the intruder blurted. "What the hell?"

"Gray?" she said blankly.

"Helen?"

Her arms fell away from him, and she stumbled back. "What are *you* doing here?"

"Last time I checked, I live here," he retorted. "Is that a gun?"

"Oh. Um, yes. There was a robbery at my mom's place last week, and I've been a little jumpy being in this big house all alone." She went to her nightstand and deposited the pistol in the drawer by her bed, taking the moment to compose herself and try to get her pulse and breathing under control.

She turned to face her husband in the dark. "Why didn't you tell me you were coming? I almost shot you, for crying out loud."

"Last-minute change of plans."

"Why did you come home?" She was having trouble computing the fact that he was here. In the flesh. Now.

"I came because you asked me to, Helen."

"Huh?"

"You've never done that before, you know. Not in all the years we've been married."

Something cracked open painfully in her chest. He'd come home for *her*? Because she'd needed him? Was it possible? Beneath all the layers of resentment and hurt calcified between them, could he still care about her? Enough to mend their marriage one day?

Hope exploded in the void left by that giant crack in her heart.

"I—never?" she asked blankly.

"Never."

"Oh." She wasn't quite sure what to say to that. "Did you finish your business in Brazil then?"

"Sort of."

She frowned at the evasive note in his voice. "Did you get in trouble? Get kicked out of the country?"

"Something like that."

"Oh, Gray. What did you do?"

"I might have gone on national television and said what needed to be said about corruption in the Brazilian government and the disaster it's causing in the Amazon."

She laughed ruefully. "And people say I have a talent for getting into trouble." She strode toward him as he moved toward her at the same moment. They met in the middle and wrapped each other in a long, tight embrace.

"I've missed you," she murmured. "I'm glad you're home."

"You're sure about that?" he replied against her temple.

"Positive."

"How's Nancy?' he asked.

"You heard about that?" she blurted, leaning back to look up at him.

"It's the other reason I raced home. If the kids are in trouble, I need to be here."

"You always were the best father ever." Even in the times she'd been an absentee mother, he'd never failed to step up for their children. She smiled up at him apologetically. It took her a moment to recall that he'd asked her a question. "Nancy's going to be fine. The bullet passed harmlessly through her side. Didn't hit anything vital."

"Wow. That was lucky," he exclaimed.

There wasn't anything the least bit lucky about it, but she kept that comment to herself.

"It's late, Helen. Why don't you get ready for bed and join me? And while you do that, you can tell me about your evening. Were you at a fundraiser for Mitch?"

She hustled into her walk-in closet and mostly closed the door before turning on the light. No need for Gray to see how disheveled she was and ask a bunch of awkward questions.

She called out, "It was a fundraiser, but for the Hirshhorn Museum. Yosef and Ruth used to go to it every year."

"How's she doing?" Gray called back.

As she stripped out of the destroyed gown and ruined stockings, balling them up and stuffing them in the back of her closet, Helen answered, "Ruth's nearing the end, and Yosef asked me if I would go in her place, for old time's sake."

"How's he holding up?" Gray asked.

She pulled on pajama bottoms and pulled a T-shirt partially on, stopping with it over her head. Padding through the bedroom, making a production of looking for the sleeves of the T-shirt, she made it to the bathroom without Gray seeing all the grass in her hair or mud on her face. When she got into the bathroom, she kicked that door mostly closed as well and turned on the sink faucet.

Scrubbing her face and hands, she replied, "Yosef's showing the strain of caring for Ruth. I'm worried about his health."

"Is he eligible to retire from the State Department?" Gray asked as she commenced brushing out her hair.

"I imagine he is, but he needs the income and health insurance to care for Ruth until she passes. Also, I think having a job keeps him from dwelling on . . . what's coming."

"I don't know how I would manage if I knew I was going to lose you," Gray said.

The evidence of her brush with death removed, she stepped into the bedroom. As she slipped under the covers, Gray turned out the lamp on his nightstand. She rolled over and sighed in profound relief as his strong arms wrapped around her.

He rolled onto his back, taking her with him, tucking her against his side. She threw her arm across his ribs and just breathed in his presence beside her.

It had been so long since she'd let down her guard for even a moment. "You're not going to lose me, Gray. Not as long as you'll have me."

He chuckled, a low rumble in his chest against her ear. "You drive me crazy, but I love you anyway, *mi tesoro*."

She still smiled every time he called her his treasure. He was so generous with his affection. Always had been. It was perhaps her favorite quality of his.

Full stop, she didn't deserve this man or his love. But soon she would find Scorpius and eliminate that final threat to her family. And then she would spend the rest of her life trying to be worthy of Gray and the kids. No more secrets. No more lies.

As Gray's breath settled into sleep beneath her arm, though, she registered the risk she was taking by staying here with him tonight. She ought to slip out of the house, go to ground, and stay far away from her family until Scorpius was eliminated.

Her husband's return home in the middle of this crisis was a complication she really didn't need right now. She was going to have to lie to him. Make up some story about a trip out of town to finish this one last trade deal. It would mean skipping out on Mitch's campaign. Hiding from her family.

She would also have to hide from the press and anyone who might tell Gray and the kids that she was still in Washington.

Lying in the dark, listening to her husband's slow, even breathing, she made a list of last-minute loose ends she had to take care of before she went to ground and hunted down a killer. And then she mentally girded herself to walk away from her family one last time.

Tomorrow, she would go to war. But for tonight, she would rest.

Just one night with Gray. And then she would leave. Do what had to be done.

CHAPTER 43

GRAY WAS ALREADY UP AND AROUND WHEN SHE ROLLED OUT OF bed the next morning. Last night's excitement at the Hirshhorn had left her arms and shoulders practically immobilized with stiffness, and she took a long, hot shower to loosen them up. She dressed for work, today's granny disguise consisting of loose yoga pants, a white turtleneck, a crocheted vest, and more temporary gray stage coloring combed into her hair.

She heard the exercise bike whirring and ducked into Mitch's old bedroom, which had been converted into a home gym. Gray was shirtless, his muscular torso glistening with sweat. She was mightily tempted to drag him back to bed and have her wicked way with him.

Gray let go of the handlebars and sat upright, still peddling as she advanced toward him, smiling. He said cautiously, "That's an, um, interesting look. Did your mother lend you that outfit?"

She laughed and then dramatically grabbed at her back and pretended to hobble the last few steps to his side. "It's a negotiation tactic. The other side thinks I'm some old lady in my dotage. They're totally underestimating me."

"Thank God. I was worried for a second there that you'd contracted some bizarre disease that aged you twenty years overnight."

She strolled over to the bike to loop an arm around his neck. "Will you still love me when I'm gray-haired and frumpy for real?"

"You will never be frumpy, babe."

"Just for that, I'll put on black leather for you tonight," she murmured against his lips.

"Deal," he replied, grinning. "Speaking of which, what's up with that godawful Eldorado in the garage?"

She laughed gaily. "Do you like my new car?"

He answered cautiously, "I have to be honest. It's hideous. Are you having some sort of midlife crisis I should know about?"

Still smiling, she replied, "It's a loaner. Only one my mechanic had on hand."

Gray sagged in relief. "Thank God."

"I'll try to finish up early," she said, stepping back from the temptation he represented.

"Oh, I forgot," Gray said abruptly, snapping his fingers. "Mitch wants us to come over to his and Nancy's place for supper. She's getting out of the hospital today. Peter and Li are coming, and Mitch was going to call Jaynie when he got off the phone with me. It'll be a family shindig. You know, to welcome Nancy home. "

"You mean a photo op for the press?" she commented dryly.

Gray shrugged, and a shadow entered his eyes.

"This isn't the 1950s, darling," she murmured. "You're his father, and Mitch is as proud of you as can be. And so am I. You'll be a huge asset to his campaign."

Gray pulled her close and kissed her hard. "Maybe don't wear leather to Mitch and Nancy's. We wouldn't want to shock the children."

"We're not on our deathbeds. You and I are healthy adults with a healthy marriage. The children can get over it," she retorted.

"Okay. Leather it is. I can't wait to see who clutches their pearls harder—Nancy or your mother."

"My mother's going to be there?" she exclaimed in dismay.

"Did I forget to mention that? I'll charm her into behaving," he said sympathetically.

"You were always better at managing her than I was." Of course, he was better at managing everything when it came to family.

"Kick butt and take names today, Grandma," he teased her.

She swatted his shoulder and headed out, pausing in the doorway to blow a sexy kiss at him. Lord, she loved that man.

She was still smiling a little as she signed into the Box. She saw on the entry log that the entire team had already arrived. No surprise. It was nearly 10:00 AM. She passed the clipboard back to Bill and headed into the main warehouse.

She noticed immediately that it was atypically quiet. She didn't hear any forklifts today. *Weird.* She was about halfway to the bank of elevators when a fast-moving shape burst out from between two rows of shelves, coming straight at her.

Her many years of aikido training kicked in, and she sidestepped fast. It was only as the object rushed past that she registered it was a man. This was an attack!

She jumped after him, shoving him in the back as hard as she could, helping along his momentum. He took several staggering steps and ran into a pile of boxes that tumbled over before regaining his balance and spinning to face her.

The attacker wore a black ski mask. His hands were big and hard-looking, and he gripped a wicked-looking military field knife in his right fist.

He charged her, and she ducked low, squatting almost on her heels to avoid the blade as it arced toward her. He slammed her left shoulder with his knee as he passed by, knocking her head over heels.

She completed a backward somersault, fetching up against a stack of boxes. She shoved fast to her feet as the boxes fell over. She grabbed the corner of one and tried to send it in her attacker's direction. As he charged her again, she leaped sideways just in time. He buried his knife in the side of a wooden crate and spun to face her once more.

Unfortunately, he was getting wise to her dodging tactics. This time, he threw his arms open wide just as he raced past her. He snagged her across the collarbones with his left arm, spun in a fast one-eighty, and swung the knife at her.

She threw her forearm up and back over her shoulder as hard

as she could, and her wrist connected painfully with his hand, bone on bone. Her strike knocked the knife out of his fist. It flew harmlessly past her head and clattered to the floor behind her.

The attacker managed to bring his empty hand down and grapple her from behind, wrapping her in a crushing embrace that trapped her arms at her sides. She felt his upper body rear back. She threw her head to the side, turning it to give him her ear. The glancing blow from his forehead still snapped her head forward painfully, but it didn't knock her out the way it would have if he'd hit the base of her skull.

She struggled frantically to pull her right hand back, not to free it but to angle it into her cross-body purse.

He leaned back, lifting her all the way off her feet, and she mule-kicked his shins as hard as she could.

He threw her down violently, and her forehead cracked against the concrete floor. Blinking hard as involuntary tears of pain filled her eyes and her vision swam, she saw him scramble past her left side.

Crap. The knife.

She groped at her hip. *Thank God.* Her purse was still there. Shoving her hand into it, her fingers wrapped around the butt of her pistol. The man dropped to his knees beside her, and she flung herself to the right, away from him, rolling across her purse and hand.

Coming to a stop on her back, she pointed the pistol up at the assailant, who stopped in the act of raising the knife high over her belly.

"Freeze!" she yelled.

She saw it in the attacker's eyes. He was debating gutting her anyway, the risk to his own life be damned.

"Don't do it. I'll kill you before your blade ever scratches me," she panted. "At this range, I can't miss."

He hesitated.

"You brought a knife to a gun fight," she said icily. "Give it up."

If he could've killed her merely by glaring daggers at her, she would already be dead. She sat up slowly, never taking her aim off his face. She scooted backward a half-dozen feet on her rear end. When she was well out of range of him, she climbed carefully to her feet.

"Drop the knife," she ordered.

It clattered to the floor again.

"Take off your mask."

The man scowled and didn't comply.

"You have two kneecaps," she bit out. "I can take them both out and make sure you'll never walk normally again. The mask. Lose it."

"You take it off," he snarled.

American accent. Not a Russian hit man then. One of Scorpius's guys, perhaps.

As if she was dumb enough to approach close enough to grab his mask and put herself in range of him again. *Not.*

She shifted her aim quickly and fired a shot so close to his head that it grazed the ski mask in question. The report of the gunshot was incredibly loud in the echo cavern of the warehouse.

Someone on the far side of the warehouse shouted incoherently.

"The mask. Now," she grounded out. "Or I *will* cripple you." She shifted her aim to his right knee.

Her attacker reached up sullenly and pulled it off.

"Ben?" she blurted. What the hell was her own security specialist doing trying to kill her? "You work for Scorpius?"

He scowled. "Not me."

"Then why?"

"You killed Kyle," he snarled.

"No, I didn't," she answered evenly. "But someone is trying to frame me for it."

Bill from the cage careened around the end of the aisle and screeched to a halt at the sight of Ben on his knees and her pistol trained at him. "Put the gun down," the security guard ordered her.

She never took her gaze off Ben. "I think not, Bill. How about you put Ben here in handcuffs instead?"

"Ben? Benjamin Cabelo?" Bill said blankly. "But he's one of us . . ."

"Handcuffs. Now," she said, a little less pleasantly. "Ben and I need to have a conversation, and he needs to be properly restrained first, so we can have it without more violence."

Bill moved forward slowly, frowning heavily.

"I'm in charge of this team," she said firmly. "Ben is my employee, and I'm ordering you to restrain him."

Bill reluctantly put Benjamin into a pair of steel handcuffs. "Now what?"

"Now you're escorting us to the Box so I can talk with him," she said patiently. "Call the elevator, will you?" To Ben, she said, "Stand up. It goes without saying that if you make any sudden moves or try anything stupid, I'll drop you where you stand."

He made a disgusted noise she would take as acknowledgment of her warning and rose awkwardly to his feet.

The elevator dinged nearby. She gestured with her head at Ben. "Move."

She followed him to the elevator and got inside.

"Face the corner. On your knees," she ordered him. While he did that, she backed as far away from him as she could in the confined space.

"Bill, you're coming with us. Keep your weapon trained on Ben. If he even flinches, blow his head off."

"Yes, ma'am."

The elevator ride was tense but thankfully uneventful.

She had Ben precede her and Bill from the elevator and ordered him into the conference room. The other team members exclaimed and asked a flurry of questions, talking excitedly over one another, as they realized Ben was handcuffed and she had a weapon trained on him.

She ignored everyone and stood back grimly as Bill handcuffed one of Ben's wrists to the arm of a chair and zip-tied Ben's left wrist to the other arm of the chair.

"Thank you, Bill. I'll be upstairs in a bit to fill out whatever reports or paperwork this incident generates."

The security guard left, and her team crowded into the doorway.

"Everyone out," she said firmly. "Ben and I need to talk in private."

The conference room emptied, and she watched her entire team retreat to the far end of the Box around Ritika's desk.

"Polina can read lips," Ben said sullenly.

"I'm aware of that. Which is why I'm putting my back to her. I frankly don't care if she reads what you say."

His expression went closed. Stubborn. This guy would die before he told her anything he didn't want to share. She had faith torture wouldn't move the needle of his stubbornness one iota.

"You listen, Ben. I'll talk."

She caught the flash of surprise in his eyes. "I didn't know Kyle Colgate very well. But the man I met last week was a good guy. Forthright and honest. No way was he Scorpius."

Ben shifted in his seat and tested the restraints lightly.

She added, "Given that you were prepared to kill me to avenge his death, I gather you were his friend, or at least worked for him."

"I wasn't going to kill you," he muttered. "At least, not until you told me why you shot him."

Which would explain him bringing a knife to the fight and not a gun. She was inclined to believe him. And now that she thought about it, he never had made any actual attempt to gut her. She continued, "I'm guessing Kyle put you on this team to watch it and me. How am I doing so far?"

Ben nodded his head infinitesimally. It wasn't much of a concession, but it was enough.

She continued, "I assume everyone on this team is working for somebody else in the agency. It's a total political shit show. Agendas within agendas. Nobody can trust anybody. You didn't trust me, and I sure as hell didn't trust you."

His shoulders were coming down from around his ears slightly.

"I'd like to show you something," she said, reaching into her purse for the CD-ROM holder containing the security videos from Skidmore's building. "I haven't seen it yet, but I've been told what's on it. Hang on a minute while I figure out how the projection system in here works."

Dryly, he instructed her from his seat on how to turn the system on, load the CD into the laptop, and send the image up onto the wall.

She did white out the conference room walls then. Using the remote control she'd seen Polina use, she hit play. The date stamp on the first video images that popped up was Monday, April 11, the same day she'd seen Polina enter Skidmore's building, but the time stamp placed it in the morning.

While she fast-forwarded to later that day, she said, "I was attacked by a man at the restaurant the night Andrew Mizuki was poisoned. I got a picture of him and IDed him as one Roger Skidmore. This security footage comes from his building. I stole the CD yesterday."

Ben's handcuffs rattled at that, but she didn't take her gaze off the video speeding by.

"I followed Skidmore to his apartment on the evening of April 11th. While sitting in my car across the street, I spotted Polina Semyonova entering the building."

The outdoor video shots went dark, and she slowed down the fast forwarding. "It would've been around 9:00 PM when I saw her . . ."

She hit pause. "Bingo." An image of a woman entering the lobby filled the wall.

Ben leaned forward in his chair. "That's her, all right. What was she doing there?"

"An excellent question. As soon as I saw her, I left. I didn't want her to see me and recognize me. I drove away from Skidmore's and didn't return."

She resumed fast-forwarding. "Let's see how long Polina was in the building, shall we?"

She fast-forwarded again. As the time stamp sped past midnight, all traffic in or out of the building stopped. She was surprised at how long it took for anyone to come out of the elevator.

At a little past 4:00 AM, an elevator door in the lobby opened.

A blond woman matching Helen's height and general build stepped out of it. She paused and glanced up at the security camera.

Helen gasped as Ben snarled, "That's you. You killed Skidmore and then killed Kyle."

She looked over at him and waited until he lifted his furious gaze to hers. "Like I said. Someone's trying to frame me. I promise you, that's not me."

She glanced back at the woman wearing black jeans and a black leather jacket identical to the one she sometimes wore. "Is there a way to clean up this image on this laptop? Enhance it?"

Ben bit out, "I believe that computer has an image enhancer." He told her where to find the program and how to start it.

She loaded the image and sat on the corner of the conference table while the program slowly enhanced what surely did appear to be a photo of her. She had to admit Polina—if that was who this was—had done a terrific job of transforming her own somewhat narrower face into Helen's. The wig was a dead match for her hair, too.

Over the next minute or so, the picture came into sharp focus.

"Let's see if we can zoom this in on my face," she murmured. She blew the image of her face up until it filled nearly the entire wall. It took her a minute, but finally she found what she was looking for.

"Ben," she said quietly. "Take a look at that woman's right ear."

"What about it?"

"Now, take a look at mine." She tucked her hair behind her right ear and turned her head to show it to him.

It took him a few seconds, but then he sucked in air hard between his teeth. "Her ear is pierced. She's wearing that little stud in her ear. And your ears aren't pierced."

"Do you want to take a closer look at my ear to assure yourself of that?" she offered.

"No. I can see from here." He added, "Your ear is a different shape, too. Hers is longer. More pointed at the bottom. Yours is rounder. Smaller."

"Convinced?" she asked soberly.

The tension went out of him all at once. As for her, she turned back to the image, trying to make out Polina's features under the prosthetics and makeup her imitator was using. The disguise really was top-notch. She couldn't see anything but her own face staring back at her.

"Just out of curiosity, Ben, how did you find out that I'd supposedly killed your boss?"

He swore under his breath. "I got sent video of the kill shot and of you packing up your shooting gear in your car and driving out of the parking garage across the street from his place."

"Who sent it?" she asked quickly.

"No idea. It came anonymously."

"So somebody pointed you at me in expectation of you trying to kill me," she commented thoughtfully. "Who knew you and Kyle well enough to know that you were that deeply loyal to him?"

Ben stared up at her.

She prompted, "This person has your email address. Knows you're protective of your friends. Knew how to set you off."

"I'm not usually the type to get set off," he mumbled.

"Nobody is in your line of work. But somebody made this personal for you. Guessed you would come after me."

He shook his head. "I've got no idea who it could be."

It sounded as if he was telling her the truth.

She collected the CD from the laptop, erased the cache memory from the laptop, then moved over to her purse sitting on the podium to rummage in it as she asked, "What am I going to do with you, Ben?"

He met her gaze grimly. "I messed up. Lost my cool. You should throw the book at me."

She sighed. "I suppose I should." As she moved over to him, she unfolded the blade of her pocketknife. Slipping it under the zip tie, she gave it a sharp yank and cut through the plastic, freeing his left hand.

"Have you got a handcuff key?" she asked him.

"In my wallet."

"Can you get it out yourself, or do you need me to help?"

Already leaning on his left hip and reaching back with his free hand, he muttered, "I've got it."

"I'll leave you to it then."

"You gonna press charges? Write me up?" he blurted from behind her.

She paused and looked over her shoulder at him. "Should I? Or are we good?"

He stared at her for a moment. Then, "We're good."

She walked out of the conference room and, as she expected, was practically assaulted by the rest of her team.

She raised a hand to silence them all. "Ben and I had a little misunderstanding. It's sorted out now. Carry on with whatever you would normally be doing, please."

She pushed through them, and Ritika fell back, opening a path for her. She got in the elevator, and as the doors closed, the last thing she saw was Polina frowning heavily at her.

Was Polina the person who'd sicced Ben on her? It made sense. She would know the guy well enough to push his buttons by showing him his boss's gruesome murder. Which begged the question, who was pulling Polina's strings? Richard Bell? Had he told her to imitate Helen Warwick, frame her for murder, and set up Ben to come after her?

CHAPTER 44

THANKFULLY, HELEN WAS ABLE TO HALF-TALK, HALF-BULLY BILL INTO round-filing his weapon discharge report in the trash can before she left the warehouse. She was just pulling out of the Box's parking lot when her phone rang. It was George Vincent.

"Hey, George. Please tell me you don't have another body for me to look at."

"I need you to come into my office, Helen. "

"Why?"

"We need to talk."

He was hiding something. She could hear it in his voice. "I'm booked solid today, George. If this is an emergency, you're going to have to give me more than that."

"Just come to my office. Now."

She frowned as a sudden suspicion slammed into her. "Did you by any chance get an anonymous video sent to you? Maybe of someone who looks a lot like me doing something bad?"

George swore under his breath. She was tempted to join him.

"How long ago did it come in?" she asked.

"About two minutes."

She thought fast. It had been long enough for Polina to talk with Ben and for him to tell her the woman in the video had pierced ears and Helen didn't. Had Polina called someone, or had she personally sent the same video Ben had gotten to the metro police?

"Did the video come to you specifically?" she asked.

"It was sent to the Metro Homicide Division. When the BOLO went out for a woman matching your description, I asked my boss to let me see the video."

"And you recognized me right away. Have you given the police department my name yet?" she asked in resignation.

"I thought we'd have a little chat first," he replied.

"The kind of chat where I need my lawyer?" she retorted.

"Mom's in court today. She couldn't join you even if you called her. And no, not that kind of chat. Not yet."

"I didn't do it. I'm being framed for Kyle Colgate's killing and the murder of a man named Roger Skidmore. A female assassin is dressing up to look like me and making sure to get herself caught on camera leaving the scenes of the crimes."

"Skidmore, you say?"

"He lives—*lived*—in Arlington. I can send you his address. I don't think his body has been discovered yet. Although honestly, it may not be there anymore."

"And how do you know he's dead if you didn't do it?"

"A little birdie told me." She added, "As for Kyle Colgate's assassination, I'm told it happened right at midnight on Wednesday, yes?"

"That's what the time stamp on the video says," George replied cautiously.

"Perfect. I was with your mom's PI Clint not long before that, well outside of the city. He can vouch for me."

"He might not be the most reliable witness—"

"He's reliable enough. Clint and I were meeting to talk, and somebody tried to kill us. We fled, and I drove from there directly to a car dealer to drop off my car for repairs after it got shot up. I was at the car dealership at midnight. You can do the math from my meeting place to the car place and figure out that I drove straight there with no detours to kill anyone."

"What car dealer was open after midnight?" George challenged.

"He runs an after-hours chop shop. While I would hate to burn him, I'm confident he has security cameras all over his business and can verify my whereabouts that night. Also he can testify that he dug a slug out of my car."

"Come in, Helen. Give a statement. Let us question you. If you didn't kill these guys and you're not the lady on the tape, let me help you clear your name."

"Check the video, George. The lady who killed Skidmore and impersonated me has pierced ears. Mine are not pierced. You don't need me to make a statement or undergo interrogation to prove that. I've been all over the news at Mitch's campaign events. Find a picture, any picture of me, and look at my ears."

With that, she hung up. Just to be safe, she turned off her phone and popped the SIM card out of it. No sense making it easy for the cops to find her and arrest her.

Speaking of which, she needed to ditch the Jiggilac. The car was a rolling look-at-me billboard. She headed over to Manny's place, praying her car was ready for pickup.

It was. He'd painted her car white this time, and the passenger door looked as good as new. He'd even put a new set of license plates on it for her.

"Promise me those plates aren't hot," she told him.

"They're clean as a whistle," he declared.

"One last request, my old friend," she murmured.

Manny looked at her sharply. "What's that?"

"Save your security tapes from two nights ago. The ones that have me on them."

"Why?"

"I need an alibi for that time. If the police come around asking about me, by all means hand the tapes over to them."

He blinked, looking startled. "It's not often my clients beg me to cooperate with the police, but you've got it."

With a quick hug for him, she handed over the Jiggilac's keys and took hers.

It felt good to be back in her own safely anonymous car. Where to now? It wasn't as if she could drive around with a sign on her back inviting Scorpius to come and get her.

Something George had said in the car had caught her attention. She replayed the call in her mind and snapped her fingers when it hit her. Angela was in court today. Which meant she wouldn't be at her office.

Helen headed for east DC and parked one block over from Angela's place. Familiar with the alley behind it, she approached the building from that direction. Taking the fire escape to the top floor, she jimmied open the window to Angela's crash pad. With a quick look around to make sure the alley was empty, she stepped over the sill and slipped inside.

It didn't take long to find an index card in the top drawer of the desk in Angela's bedroom with a series of numbers scrawled on it. From its easy-to-find position, she took it to mean that Angela had finally gotten around to opening Derek's safe.

Wincing, she headed for the closet.

Pulling out the pile of folders, she carried them over to Angela's desk and sat down. The very first folder she opened was the one she sought. Mitch's name jumped out at her immediately.

Frowning, Helen read a campus police report documenting a girl going missing from the Sigma Rho Alpha bacchanalia during Mitch's senior year of college. A long list of names of boys at the frat who'd been questioned was in the report. Mitch's name and the three names from her father's files were in the list.

She turned the page. Next came paperwork passing the case off to the local police. There was a brief investigation of the sister, who was ruled out as an accessory or suspect in the missing girl's disappearance . . . and a notation added later that the sister had committed suicide.

That poor family.

Near the back of the file, Helen stared at a handwritten note saying the case had been closed for lack of evidence of a crime. There was no body, no evidence of foul play where the missing girl was concerned, no suspects who could be charged with any crimes related to the girl's disappearance. The district attorney's name was signed to the affidavit.

Except she recognized the handwriting. It wasn't some long-departed DA's. That was Mitch's scrawl.

She turned back to the front of the file, pulled a burner phone out of her purse, and photographed every page in the folder. She considered photographing the contents of some of the other files but decided not to push her luck. She'd been here long enough and had gotten what she'd come for.

Returning the files, putting the index card back where she'd found it, she returned the desk chair to the exact position she'd found it in and retraced her steps to her car. *Well, well, well.* That conversation she needed to have with her son had just gotten quite a bit more interesting. And urgent.

CHAPTER 45

*D*ANNY CAME HOME FOR LUNCH AS USUAL, GRABBED A SANDWICH, and waited in his room until he heard his mother leave for her yoga class. The house went silent around him. This was his chance.

The day that Christine had browsed the computer files she'd stolen to look for some problem Danny could fix for their father, she'd briefly opened a document that had been nothing more than a series of two-digit numbers.

He might not be the smartest guy in the family, but he had a great memory for numbers. Especially when they looked like the combination to a safe.

Richard had mentioned having a safe in his office once, but Danny had never seen it. Not that he snooped around in there, like, ever.

He headed downstairs and let himself into his father's office. If his dad had anything in the house about this Helen Warwick woman that could help him find her and take her out, he would bet it was in here. He looked around the perfectly neat office but didn't spot anything that looked like a safe.

A close examination of his father's bookshelves and desk didn't yield any false fronts hiding a safe either.

Danny jumped nervously as his father's new computer beeped on his desk. The monitor lit up as well. He moved over to look at it and was surprised to see a popular computer game open on the screen. His father played video games? No freaking way.

A chat opened up in a corner of the screen. He leaned closer to read it:

Helen Warwick sends you a message: Come and get her yourself or she'll wipe out all your people. She knows about Whitehorse.

Danny gaped. *Ho. Lee. Crap.*

Triumph surged through him. He was totally on the right track. If he took care of this madwoman who dared to taunt and provoke Richard, his old man would be thrilled. The one thing Richard hated above all else was defiance of any kind toward him.

The word *Whitehorse* tickled at his memory. He'd heard that word before . . .

He snapped his fingers as it came back to him. The phone call he'd overheard Richard having a couple of days ago. His father had mentioned Whitehorse. Richard had been worried the man he'd seen with Helen Warwick knew something about it and had told her.

Obviously, the sender of that message now blinking on his old man's computer thought Richard would be mad that she knew about it, too.

Which gave him an idea. If he could find his old man's files, he should look for information about this Whitehorse. Obviously, he could use it as bait to draw out the Warwick woman.

He was sure his father had said the safe was in his office. It had been late, after a family movie night. All four of them were about to head up to bed. Dad had told Mom he had some files on his desk that he needed to put into his office safe before he came upstairs. It had to be in here somewhere.

Frustrated, Danny stood in the middle of the office and did a slow three-sixty. His gaze lighted on the door in the corner.

He opened the deep, narrow closet, turned on the light, and crowed in triumph. A tall floor safe filled the whole back of the space. He dialed in the memorized combination and gave the handle a tug. The heavy door opened smoothly.

"Damn, I'm good," he congratulated himself.

His pulse leaped as he spotted a handgun lying on the top shelf of the safe in front of a two-inch-thick stack of cash. *Whoa.* Were those all hundred-dollar bills? He reached for the pile of money but jerked his hand back sharply as he remembered why he was here.

Most of the safe consisted of deep drawers full of manila files. No surprise, his OCD old man's files were all neatly labeled and arranged in alphabetical order.

He checked through the *W*s. No Warwick. There was no White-horse either.

Irritated, he started at the beginning and read each label in turn. He felt time ticking by. His mom's yoga class was only an hour long, and he'd been in here a while. Faster and faster, he read through the labels.

He'd reached the *O*s when he swore under his breath. White-horse was filed under Operation Whitehorse.

The sound of a motor activating on the other side of the closet wall made Danny jolt. The garage door. Mom was home, and he was out of time.

Snatching the Operation Whitehorse file, he hastily closed the drawer, closed the safe, turned out the closet light, closed the closet door, and raced for the office door. Was there anything else he'd forgotten to do? This time he wasn't going to screw up and forget anything.

The kitchen door opened as he raced down the front hallway and up the stairs. Stuffing the manila folder under his pillow, he leaped onto his bed and threw himself flat on it. Closing his eyes, he pretended to be asleep.

His bedroom door opened quietly, and he listened as his mother peeked in on him, backed out, and closed the door behind her.

Whew, close call. But he'd done it!

Padding over to his door, he locked it and carried the file to his desk. He opened the thick file and started reading stuff about some program to train snipers. *Sweet.* Sounded like fun.

He found a bunch of glossy eight-by-ten pictures, head shots of a bunch of men and a few women. On the back of each one was a number and some dates.

In the back of the folder was a long list of names written in his father's hand with dates beside them. The dates started about fifteen years ago and were listed in chronological order. He didn't bother to read the whole list. It looked important, and that was all that mattered.

He stuffed everything back in the folder and closed it, considering what to do next.

For the moment, he hid the folder in the bottom of a desk drawer under a bunch of comic books everyone else in the house thought were stupid.

Now, to bait the hook. By himself. Like a freaking adult. Best of all? He got to hunt the most dangerous prey there was. A human. It was scary, but it was also weirdly exciting.

CHAPTER 46

SUPPER AT MITCH AND NANCY'S WAS GOING TO BE CASUAL TONIGHT.
Peter and Li had volunteered to pick up takeout food and bring it
over, so nobody had to cook. But Helen suspected the press
would be camped outside anyway, and she put on dress slacks and
a cashmere turtleneck, which she threw a nice blazer over.

Gray grumbled about having to wear a suit and tie to dinner
with the kids, but she didn't relent. He wasn't used to the way the
press followed Mitch around nowadays.

The drive to the kids' house in Gray's SUV wasn't nearly long
enough for her to mentally gird herself to deal with both journalists and her fractious family. Hopefully, the children would be so
pleased to see Gray they wouldn't give her the third degree as
they were wont to do.

The press presence in front of Mitch and Nancy's house wasn't
as bad as she'd feared, although she did spot Tyler Jenrette
among the milling journalists. Gray stopped the SUV and rolled
down his window as he pulled into the driveway to say hello to the
reporters flagging him down.

Pasting a smile on her face, she managed not to roll her eyes.
Gray was such an amateur at this stuff.

Except as he chatted pleasantly with the journalists and told
them how relieved the whole family was that Nancy was recovering from her ordeal and able to come home so quickly, Helen

couldn't help but notice how the journalists were warming up to Gray.

Outstanding. She would be thrilled to hand over proud parent duties to him for the remainder of the campaign. In fact, she had a long list of mandatory appearances that Mitch's campaign manager had foisted off on her when this whole circus got rolling. Gray was welcome to do them all in her stead.

The car door beside her opened and Gray stood there, looking at her quizzically. "Everything okay?" he asked.

"I was just thinking about all the campaign events I'm going to pass off to you, given how deftly you handled those reporters. You're much better suited to be a political parent than I am."

He laughed heartily. "Not me. I have a bad habit of telling the truth."

She patted his cheek fondly as she stepped past him. "And that's why I love you, darling."

They walked around to the back of the house to go inside, out of view of the press. Peter opened the kitchen door and gave Gray a big welcome home hug. The hug her son gave her was much more restrained. But hey, any hug at all was progress.

A whirlwind of jeans, long hair, and laughter flew into the kitchen just then, and their youngest, Jaynie, threw herself at Gray with a squeal of delight. She always had been a daddy's girl.

Gray laughed and hugged Jayne tight, picking her up and spinning her around before setting her back down. Jaynie launched a barrage of questions at Gray immediately, blessedly taking over the conversation and drawing any attention away from her mother.

Helen set down the apple pie she'd made this afternoon on the kitchen counter next to a gigantic array of Chinese takeout boxes. Liang came over to say hello to her beneath the din of laughter and talking.

"Hello, Mrs. Warwick. I see you've gifted us with another pie."

She rolled her eyes at him. "What am I going to have to do to get you to call me Helen?"

Li just smiled. Respect for his elders was too drilled into him to consider calling her by her first name, apparently. "Did you bake this pie as well?" he asked.

"I did. And I didn't burn it this time. Although I admit I'm worried about whether the apples are fully cooked."

"I like a little crunch in my apple pie," Li replied chivalrously.

"Such a gentleman you are." She looked up at him ruefully. "Since you didn't get to taste the first pie I made for you, I figured I owed you boys another one."

"Here's hoping this one doesn't get shot up and buried in broken glass," Li said blandly.

She rolled her eyes at him.

A quick smile flashed on his face and disappeared.

"I do love a man with a dry sense of humor," she commented. "I see why you and Peter are such a good fit."

Li nodded, and she asked, "And how's my grand-dog?"

"Growing like a weed. He graduated from puppy kindergarten last week and had his first big-dog obedience class yesterday."

"My goodness. He *is* growing up in a hurry," she commented.

Gray said from behind her, "All kids grow up in a hurry. You have to enjoy every moment with them that you can."

Peter piped up from the other side of the kitchen island. "Too bad Mom didn't learn that lesson thirty years ago."

Helen opened her mouth to defend herself, but Gray beat her to it. "Your mom's work was very important, and I'll have you know she paid a lot more of the bills than I did. If not for her, you wouldn't have had that nice house to grow up in, or that fancy private education, or had your college paid for. For that matter, I wouldn't have been able to spend so much time with you kids. So maybe show a little gratitude."

She blinked, startled. It was a rare event when anyone stood up for her, and she rather liked it. As the conversation moved on to other topics, she looked back over her shoulder and mouthed a silent thank-you to her husband. He blew her a kiss and then waggled his eyebrows suggestively.

Gray asked, "So, Jaynie-kins, what are you up to now that you've got that fancy PhD in whatever it's about?"

"Social media and authoritarian regimes," Jayne replied. "And I got a job."

Exclamations of congratulations burst out.

"Tell us all about it," Helen said, pleased that the last of her chicks seemed to be launching into the world successfully.

"It's called the Polarus Group. It's more or less a think tank. We sell reports on the business and political conditions in various countries to corporations who are thinking about investing there."

"Sounds rather dry, but if you enjoy it, I'm delighted for you," Helen replied.

"This from the woman who negotiated trade deals for a living?" Peter responded.

Helen shrugged, refusing to rise to his bait. "I'm so pleased for you, darling." She gave Jayne a hug. "And it really does sound right up your alley."

Jayne smiled, but the expression in her eyes suggested something else. Helen studied her daughter as she turned away to accept a hug from Gray. Jayne's gaze was closed. Polite. Not deceptive, but not sharing everything.

Exactly the way her own eyes looked when anyone asked her about her job.

Helen considered what Jayne had said. Polarus sounded like one of the private intelligence firms that had cropped up in recent years to sell information to corporate clients. Although employees of those firms were known to develop networks of informants in global hot spots, they weren't generally boots-on-the-ground types, gathering raw intel directly. Jaynie should be safe enough as long as she stayed at her desk here in DC.

Nancy and Mitch came into the kitchen just then. She moved gingerly, and he hovered protectively. The whole family moved over to the kitchen table where Mitch carefully installed Nancy in an armchair with pillows at her back and uninjured side.

Constance arrived, and Helen was happy to hang back from the general hubbub. Hugs and kisses were exchanged, and everyone served themselves buffet-style before sitting down at the big table.

Helen made it all the way to Jayne carrying the apple pie over to the table with a knife, forks, and plates before Peter took another potshot at her. "Seriously, Mom? When are you going to give it up and stop trying to pretend you know anything about being a parent?"

Hurt and startled by the ambush, she looked up. Even more startling, though, was Jaynie jumping in to snap, "Oh, grow up, Peter. I'm so sick of your petulant whining and 'poor me' act. Our parents may give us our emotional baggage, but at some point we have to become adults and take responsibility for dealing with it ourselves."

Mitch jumped in to referee what looked about to become a sibling fight. "Wow, Jaynie. Did you take some psychology classes or something? I thought you studied how to be a media influencer."

"Real media influencers study human psychology, thank you very much," she retorted. But her irritation with Peter was derailed. Helen glanced down the table, caught Mitch's gaze, and nodded a silent thanks to him. He nodded back.

Constance asked for an update on how the campaign was going, and the conversation blessedly pivoted to that.

It turned out the apples were, indeed, close to raw. Maybe she just wasn't cut out for baking. Everyone was polite enough to eat their crunchy pie, but no one asked for seconds.

Constance and Helen volunteered to carry the dessert plates and coffee cups over to the sink to rinse and pop into the dishwasher. As they stood side by side, Helen said, "One of these days, Mom, I'd love for you to show me how you make a decent apple pie."

Constance stopped mid-rinse to stare at her. "Why, I'd be delighted to, dear. I think that's the first motherly thing you've ever asked of me."

"Surely not," she murmured. Although now that she thought about it, Constance might be right.

Nancy stood with Gray's help and shuffled slowly into the family room while the rest of the clan trailed along.

"Mitch, do you have a minute?" Helen asked him in a low voice, hanging back from the others.

He glanced at her, and his brows came together.

"Meet me outside when you've got Nancy settled," she muttered. He nodded and followed his wife out of the kitchen. When the others disappeared from view, she slipped out the back door and waited behind the garage for her son.

"Now what?" Mitch asked in a long-suffering tone as he joined her.

"Come with me. I have something to show you in your dad's car." She led him to Gray's SUV. "Climb into the driver's seat." She went around and climbed into the passenger seat.

"Really? Does everything always have to be all cloak-and-dagger with you?" Mitch groused.

"When is the last time you swept your house for bugs?" she asked him tartly.

"Uh, never."

She shrugged. "Hence the car."

He just shook his head.

"I went back to the country club where Nancy was shot to have a word with the police. Turns out a professional took that shot."

"But he missed," Mitch replied blankly.

"Exactly. Which probably means whoever took the shot at you at the theater also meant to miss. I have to ask, did you hire someone to shoot at you to boost your campaign?"

"I would never!" he exclaimed, sounding genuinely aghast.

She studied him closely, looking for the slightest sign of deception. At length, she nodded, relieved. "Any idea who did hire the shooter?"

"No. None. He's missing me intentionally?" Mitch responded.

"Perhaps you should make some sort of public statement about not wanting to win the election on sympathy but on the strength of your qualifications?" she suggested. "Maybe the shooter would catch a clue and stop taking potshots at you and Nancy?"

"Maybe," he said doubtfully.

Hell, she could see it in his eyes. He might not have hired the shooter, but he was loathe to give up the sympathy vote the incidents were garnering for him.

She said heavily, "There's something else." She reached under her seat and pulled out the manila envelope holding the print-outs of the pictures she'd taken in Angela's apartment earlier. She handed it to him silently.

Frowning, he opened it and pulled out the sheaf of papers.

As he started reading, his entire demeanor went still, then afraid. The fear rolled off him in palpable waves. Honestly, she couldn't remember the last time she'd seen her son well and truly scared. Not even being shot at had shaken him this badly.

"Where in the hell did you get this?" he finally demanded when he'd finished reading the last page.

"I think it's time you tell me about it," she said quietly.

"Damn it, I had the situation handled. It was totally buried. *Where did you get this?*"

"I'm going to have to respectfully decline to answer that. You are the district attorney, after all."

"You stole it?" he exclaimed.

"No comment." She sat back, waiting, her posture making it clear neither of them was getting out of this car until he spilled his guts. She might not have been a great mom, but she had her moments. She knew how to maneuver her kids into confessing their crimes without ever having to say a word to them.

It took a minute, but finally Mitch made a sound of disgust. Then, "Spring term of my senior year of college, a girl died at the SRA bacchanalia. Whether she OD'd or died of alcohol poison-ing—or had a heart attack, for all I know—she was found unre-sponsive in a guy's room. We tried to revive her, but CPR did nothing. She was dead."

Helen nodded, her posture not changing. He didn't get off the hook until he'd told her *everything.*

Mitch continued, "We were always told to call certain parents before we called the police. You know the ones—rich, powerful parents who could make problems go away. Avoid scandal. Keep their kids out of trouble."

She nodded.

"A couple of dads came over to the frat and carried the girl out. I have no idea where they took her or how they disposed of her body." He added in a rush, "I didn't know they would *hide* her body. I thought they were going to make it look like she had an accident. Give her family closure."

"But?" she prompted.

"Her remains have never been found."

"I gather that wasn't the end of it?"

Mitch sighed. "The dead girl's family demanded an investigation. Made a lot of noise. One of the dads pulled some strings. Got the campus police to whitewash the investigation and drag their feet at handing the missing person case over to the local police. All the police involved declared there was no evidence of foul play, and as far as they were concerned, she was a runaway."

"Then what happened?"

"I graduated. Got a summer internship at the DA's office. And then the sister of the dead girl showed up, demanding that the investigation be reopened. She had affidavits from the dead girl's therapist saying she was no way suicidal, definitely not the type to run away, and of sound mind. The DA was inclined to grant the sister's request."

He paused and then said in a rush, "It would've ruined everything! Not only did she die on my watch, but there was a cover-up that could be traced back to the frat and the student officers of the frat, of which I was the leader."

"What did you do?" she asked grimly.

"I called Grandpa Stapleton. Asked him if he could make the sister go away. Stop demanding a new investigation. She was threatening to talk to the FBI and the national media. Make a huge stink about it."

A bad feeling settled in the pit of her stomach. "What did my father do?"

"He said he knew a guy . . . someone who had come before the House Intelligence Committee . . . who had the resources to silence people quietly. Gramps told me he would take care of everything."

"What happened?" she prodded when Mitch didn't continue.

He shot her a miserable look. "I think I destroyed his career.

Next thing I knew, Grandpa told me never, ever to speak of the dead girl or her sister again. To forget it had ever happened. He told me it would never harm me or my career. And the next day, he announced his resignation from Congress. I got the distinct impression someone blackmailed him into leaving politics."

"Any idea who?" she asked. "Did he happen to mention the name of the guy he knew? The fixer?"

"I overheard Gramps talking to someone on the phone the night I asked him to help me. I think he called the guy Bill."

Her shoulder banged against the car door as she lurched. What were the odds he'd actually said Bell? If so, Richard Bell *had* ruined her father's career.

Mitch asked anxiously, "Is there any way you can find out what happened to the sister? Use your connections . . ." He added in a rush, "I've wondered all this time what happened to her."

Helen answered gravely, "If my dad called the guy I think he did, that's the reason she's dead."

"Oh, God," he groaned.

At least he had the decency to show a little remorse. She said heavily, "When people are desperate or terrified, they either make the best decisions of their lives or the worst. You and your fraternity brothers made some bad decisions that night, and you compounded them with more bad decisions that were extremely costly to people around you. My dear boy, you have blood on your hands."

Not that she was in any position to lecture him on it. She had plenty on her hands, too. And she knew all too well the weight of ending human lives.

No matter how well she compartmentalized killing in her mind, no matter how well she understood that the only people she killed were deemed by her government to be threats serious enough to die, there was still a cost to having taken another life.

Mitch stared at her in horror as that cost began to make itself felt to him. Dismay and a certain amount of sympathy rolled through her. He'd obviously never faced up to his role in the sister's death before.

"We all make mistakes, son. But we have a responsibility to face up to our mistakes, too. Who knows where my dad's career would've gone if you hadn't ended it? He would've made a good president and done good things for this country. And who knows what that young woman would've done with her life? She obviously was a good person and loved her sister, if she was willing to fight for answers."

"I didn't know she would die!" Mitch exclaimed.

She sent him a withering look. "What did you think was going to happen when you asked my father to make her disappear?"

"Not that!"

"Then you were naïve and stupid in addition to being selfish." They were not words she relished saying, but they were the truth. And it was high time Mitch took a hard look at what he'd done.

His expression was angry, but he had the good grace not to argue with her.

She continued soberly, "As your mother, I'm compelled to ask myself if you're cut out for elected office, particularly as the chief officer of the court for a major metropolitan area."

"You wouldn't tank my career, would you?" he asked, aghast.

"This isn't about your career, Mitchell. It's about your moral fiber."

He opened his mouth. Closed it. *Smart boy.* She was not above releasing the file herself if he screwed up this conversation much more.

He was silent a long time, thinking. She didn't interrupt him. God only knew if she'd gotten through to him and the ambition that had always blinded him.

"What do you want from me, Mother?"

"This isn't a transaction," she snapped. "All I want is for you to acknowledge to yourself that you made a big mistake and followed it up with a huge mistake. Learn from what you did. Be a better man."

He exhaled hard. "Fair." Another big exhale. "Are we done here?"

"You've got another problem. The person I copied that file from is in an ideal position to blackmail you."

His gaze snapped down to the sheaf of papers in his lap. She watched with interest as his legal mind engaged with the problem.

"How sure are you the sister was murdered and the first girl will never be found?" he asked.

"One hundred percent."

"Seriously. Will this Bill guy have disposed of the first girl's body in a way that she can never, ever be found?"

"He would certainly know how to do it. That doesn't mean he did so, however. He could be holding pictures, personal effects, maybe DNA samples, to prove he knows where the girl's body is."

"How likely is he to blackmail me?" Mitch asked pragmatically.

"Extremely, if he needs your help for some reason."

"What does he do? Who does he work for?"

"I believe he's a senior CIA officer."

"Oh. Well, then. I'm good. The DA's office doesn't get involved in CIA activity. If there's a legal case associated with those guys, the Department of Justice has jurisdiction. The odds of some CIA dude ever needing my help are close to zero."

"But not zero," she pointed out.

He shrugged. "Very little in life is absolutely certain."

She said carefully, "The person who holds the originals of those documents is very likely to encounter you professionally."

"So, we're talking about a lawyer." He broke off, but after a moment, his face cleared. "Your friend, Angela Vincent."

Helen held her facial features still, trying not to give away that he was right.

"I can handle her," Mitch declared confidently.

"Are you sure about that? She's a very sharp attorney."

"Yes, she is. But so am I. She swears up and down that she's ethical. If she tries to blackmail me, I could ruin her reputation."

"And she could ruin yours."

He shrugged. "Where's the proof of any of this? These are just a bunch of statements by kids, who by their own admission were drunk off their asses at a party, and allegations by grieving relatives of the missing girl."

"You just told me she died. Surely a bunch of your frat brothers know that."

He shot her another look she recognized all too well. Sometimes he was so much like her it was scary. He said, a shade scornfully, "I knew how to do damage control even back then. Only three guys besides me know that girl died."

Which would explain the three names of Mitch's frat brothers tucked into her father's secret files.

"They were the other officers of the frat that year and would be as ruined as me if the truth ever came out." He added, "And before you ask, I stay in close touch with all three of them. They're all too rich to be bought off by some reporter and have jobs where that kind of scandal would ruin them. They'll never talk."

"It's a big risk to trust them with your career," she commented.

"A risk I'm willing to take," he said bluntly.

"You always have had big political ambitions, Mitch. The higher you go, the more incentive one of your buddies has to turn on you. Secrets have a way of coming out, whether you want them to or not."

"I'm not walking away from elected office before I even get there," he declared.

She said heavily, "All right, then. I've still got your back. If any of your frat brothers ever do turn on you, though, promise you'll let me know."

"Why? Are you gonna call Bill and have him off them?" he threw out.

"There are other ways to silence people," she replied dryly.

"Does Angela know you copied these documents?" he asked her.

"Of course not."

"Okay. I'll handle Angela from here on out."

"You're sure?"

He sent her another look that she'd seen in the mirror more times than she could count. She smiled in spite of herself and threw up her hands. "All right. I'll leave you to it. You know what you're doing. Just try to be an honest DA."

That made him blink rapidly. "Does Angela have other files besides this one?" he asked shrewdly.

"I'm sure I don't know," she blurted.

"She does," he accused. "Derek Cahill did what he could to clean up the district attorney's office, but he inherited a lot of dirt. Some of it was too big for him to handle."

"Don't make the same mistake, Mitch." She added reluctantly, "Mark my words. Angela will use this file against you someday."

He shot her a look that she expected made defense attorneys quail. Here was the aggressive prosecutor she knew her son to be. "Mom, you and Grandpa Stapleton taught me how to swim with sharks. I can look after myself and take down anyone who tries to mess with me."

"Honey, there's always a bigger shark in the ocean than you."

He snorted. "As DA, I'm the biggest shark in this town. I'm Jaws."

She seriously doubted that, but she wasn't going to argue with him about it. An image flashed through her mind of those men chasing her across the roof of the Hirshhorn, shooting over the edge of the roof at her, the panicked flight for her life.

Nope, she stood by her statement. There was always a bigger shark. And she would be wise to remember that herself.

CHAPTER 47

SINCE THE SHOOTING AT HER HOUSE, CONSTANCE DIDN'T LIKE TO go home by herself after dark. Not that Helen blamed her. Gray volunteered to drive Constance back to her place and check the rooms for her, which left Helen to drive his SUV home.

As Gray handed her the keys in the driveway, she murmured, "We're close to Yosef and Ruth's house. Would you mind if I swing by there to check on them? Yosef said Ruth is slipping fast, and I'd like to see her before she passes."

"Of course. I'll grab a cab from your mom's place to ours."

She kissed him quickly. "Thanks. You're the best."

"And don't you forget it."

She laughed at him. They hadn't gotten along this well in years. If she'd known all it would take was her retiring and stopping traveling, she would've done it long ago—

Well, she would've more seriously considered retiring long ago. She'd loved her work in her day. But she was tired. Ready to slow down and not live on the edge of her seat, adrenaline pumping all the time, her hair on fire.

She backed out of the driveway, waved cheerfully at the handful of reporters out front, and headed toward Old Town Alexandria where Yosef and Ruth's townhouse was. She watched her rearview mirror out of habit. Yep, she was ready to stop looking over her shoulder all the time. It would be nice to forget how to do evasive maneuvers, how to spot a tail, or how to lose one.

With a sigh, she parked a block over from Yosef's house and slipped out into the night, walking quickly down the alley behind the Mizrah home. She let herself into the backyard.

She texted Yosef that she was standing on his porch, and in under a minute, the back door opened without a light ever going on in the kitchen. She joined him inside and followed him to the living room in the front of the deep, narrow house, where a reading lamp was on beside his favorite armchair.

"To what do I owe this late visit?" he asked after she declined his offer of tea.

She sank into the matching armchair. "I'm worried about you and Ruth. Please, please reconsider moving her somewhere safe and maybe going to ground yourself for a little while. At least until I've found and taken out Scorpius."

"How's that going?" he asked.

"I'm fairly sure I know who he is. But now I have to prove it."

"Really?" he exclaimed. "That's fantastic. Are you able to share his identity yet?"

"Richard Bell."

"Indeed? That's alarming."

She blurted, "Did you know he recruited people with antisocial personality disorders out of the military and trained them to be snipers?"

"I heard some whispers to that effect a while back," he said. He shook his head. "Sociopaths should never be trained how to kill effectively."

Leaning forward in her chair, she asked, "Did you ever hear what happened to the snipers who graduated from his training program?"

"There were successful graduates?" he replied, sounding surprised. "The way I heard it, they all died, and Congress shut down the funding."

"Nope. There were about a dozen successful graduates of the initial program. And if I'm right, he may have actually started selling information to Russia to keep his program funded off the books. There's no telling how many of these unstable assassins he has trained. He could have a whole army of them by now."

Yosef stared at her in dismay.

"The last notation I saw in the CIA's Operation Whitehorse archive said he was having trouble finding candidates out of the military. Apparently, sociopaths with an interest in sniper school aren't a dime a dozen."

"Thank God for small favors," Yosef murmured.

She finished, "He tried training civilian sociopaths, but they weren't able to abide by the strict rules he set for them, and all failed the training program."

"Meaning they were killed?" Yosef asked.

She nodded tersely.

He steepled his fingers under his chin, a sure sign he was thinking hard. "That sounds like Bell. I'm convinced he's a sociopath himself, by the way."

"Given how he trained his recruits, I'm inclined to agree with you." She briefly described the various way he'd triggered his recruits to become killers and how he tortured victims in front of his people to keep them afraid of him and in line.

"How do you intend to prove he's Scorpius?" Yosef asked.

"I'll have to find someone I trust to set up round-the-clock surveillance on Bell. Tap his phones, computers, bug his house, car, and office, the works."

"Bell will spot any surveillance you put on him. He's a paranoid bastard."

"Scorpius slipped up a couple of weeks ago and sent a message to his Russian handler without properly encrypting it. My team caught it. Maybe he'll slip up again."

"Do you know Bell sent the message your team intercepted?" Yosef asked.

"No. Scorpius destroyed the computer it came from before my tech guy could locate it."

"How did Scorpius know to destroy the computer?" Yosef asked.

"I'm convinced Polina Semyonova and Mason Chunenko work for him, and possibly Jack Zellner. Although Jack may just be a wannabe. He follows Polina around like a puppy dog. Until earlier today, I thought Benjamin Cabelo worked for Bell, but when he attacked me, I revised that assessment."

"He attacked you?" Yosef blurted.

She filled him in quickly.

"For what it's worth, Ben had no intention of killing you. He's a top-notch operator. If he'd wanted you dead, we wouldn't be sitting here talking right now—"

The lights went out, and the living room plunged into darkness.

Helen glanced out the front window, saw the streetlights were still on outside, and swore under her breath as she flung herself out of the chair onto the floor. Yosef did the same, albeit not as quickly as she had.

"Can Ruth be moved?" she asked him urgently.

"In an emergency."

"This is an emergency," she confirmed.

"I'll have to carry her downstairs," Yosef said.

She winced. He wasn't recovered yet from the gunshot to the chest that had cracked his sternum. "You're sure you can handle her?"

"She barely weighs eighty pounds. And she's my wife."

She wasn't about to argue with him, for she felt a breath of cool air move on her skin. Someone had just opened a door or window somewhere in the house.

"Do you have a weapon in this room?" she whispered.

He reached up to the cigar box on the table between the armchairs and pulled out a pistol. But when he held it out to her, she shook her head, breathing, "You take it. The intruder may be upstairs."

"The intruder is coming for me. Not Ruth." He shoved the weapon in her hand.

She switched the small handgun to her off hand and pulled her larger, heavier Wilson pistol out of her purse. Rising to a crouch, she told him quietly, "Follow me. I'll take you up to Ruth."

He nodded and rose as well. The staircase was directly outside the living room, and it was an easy matter for her to clear the long central hallway and wave him across to the foot of the stairs.

"Fifth tread squeaks," he breathed.

She nodded and headed upstairs, bypassing the noisy step. She moved swiftly until she reached the landing, pausing with her head at floor level to scan the space. She didn't sense anyone up here. She heard only the quiet beep of Ruth's heart monitor and the rhythmic whooshing of her oxygen pump.

She ran across the hall to Ruth's door and opened it fast, swinging in low and clearing the room, pistol at the ready. The high hospital bed was easy to see under, and she moved past it.

She had a momentary fright when she opened the closet. A row of Styrofoam forms in the shape of human heads were covered in women's wigs. *Oh, right.* Ruth had been raised as an Orthodox Jew. She wouldn't show her hair in public after she was married and had used scarves or wigs to cover it.

She whispered to Yosef, "Clear."

He was already unhooking leads and gently lifting the oxygen mask off Ruth's face. When he slipped his hands underneath her and lifted her, Helen mentally gasped at how frail Ruth was. She also noted sadly that she didn't rouse when lifted. Ruth's head fell limply to Yosef's shoulder.

He nodded his readiness to move.

"Fire escape?" she breathed.

"Main bedroom," he answered as quietly.

Once more, she cleared the hall and darted down it toward the back of the house. She'd finished clearing the bedroom by the time Yosef joined her.

"Can you get Ruth outside by yourself?" she asked.

"I'll manage. You do what you have to."

"I may destroy your house."

"Do it," he allowed. "Be careful. He's here to kill me."

She paused at the hallway door to glance back and saw Yosef straddling the windowsill, angling Ruth awkwardly through the opening. Then she opened the door and slipped into the kill zone.

With Yossi and Ruth out of the house, there were no innocents to avoid shooting. Anything that moved needed to die.

She thought fast. She really didn't want to get into a fast-draw contest with the intruder by stepping out in front of the killer face-to-face. There had to be some way to gain an advantage. To hide until she spotted her quarry.

She had an idea. But she would need to move fast. The house wasn't that big. The killer had to be about done clearing the ground floor and would head up here next. She raced back to Ruth's room and slipped inside, closing the door silently.

She grabbed a wig out of the closet and yanked it on her head, quickly tucking her blond hair under the dark wig. She lay down fast in Ruth's hospital bed, pulling the sheet up to her neck. Helen grabbed the IV line and the leads Yosef had disconnected and pulled them under the sheet with her.

Working fast, she passed the lead that went to the heart monitor down the neck of her sweater and pressed the adhesive paper circle against a spot over her heart. The monitor started beeping quietly, albeit very rapidly. She pressed the oxygen mask to her face and pulled its elastic strap over the wig.

She would have to pretend to be unconscious. If the killer peeked in here and saw Ruth looking back at him, he would kill Yosef's wife on the spot. But she guessed the killer would bypass Ruth if she posed no threat. If nothing else, the assassin wouldn't risk the noise of a gunshot, even the whisper of a silenced weapon, warning Yosef.

Lying in the faint light of a streetlamp creeping around the curtains, staying perfectly still, perfectly exposed like this, was nerve-racking. She tried to slow her heart rate, to relax, but it was a futile exercise. The heart monitor continued beeping quickly, like a bird chirping.

A stair tread squeaked for an instant and then went silent. The shooter had tested it but lifted his foot off it the second it made a sound.

Here goes nothing.

She braced her entire body to throw herself off the far side of the bed away from the door. The doorknob started to turn, and she closed her eyes hastily. Very carefully, she slitted open her eyes just far enough to peer through her lashes at the ceiling. She made out fuzzy patches of light and dark, but that was about it.

She felt the intruder move slowly, cautiously, into the room, but as much as she strained to hear him, she didn't catch the slightest hint of sound. The assassin was good.

A black shadow eased into her line of vision. It was almost impossible to keep her breathing light and even, to hold her body perfectly still as she waited for the killer to retreat or raise a weapon to kill her.

She counted four breaths. Five.

And still he stood there. Undecided, was he, on whether or not to kill her? The tension stretched nearly to the breaking point.

Then the shooter turned around to leave the room, leaving as slowly and silently as he'd entered.

Helen eased the bed sheet back silently. Step by step, the killer crept toward the door, while Helen sat up carefully, swung her feet to the floor, and rose specter-like to stand behind him.

She'd just brought both pistols up to chest-level when, all of a sudden, the killer whirled around to face her.

Helen experienced an instant of complete, paralyzing shock as she stared at . . . herself.

A woman with blond hair, wearing black slacks and a leather jacket over a black turtleneck stared back at her.

She looks. Just. Like. Me.

The shooter whipped up her gun.

Helen shot her with both pistols before the gun cleared the woman's hip. Pulling both triggers again, she put two more shots into the woman before the killer's knees finished buckling and she dropped to the floor.

The assassin's pistol fired as her hand spasmed in death, and Helen leaped to the side reflexively. Not that it would've done any good. By the time her brain had registered the noise and sent a signal to her body to jump, she would've been hit.

Keeping her pistols trained on the crumpled woman, Helen

did a quick health check on herself. No pain. No numbness. No impacts on her body. That stray death shot had missed her.

Cautiously, she moved forward, aiming the toe of her shoe at a spot just below the woman's kneecap. She kicked it hard. If the woman was alive, hitting her funny bone like that would cause a reflexive jerk of the woman's foot.

Nothing. The killer was still.

Using her foot again, Helen shoved at the woman's shoulder, rolling her onto her back. Sightless eyes—her eyes—stared back at her.

God Almighty, it was creepy staring down at her own dead face.

She moved quickly behind the hospital bed and waited for several long minutes for anyone else to respond to the sound of the gunshots. Nobody else burst into the room.

Helen 2.0 had been a solo assassin then.

Emerging cautiously from behind the bed, she approached the shooter. Pressing her left-hand pistol against the woman's ear, she stuck her other pistol in the back waistband of her pants and reached down to check the woman's throat for a pulse.

There was no throat left to check. One of her shots had blown it to kingdom come. The entire area was the texture of ground meat. Helen's hand came away sticky with still hot blood. Out of an abundance of caution she grabbed the woman's wrist and verified that there was no pulse. If nothing else, the large volume of blood spreading around the body was certainly commensurate with a dead person.

Out of curiosity, Helen wiped her hand free of blood and then ran her fingertips across the woman's face. She felt the edge of a prosthetic along the woman's jawline. Prying it up with her fingernails, she peeled it off the left side of the corpse's face. It came away with a sticky, tearing sound as the spirit gum holding it down released.

She stared in shock.

Polina Semyonova.

Well, hell. She'd been hoping to interrogate Polina. Force her to admit that Richard Bell was Scorpius and that she was one of Bell's sociopath assassins.

Helen texted Yosef quickly to let him know the problem was taken care of and she was safe. Then she found a container of alcohol wipes on the medical supply shelf on the other side of the bed and used them to wipe down the bed, oxygen mask, and other leads, the wig form, the doorknob—anything she might have touched or left a fingerprint on.

Last, she wiped down Polina's wrist and throat to erase any fingerprints in the woman's blood. Pocketing the wad of wipes, she pulled her pistol and made her way downstairs cautiously.

Only when she was driving in her car, safely clear of the entire Old Town neighborhood, did she pull out her cell phone and dial George Vincent.

"Helen? It's late—"

She cut him off. "You'll find Kyle Colgate and Roger Skidmore's killer at the following address. I'm confident that, after you examine her, you'll be convinced I'm not the person you're looking for."

"Why's that?" He sounded as if he was moving, quickly, while talking.

"It'll be self-evident when you find her."

"Is she armed?" he bit out.

"Yes. But she's also dead."

"Did you kill her?"

"You will find no evidence to that effect at the scene. Also, let me save you some time, paperwork, and red tape. She was a CIA officer. You might want to go ahead and call them after you take all the pictures you want of her body. Oh, and be sure to send yourself and your precinct copies of the pictures before you call the CIA. They'll confiscate everything at the crime scene, including your cameras."

"Good to know." She heard a car start in the background.

She was pulling the phone away from her ear to disconnect the call when George surprised her by saying, "The medical examiner says our two tortured druggies and Skidmore exhibit nearly identical torture markings."

"Did the killer leave a fingerprint behind on his forehead?" she asked.

"Not this time."

She replied, "The woman you're about to find in Alexandria is probably at least one of your torturers then. She spent several hours inside Skidmore's building the night he died. Plenty of time to have tortured him thoroughly."

"Do you know the vic's name?"

"Polina Semyonova."

"Thanks." George added, "This one's gonna be a piece of cake. Already got an ID. Already know who killed her. And the cherry on the sundae, I get to hand the whole thing over to the CIA. I won't even have to file a report."

Alarmed, Helen blurted, "I have *not* admitted to killing her, nor will I. Furthermore, there's no evidence whatsoever to tie me to the killing. This one is going to be strictly CIA business."

"As long as no evidence points at you, your name won't show up in any police report of mine. As far as I'm concerned, you're just a CI giving me a tip on a possible crime."

She did disconnect the call then. She was confident of her ability to properly clean a crime scene. It had been an important part of her training, and she'd been doing it for many years. Nothing would link her to Polina's death.

Somewhere in the drive northward, her adrenaline abandoned her. She felt wrung out like a washcloth as she bagged up her blazer, the wipes, and both pistols, and tossed them into a nearly full dumpster behind a fast-food restaurant. Finally, she pointed Gray's car toward home.

Gray had left the light on over the stove for her. She turned it off wearily and climbed the stairs. She tiptoed past his sleeping form into their bathroom, closed the door, and turned on the bathroom lights.

Drat. The knees of her slacks were bloody. She must've knelt in Polina's blood. Her sweater also had bloody smudges on the back of it where she'd pulled her weapon from the waistband of her slacks. This outfit was a total loss. She stripped to her skin, gathered all the clothes and her shoes, and stuck them inside her secret storage room for tonight. She would burn them the next time she was home alone.

She took as hot a shower as she could stand, letting the water wash away the blood and horror of staring at herself . . . and pulling the trigger.

Did her eyes look that cold and flat when she killed someone? Polina's eyes had been completely devoid of expression or humanity in that instant they'd stared at each other.

Did she move like Polina had? Like a predator on the hunt? Did she hold a weapon like that, as if it was an extension of her arm? Did she look like a cold-blooded killer, too, when she stalked her victims?

For thirty years, she'd done her job and never stopped to think about what she looked like to other people, what they would think of her, what they would see when they looked into her eyes.

Am I the soulless monster Polina portrayed me as?

CHAPTER 48

*H*ELEN WOKE UP LATE, RELISHING SLEEPING IN ON A SATURDAY morning. The smells of bacon frying and coffee wafted upstairs, tempting her out of bed. She dressed and followed her nose to the kitchen, where Gray was currently flipping pancakes on the stove.

"You are a god among men." She groaned in delight.

"Everything go okay with Ruth and Yosef?" he asked.

She stiffened for a moment before catching herself and relaxing. "Ruth is skin and bones. So frail. I don't think she'll be with us much longer."

"Aw, that sucks. Sorry to hear it. How's Yosef?"

"More devastated than he's letting on."

"We should have him over for dinner soon," Gray suggested.

"As long as you're cooking."

He grinned and plated a stack of pancakes for her.

She'd just sat down at the kitchen table to dig in when her cell phone rang. "Hello?"

"Helen, it's James."

"One moment," she told him. To Gray, she murmured, "Work."

"Seriously? It's a weekend," Gray grumbled as she strode past him. She shrugged and headed outside onto the front porch. It was a beautiful morning, and she sat down in the swing.

"What's up, sir?"

"Lester Reinhold is missing."

"Missing? What does that mean?"

"He was supposed to get home from his vacation three days ago. A search party went out looking for him, his two sons, and their bush pilot. The searchers found nothing."

"Where were they?"

"Alaska."

"It's easy to get lost up there. Weather's unpredictable. Maybe they just got stuck out for a bit."

"We found their campsite. They had a float plane. Looks like they broke camp and flew out. Should've landed in Anchorage Tuesday afternoon. Never showed up."

"Do you think Scorpius did this?" she asked.

"What else am I supposed to think? My senior staffers are dropping like flies. Where are you with the investigation?"

"I'm convinced I know who Scorpius is, but I don't have any solid proof yet."

"Who?" Wagner demanded.

"Richard Bell."

He swore volubly. "I just sent the paperwork up to the Hill naming him my acting deputy director in Reinhold's absence."

She winced. *Yikes.*

"Why do you think it's him?" Wagner asked tersely.

"It's all circumstantial. For example, one of the members of my team seems deeply loyal to Bell and might be the same person who leaked to Scorpius that my team intercepted a message from Scorpius to his handler. I thought for a while that Scorpius's inside guy on my team might be Benjamin Cabelo, but I've been able to rule him out recently."

"Who is this team member who may work for Scorpius?"

"Polina Semyonova."

"Let's bring her in. Question her—"

"She's dead, sir." Helen glanced at the front door to make sure it was still closed and lowered her voice, "I shot her last night when she tried to kill me."

Charged silence filled her ear for several long seconds.

"Now what?" Wagner asked.

Helen sighed. "Have you ever heard of an Operation White-horse? It was an experimental training program the agency ran about fifteen years ago."

"No. Should I have?"

"Do you want plausible deniability, sir? If so, we need to end this conversation now."

"What I want is Scorpius's head on a platter. Keep talking."

She filled him in briefly on what she knew of Operation White-horse.

"So Bell is running an off-book team of assassins that report only to him?" Wagner exclaimed.

"Looks that way."

"How many of them?" he demanded.

"No idea. He had a dozen by the time the initial program ended. Maybe twenty or thirty by now? But that's purely a guess. Interesting side note: Scorpius was first known to be active right about the time the funding for Operation Whitehorse ran out. If Bell is, in fact, Scorpius, it's possible he started working for the Russians to get money to keep funding his program."

Wagner swore. "I'm heading to my office now to look up the status of this program. But I'm pretty sure it's not on my current books and is defunct."

She replied, "If Bell is Scorpius, and he is getting the funding he needs for Whitehorse from Russia, he would've let the congressional funding expire."

Wagner swore eloquently at that.

She asked, "Is there any way you can hold off on appointing him for a while?"

A pause. "No."

Wagner's pause was just a bit too long, his "no" a bit too grimly churned out. Damn it, Bell had dirt on Wagner and could force the DCI to appoint him. Senator Veenstra had said Bell had dirt on everyone in Washington and Capitol Hill in its entirety was scared silly of him. Apparently that dirt extended into the intelligence community, too.

Wagner said, "I need you to get me proof ASAP that Bell is Scorpius."

"I'm working on it as fast as I can."

"You don't understand. He's possibly the most powerful man, the most feared man, in Washington, even without being Scorpius. He's got his claws into everybody in this town. *Everybody*. If he's also working for the Russians, if he has his claws into them the same way he does our government . . ."

She grimaced. She really didn't want to hear how Wagner would have finished that sentence. If Bell was Scorpius and he could pull the strings of both the US and Russian governments, there was no limit to his power or to the trouble he could cause.

"Listen, Helen. I need to activate you. In your old job. You'll be working directly for me. Understood?"

"But I'm retired—"

"You just told me the most dangerous man, maybe on the whole planet, has been training a private army of psycho killers."

"But—"

He cut her off again. "Bell aside, a Russian mole is systematically wiping out the senior leadership of the CIA. We have no choice but to retaliate. And I'm not giving you a choice. I'm ordering you to come back."

"Use the Special Operations Group. Killing Russians is their job—"

"I can't respond officially. It has to be completely off the books. You'll be totally dark. No record of you working for me. As of now, I'm issuing sanctions to you for all senior Russian intelligence officials on US soil."

"Including Scorpius? He's American, after all."

"Especially Scorpius."

"What about his team?" she asked.

"Do what you have to do to take him out. We'll worry about mopping up the rest of his people later."

"Is this Scorpius sanction also off the record? I was counting on having agency support when I go after him."

"He's official. You can have all the resources you need or want for that job. But I want Scorpius's handler dead, too. And that can't be an official hit."

She frowned. "As I understand it, Anatoly Tarmyenkin is probably handling Scorpius."

"Then kill him."

"If that's an order, I'll obey it. But I spoke with Anatoly night before last, and he stated unequivocally that he doesn't want a war with the CIA. He indicated that his boss was the one supporting the recent killings of senior CIA officers."

"Who is Tarmyenkin's boss?"

"I don't know, but that should be easy enough to find out."

James growled, "Fine. We'll start with the boss. Identify him and kill him. When you're done with him, I'll have other names for you."

She stared at her phone as the line went dead in her ear. Did he even have the right to order her back onto active status with the agency? Monday morning she would have to call one of the agency's lawyers to ask. She wasn't about to run around assassinating any Russian government officials without verifying he'd given her a valid sanction and that she was obligated to execute it.

She wandered back inside and sat down thoughtfully at the breakfast table.

"Anything important?" Gray asked.

"Nothing that can't wait till Monday."

"Then eat your pancakes before they get cold."

But it was not to be. She'd no sooner poured maple syrup over her now lukewarm pancakes when her phone dinged an incoming text. It had better not be Wagner giving her more names for his kill list—

She jolted as she read the message. It was short and to the point.

Come and get it.

Below the text was a set of latitude and longitude coordinates, and a picture of a manila file folder lying open. The handwritten page said merely *Whitehorse Notes*.

And she recognized the block-script handwriting. It was Richard Bell's.

CHAPTER 49

HELEN, CROWDED INTO A CORNER OF THE COMMAND TENT, SMELLED the sharp odor of sweat and tension. The tent was illuminated with red light to preserve the night vision of the operators filling the space. Their faces were painted dark green and black, and only an occasional flash of white teeth interrupted the sea of shadowed faces.

She glanced at the bank of flat-screen monitors filling the far wall. A metal pole barn, perhaps forty feet square, showed on the center screen. Both barn and the area around it were completely still, exactly as they had been since she arrived in this isolated forest in western Maryland.

The building stood on the property of a hunting and fishing company that had once run tours out of it. However, that outfit had folded a few years back, and this place was deserted as far as anyone could tell. Neighbors who'd been questioned claimed not to have seen anyone on this land for several years except for the occasional kids driving through on dirt bikes.

The silent, focused operators around her mostly stared at the bank of monitors, memorizing the building, the terrain close to it, and the features of the area around the target.

A satellite feed showed an area perhaps a half mile across, with the barn in the middle. The guy running the monitors was using some sort of look-through feature that stripped away the foliage, showing the terrain below in amazing detail. Every boulder and gully was visible.

Another camera, a long-range surveillance model on a tripod in the woods, pointed into the invitingly open sliding door on the north side of the barn. On the monitor dedicated to it, a folding table was visible smack-dab in the middle of the barn. And lying in the middle of the table was the Operation Whitehorse file.

Of course, the whole thing was a trap. The trick was to find the trap and disarm it before she and the team went in and caught or killed Scorpius.

As much as Wagner wanted the Russian mole dead, Helen and the operators around her understood the value of keeping the bastard alive and debriefing him thoroughly—which was to say, interrogating him and torturing him if necessary to get him to talk—before taking him into some distant jungle and leaving his corpse for the animals and insects to erase.

Wagner was a political appointee, not a career operator like everyone in here. He was emotional after the murders of his close associates. Afraid for his own life. He wasn't thinking rationally about the intelligence that could be gleaned from a man like Scorpius.

Helen got it. Scorpius had frightened and embarrassed Wagner and was killing the DCI's top lieutenants. She would be mighty torqued off if she was in Wagner's shoes, too. But for her, and for the men around her, killing was not an emotional thing. It was a cold business and accorded the serious, focused attention it deserved.

She rarely worked with a team like this. She specialized in solo kills, particularly at long range, which involved quietly slipping into position, taking a single kill shot, and quietly slipping away.

This business of taking along an entire team of commandos, fully equipped with all the latest surveillance technology, tactically planning an attack, and rehearsing scenario after possible scenario, anticipating every eventuality, was neither familiar nor particularly comfortable to her.

She would just as soon leave the whole job to this strike team. But Wagner wanted her here as his personal eyes and ears to make sure Scorpius got taken down. Honestly, it was better that she was here and not the big boss. He would've only gotten in the way of the smooth functioning of this group.

The team leader was Ben Cabelo. He'd asked her—in front of the whole strike team—if he could make up for their earlier misunderstanding and put his life on the line for her.

She would've said no out of hand except he ordered his team, if he did anything at all to endanger the mission or Helen, to kill him immediately. She had to give the guy props for trying hard to make amends.

His request to her and the order to his men had put her in the uncomfortable position of either trusting the whole team, including Ben, or trusting none of them at all.

She gazed around speculatively at the ten men and two women. What were the odds all of them were Bell's sociopaths? The irony of this whole mission was that the answer to her question was probably sitting in the very file this team was tasked with retrieving.

Above and beyond the identities of Bell's sociopaths, she prayed there was proof inside the file that Richard Bell was, in fact, Scorpius.

She'd never been so sure of something in her life that she had no proof of. Her intuition, her gut feeling, shouted at her that Bell and Scorpius were one and the same. It was the only thing that made sense.

She'd tried to impress on Wagner the importance of retrieving the file, and she had gone so far as to ask him to make the file the primary target instead of Scorpius, but Wagner was laser-focused on finding the mole and rooting him out.

Not only did she strongly suspect Richard Bell had dirt on Wagner personally, but Wagner was clearly convinced he was next on the mole's kill list.

A quiet voice murmured into her earpiece, "I've got movement at corner one-two. Infrared shows it to be a deer."

The north wall of the barn, with the open door, was side number one, the east wall was side number two, the south number three, the west number four. So, corner one-two would be the northeast corner of the structure.

The man calling out the deer was one of two snipers positioned about two hundred yards away from the barn, performing overwatch duty tonight. They would stand off and observe, calling out whatever threats they spotted and standing by to kill anyone who threatened Helen's safety when she went in to retrieve the file.

Of course, long before she made the attempt, the ground-penetrating radar sweep around the barn would have to happen, plus a detailed infrared scan from a satellite, and a second scan closer in from an ultraquiet drone equipped with surveillance cameras.

Then the team would move out, scouting for traps, trip wires, and anything else around the barn that the technology failed to pick up. Last, a bomb technician would be sent into the barn to check the table and file folder for any booby traps. Only when that technician had declared an all clear would she be sent in.

Her guess was that the barn was outfitted with a small camera whose feed Bell would be watching remotely. There might even be a speaker or something similar for him to talk to her through.

So far, nobody had been inside the barn, which meant nobody had visual on the corners or rafters yet.

Full dark had finally settled in, which meant the team's sophisticated night optical equipment would give them a distinct advantage over anyone with civilian night vision gear or no night vision gear at all.

Ben told the team to get ready to roll in two minutes. There was a flurry of activity as the last bits of gear were donned and checked, weapons slung over shoulders, and the operators ducked outside.

For her part, Helen moved over in front of the monitors and sat down in one of the now vacant camp chairs to watch the team do its thing.

Three of the monitors shifted to a split-screen view, each quarter of the screen showing a body cam image stream from one of the operatives dispersing into the night and fanning out around the barn.

"When is the intel satellite due to pass over?" Helen murmured to the guy manning the monitor array.

He looked at his watch. "Twelve minutes. Time enough for the team to get into position."

She watched with interest as the team glided through the night, wraithlike, blending in seamlessly with the darkness. The body cams also had audio feeds, but none of them were picking up any noise to send back to the command tent. Not that she expected any less of Ben and his team.

The satellite passed overhead, and its advanced surveillance features showed no human activity in or around the barn except for the special operators ringing it. More importantly, it looked through the metal roof and confirmed that nobody was hiding inside the structure.

The guy manning the monitors vectored in a high-altitude drone to loiter several thousand feet above the barn, high enough that it could not be heard or seen from the ground in the dark. It, too, reported that all was quiet in and around the barn.

"Who's flying the drone?" she asked during a lull in the search for traps.

The comm guy/camera operator answered, "Tonight, our RPA pilot is operating out of Nevada."

"RPA?"

"Remote Piloted Aircraft."

Helen and her companion watched in silence as the team painstakingly cleared the area around the barn, using metal detectors, electronic signal detectors, and other gear to check for traps or surveillance of any kind.

The closer the team got to the barn, and the longer they went without finding anything, the more tense Helen became. Just how sophisticated was the trap Richard had laid for them? Did he have access to some new and heretofore unknown technology they were failing to spot?

Finally, the team ringed the tiny clearing around the barn itself. The comm guy transmitted quietly, "Deploy the Hornet. Something's not right about this whole setup."

"What's a Hornet?" she asked him.

"Black Hornet. A nano-drone. A pair of them are charging in that case over there if you want to look at one."

Antsy, she was happy to have something to do. She went to the briefcase-sized plastic case lying on a camp table and opened the lid. Nestled in foam were two tiny, identical helicopters. She reached out to touch one lightly.

The body was about one inch wide and high by slightly more than that long. The tail extended maybe four inches behind it, giving it an overall length of about six inches. A pair of rotor blades, each about three inches long, extended over it. She spied a thin wire about six inches longing hanging below the belly.

"Does it have a camera?" she asked.

"It has three. One that looks straight ahead, one that looks straight down, and one that looks down and ahead at a forty-five-degree angle. They transmit directly to the operator and store no data, which is great if it's captured."

"How fast can it go?" she asked curiously.

"Top speed is about thirteen miles per hour. And they can hover, of course. Battery is good for twenty to twenty-five minutes. Which is the same time it takes its battery to charge. That's why we deploy them in pairs. One charges while the other flies, and then they swap out. We can always keep eyes on a target that way."

"Nice. What does one of these little beauties cost?"

The guy grinned. "Almost two hundred grand."

"Apiece?" she squawked, yanking her finger back.

"Yep."

Just then, one of the monitors lit up. An image of the barn looming tall in front of the camera popped up.

"How loud is the Hornet?" Helen asked. "Would a receiver inside the barn hear it?"

The guy shrugged. "They're pretty quiet. I doubt ours will be audible over the regular night noises of crickets and wind."

She nodded, moving over to the bank of monitors to stare at the images as the tiny drone flew toward the barn door.

She was startled when it abruptly dropped down toward the ground. "Is it okay?" she blurted.

"Yeah. Operator's gonna take her in low."

The little drone skimmed along the weeds. Its belly must be hitting the grass stems.

"Nice flying," the cameraman murmured. "A stalk of grass that gets tangled in the rotors can bring one of these down."

The Hornet reached the bare dirt just beside the barn and stopped. A female voice murmured, "Motion sensors on either side of the barn door. Mounted about eighteen inches above ground."

The Hornet, skimming the bare ground, eased around the corner into the barn. The straight-ahead view showed the table legs.

The operator moved the Hornet deep into the one-two corner. It began to rise vertically, like an elevator. As the Hornet ascended, more and more of the barn came into view.

The interior was ringed with shelves that held an assortment of camping gear and general junk. A pile of canoes was stacked haphazardly in one corner. The middle of the space was clear, though, empty except for that lone folding table with the file lying on it.

A steady stream of low chatter came over the radios from the female voice. Helen gathered the woman was receiving the imagery from the Hornet as well and giving a blow-by-blow report to the rest of the team on what she was seeing inside the barn in real time.

"No tangos. No weapons. Concrete floor. A lot of shelves ringing the perimeter, full of junk." Then, "Wait. Don't leave the corner."

Helen gathered that was an instruction for the Hornet operator.

The woman, who must be a real-time photo intelligence analyst, said in a hush, "Stay in the shadows. Pivot a bit right to face the three-four corner. I think there's a camera mounted in the rafters."

The view shifted to the right. Rose by maybe another foot.

"I think if you hug the rafters, you'll stay above the camera angle," the woman said quietly.

A male voice breathed, "Watch this."

Helen held her breath as the tiny Hornet ascended into the rafters. Carefully, the operator flew between a pair of ceiling joists, crossing over the big barn door opening, and easing toward the adjacent corner.

"Don't get too close," the woman responded. "It probably has an audio pickup."

The drone stopped its forward progress just past the main door. Then it gently descended until the forward-looking camera just cleared the bottom of the rafters. Dead ahead, a camera was pointed down from the corner at the table.

"Make and model?" Ben's voice murmured.

"Stand by," the guy beside Helen answered.

She watched as the comm guy frowned and leaned in close to the monitor, captured a still image, and increased its size.

Off radio, he muttered, "Dang, that's stripped down. Maybe a new military model I've never seen before . . ."

He opened a laptop computer and typed rapidly. A bunch of images of small video cameras popped up on his screen. He glanced down at those, back up at the still image, and scrolled down the page. It took him a lot of scrolling to finally stop on an image and blow it up on his laptop. He actually lifted his computer and held it up beside the still image.

Then he startled Helen by bursting out, "Son of a bitch."

"What?" she asked quickly. "Whose is it? Ours? Russian?"

"RadioShack."

"I beg your pardon?" she blurted.

"That's a cheapo little model you can buy anywhere," he said in disbelief. "Mounted on a simple, motorized swivel. Bloody thing can only turn left and right. Can't even tilt up or down."

He sat back down and transmitted, "Civilian video camera with a left-right only swivel mount. Looks like someone wired it to the motion sensors on the north doorway to activate it. It's got some sort of transmitter wired to it that is sending video elsewhere. Crappiest setup I've ever seen on an op."

The woman interjected, "The camera does not appear active now."

The Hornet operator approached the camera from above, getting within six feet or so of it. If only motion turned it on, they weren't worried about noise activating it, apparently.

The man beside her identified the swivel model and actually read the name of the motion detector off its case beside the camera. The entire setup was available online or from any hobby store. He also read online that the model of transmitter attached to the camera had about a two-mile maximum range.

She did the math fast in her head. A radius of two miles squared was four. Times pi, that meant something like twelve and a half square miles around them in which Bell could be holed up. That was a lot of land to search, particularly on foot, in the dark, seeking someone who didn't want to be found.

Helen sat back, thinking hard. Why on earth would Richard Bell use some crappy camera like that when he had full access to the best technology the CIA had to offer? For that matter, if he was Scorpius, he undoubtedly had access to Russia's best technology, too.

"Something is very wrong here," she announced to her companion.

He glanced at her grimly. "I'm inclined to agree."

Someone on the radios murmured, "Want us to catch a critter and turn it loose in there? See if the camera lights up and if there's some booby trap inside we haven't spotted?"

The cameraman looked over at her questioningly.

They risked blowing up the all-important Whitehorse file. But the alternative was to risk blowing up herself and a bunch of these operators.

She frowned. "Can we have the drone—the big one loitering overhead—expand the search area? See if maybe we can find whoever's receiving the signal from that camera?"

"To be clear, it's easy to pinpoint a source that's transmitting an electrical signal. The Hornet, or the camera in the barn, for example. But it's very hard to track a receiver. They only passively receive signals, putting out nothing to track."

"What if we wake up the camera? Might Richard Bell send it a signal to swivel or something?" she asked.

He frowned. "It's worth a try." He murmured instructions to the RPA pilot to take his drone up higher and expand the surveillance radius to two miles. Then he radioed the SOG team, "Affirmative on the critter."

"Roger. Give us a few to find one."

"What? Your guys don't have live rabbits in their backpacks they can just whip out?" she quipped.

The cameraman rolled his eyes.

In an impressively short amount of time, someone announced, "I've got a possum. They ain't fast, but this one's a big sucker. Should trigger the motion detector."

Helen shook her head. Sometimes she forgot just how resourceful guys like this could be. Most of her kills, particularly those later in her career, were set up for her in advance. She usually had little more to do than stroll into a prebuilt shooter's hide, wait for the target to appear, take the shot, and walk out. She often didn't even have to break down her weapon and take it with her.

Since many of her shots exceeded a thousand yards, she usually had plenty of time to exit the area before anyone figured out where the shot had come from, let alone from how far away it had been shot.

"How are they gonna get the possum to go into the barn?" she asked the guy beside her.

He shrugged. "They'll head for a dark place if they're scared. And our guys will probably toss in some food to get it to head toward the table."

She watched, impressed to death as a large, scruffy opossum waddled into the barn a few minutes later. The guy who'd turned it loose in the doorway reached around the edge of the door to wave his hand in front of the motion sensor, which was mounted too high for the possum to activate. The operator raced away from the building and headed for the woods in case the building blew up in the next few seconds.

"Camera's live," the female operator announced.

Helen watched with interest as the camera pivoted slightly to the left toward the possum.

"Did you get it?" she asked the guy beside her tensely.

"Yep. I got a location on that transmission. About a mile due east of here. He pointed at the monitor. "Top of that ridge."

She yanked out her cell phone and took a picture of the monitor with his finger jabbing at Bell's location. "I'm heading over there. If you wanna send some guys that way, tell them I'll be moving fast."

She grabbed her rifle and made it to the door of the tent before the guy behind her called, "Wait!"

"What?"

He carried over a device about the size of a garage door opener and tucked it in a pocket of her utility vest. "IFF radio. Identification-Friend-or-Foe. It'll ping a signal our guys can see in their optical gear so they don't shoot you."

She nodded and headed out. The command post was south of the barn, so she had only about a mile to travel. She jogged most of the way, slowing as she circled wide of the ridge to approach it from behind.

Lord, she hated running around in the woods. Give her a nice urban kill any day of the week over this terrain. Huffing, she paused partway up the ridge to catch her breath and let her burning legs take a break. When she felt recovered from the run over here, she eased forward cautiously. She didn't much care if the SOG team had caught up with her and was nearby. She was totally focused on her quarry. And he was somewhere in front of her.

Given that he hadn't shown up on heat-seeking scans earlier, she figured he was under some sort of tarp that masked heat. She scanned the ground carefully as she glided forward. She wasn't nearly as stealthy as the SOG guys, but she was stealthy enough.

There.

She spotted the low hide in front of her and froze. The tarp was propped up front and back into a low, triangular tent. The glow of a laptop screen silhouetted a long shape lying under the tent.

Bingo.

CHAPTER 50

*S*LOPPY, *RICHARD*. *VERY SLOPPY*.

She brought her rifle up into a firing position and advanced. Wary of her foe having placed trip wires, mines, or other traps out here, she moved one cautious step at a time, testing the ground before transferring any weight, moving each foot forward gently, feeling for trip wires.

It was glacially slow approaching the hide without being discovered and took all of her considerable patience. But finally, she stood only a few yards behind Bell.

Except . . .

Bell was a big man, a few inches over six feet tall. Barrel-chested. Muscular. The form stretched out on the ground before her was slim. Wiry. No more than five foot ten or so. Frowning, she eased forward. Knelt down on one knee.

Using the tip of her rifle barrel, she bumped the sole of his tennis shoe and resumed her shooting stance. For his part, the person in the hide's head whipped around.

Not Bell.

Upon seeing her, the young man lurched up, banged into the tarp hard, and brought the whole thing down on top of himself.

Swearing, Helen jumped forward, on top of the tarp, to immobilize him. As she sprawled on top of the guy, she discarded her rifle and pulled her pistol out of its holster. She yanked down the top edge of the tarp and planted her pistol against the side of the kid's head as he stared up at her in horror.

"Who are you?" she snarled.

"Danny. Danny Bell." He added, "Mrs. Warwick?"

What the heck? How did he know who she was? "Richard Bell's boy?"

"Yes."

"How did you get the Whitehorse file?"

"I stole it from my dad's safe."

"Why did you bring it out here and send me that text?" she bit out.

"I was going to kill you."

A dozen questions erupted in her head. She settled on, "How?"

"Shape charges of C-4 under the rafters. I was gonna blow you up."

She reached up with her left hand to press the transmit button on her throat mic. "Did you hear that?"

In her earbud, Ben's voice said grimly, "Copy."

"Why were you going to kill me, Danny? Did your father put you up to this?"

"Sort of."

"Explain."

She felt his sigh beneath her. "I messed up really bad. My old man found out and was furious. Told me to show him why he shouldn't kill me."

"And you thought assassinating me was the way to do that?" she blurted.

"I overheard him on the phone saying you were a big problem. I figured if I took care of you for him, he'd let me live."

What kind of parent threatened to murder his own child?

"Do you *want* to kill me?" she asked quietly.

He frowned up at her. "I've never killed a human. It's exciting to think about hunting one . . . Dad says they're the ultimate test for a hunter. But I didn't really want to."

Spoken like a true sociopath. Like father, like son, apparently.

"Do you want me to kill you?" she asked evenly.

"No."

She looked into his eyes from a range of about eight inches and asked, "Do you have a gun under the tarp?"

"No. My dad says you're a sniper. I figured if I tried to outshoot you, I'd lose."

She saw no sign of dishonesty or evasion in his eyes. Of course, sociopaths were typically outstanding liars. Having no capacity for remorse, guilt, or empathy made lying much easier, as it turned out.

"I'm going to climb off you and let you sit up. Okay? But I want you to put your hands on top of your head and move very slowly. I don't want to shoot you, but I will if you make me. Understood?"

"Yes, ma'am."

Without warning, she rolled fast to one side and came to her feet in one quick move. In the blink of an eye, she was standing over Danny, her pistol in both hands, pointing down at him. She watched warily as he sat up. Using her foot, she slowly pulled the tarp off his legs. Lord, he looked like a baby. Younger even than Jaynie.

"There are several men in the woods around us right now," she told him. "I want you to keep sitting where you are and your hands in plain sight resting on your knees. If you reach for anything or they lose sight of one of your hands, they're going to kill you. And we don't want that, do we?"

"No, ma'am."

He sounded like a scared little kid. What the hell was he doing out here, playing with the big dogs? What was Bell thinking, sending his son into this deadly situation?

She glanced around and spied a boulder a few feet away. She moved over to it and sat down. She laid the pistol on its side on her right knee, still pointed at the boy, a position she was perfectly comfortable firing from. But Danny Bell didn't know that.

That, and she wasn't lying about there being operators in the darkness around them. She had faith they'd caught up with her long before she'd scaled that ridge and had been shadowing her the whole time.

"Talk to me about your father, Danny," she said evenly. "What's he like?"

"He's an assho—" He broke off. "Sorry."

"It's all right. I imagine my kids call me an asshole from time to time, too. My youngest is only a few years older than you."

"I'm twenty," he volunteered.

"What else did your father say about me in that phone call you overheard?"

"He said he didn't have the resources to deal with you right now and that he would take care of you later. He wanted that man he saw you with on TV shot."

She frowned. *On TV?* That morning in the park, where the dead girl's body had been found. There'd been a bunch of news crews with cameras. "Kyle Colgate?" she blurted.

"Yeah! That's it!" Danny threw a hand up, and she yanked her pistol up off her knee.

"Don't move that fast again, Danny. I almost shot you, and I expect the men in the woods almost did, too."

"Oh. Um, sorry." He looked around fearfully.

"Did your father say anything else?"

"He said he couldn't come after you in a half-assed way because you're . . . I think he called you sharp."

Bell respected her skill, did he? *Good to know. And bad.* It meant he would come after her with a good plan and plenty of firepower if and when he did decide to take her out.

"Does your father know you're here? Doing this?"

"No."

"What would he think about it if he did know?"

"He would think I'd better not screw it up," Danny said miserably.

"Would he be worried about you?" she tried.

"Doubtful. He's still royally pissed off at me. Hasn't spoken to me since he told me to show him why he should let me live."

"Does he get that mad often?"

"Not hardly. He gets even, but he doesn't get mad."

"Gets even how?"

"Well, if any of us—my mom, my sister, or me—breaks the house rules, he punishes us. Not that my sister ever breaks a rule."

Her hand tensed on the pistol as he reached slowly for the

sleeve of his mock turtleneck. "I don't know if you can see them in the dark, but the time he caught me smoking, he lit the whole pack of cigarettes I had one by one and put them out on my arm."

"He burned you?" She wasn't sure she managed to mask her dismay. Bell tortured his own children? *Cripes.*

Keeping her voice as even and conversational as she could, she asked, "What do you think of your father?"

"What do you mean?"

"Do you like him? Think he's a good guy?"

Danny burst out, "I hate his guts. He's a monster. I would kill him if I thought I could pull it off. But he's so paranoid and suspicious, I think he'd catch me. And then he would kill me for sure."

The pain on the young man's face called strongly to the mother in her. "No parent should burn their child or terrorize them. Your father is not a good parent or a good man."

"You're telling me," Danny replied fervently.

"I'm sorry he's been terrible to you, Danny."

He shrugged about like one of her sons would've when they were that age in response to an expression of sympathy.

She was silent, thinking, for a bit. Then she asked, "Do you know what your father's job is?"

"He works for the CIA."

"Have you ever heard him use the word *Scorpius*?"

Danny frowned, thinking. "I don't think so."

"You said you got the Whitehorse file out of your father's safe. Were there other files in it?"

"Uh-huh. Drawers full of them. Hundreds of 'em."

What she wouldn't give to have a look through all of those. She pondered the odds of getting a search warrant to seize them. Probably low in the absence of any solid evidence whatsoever that Bell was a Russian mole.

"So, Danny. What am I going to do with you?"

"Turn me loose?" he suggested hopefully.

"Do you want to go home to your father without having killed me?" she asked gently.

The stark fear that wreathed his features was wrenching to witness. He really was terrified of his father. *Smart lad.* Danny shook his head vigorously in the negative.

"What do you want to do?" she asked him.

He lifted his anguished gaze to hers. "If I could, I'd leave home and get as far away from my old man as possible. I'd never come back. And I'd never speak to him again."

She tilted her head to study him intently. "What if I helped arrange that for you?"

"I told you. He's in the CIA. He could find me no matter where I went."

She pursed her lips. "Oh, I expect I could figure out how to hide you from him permanently. If that's what you wanted."

"I do want that! I *hate* him." A pause, then he added, "But why would you help me? I was going to kill you."

"Were you lying when you said you didn't really want to kill me?"

"No, ma'am."

"Well, there you have it. I was just talking with my son about this very thing. I was telling him how, when people are at their most desperate or most terrified, they either make the best decisions of their lives or the worst ones. I think we can both agree that trying to kill me was not your best decision ever."

He nodded. "Christine—she's my sister—says I'm too impulsive. Disorganized. That I'm going to get myself in trouble."

"Organization and impulse control can be learned," she commented. "Would you like to learn them both?"

"Yes."

His answer was firm. No hesitation.

"Fair warning. They aren't fun to learn."

"I don't care, Mrs. Warwick. If I could learn those and get away from my old man, I'd be the happiest person ever."

"Here's the thing, Danny. I agree with you about your father being able to track you down pretty much anywhere. The way I hear it, the CIA is very good at that kind of thing."

All the hope visibly whooshed out of him, and he slumped in dejection.

"What I think we need to do is convince your father you've died."

"Died?" he echoed. "How?"

"What if we fake your death and then I send you far, far away? To someplace you can learn self-discipline and self-control."

"You'd do that for me?" Danny asked in a small voice.

"Well, it's better than me killing you and making a mortal enemy of your father, don't you think?"

"It sure is."

"I'm going to ask my friends to come out of the woods, and I'm going to step away to have a conversation with them. They may want to restrain you . . . for everyone's safety. Is that okay?"

"Anything, if you can get me away from my old man for good."

In short order, two of Ben's guys materialized out of the shadows. They zip-tied Danny's hands and ankles, picked him up, and carried him away from his gear. While one of the men pulled back the tarp and secured Danny's laptop, Helen moved out of the young man's line of sight.

Ben and a half-dozen of his operators were waiting for her in the trees.

"What do you have in mind?" Ben asked her in a low voice.

"Use the boy to bait a trap for Bell."

Ben frowned. "The kid said his old man wants to kill him. Are you sure Bell will bite?"

"Only one way to find out."

The SOG operators, all experienced at planning complex special operations on the fly, quickly laid out a plan. In their scenario, Danny would appear to be positioned in the building with the Whitehorse file. When Bell approached and was in visual range, Helen would go inside the barn. She would "find" the trap, bolt from the building, and the barn would blow up, with Danny apparently still inside.

They didn't have time tonight to pull one of Danny's teeth—at least not humanely—but tomorrow, a dentist would extract one of the youth's molars. It would be planted in the wreckage of the barn for a medical examiner to find and run DNA testing on.

"How are we going to draw Bell out here?" she finally asked.

"The kid's cell phone. If he turns it on, Bell ought to be able to geolocate it."

Helen frowned. "I think it'll take more than that. We have to get word to Bell that Daniel is going after me tonight."

Silence reigned around the circle of operators. Nobody had any ideas on how to do that believably.

"Let me ask Danny," she finally suggested.

She walked over to him and explained the problem.

He had an immediate idea. "If I call my sister and tell her what I'm doing, she'll tattle on me instantly. Always does. She thinks she's keeping me out of worse trouble by telling the old man whenever I break a rule and not giving me a chance to cover it up."

Given what the boy had said about Bell, she was inclined to agree with the sister.

Helen ran the idea past Ben, and he approved it.

Danny turned on his cell phone and made the call to Christine. As he ended the call, he said in satisfaction, "Oh, yeah. She's running straight to the bastard as we speak. She was spitting mad at me."

And now it was a waiting game.

While she waited, Helen made some phone calls and finalized a plan for the young man. He would probably need facial surgery to foil the facial recognition technology that was becoming prevalent. After he healed from that, a general in the Israel Defense Forces who owed her a favor would see to it Danny got a new identity and spent a couple of years in the Israeli army.

The fact of the matter was that people of a certain psychological profile were very useful to the government, and very rare. Whereas Bell had recruited sociopaths who were just organized enough to follow his rules but would kill without compunction, the government wanted people with milder sociopathic tendencies, people who were capable of self-regulating while doing dirty work for Uncle Sam. People who, to put it in Danny's terms, were organized and had excellent impulse control.

If Danny could be taught those, someday he could be a very useful asset to the United States. The fact that he'd honestly expressed excitement at the idea of killing her but had also not particularly wanted to follow through on it gave her hope that he was a trainable sociopath.

And then there was the added satisfaction of stealing Richard Bell's son from him. The man deserved to lose his child after the way he'd treated the boy.

For a moment, the uncomfortable question of whether or not she deserved her children flitted through her brain.

No. She was not Richard Bell. She was not a cold-blooded sociopath. She loved her children and would never hurt one of them. She'd been the best parent she could be in and around the demands of her career.

Her thoughts turned back to the burning question of how to prove what she already knew—that Richard Bell was Scorpius.

CHAPTER 51

HELEN HAD SET UP A TEMPORARY SHOOTER'S NEST ABOUT FOUR hundred feet north of the barn, as far back as she could go and not lose sight of the building through the thick forest. From here, she could look straight inside the big, open sliding door on the north side of the structure. Even if Bell wasn't interested in hunting her tonight, he would surely be very interested in retrieving the Operation Whitehorse file.

Before she'd made her way into the woods, she'd swung by the barn and photographed the entire file with her phone. It had taken a while to do—there were over a hundred pages of documents and pictures. And now that she was hunkered down behind a fallen log, her face greasepainted, chilling under a ghillie net until Bell showed up, she had some time to kill. She pulled out her phone.

The front section of the file was mostly profiles of the candidates, with detailed notes—much more detailed than in the CIA archive file—on their performance in training and methods he'd used to trigger them to kill. She skimmed through those, interested to discover that every graduate who survived the training was given a new identity. She made a mental note to read all the training notes later when she had more time.

Next up in the folder was a pile of eight-by-ten head shots. Danny had mentioned there was writing on the back of each picture, and she'd made sure to snap pictures of the backs as well. One by one, she scrolled through the photographs. They were numbered sequentially, and each one had several dates written on the back of it.

She guessed the first date was the recruitment date. The second, usually delayed for a while, was probably the start of training date. The third date was usually exactly three months after the second date, and she guessed that was the end of training date.

For the pictures that had no fourth date, the third date was always less than three months after the second. She gathered those were the candidates who didn't make it through the full three months of training and were terminated somewhere in the middle of the program.

All of the pictures that included a fourth date had three full months between the second and third dates. Clearly, they'd graduated from Bell's twisted little program. The fourth date, then, must be an activation date for the candidates who'd survived the program. Those dates were always at least six months after the graduation date. Was that because the assassins had to recover from facial reconstruction surgery and assume their new identities before they were considered active?

She scrolled back to study each picture more closely.

The fifth picture was the face of an unsmiling young woman. Was that Polina? The eyes looked similar. If this woman had plastic surgery to elongate the shape of the eyes, narrow the nose, widen the mouth, round off the forehead, soften the jaw . . .

This was definitely Polina Semyonova, pre-surgery. Interesting. She'd been the first candidate to survive the training program.

Helen studied the next several photos in detail. Her job had required her to be an expert at identifying faces. Often, her targets had changed hairstyles, aged, or even disguised themselves. At a minimum, she usually had several photographs from different angles and distances to go off when she made an identification before taking her shot. But sometimes only a single photo, or perhaps an old one, was all she had.

She wasn't sure who she might be able to identify from these pre-reconstruction pictures, but she memorized the faces carefully.

When she got to the one labeled *No. 10*, she frowned. The man looked vaguely familiar. Was that . . . Roger Skidmore? It was harder to see Skidmore in this guy's features than it had been to see Polina in her picture, but she was fairly sure it was him.

If she'd been sent out to kill Skidmore, she wouldn't have taken the shot had she seen this guy, but she would've called in a possible sighting and asked for verification from Yosef.

The facial recognition team at the agency was going to have a field day trying to figure out who these people had become.

She thought number eighteen might be Mason Chunenko, the hacker on her Scorpius hunting team, but she wasn't sure of that identification.

Subjects nineteen through twenty-four, all young men, differed sharply from the others in that they had longer hair. There wasn't a military regulation haircut among them. The backs of all six pictures had only three dates written on them in Bell's blocky script. In every case, the pairs of dates that indicated the start and termination of training were only a few days—or a week at most—apart.

She recalled from the CIA's archived Whitehorse file that Richard had recruited six civilians for Operation Whitehorse, but the experiment had been a total failure. She made a mental note to read Bell's notes on their training later. If she was going to try to help Danny Bell function in the world safely as an adult, maybe she could pick up a few hints from Bell's notes on why these young, murder-curious sociopaths had failed.

Did the six dead civilians' families ever find out what happened to them? Probably not. Bell didn't strike her as the kind of man who would bother coming up with a compassionate cover story to explain their deaths, let alone shipping the bodies home for burial.

And it wasn't as if the CIA was about to run back to the families and confess that their sons had met untimely ends in a wildly unethical CIA training program run by a monster.

Number twenty-five made her pause for a long time. She was sure she'd seen a similar face before. But she couldn't put her finger on just where.

It took several minutes of staring at the picture, and finally squinting her eyes to blur the image, for it to hit her. It was the man she'd killed last winter in the woods near where the DaVinci Killer crucified Ryan Goetz.

Everyone had thought initially that she'd killed Scorpius, but he'd turned out to be a John Doe wearing the distinctive hat and coat she'd seen on Scorpius the one time she'd glimpsed him in person—the same John Doe that Greg Ford had failed to put a name to after months of research. If the man she'd killed had been number twenty-five, that would explain his complete lack of an identity.

More importantly, if Scorpius had used one of Bell's assassins to impersonate himself at the Goetz killing, it was yet another bit of circumstantial evidence for Scorpius and Bell being one and the same.

In all, there were thirty-seven pictures.

A total of sixteen had only three dates on the back, meaning they'd failed to complete the training and died.

Of course, two of those who'd made it through, Polina and number twenty-five, were also dead. Helen winced. It couldn't have endeared her to Bell that she'd personally shot two of his assassins.

A possible third—Skidmore—was also dead, which left Bell with eighteen active assassins. How many more of Bell's killers had died along the way? Surely at least a few. Maybe Bell had recorded that somewhere in these meticulous notes.

The last picture, number thirty-seven, was definitely of someone from the military and had only two dates on it, spaced some six months apart—clearly a recruitment date and a training start date just over a month ago. Which, if she was guessing correctly, meant the guy was currently in training. So Bell was still recruiting sociopathic assassin-wannabes when he came across them.

Where were they being trained, anyway? She made a mental

note to ask the CIA to research private property owned by Richard Bell, particularly a large parcel of land in a very remote location.

At least Bell's success rate at getting his candidates through training without having to kill them had gotten significantly better over the years. Of the last ten candidates who'd started the program, only one had been terminated.

There was no specific mention in the file of who was spotting candidates for him, but Bell had to be using a psychiatrist or psych-test administrator to find potential assassins. The CIA shouldn't have too much trouble figuring out who that was . . . and turning him or her.

Behind the photographs were pages and pages of encrypted data stapled into four-and five-page packets. She would lay odds these were the new identities that had been built for Richard's killers. They were about the right length for a detailed legend, and some of the encrypted information looked grouped, like addresses and phone numbers.

She counted, and there were thirty packets in all. If she was right about what they were, he had pre-ginned identities ready and waiting for the next dozen graduates of his sick school for sociopaths.

At the very back of the file was a paper-clipped sheaf of hand-written pages on lined notebook paper. It was a list of names, followed by a one- or two-digit number, and a date.

Oh. My. God. Is this the Operation Whitehorse kill list?

The dates ran in chronological order, and the numbers beside each name ranged from numbers five to thirty-six. Those must correspond to which assassin had made the hit.

Frowning, she glanced at the very end of the last page of names. And stared. The last name read *Colgate, Kyle, no. 5, April 13.*

More chilling than that was the second to last name. *Reinhold, Lester, no. 26, April 12.* So Reinhold *was* dead, and not merely lost in the wilds of Alaska.

The entry above Reinhold was *Mizuki, Andrew, no. 10, April 2.*

She flipped back through the photographs to the back of the

picture she thought was Roger Skidmore. He was Subject no. 10. So Skidmore *had* put the poison in Andrew's sake. The same sake she'd presumably been going to drink, too.

Had she been a target of that kill, too? She would probably never know. Bell obviously wasn't recording the names of people who were collateral kills to the primary ones. Otherwise, Reinhold's two teenaged sons and the bush pilot would also be named on Bell's kill list.

She shook her head and pocketed her phone. The worst of it was that Operation Whitehorse had been approved by the House Intelligence Committee. The whole program had been completely legal, at least initially.

For that matter, it still might be legal. The CIA encouraged officers to freelance funding for projects if they could. As long as the project was approved, which Whitehorse definitely had been, someone like Bell could continue to run it and finance it until someone else told him to shut it down.

A voice came through her earpiece, startling her back to the present. The comm guy said, "The drone is ready to go, Mrs. Warwick."

"Thank you," she murmured. She had a little surprise in store for Richard when he arrived. He was too careful a man to just barge into the woods to retrieve his file and possibly kill his son while he hunted her. The meticulous notes he'd kept on Operation Whitehorse were proof enough of that.

The way she figured it, he would bring all the high-tech gear he had, reconnoiter the area thoroughly, and only move in when he was sure he had the advantage.

And she planned to use that against him if she could.

She listened to a flurry of radio check-ins as the SOG team reported in individually that they were in place and ready to go. There had been a debate over whether or not to mic up Danny, and it had ultimately been decided not to risk Richard Bell spotting an earpiece.

Ben was the last to report in. "The decoy's in place, and the kid's clear. Going silent."

Tactical operations such as this were generally run under complete radio silence rules. Only a life-threatening crisis would pro-voke any of the team members to transmit from here on out.

Which was fine with her. She wasn't used to working with a big team, and frankly, a bunch of radio calls in her ear would distract her more than they would help her. She checked her watch. It had been a little over two hours since Danny called his sister. From here on out, they could expect Bell to show up at any time.

Using her rifle scope, she surveyed the area in front of her. Somewhere out there, Ben and his team were hunkered down just like her, waiting and watching. They had set up a perimeter about four hundred yards out from the barn and would be facing outward, looking for Bell and anyone he brought with him.

The drone was still somewhere overhead in the dark, looking down on them all, and the comm guy in his tent would be moni-toring the live feed from it. He should be the first person to spot Bell, well outside the SOG team's perimeter.

The night sounds had never really stopped—Ben and his team were silent types even when they weren't trying to be—but the frogs, crickets, and other night insects became noticeably louder around her.

Back-to-nature hides were not her preference, but snipers had to take what they could get. This was certainly not the first time she'd lain on the cold ground, getting poked by sticks, her body going stiff with the damp and chill in the air. Although she did fervently hope it was the last time she had to do this.

As the night settled around her, she, too, settled into the wait. It wasn't uncommon for hours to go by between the safe window for her insertion and the moment when she took a shot.

She passed the next hour trying to figure out various ways Richard and his men might approach the barn. It all boiled down to whether or not he chose to come for her tonight. Given that Danny reported overhearing his father say he wanted her dead but didn't have the resources to spare to go after her properly, her guess was that Richard would make a run at her. If she wasn't mistaken, he wasn't the kind to walk away when an opportunity landed in his lap.

She did wonder who he would bring with him. If he was Scorpius, he might commandeer whatever was left of the Spetsnaz team in town to kill her. Of course, he might have a few of his private assassins hanging around DC and bring them along.

Indeed, the more she thought about it, the more certain she was that he would prefer to work with his own people instead of a Russian team he didn't know very well. Also, he would be able to call all the shots with his own team. A Spetsnaz team wouldn't want to take orders from some American civilian, even if he was a famous mole for their side.

A voice over her earpiece startled her back into the present. "Look sharp, everyone. Incoming."

That was the comm guy.

"I've got a step van pulling off the main road, headed this way," the comm guy added.

Given that the dirt road leading to this place went nowhere else and dead-ended at the barn, odds were excellent Bell was in the van.

The comm guy announced, "Going dark now. Good hunting."

The downside of her plan to mess with Richard Bell was they, too, would lose the live video feed from the drone while Richard and his team moved into position.

The Hornet pilot would put up the nano-drone and do his best to spot and track the incoming hostiles, but it wasn't ideal. For the next few minutes, the good guys would all be operating in the blind.

But if Danny was to get away from his father and make a clean start in life, they had to convince Richard his son had died. And doing so was going to take a little trickery.

Helen scanned the area in front of her continuously, looking for the slightest sign of movement. As the minutes ticked away— ten minutes, then twenty—her tension mounted. She never heard the van, so it must've stopped well away from the barn. Which put Richard on foot, approaching the building.

C'mon. Show yourself. Where are you?

Another ten minutes passed. Something was wrong. Richard's team must be fanning out through the woods to set up their own perimeter before he went in. But it was taking them too long. Experienced special operators could cover a mile in rough terrain in less time than his team had been here.

What are you doing, Richard?

Of more concern was the fact that none of Ben's guys had clicked their microphone to indicate they had a visual on anyone.

Was Richard standing off, trying to get a visual on Danny before he moved in? Or had he gone straight to the part where he combed through these woods hunting for her?

The ghillie net she was under had reflective fibers woven into it that would disguise both her heat and her visual signal from scans. If Richard had put up a drone of his own or tried to hijack the SOG drone, he shouldn't be able to spot her—

She was so tense that the faintest of noises behind her made her freeze. She felt goose bumps rise on her skin, and the hair on her forearms stood up.

Crap. Crap, crap, crap.

None of Ben's men were stationed behind her.

CHAPTER 52

*T*HREE HOURS EARLIER . . .

When Ben agreed to help her stage Danny's death, his guys cut off Danny's zip ties, and the whole group hiked back to the barn to reset Danny's trap, this time to catch Bell instead of her . . . and with significantly more sophisticated gear in place of Danny's cheap setup.

As the SOG team went to work carefully unwiring and rewiring Danny's explosives and installing their own cameras and motion detection gear, Helen peeled away from the group and headed for the command tent.

When she ducked inside, the comm guy looked up at her in surprise. "Thought you'd be setting up your hide."

She shrugged. "I might have an idea. Am I right that the imagery from the drone you've got loitering overhead is encrypted when it's transmitted to you?"

"Yes."

"Is it possible to unencrypt the video feed?"

He frowned. "Yes. But why would I do that?"

"Which brings me to my second question," she said. "Do you have the capability here to take prefilmed video and loop it, then upload that video to the drone and have it replay the looped video?"

"We don't usually do stuff like that in the field." He sounded grumpy—or perhaps just puzzled.

"I'm sure you don't. But is it possible?"

His frown deepened. "Yeah, I guess so. It would take a little fiddling with the uplink, but I think I could do it from here."

"So if we were to put Danny in the barn for the next ten or fifteen minutes, you could film him sitting in there with the drone's look-through-walls camera. Then you could make a loop of that video and send it to the drone to broadcast unencrypted?"

"You think Scorpius will try to intercept the video feed?" the comm guy asked, starting to smile a little.

"I think it's worth a try. He and his guys have access to the same gear and toys you guys do. I'm assuming Ben and his team can intercept drone signals?"

A short nod from the comm guy. "That's my job, in fact."

"Do you always need this tent and fancy setup to do it?" she asked.

"Nah. I've got portable stuff I can use in the field."

She smiled brightly. "Well, then! I'll let you get to it. I'm going to tell the team to plant Danny inside the barn for, say, ten minutes? Is that long enough for you to get a good loop?"

"Yep. That's plenty. How long until Scorpius gets here?"

She considered quickly. "Two hours, give or take. It's about an hour drive from his home to here, and I figure he'll gear up before he heads out."

"Will he come alone?" the guy asked.

"No idea. If he thinks his kid is out here alone, he might. But if he intends to kill me while he's out here, he'll bring help."

"How much help?"

"Again, no idea. We're gonna have to wing it."

He smiled grimly. "That's what we do best."

Helen strained hard to pick up any more movement behind her. *There.* Another faint scuff of sound.

The comm guy wasn't reporting any hostiles out here, which meant he was still looping the video of Danny hiding in the barn behind a pile of canoes. Which also meant Richard's guys had indeed hacked the drone and were watching the fake video. The good news was the video wouldn't show any of Ben's SOG guys currently positioned around the barn.

The bad news was whoever was behind her was headed this way.

She dared not make any fast moves. It was torture, rolling over at the speed of a glacier, inch by inch, knowing someone was close. Very close now.

Close enough for her to hear leaves rustling. Which placed him no more than a hundred feet from her, and probably closer to fifty.

Finally making it onto her back, she eased a small portion of the ghillie net aside so she could poke her scope through the netting and weeds woven into it.

Holy crap. A man was directly in front of her, no more than forty feet away, creeping forward step by stealthy step. If she shot him, even with the sound suppressor on her weapon, Richard would surely hear the shot. He would either run or he and his team would unleash all their weapons on her. Neither was an ideal outcome.

The man in front of her scanned the area before him through the scope of his rifle.

Please, God, ghillie net. Do your thing and hide my body heat.

She held her breath, finger poised on the trigger, her gaze riveted on the barrel of his weapon, swinging left and right. The moment it trained on her, he was dead.

Closer and closer he came. Thirty feet.

Twenty.

Ten.

How on earth wasn't he seeing her? She could actually hear him breathing.

He took another step, veering to his right.

What was he doing?

Another step to the right.

Then it hit her. He was going around the end of the giant log she was tucked up against. Did she dare try to move, to track him with her weapon, or should she lie perfectly still and let him move out of her line of sight?

Caution won out, and she lay under the camouflage net, perfectly still, her rifle pointing uselessly at the woods behind her. She strained to look to her left with her eyes while not moving her head. He took another step and moved out of view. She squeezed her eyes tightly shut, the tension almost too much to bear.

She was a sitting duck. Completely defenseless.

She heard him take a quiet step.

Another.

Was he past the log? Did she dare turn her head to look?

A rustle of leaves.

Okay, that was definitely on the other side of the log.

Slowly, slowly, she rolled to her belly.

The man was kneeling on one knee about fifteen feet beyond the log, gazing intently at the barn through a sophisticated telescopic sight—

She recognized that model. It had state-of-the-art heat sensing technology in it. Even through the metal wall of the barn, it would light up Danny's hiding spot.

A spot Danny was no longer in.

Swearing silently, she reached down to her ankle and pulled out the field knife strapped there. She rose to her feet, the ghillie net still draped over her head. But she had no time to get rid of it.

She sat her right hip on the giant log and swung both feet over it silently. She came to her feet smoothly, knife brandished before her.

One careful, silent step.

Another.

The man lowered his rifle and reached for his throat. *Crap.* He had a microphone and was going to report that Danny wasn't in the barn.

She lunged forward.

The man heard her at the last moment and started to turn

around and come to his feet. She barreled into him, knocking him forward onto his face. His hands flew up to catch himself.

Which meant he wasn't pressing the transmit button on his throat mic, at any rate. She sprawled on top of him.

Being a trained operator, he flung himself to one side before he'd barely hit the dirt, rolling on top of her. However, she'd anticipated the move and flung her left arm up over her head and her right arm—the one with the knife—out to the side.

She grabbed a handful of his hair with her left hand and yanked back hard. As his hands came up to grab for that, she reached around his right forearm with the blade of her field knife and slammed it against the left side of his neck as hard as she could.

He actually helped her slit his throat by throwing his forearm forward hard against the inside of her elbow. The tilt of her wrist meant the razor-sharp blade slid along the side of his neck just under his jaw, slicing through everything in its path.

He let out a gurgling cry and flung himself in the other direction, rolling off her. She pushed up, not as fast as he did, but fast enough. She threw herself across his back and stabbed at the right side of his neck.

It wasn't a pretty blow and partially missed its mark, piercing the front side of his neck at the larynx. He tried to shout, but with a steel blade buried in his voice box, he managed only a choking sound.

She leaned into the blade, twisting it toward the back of his neck and driving it deeper.

He made horrible gasping noises as she severed his trachea, and he commenced gasping through the impromptu tracheotomy.

She shoved up off his back and stumbled to her feet, watching him clutch at his throat with both hands. Black liquid gushed between his fingers. He fumbled at the wound for a few more seconds and then collapsed as his life's blood poured out onto the ground. His right hand fell, palm up, fingers slightly bent.

In her night optical goggles, she saw something that froze her in shock. She reached down to rub her thumb across the pad of the dead man's thumb. She wiped away most of the blood, but enough remained in the crevices of his skin to bring his fingerprint into sharp, black relief against the lime green of his still warm flesh.

A V-shaped scar was clearly visible in the dark lines of his bloody fingerprint. So her intuition had been correct. Bell and his killers were behind the tortures and murders. George Vincent was going to be ecstatic when she delivered the body of this guy to him.

Giving herself a mental shake, she felt quickly at the dead man's ears and pulled out the earpiece she found in his left one.

Pulling out her own left earpiece, she stuffed the dead man's awkwardly into her own ear. She'd hadn't even risen to her feet yet when she heard a male voice say low, "Verify visual on Danny in the barn."

She waited for a few seconds, praying someone else would answer.

Nada.

Drat. That order was directed at her dead guy.

No way could she successfully fake being the dead man over a radio. She shoved frantically at the dead man's shoulder to roll him partly onto his side. Grimacing as she reached into the wreckage of his throat, she felt around for a microphone on a neck strap. Hot blood still seeped sluggishly from the wound, but without his heart pumping it out the severed arteries of his neck, the flow had all but stopped.

There. His throat microphone. She fumbled for the transmit button, and when she finally felt it, pressed it once. Hopefully, the voice on the other end would take that for an affirmative.

Either way, she needed to move. The insects around her had gone silent in response to the sound of their fight and his muted cries.

She grabbed the ghillie net, which had fallen off her back in the struggle, moved swiftly around the log, and scooped up her rifle.

Draping the ghillie net over her head and wrapping it around her like a cloak, she shrouded its ends over her arms and moved out cautiously to the east.

She stopped in the lee of a tree trunk with a branch coming off it, chest-high. She wasn't quite at a ninety-degree angle from the barn's open door, but she was close. Propping her rifle in the crook of the branch and tree trunk, she gazed down at the barn, where she knew Danny's clothes had been stuffed with leaves and posed in a crouch in the corner of the barn. His cell phone, turned on but silenced, would be lying on the floor beside the decoy dummy.

She was looking into the barn from about as oblique an angle as possible, and she couldn't see the decoy from here. Which meant in the absence of Richard or one of his men actually stepping inside the barn, they wouldn't be able to visually verify Danny's presence or absence.

Would Bell move in on the barn now, in the belief that his son was indeed inside?

Or would he send in a flunky to take out his boy?

She still had a hard time wrapping her head around the idea of a parent killing his own child.

A microphone clicked several times fast in her right ear, and she froze. One of Ben's guys was in trouble.

It *click-click-click*ed again. Or maybe that was another mic. Those clicks had been slower than the first set. *Damn.* What was happening around her?

The comm guy's voice said in her right ear, "RPA drone's being jammed by hostiles. I've taken all the cameras offline. Everyone's running blind."

Satisfaction coursed through her. She'd guessed right that Richard would mess with the drone. Now if only he'd bought the faked video.

Ben's voice barely breathed, "Check in."

She counted the clicks one by one . . . six . . . seven . . . eight. She waited for any more clicks.

Nothing.

Crap!

She reached up and clicked her mic once. Four of Ben's operators were down. What the hell was going on out here?

Of course, she knew the answer to that. Richard's assassins were out here, hunting. And clearly, they were having some success.

She considered coming up on mic to tell the team to pull back. That killing Scorpius tonight wasn't worth the lives of good men and women. She could keep her investigation going. Find a way to prove Bell was Scorpius and let the legal system take him down—

A movement in her scope riveted her attention.

Something lurked at the far edge of the clearing beyond the barn. She was at the one-two corner—the northeast one—and the movement had been near the four-one corner—the northwest corner of the barn. The trees came within about fifty feet of that barn at that point, and the canopy of overhanging limbs came within about twenty feet of the barn wall, creating deep shadows beneath them.

She rarely practiced shooting through night optical devices and, in frustration, flipped them up. For a moment, the forest around her was nothing but blackness. But then shapes and shadows and textures resolved before her.

Placing her eye to her rifle sight again, she focused in on the spot where she'd seen that movement.

She estimated the distance at 250 feet, close enough she didn't need to bother with windage adjustments, particularly since only the lightest of breezes caressed her cheek.

A shadow within the shadows moved. A man.

About six foot two. Big guy. Thick.

Was that Richard? The man in her sight had the right build to be him.

She watched in perfect, predatory stillness as the man raised a rifle wrapped in shredded camo fabric. Slowly, he scanned 270 degrees around him, taking in the whole clearing and trees beyond.

She had almost the whole tree between her and him, and a length of ghillie net still draped over her exposed arm. She held her position, not moving a muscle.

The man lowered his rifle. Eased toward the door of the barn.

Kill him now or try to move in on him and incapacitate him without killing him? Logic said to keep him alive. But the fear that had been simmering in her gut for weeks argued for just killing him and being done with it. An image of Jaynie laughing and hugging Gray flashed through her mind. *Right. Her family. Bell would kill them all to get to her.*

Reaching for her throat, she breathed into her mic, "On my mark, blow the barn."

The comm guy had the detonator the team had rigged to the rewired explosive array. They'd assured her they'd placed Danny's dynamite to maximum effect and the entire structure would blow to Kingdom Come, with nothing left but fragments no larger than her hand.

She needed to wait until Bell was all the way in the barn to make sure he got caught in the main blast. But she also didn't want to give him time to spot the decoy and report it to the others as a setup.

Just a few more steps. She wedged her rifle in the crook of the tree and clapped her hands over her ears as Bell took the last few steps toward the barn.

He disappeared inside the structure.

"Mark," she breathed.

She barely had time to squeeze her eyes shut before the whole barn blew up and a spectacular explosion rocked the night. Searing heat slammed into her, and the concussion nearly knocked her off her feet. And she was behind a tree that had absorbed the brunt of the blast wave.

Her ears rang like crazy, and even with her eyes closed, her night vision was shot. She flipped down the night optical devices and saw only a sea of blindingly bright green.

Quickly, she reached up to her temple and dialed down the goggles' sensitivity. She was abjectly grateful as the forest looking away from the blast came into green and black relief. Bell might've been vaporized, but his killers were out here somewhere.

Time to go hunting.

CHAPTER 53

*T*HE FIRST ORDER OF BUSINESS WAS TO GET THE DRONE UP AND RUN-
ning again. To that end, she crouched behind her tree and whispered, "Bell's dead and decoy Danny with him. Can we bring up
the drone and re-encrypt its live feed?"

"On it," the comm guy answered. He sounded rather harried at
the moment.

She headed out into the forest cautiously. A Special Forces operator she was not. But Ben's team was out here dying to protect
her. The least she could do was lend her skill with a rifle to them.

She moved a couple of hundred yards directly away from the
fire, heading north. Behind her, the debris had settled, and the
contents of the barn were burning in a low, wide fire filling most
of the clearing.

She turned east to start a big, circular sweep of the area around
the fire. Something—someone—moved in the distance to her
left, and she veered right, away from whoever was out there. She
really didn't want to go head-to-head against one of Richard's
guys if she could help it. She would much rather sneak up behind
one and ambush him without a fight.

She zigzagged along a general course around to the east side of
the barn, sometimes drawing within a hundred yards of the
wreckage of the barn, sometimes heading directly away from it.
Always she kept her path random. Unpredictable. Sometimes she

moved fast, and sometimes she stood still for several minutes before creeping forward at a snail's pace.

She'd passed what she guessed to be due east of the barn and was starting to angle to the south when she thought she detected motion ahead of her and turned toward it. But before she spotted whomever she'd heard, she caught another movement off to her left side, about the same distance away as the first time.

Frowning, she turned hard to the right, away from both sounds.

She continued her wide arc and, a few minutes later, spotted yet another glimpse of the person shadowing her. Again, he was directly off her left shoulder at a range of perhaps two hundred feet.

A suspicion that she was being herded toward some destination took root in her gut.

The comm guy still didn't have drone overwatch restored, so she had no way of knowing what waited ahead of her.

How did the person off her left flank keep showing up at that exact distance away from her, staying even with her forward progress? It was almost as if he knew where she was.

But she'd been zigzagging randomly, and changing speed randomly, too, since she'd first sighted him. It was almost as if he was tracking her . . .

She swore under her breath.

The IFF tracker the comm guy had put in her pocket hours ago. If Richard's guys could jam a drone transmission, they could surely hack an Identification-Friend-or-Foe frequency.

Reaching into her vest pocket, she pulled out the transmitter. In her night vision goggles, it put out a bright white light. Cripes. If the guy off to her left could see that, no wonder he was having no trouble keeping pace with her so precisely.

Frankly, she was shocked he hadn't shot her already.

She looked for an off switch but couldn't find it. Her initial impulse was to jam it under a rock and run. But then she thought better of it.

She must have rope somewhere in this utility vest they'd given her. It took opening several pouches until she found it. Quickly, she tied one end around the garage-door-sized transmitter, criss-crossing it in both directions so the rope was securely fastened around the radio.

She unwound the entire rope and was disappointed to see it was only about thirty feet long. She looked around. *There. A nice thicket with lots of underbrush.*

She set the transmitter on top of a knee-high boulder in front of the thicket, playing out the nylon line as she backed up. When she reached the heavy brush, she painstakingly lifted vines, bram-bles, and low branches and crawled backward under the mess.

All the while, she wove aside branches and obstructions, creat-ing a narrow tunnel no bigger around than her arm that led straight back to the IFF radio.

Her hair caught painfully and her sleeves ripped, but she kept going until she reached the end of the rope. Then she scooped up a pile of dirt and leaves to elevate her chest, stretched out atop the tiny rise, unfolded the integral bipod attached to the barrel of her rifle, and draped her right arm around the stock of her weapon.

Her finger came to rest on the trigger.

Nothing like going fishing for humans. Literally.

It took about ten minutes, but the guy tracking her finally couldn't resist moving in for a closer look at why the IFF trans-mitter had gone motionless.

Oh, he was cautious and came in slow. And he was good. She never heard a thing, and she wouldn't have seen him at all had she not been looking directly over the boulder and IFF transmit-ter in the direction he came from.

His utter silence only reinforced her certainty that he'd been herding her toward some sort of ambush.

She waited until he was perhaps twenty-five feet from the IFF transmitter, close enough to see the infrared signal clearly, but not close enough to make out the radio itself. And then she gave a yank on the rope, pulling the transmitter off the rock. It fell harmlessly to the ground behind the boulder where she could see it but he could not.

The man froze, his rifle plastered to his cheek.

She would get one shot at him. If she didn't kill him, he was plenty close enough to return fire and take her out.

She lined up his nose carefully in her sight. A shot directly through the nose would send the round straight through his head and out through the medulla oblongata—the bottommost part of the brain where it joined the spine. All of life's vital functions were controlled from the brain stem, and a shot through it caused the target to simply drop dead without triggering any reflexive clenching of the hand that might cause her target to fire off a shot at her as he died.

He took one slow, cautious step forward, rolling carefully from heel to toe. He paused.

She squeezed the trigger.

He dropped like a marionette whose strings had all been cut at once.

The sound of her shot was impossibly loud, though, and would draw everyone and their uncle. She pushed up to her feet and bolted forward, straight at the guy she'd just killed.

She tore clear of the thicket and turned left, sprinting for all she was worth back in the direction she'd come from. Panic dug its spurs hard in her sides, pushing her to a speed she didn't know she possessed.

Behind her an enormous volley of gunfire burst out, some close, and some more distant. It went on for perhaps a minute, shot after shot ringing out in the night, but she just ran and ran.

Finally, when she thought she'd run all the way back to nearly where she'd started and her lungs felt on fire, she stopped and doubled over, panting in great heaving gasps.

She'd lost her ghillie net somewhere in her mad dash. She didn't know where Ben's guys were, and she had no idea where to go now.

Finally catching her breath a little bit, she straightened painfully to have a look around. All she saw were trees and more trees. She didn't recognize the terrain. A wave of disorientation rolled over her.

Great. She was lost in the middle of a great, hulking forest full of assassins who wanted to kill her.

And without her IFF transmitter, Ben's guys couldn't track her and find her.

Still panting hard, she radioed in a raw whisper, "Hostiles have hacked our IFF frequency. Go to backup."

She didn't remember anybody briefing a backup frequency, but surely the SOG team had one.

Another voice came up quickly. It was the comm guy. "I've got overwatch up."

Thank God.

She leaned back against a tree, still working on catching her breath as he began to call out rapid-fire locations of the tangoes for Ben and his remaining operators and vectoring the SOG team in on the targets.

It took a shockingly short amount of time for Ben and his guys to take out the five hostiles clustered on the southeast side of the barn.

Southeast, huh? Yep, the last guy she'd killed had been herding her like a lamb, straight into a slaughter. Any remorse for killing him evaporated.

She jolted as the com guy said, "I've got one more tango. North of the barn by about three hundred yards. Stationary at the moment. Move out heading 310, and I'll call the distance—"

"Um, I think that's me, you're vectoring the team to," she said into her radio.

"Head for the barn," the comm guy instructed her.

"I'm a bit turned around. Not sure which way is south. But I'll walk in circles if that'll identify me."

To that end, she stepped away from the tree and paced in a circle about ten feet across. She made two full laps of it.

The comm guy came up, humor in his voice. "The tango is Mrs. Warwick. I'll vector you to her position so you can lead her out of the woods."

It was an ignominious way to end the mission. But Ben and six of his guys appeared out of the darkness in about ten minutes. Ben merely gestured for one of them to take her back to the command tent. The others veered off into the trees, presumably heading for their downed teammates.

It was all she could do to keep up with her guide, who set a blistering pace. She was panting again by the time the tent finally came into sight ahead. Ben's guy left her there and took off at a run into the woods to help with the rescue effort.

She was ready to sob with relief by the time she stepped inside and sank into one of the folding camp chairs. This running around in the woods stuff might be all in a day's work for the SOG guys, but she was completely out of her element and wiped out by the past few hours.

And this night was far from over.

CHAPTER 54

HELEN WAS SHOCKED WHEN SHE GLANCED DOWN AT HER WATCH and realized it wasn't even 1:00 AM. It felt as if dawn must be only minutes away.

Ben and his guys, guided by the drone, had found their downed teammates and were rendering first aid or carrying the bodies back.

The woman who'd done the live photo analysis from the Hornet had died, along with one of the men.

The Hornet operator had taken a round under his armpit into his chest and was in a bad way with a collapsed lung and internal bleeding. A helicopter was called in to airlift him out.

Three more guys from the SOG team had taken incoming fire. One was shot through the thigh and had a shattered femur. He was in a ton of pain, and the SOG medic loaded him up with a bunch of morphine before putting him in a black van that pulled up. The interior of the van was fully decked out as an ambulance, but no exterior markings announced it to be that. He was whisked away into the night.

A second black van, also an unmarked ambulance, took in the remaining wounded, who'd been stabilized in the woods, and left with them.

Then it was time to look at the barn and see if they could find any remnants of Richard Bell from which DNA could be lifted and a positive identification made. It was a grim business sifting through bits of concrete, burned lumber, and twisted scraps of metal.

One of Ben's guys found a chunk of—for lack of any better description—cooked meat. It was bagged up and loaded in the SOG van. A few of Ben's guys helped the comm guy take down the communications array and load it into the van. Helen was deeply impressed at how fast that happened.

Ben's guys were just winding up and getting ready to roll when a small convoy pulled up, consisting of a large step van and three black SUVs with blacked-out windows. Eight men in rough civilian clothing climbed out of the various vehicles.

"And who are you?" Helen asked.

"Cleanup crew," one of them answered.

Ah. They were here to collect the bodies of Richard's men and make them disappear.

She reported roughly where the bodies of the men she'd killed could be found, and Ben and his guys did the same. She gave a blind email address to one of the cleaners with instructions that photographs of all the deceased hostiles be sent to it.

Last, she asked the guy in charge of the cleanup crew, "Could you guys do me a favor and plant one of the bodies somewhere in Washington, DC, where it'll be found relatively quickly and reported to the police?"

The cleaner sent Ben an alarmed look.

Ben frowned. "Why?"

She explained, "The first guy I killed has a distinctive scar on the pad of his right thumb. It identifies him as the person who tortured and killed two civilians in DC in the past few weeks. Maybe we could throw the DC metro police a bone and give them their murderer? And, you know, give the families of the victims some closure?" She added lamely, "Also, it might stop rumors of there being another sicko serial killer on the loose. It could take some pressure off the police and the DA's office to catch him."

The cleanup crew looked over at Ben for permission.

He asked them gruffly, "Can you dump the body without putting yourselves in any danger of being spotted or caught?"

There was a chorus of "of courses."

He glanced back at her. "What weapon did you use? Do we need the crew to deep-six your gun?"

She shook her head. "I slit his throat. Standard field knife. Won't be traceable."

"Badass," one of Ben's guys murmured.

Ben shot his guy a quelling look.

"Do it," he told the crew.

She sent a silent message out to Mitch, wherever he was sleeping tonight. *You're welcome.*

The cleanup crew hiked off into the woods, carrying a bunch of stretchers. They had six bodies to retrieve.

A good night's work, that. By her count, Richard Bell's hit team was down to around a dozen guys. And with the pictures she'd taken of the Operation Whitehorse folder, hopefully the CIA could round up the rest and get them off the street. Especially now that Richard was dead and they had no one to give them orders . . . or keep them in line.

"That's it, then," Ben said, sounded profoundly exhausted.

"Speak for yourself," she replied. "I've got to send off Danny."

Ben asked quickly, "Do you know someone who can spirit him out of the country? Get him a new identity?"

"I called in some favors while you guys were filming Danny hiding in the barn. My guy's waiting for us now. As soon as we get back to town, I'll drive Danny over to Baltimore."

"Take one of the SUVs," Ben said. "The sooner he's gone, the better. Oh, and don't tell him his old man is dead, eh?"

She frowned. "Why not?"

"A kid like that benefits from being afraid of someone. He needs to keep looking over his shoulder. It'll keep him honest."

"You know the type?" she asked shrewdly.

He shrugged. "A lot of those types end up in my line of work."

"Same," she murmured.

She collected a set of keys and fetched Danny out of the SOG team's van, where he'd been gagged, zip-tied, and secured to a bench for the duration.

He had a thousand questions, all of which he spewed at her as she guided the SUV out to a main road and from there to a highway.

When she could get a word in edgewise, she told him the ruse had worked. "Your father thinks you died in the blast. The man I'm taking you to now will get you out of the country, help you set up your new identity, and deliver you to Israel."

"Israel?" Danny exclaimed. "I'm not Jewish!"

"You are now. And you're going to enlist in the Israel Defense Forces. They're the sharpest military group on earth. They can teach you all the self-discipline and control you'll ever need. And, if you're so inclined, they can also put you into all the combat you want."

"Like shooting at bad guys?"

"Only at bad guys, but yes."

"Sweet."

The remainder of the drive to Baltimore was silent. As they pulled up at a crappy little pier on the edge of Baltimore Harbor, Danny looked over at her, a strange look on his face. "There's something I think I need to tell you."

"What's that?"

"About my old man."

It was interesting how he never called Richard his father. "What's that, Danny?"

"The day I overheard him on the phone talking about you. When he said he couldn't kill you yet."

"Yes?" she prompted him.

Danny frowned. "I think he's doing something bad. Really bad."

"Like what?"

"I don't know. But he talked about how he wasn't about to let you derail his life's work. He said he's spent decades putting the pieces in place and the plan is already in motion."

"Did he say anything else?"

Danny frowned. "Not on that call. But when you live with a man like him, you watch him all the time. Read his moods. Stay out of his way. Try not to make him mad."

Helen nodded. She could only imagine what that must've been like for Danny.

The youth continued, "He thinks all politicians are stupid. That our whole government is run by stupid people."

She smiled a little. "Lots of people might agree with him."

He shook his head. "You don't understand. He despises stupidity. Like, really hates it. He doesn't tolerate it. At all. He talks casually over dinner about how he destroys people's careers for being stupid. And if they try to fight back, he destroys their lives. It's more than a pet peeve. It's, like, an obsession, with him— eradicating stupidity."

Where is Danny going with this?

"I think he might . . ." Danny trailed off.

"Finish that thought," she urged him gently.

"You're gonna think it's crazy, but I think he might be planning to do something to the politicians he thinks are stupid."

"But you said he thinks they're all stupid."

"Just so."

The boy's simple answer chilled her to the bone.

"Can you think of anything else you've heard, anything that might tell me more about what this plan of his might be?"

Danny frowned, thinking hard. "My sister has a bunch of his computer files on her laptop. She stole them to blackmail him with if he ever comes for her. She told me once that he's planning something huge. She was really scared by whatever it was. Like terrified. I mean, I suck at telling how other people are feeling, and even I could see how scared she was."

"If you think of anything else that could help me figure out what Richard is up to, I'm going to give you the name of a man to call in Israel. You can tell him what you remember, and he'll pass it to me. Okay?"

Danny nodded.

She pulled out a small notebook from her purse and wrote down the name and number for him. "Don't lose that."

He grinned. "I can memorize numbers like nobody's business." He rattled the long phone number back at her to demonstrate his point, and he'd only glanced at the paper once.

Her guy on the freighter had come ashore and was walking toward the SUV.

She gave Danny one last warning. "Remember, you're dead. You must have no contact whatsoever with your family. None. Not your mother. Not your sister. And definitely not your father. In fact, when I leave here, I'm heading over to your family's house to break the sad news that you've perished in a tragic accident. They will believe you're dead. If you ever attempt to contact them, they won't believe you're you. Understood?"

"Yes, ma'am."

"I'll be keeping an eye on you from a distance. Maybe one day, our paths will cross again."

He nodded and opened the door to join the man waiting silently in front of the vehicle.

"Thanks, Mrs. Warwick. I owe you one."

"Who knows? Maybe I'll collect on that favor someday."

With a brief smile, he turned away and jogged over to the freighter captain. He didn't look back.

She had one more stop to make tonight before she could go home and crawl in bed for a week. And she didn't relish it.

She spent the entire drive over to Richard Bell's house trying to figure out what huge plan Richard already had in motion that could scare his kids half to death and would constitute his "life's work." What would be the ultimate goal of a man like Richard Bell?

If he was Scorpius as well, did his plan involve manipulating not one but two world powers? What was he after?

Money? Power? War between the United States and Russia?

Given that he had a cadre of sociopathic killers working for him to help achieve it, she had a very bad feeling it might be some combination of all three. Particularly since Bell was behind the recent killings of three senior CIA officers.

Whatever it was, his conspiracy was already in motion. It was clearly violent, given that blood had already been spilled, and it seemed aimed at the US government.

Her gut shouted a warning at her that she *had* to figure it out, and soon.

Even if Bell was Scorpius and he was dead, would the plan continue on? Did he have a lieutenant who would step in and take over? Maybe inherit Bell's blackmail files and take up right where he'd left off?

She prayed his second-in-command was in the Operation Whitehorse files on her phone. She *had* to find out what he'd been planning.

She parked in the Bell driveway, staring reluctantly at the darkened house. She waited until the police cruiser she'd requested had arrived and briefed the policemen quietly that she was here on behalf of the US government to make a death notification. The uniformed officers nodded and followed her up the front sidewalk.

She stared at the doorbell reluctantly. Procrastinating wasn't going to make this any easier. She reached out and rang the doorbell.

"First one of these?" one of the cops asked from behind her.

"Does it show?" she replied.

"They won't care about you as soon as they hear the news. Just stay calm, say something sympathetic, and then you can leave. We'll take care of getting neighbors or family to come over. We do this stuff all the time."

"For which I am grateful on behalf of the public," she murmured.

Nobody came to the door right away.

She waited a full minute and rang the bell again. A light went on upstairs, but still nobody came to the door. She was just about to ring the doorbell for a third time when the porch light went on.

The front door opened . . .

And she stared in utter shock . . .

At Richard Bell.

CHAPTER 55

*I*T WAS ONLY HER LONG YEARS OF LYING TO HER OWN FAMILY THAT kept her facial expression from devolving into open-mouthed, gaping shock.

The good news was, for just an instant, he seemed fully as shocked as she was to see her alive and well, standing on his front doorstep.

So she and the SOG team had successfully taken out all of his men. None of them had reported back to Bell, and he'd assumed they'd killed her.

Surprise. I'm a tough old bird to kill.

Richard's cold gaze narrowed in calculation, and if she wasn't mistaken, his chin dipped ever so slightly, as if in acknowledgment of a worthy foe. Startled, she nodded back infinitesimally.

"I'm sorry to bother you at this ungodly hour, sir," she said politely. "But I'm afraid I have some bad news. May we come in?"

He unlocked the storm door and stepped back.

She entered the house with the policemen on her heels. Richard led them past a curving staircase into a painfully formal and achingly neat living room. Somehow, this was what she'd expected of his home.

"Would you like to fetch your wife?" she asked gently.

His brows twitched into a frown. "No. Whatever news you have, you can give it to me. I'll tell her what she needs to know."

That was weird. But if that was what he wanted . . .

This was not going the way she'd expected. At all.

She glanced over at the cops, who also looked mightily confused. One of them said, "Sir, I think your wife should be here with you."

"No." Richard's voice was flat. Implacable.

The officer looked at her and shrugged.

Well, okay then. She took a deep breath. "Mr. Bell, I'm sorry to inform you that there was a tragic accident earlier this evening. I'm afraid your son, Daniel, didn't survive."

Bell went utterly still. She wasn't even sure he was breathing. Then, after many long seconds, he let out a long slow breath. It almost sounded like relief.

Had Danny not told her that Richard was threatening to kill him, she might've guessed that big sigh was a sound of shock or grief. But as it was, she had to wonder.

He looked past her to the pair of police officers. "The two of you may go. I assume you can show yourselves out?"

"Excuse me?"

"Are you sure?" they blurted simultaneously.

"Mrs. Warwick and I have a few things to discuss in private. And I will take care of notifying my wife and daughter of my son's passing."

"Don't leave!" she blurted to the police. No way was she going to be alone with this man!

"Leave," Richard ordered them firmly.

"Stay in the front hallway," she demanded. "Or I'm leaving with them," she threatened Richard.

He shrugged and leaned back in the big leather armchair he sat in, locking his fingers across his stomach.

She looked nervously at the policemen, who nodded back reassuringly at her. "Stay where I can see you, please," she asked them.

The cops moved into the front hallway, on the far side of the staircase but still in her line of sight. To their credit, both men kept their stares locked on her. They might not know what was going on, but they'd definitely picked up on her panic at the idea of being alone with Bell.

She turned her attention to Richard.

No way was she breaking the silence first. She waited him out, prepared to sit here for an hour if she had to.

Finally, he asked in what sounded like resignation, "How did he die?"

"There was an explosion. In a small storage building of some kind."

"Did you kill him?" The question was delivered so mildly, so casually, it took her a moment to register what he'd asked.

"No!" she blurted, her dismay genuine.

"But you were there."

It was a statement of fact. She had no way of knowing what his team had reported back to him before they'd died, so she decided to stick as close to the truth as possible.

"I got a text. From an anonymous sender, earlier today. In it, the sender offered me a file of information."

"Pertaining to what?"

"I'm not sure. But the sender seemed to think it might help me with the investigation I'm conducting for James Wagner."

"Ah, yes. The hunt for the elusive Scorpius. How's my team coming with that?"

She didn't rise to the bait of him calling it his team. Instead, she answered pleasantly, "It's going nowhere fast. Scorpius is nothing if not adept at covering his tracks."

"And how does this anonymous text relate to my son?"

He already knew the answer to that, of course.

She shrugged, calling on her best acting skills to keep her voice light. "I believe it was your son who texted me. How he got hold of my private phone number is a mystery to me, though. At any rate, I drove to the location that was texted to me."

Richard's expression was completely neutral, but she thought she sensed a certain . . . *something* about him. Tension. Or maybe anger. The man was impossible to read.

"Obviously, I wasn't going to just waltz up to this spot in the middle of nowhere and stroll right into what could be a trap. I set up shop in the woods to watch the area for a bit. Get the lay of the land. See if anybody showed up."

"And did they?" She gave him her best blank look, and he added impatiently, "Show up. Did someone show up?"

"Eventually, your son arrived. He went into the barn. He was inside for a few minutes. And then . . ." She broke off, reliving the moment the barn had exploded in her mind's eye. "And then the whole place blew up. I don't know if there was some sort of gas leak or the like. Honestly, the ferocity of the explosion leads me to believe that perhaps he had something with him of a combustive nature. He must've set it off by accident."

She added sincerely, "He never knew what happened. It was instantaneous." A pause. "You'll be sure to tell your wife that, won't you?"

"Of course."

"I'm so sorry for your loss." She started to stand up.

"Sit."

She sat. Dang, that man had a command voice that was hard to ignore. No wonder everyone who knew him was scared silly of him. The coldness in his eyes when he snapped that order at her had promised severe pain if she didn't comply. An image of that row of circular scars on his son's arm flashed through her mind. Images of dead bodies on slabs at the morgue. The look in Polina's eyes as she'd pulled the trigger—

"Mrs. Warwick. It has come to my attention that you've been poking into my affairs."

"I've poked into a lot of people's affairs over the course of my investigation," she said as evenly as she could.

"Have you found Scorpius?" His voice was whiplash sharp.

"I've found no evidence to prove who he is."

"Nor will you. I gave finding him my best shot. And if I couldn't find him, you certainly won't."

That last bit was delivered with enough scorn to set her teeth on edge.

"I must advise you to refrain from poking any further into my business dealings."

Warning her off, was he? Worried she might uncover his conspiracy, perhaps? *Good.* That meant she was getting closer to it than she knew.

He continued icily, "You were a small fish in the agency during your career. If a little minnow like you continues trying to swim with the sharks, you'll get eaten alive."

The implication was clear: he was the shark that would be doing the eating.

She shrugged. "You're right, of course. I want nothing more than to retire and take up baking and spoiling my future grandchildren. I have yet to master making a decent apple pie, and I would like to get on with that project."

He studied her as if measuring the truth of her words. She looked back at him openly. After all, her statement was completely true.

A frown momentarily marred his brow.

"Then we understand each other. We will each go our separate ways. I would hate to think what might happen if our paths cross again. After all, I have lost a child this night."

She leaned forward, all pretense of politeness gone. "Mr. Bell, if you ever threaten my family, if you ever even think about harming one of my children, this minnow might just turn out to be a piranha."

That sent his eyebrows—the only part of him that seemed to express anything resembling emotion—skyward.

She did stand up then. "Again, I am truly sorry for your loss. Please convey my sincere condolences to your wife and daughter."

His stare, colder than ever, locked with hers.

She saw it in his eyes as clear as day. He knew that she knew he was Scorpius. And he was silently daring her to prove it.

Just as coldly, just as silently, she accepted the dare. She would find out what he was up to, and when she'd stopped his grand plan, she was going to put him down like the vermin he was.

The only emotion that lit his eyes as she turned away from him was sardonic amusement. Apparently, he looked forward to the coming battle between them.

He thought he was the predator, moving silent and unseen toward his target. But he had it all wrong. He was the prey. She knew who he was now. She'd seen his true colors. Understood him. Knew what made him tick. Oh, yes. She had his number now.

One day.

One day she would take his secret conspiracy down, and then she would take *him* down.

That was a promise.

Don't miss where it all started, in

SECOND SHOT

Available now where books are sold.

CHAPTER 1

HELEN WARWICK STARED AT THE GLOSSY BLACK DOOR WITH ITS period-accurate brass knocker and kickplate. It was as carefully understated as every other door in this upscale Georgetown neighborhood and screamed of wealth and privilege.

Since when did her middle child become all of this? For that matter, when did Peter grow up? One minute he'd been a bright, charming child with no talent for sports but a discerning eye for everything and everyone around him, and the next he was an upwardly mobile Gen Whatever-they-were up-to-now'er with a live-in boyfriend, an art collection, a prestigious address, and a puppy.

It was her fault, of course, that she'd missed so much of his childhood. She'd missed far too much of all her children's lives. But, at long last, this was her chance to make up for it in some small measure.

Retirement. Motherhood. She could do this.

She lifted the knocker and let it fall.

Liang—Li to the family—opened the door immediately. "Mrs. Warwick. So good of you to puppysit for us tonight."

She air-kissed him on both cheeks and held out a slightly singed apple pie balanced in her left hand. "Housewarming gift."

"Did you bake this?" he asked in genuine surprise, taking the pie as she set her purse down on the impeccable Louis XV credenza.

"I did. Eat it at your own peril."

He laughed warmly and led her into the kitchen where a small Renoir pastel casually filled a wall beside the refrigerator. It was the study for part of a more famous piece, but still a work of art in its own right. Where the boys got the money for such things, she didn't know and didn't ask. Of course, it didn't hurt that Peter was an art dealer in an auction house that sold antiques and fine art. But still. Renoir?

"Don't you look nice tonight, Mother," Peter said coolly, sweeping into the kitchen with all the style he usually did. He wore a crisply tailored black suit that was just shy of being a tuxedo.

She'd agonized in her own closet for longer than she cared to admit, pondering what to wear to a puppysitting date. What clothing struck a tone of apology, commitment to building a relationship, and motherly love without sacrificing the cool sophistication she knew Peter cherished in all things? She'd settled on black wool slacks, a simple cashmere sweater, and a pair of black, Italian leather, stiletto-heeled bootlets that had to have cost more than her car. Thank God the agency had footed the bill for them as part of a disguise she'd worn a few years back at an Italian opera house.

"You look dashing as always, darling," she murmured, air-kissing him as well. When did her children stop actually hugging her, anyway? Probably too many parental mistakes ago for her to remember.

"Your mother baked us a pie," Li announced to fill the silence already filling the chasm yawning between her and her offspring.

"You bake?" Peter asked blankly.

"Shocking. I know. Who'd have guessed I was capable of mastering the domestic arts?" When Peter pulled a skeptical face, she added, "Don't answer that."

The silence crept forward again.

"So, where's this new granddog of mine?" she asked with cheer she hoped didn't sound forced.

"He's having a time-out at the moment," Li supplied, gesturing toward a custom wood crate with sliding screen front doors that looked like a piece of furniture. A small Calder sculpture was displayed on top of the . . . puppy cabinet.

Peter added, in complete seriousness, "We got a little rambunctious earlier and refused to poop after our supper."

"Is that a group activity in your house?" she asked dryly.

Peter rolled his eyes as Li opened the large crate and scooped out a roly-poly blond furball that was possibly the cutest creature she'd ever seen.

She cooed in genuine adoration of the twelve-week-old golden retriever. "Have you boys settled on a name for your progeny?"

Li and Peter smiled at each other and said together, "Biscuit."

"Too cute." She reached out. "May I?"

Li passed her the squirming pup, who had a fat pink tummy, sharp little claws, huge, bright brown eyes, and a black button nose. She held him up to gaze into his eyes. The little scamp stuck out his tiny pink tongue and licked the tip of her nose.

"I'm officially in love," she declared.

"Gee. If that was all it took, I'd have licked your nose years ago," Peter muttered.

"Be nice," Li murmured.

She absorbed the jab without comment. After all, she hadn't raised any of her children to be weak souls afraid to express their opinions. In that, at least, she'd succeeded as a parent.

"What's the routine with young Master Biscuit?" she asked.

"He'll need to go out once an hour on the hour," Li answered briskly. "Carry him to the backyard and put him down in the grass. Whistle until he potties. You can whistle, can't you?"

"Yes, dear. I can whistle."

"Perfect. He goes to bed at ten. Put him in his crate and close the slats. He'll complain, but ignore him. He'll go to sleep in a few minutes."

"He has already had supper, and we're not feeding him people food," Peter added. "So no snacks."

She sensed a grandmotherly rebellion forthcoming. It was

clearly her job to spoil her granddog, and she wasn't about to shirk her duty.

"Mother . . ." Peter said warningly.

"All right, already. I'll behave." *Not.*

Li took up reciting the puppy instruction manual to her. "We're staying for the fireworks but should be home by two a.m. After bedtime, Biscuit only needs to go out every two hours. If he gets hungry, at midnight you can feed him the snack I left in the fridge. It's in a bowl with his name on it."

"What's in it?"

"Ground lamb, fresh pumpkin puree, scrambled egg, and rice."

"This dog eats better than I do," she commented.

"Here is his gear drawer." Peter showed her, pulling a wide, shallow drawer in the puppy crate–cabinet-thing open. "There's a harness, leash, ThunderShirt, earmuffs for fireworks and other loud noises, teething ring, plush toys, and a spare blanket with his mother's scent on it. Emergency veterinarian's phone number is on this card, and text me if you have any questions."

"He's a puppy, Peter. He eats, poops, and sleeps. How hard can he be to take care of? I didn't kill you, did I?"

As if to make up for the dire look her son threw at her, Li kissed her on the cheek. "Hang in there," he whispered as he leaned close.

She smiled gratefully at him for the vote of support. But she knew full well how far she had to go to rebuild bridges with her family. If it was even possible.

She and the puppy walked Peter and Liang to the front door and locked it behind them. And then it was just she and Biscuit. He gave a little whimper, and she tucked him under her chin, nuzzling his silky soft fur fondly. "You don't hate me, do you, little nugget?"

The boys had purchased two town houses side by side and knocked out the walls between them, gutting and renovating them into a grand and gracious space. On the left side of the ground floor were a formal living room, dining room, kitchen, and breakfast nook. A long hall ran down the center of the house, and on the other side were two offices, a library, and a fully equipped home gym. A casual family room ran the entire width of the back of the house with floor-to-ceiling glass windows looking out on the newly landscaped formal garden and outdoor kitchen/living room.

The boys had only moved in a few weeks ago but had already done wonders with the place. In her wildest dreams, she could never pull together a space this eclectic, chic, and achingly sophisticated. Maybe she could hire them to redo the house she nominally shared with Grayson Warwick, her mostly absent husband.

She didn't want to think about that problematic relationship right now. Dealing with Peter's simmering resentment was enough for one evening.

She dutifully took Biscuit to the backyard and felt like an idiot standing there beside him in the dark, shivering and whistling until he squatted and peed. Shaking her head, she scooped him up and carried him inside.

"Congratulations on successfully training your humans to make complete fools of themselves in twelve short weeks, my friend."

Li had thoughtfully chilled a crisp, white wine and laid out a selection of old-world cheeses and sausages for her. Biscuit loved the cheese and sausage, and they reminded her of Berlin. Good times in that cosmopolitan city . . .

She noshed on the snacks and sat down to watch television in the family room, where the massive flat screen took up an entire wall. She cruised through the channels until she found a movie. *Ahh. Casablanca.* An oldie but a goodie, even if the spy tradecraft in the film was dreadful.

Biscuit curled up beside her on the overstuffed sofa and settled down to sleep. Ten o'clock came and went, along with a potty check, but the puppy didn't wake. Common sense told her not to disturb the little guy.

Rick told Louis he thought it was the beginning of a beautiful friendship, and the credits began to roll when she heard faint popping noises outside. She tensed sharply, and her gaze darted around the room. French doors to the backyard. Kitchen entrance to the left, library entrance to the right. Hallway in the middle. It had the best sight line to the backyard but no cover. Sofa would provide visual cover only. That poker table could be turned on its side in a pinch to defend against gunfire. Better to head for the kitchen with its stone counters and solid wood cabinets for protection from incoming rounds—

Oh, for the love of Mike, stand down, Helen.

It was New Year's Eve, and that was just some kids lighting off firecrackers in the alley.

Whether it was the *pop-pop-popping* or her sharp reaction to it she couldn't tell, but Biscuit jerked awake, lifting his head and listening alertly, his fuzzy, little ears perked.

"Past time for a pit stop for you, young man."

She carried him outside and set him down in the grass. The popping noises were louder out here. Amazing how much they sounded like gunfire. No wonder veterans had PTSD problems on nights like this.

Apparently, she, too, was going to have to learn not to reach for a weapon whenever she heard fireworks. Her nerves were too on edge to bring herself to whistle—one did not call attention to oneself when bullets were flying. The dog showed no interest in voiding his bladder, perhaps because she refused to mortify herself with the whistling routine.

Regardless, she picked him up and scuttled inside, eager to get under cover as yet another volley of loud pops erupted in the alley. This one was accompanied by raucous shouts and girlish screams. *Kids.* They had no idea how their commotion unsettled people like her.

It was almost midnight. She should cut herself a slice of pie and make a celebration out of her first New Year's as a retired person. That, and she would prove to the boys she hadn't poisoned their housewarming gift.

She opened drawers until she found one in the quartz waterfall island with a built-in knife rack and a dozen chef-quality knives. She pulled one out, sliced the pie, and used the blade to scoop a piece onto a plate.

A bright red glow flashed, and a second later, the distant thunder of the big New Year's Eve fireworks show on the Mall began.

Mindful of the puppy not being traumatized by the loud noises, she held him tucked under her left arm and dug around in the puppy drawer with her free hand. "Now where did your fathers put your earmuffs—"

The lights went out, plunging the house into darkness.

Adrenaline surged through her veins unbidden, and her body went light and fast, ready for violence.

What on earth?

The clock on the stove and the touch pad on the refrigerator had also gone dark. Starbursts outside sent neon strobes of green, blue, and red through the black house. Her instincts fired off a strident warning, so insistent she couldn't possibly ignore the alarms shouting in her skull.

Grabbing the pie knife, she dropped to a crouch beside the crate and listened tautly. All she heard was the steady, distant *boom-boom-boom.*

Sheesh. Overreacting, much? It was just a fireworks display. And she was a civilian, now. Out of the game—

Deafening automatic weapon fire erupted all at once. With an almighty crash, the entire glass-walled back of the house exploded inward. Glass flew *everywhere* as gunfire raked the family room.

Crap on a cracker.

Feathers filled the air as the sofa exploded. The glow of fireworks punctuated the attack, and wood and pieces of furniture flew every which way in the strobe-like flashes. Something hot and wickedly sharp sliced across her left arm with the neat precision of a scalpel. She knew that pain. She'd gotten winged by a bullet.

Instinctively, she folded over the puppy, protecting his little body with hers. Fast roll into the puppy crate. Breathe in. Hold. Breathe out.

A quiet crunch of a boot on glass. Another. A hostile was moving into the kitchen.

Quietly, carefully, she tugged the blanket inside the crate around the puppy, wrapping him like a burrito, praying it would keep him quiet and still. Gripping the knife tightly, she waited in an agony of suspense for what came next.

Legs came into her line of sight. Military-style boots, black cargo pants, leather thigh holster strapped down. A few more steps—

The gunman passed the crate.

She rolled out and stabbed with all her might, burying the sharp blade of her knife in the back of the man's knee. He screamed and went down as she jumped and landed with both knees in the middle of his back.

He was fast and strong and tried to roll over. He almost succeeded in throwing her off, but she hung on grimly as he rolled onto his side and then on top of her. He failed to trap her arms underneath him. She grabbed a handful of his hair, yanked his chin back, and slashed hard with the knife.

The assailant thrashed on top of her, knocking her head hard against the floor in his death throes. She shoved for all she was worth and managed to roll him off her. She scrambled to her feet, blinking away the spots dancing in front of her eyes, her high-heeled shoes slipping and sliding in the spreading puddle of blood.

In the flashes of fireworks, black blood welled from her attacker's mutilated throat. His hands fell away from clutching at the mortal wound, and she dived over him to snatch up his weapon, which had clattered to the floor.

It was an urban assault rifle. Russian ASh-12.7. She dropped it into place against her shoulder and rested her index finger on the trigger. Pausing to kick off her high heels, she advanced fast and silent, knees bent, on stockinged feet.

Odds were the other shooter was advancing through the far

side of the ground floor. Crouching, she swung low into the hall-way. Clear left. Clear right.

Using the tip of the weapon's barrel, she nudged open the half bath door under the stairs. Clear.

She heard a bump and a faint grunt in the library and raced down the hall on the balls of her feet, ducking into the dining room, listening hard for any more shooters than just the two.

Then the front doorknob rattled slightly, and she swore under her breath. A third hostile outside. Bastards must've planned to herd her through the house and out the front door into an ambush. By her recommendation, Peter and Liang had installed a top-notch German lock in the front door. If the guy out front thought he was picking it fast and joining the fight, he was sadly mistaken.

Gliding into the formal living room, she cleared the space quickly and eased across the foyer into Peter's office. His desk was an antique, a massive wooden beast that would stop a small tank. Crouching behind it, she propped the barrel of the weapon on the writing surface and pointed it at the door to Liang's adjoining office. Exhaling slowly, she forcibly slowed her heart rate.

Now it was a waiting game.

Then she heard a sound that made her blood run cold. Little claws scrabbling on hardwood. She swore silently. Biscuit had wig-gled free of his blanket restraint. Little scamp was running through the living room. Did she shift her aim to the foyer on the assump-tion that the shooter would be drawn to the sound of the puppy, or did she hold position, aiming at Li's office?

She had a split second to decide.

Instinct said to stay put.

In the very next breath, a black shadow spun fast through the doorway between the offices, crouching low, sweeping the office with his weapon.

She double tapped two shots at his center of mass, counting on the high-powered rounds to slam him backward against the wall and knock the breath out of him even if he had on a bullet-resistant vest.

The guy grunted and landed on the floor, leaning against the wall, but he was still functional enough to swing his weapon toward her.

Adjusting her aim a hair's breadth higher, she squeezed off two more fast shots. The hostile's throat exploded in a fountain of blood, but the weapon jammed on her second shot, the trigger balking and refusing to pull through. *Piece of crap Russian hardware.* Her target toppled over and lay still while she rapidly considered her options.

What she really wanted was her own trusty pistol, currently in her purse, sitting on the Louis XV credenza in the foyer. Laying down the Russian weapon, she eased out from behind the desk.

But then the downed man across the room moved, so she bolted forward, darting back out into the foyer and out of range of any dying-breath heroics.

The front doorknob was turning. She dived for her purse, snatching at it as she sprinted past the table, searching frantically for Biscuit ahead of her in the living room.

She missed the purse and only succeeded in knocking it on its side, the shoulder strap dangling just above the floor. But she couldn't go back. The door was opening. She lunged past it, scooped up the puppy, and dived for cover behind the sofa.

Landing hard on her shoulder—the one that had gotten hit in the initial attack—she lost her grip on the frantic, wriggly puppy, who rolled out of her arms.

Crap, crap, crap.

Peering under the couch, she saw the third hostile come in hot, charging into the foyer, aggressively swinging his weapon left and right. He raced down the hallway, his boots disappearing from her limited line of sight.

Biscuit raced after him, running into the middle of the foyer when a new barrage of fireworks, as loud and insistent as an artillery battle, peppered the night. Underneath the deafening thunder of noise, she whispered urgently, *"Biscuit! Come, Biscuit!"*

The puppy panicked and bolted straight ahead, ramming nose-first into the credenza, where he yelped and promptly got tangled in the dangling shoulder strap of her purse.

Frantic, he scrambled to free himself, to no avail.

Terrified, and completely overwhelmed, Biscuit squatted right there in the front hall and peed on the antique Aubusson rug.

The pantry and wine room doors slammed open in the kitchen.

Holding her hands out to the puppy, she tried again. *"Come to Granny. Come, Biscuit."*

Perhaps her outstretched fingers still smelled like salami, or maybe he wanted a hug, but the pup, still tangled in her purse strap, stumbled toward her, dragging her purse off the credenza. As it thudded to the floor behind him he lurched forward, dragging the purse behind him through the puddle of pee and into the living room doorway.

He finally jerked free but not before the shoulder strap fell within reach of her outstretched hand.

She was out of time. With a shove, she pushed up off her belly, burst out of her hiding place, and leaped forward. Staying low, she scooped up the dog with her left hand and her purse with her right, and bolted for the stairs.

The shooter in the kitchen leaped out into the hall and fired wildly, sending a spray of lead into the wall below her feet. She ducked as splinters of wood pelted her and dived for the steps, fumbling frantically in her purse.

Her fist closed around the familiar grip of her EDC X9 Wilson Combat handgun. She didn't bother pulling it out of the bag. She rose to her knees and fired down at the shooter below through the leather of her purse—two fast shots, one through the top of his head, the second through the back of his neck as he pitched forward, facedown.

A cloud of mist hung in the air where his head had been, illuminated by the now continuous flash of fireworks. She pushed to her feet, picked up Biscuit, and raced upstairs, tearing into the master bedroom. She paused inside only long enough to lock the door.

Sprinting for the bathroom, she locked that door as well, stopping only when she'd jumped into the separate throne room, locked that door, and sat down on the floor beside the toilet, panting.

Finally freeing her weapon from her ruined purse, she set Biscuit on the tiled floor and dug around in her bag for her cell phone. She dialed 911 as reaction set in and her fingers began to tremble.

"Go ahead," the dispatcher's voice said cheerfully.

God. He sounded about twelve years old.

She took a deep breath and reminded herself to sound like a panicked civilian. "You have to send help! There's been a shooting at the following address." She rattled it off. "Do you have anything nearby with a siren? Maybe it would scare the bad guys away."

"Ma'am, those are fireworks you're hearing—"

"I've been shot. I think I saw three bad guys. Maybe more!"

"Where are you now, ma'am?"

"Locked in the master bathroom, upstairs."

"I've dispatched a police cruiser."

"Send *all* the police!"

"Ma'am, if you'll tell me what's going on—"

She interrupted impatiently. "I told you. A gang of armed bad guys broke into my son's house and shot the place up. And they shot me, too."

"Where are you shot, ma'am?"

"In the arm."

"I've dispatched an ambulance. You should lie down on the floor until medics arrive."

"It hurts like fire, but it's not bleeding a lot. I don't think it's serious . . . not that I know a blessed thing about gunshot wounds," she added.

Her left arm was, in fact, burning as if a hot poker lay across her biceps. *Dang it.* Her new sweater was ruined, too. She tore off a wad of toilet paper and used it to dab at her wound. The hot lead must have partially cauterized her wound, which would explain the lack of profuse bleeding.

"Umm, who is this?" the dispatcher asked warily.

She ignored the question, asking instead, "When are the police going to get here?" She dropped her voice to a whisper, as if it had just occurred to her the bad guys might still be running around the house. "What if the intruders find me up here?"

"The first police cruiser will be there any time, now."

Sure enough, a police siren became faintly audible. It rapidly grew louder until it was screaming outside the house. If that hadn't scared away any remaining intruders, nothing would. Thankfully, the police turned off the siren before long, and deep silence fell over the house. The distant rumble of the fireworks continued unabated, heedless of the death and destruction going on below their star-spangled roar.

She strained to hear any movement but heard only her own breath and the puppy's anxious panting. Li'l guy had been a champ, all things considered.

Outside, police would be stacking up beside the open front door, diving in guns first, clearing the ground floor room by room. She heard them shouting back and forth. Reaction started to crowd forward in her body, a stew of mostly rage and a little fear.

Who were the shooters? Why here? Was *she* the target? She was out of the game. Off the chessboard. Why this, then? Who had it in for her bad enough to break all norms of civilized spy behavior?

A male voice spoke up right outside the commode door. "Ma'am, are you in there? The house is secure."

"What's your badge number?" she demanded, pointing her pistol at the door. He was a hostile until he proved otherwise.

He rattled off his name, rank, and badge number without any hint of hesitation.

Her body went limp with relief. She stood up, her legs protesting as she unfolded her body from the cold, hard floor. Sharp needles of returning circulation made her wince as she picked up the dog, unlocked the door, and squinted into the beam of a high-intensity, military-grade flashlight.

"Three men are dead downstairs," the cop reported. "And it appears that a fourth one fled through the alley, perhaps on a motorcycle."

Four men? She should probably be complimented that such a big hit squad had been sent in to take her out. Still, this wasn't supposed to be happening. She was *retired*.

"Who else was in the house with you at the time of the incident, ma'am?"

"Nobody. It was just me and my granddog."

"*You* shot those men?" the cop blurted.

Crud, crud, crud. Speaking in a breathless soprano, she gasped, "I was so scared, Officer. I just closed my eyes and pulled the trigger. Did I hit anything?"

"You could say so," the cop said dryly. "Since you discharged a firearm that resulted in a death, we're going to need you to come down to the station, answer some questions, and make a written statement. After a medic takes a look at your arm."

"Of course." She added a nervous, fluttery wave with her hand for effect. Although, the pistol gripped in her fist probably ruined the helplessness of the wave. "You're sure it's safe out here?" she asked nervously as she stepped into the bedroom.

"Yes, ma'am. The scene is secured." The officer snagged her gun as she waved it past him, then checked the chamber and safety before saying, "This weapon will have to be entered into evidence."

With Biscuit still tucked under her left arm, she followed him downstairs to the foyer, picking her way cautiously through the splinters, broken glass, and puppy pee. "Is there any chance I could get my shoes? I must've run right out of them, I was so scared."

"Wait here, ma'am. This is an active crime scene."

Keen observation, Sherlock. Careful to keep her eyes wide and wondering, she looked around the destroyed ground floor. It looked like a freaking war zone. As the cop held out her designer bootlets, she wailed, "Look at this mess! My son is going to kill me."

CHAPTER 2

HELEN FINALLY DROVE AWAY FROM THE POLICE PRECINCT AT NEARLY 3:00 a.m. The police were unsure of what to make of her. On the one hand, they had three dead bodies, shot with all the cold precision of the trained sniper that she was. But on the other, they had the flustered middle-aged woman sitting in a chair in front of them, wringing her hands, adamantly sticking to her story—she'd simply closed her eyes and pulled the trigger in self-defense. Poor coppers just couldn't seem to reconcile the two.

It had gotten a bit tricky to explain the knife in the back of Hostile Number One's knee, but she claimed that Biscuit had peed and the bad guy slipped in the puddle. As best she could tell, he'd grabbed at the counter as he went down, knocked the pie knife off the counter, and somehow landed on top of it, stabbing himself in the leg. Bad luck, that.

She readily admitted to using the knife to cut herself a piece of pie, of course, which explained her fingerprints on the weapon.

Her lawyer, whom she'd called from the foyer of Peter and Li's house, met her at the police station. He argued stridently that the hundreds of rounds the intruders had fired made her armed response an open-and-shut case of self-defense. Eventually, without any hard evidence to refute self-defense in response to a home invasion, the police had been forced to let her go. But they didn't like it. They smelled a rat, but they just couldn't spot it.

She made a mental note to avoid crossing paths with the Metropolitan Police of the District of Columbia—the Georgetown precinct in particular—any time soon.

She'd barely pulled out of the police parking lot when her cell phone rang. Who could be calling her at this hour? Peter had already made his opinion abundantly clear of his brand-new house being completely trashed on her watch. She doubted he would be speaking to her again this decade. At least she'd delivered Biscuit unharmed into Li's arms. That had to count for something.

The phone rang insistently. She transferred the call to her car's Bluetooth system, and it showed no name in the caller ID. Frowning, she pushed a button and took the call.

"Hello?" she said cautiously.

"Helen, Helen, Helen. What have you done?"

She sagged in relief. It was Yosef Mizrah, her longtime CIA handler. He must be calling from a burner phone. "Yossi. How did you hear about tonight's excitement? I don't work for you anymore."

"I thought I was finally rid of you, too, my dear."

She ground out, "What the heck was that? They shot up my son's house. They can come after *me* all they want. I'm fair game . . . arguably. But the bastards came after my *family*. I want names. I want *blood*."

"Metro police are saying it was a robbery gone bad. How about we figure out what happened before we jump to any conclus—"

She cut him off sharply. "You and I both know what that was. Four men armed with Russian assault weapons, who moved like a Spetsnatz team and shot out the entire back end of a house by way of entering the premises, were not trying to rob the place. They were after me. But they didn't even have the decency to wait until I was alone in my own home."

A long-suffering sigh in her ear. "I know—"

"I swear to God, if the FSB is behind this, I'll make them regret even thinking about knocking me off."

"I understand your feelings, Helen. But let's take a moment to find out who the shooters were. Collect intel on who sent them before you start a one-woman war with the Russian government."

"They started it. And I won't take this lying down."

"Let me find who 'they' are before you kill anyone else. Okay?"

She scowled fiercely. In her line of work, killing was an emotionless business transaction, but this was personal. And they'd involved her family. Still, a tiny voice of reason in the back of her head murmured that, like it or not, he wasn't wrong.

"Who's the puppy I heard about at the scene?" He was blatantly trying to distract her.

She let him, answering grumpily, "My granddog, Biscuit."

"Only you could go through a firefight badly outgunned, outnumbered four to one, with a puppy under one arm, and come out unscathed."

"I suppose you're going to need me to come into the office and make a report, aren't you?" she asked in resignation.

"'Fraid so. But Monday will be soon enough. Take the weekend to relax."

"I *was* relaxing! I was babysitting a puppy and having a piece of pie—that I made with my own hands, I'll have you know—when, poof. All hell broke loose."

Yosef was silent. The kind of silent that spoke loudly of him being as worried about this attack as she was. He, too, understood the unwritten rules that had been broken tonight.

"Promise me you won't kill anyone else before you come see me."

She rolled her eyes, even though he couldn't see them. He knew her well enough to hear them.

"Promise me, Helen."

"Fine. I promise. No murders before Monday. I'll take the rest of the weekend off."

"Nice shooting, by the way."

She snorted and hung up, without deigning to respond.

Helen turned into her driveway, and the motion-activated lights came on around the house. She waited while the steel garage door opened before driving inside. She waited for the door to fully shut, and only then climbed out of her car.

She unlocked the kitchen door and laid her hand on the bio-metric panel that deactivated the home alarm system. The network of red infrared sensor beams went off, and regular lights illuminated throughout the house.

She went over to the kitchen island and dumped everything out of her pee-stained, bullet-riddled purse. Lipstick, spare ammo mag, perfume roller, fountain pen filled with a fast-acting neuro-paralytic, powder compact, a wire garrote carefully wrapped around its rubber handles, and crumpled dry cleaning and grocery receipts that went every which way.

Opening a kitchen drawer, she pulled out a 9mm Glock 43X she kept there in case of emergency. Chambering a round, she carried it and the ruined purse outside. A quick sweep around the yard over the end of her weapon's barrel, and she laid her purse tenderly in the covered trash can behind the garage.

"Rest in peace, you beautiful girl," she murmured over her purse's corpse.

The wooded hillside behind the house was silent and still tonight, but she gave it another long, hard look anyway.

The shooters had attacked her family. They'd had no way of knowing Peter and Li would be out tonight. Outrage literally stole her breath away. *How dare they?*

The quid pro quo was ironclad: *You don't mess with my loved ones, I don't mess with yours.*

She almost wished someone would move on that hillside. Give her a reason to go hunting and kill whoever'd wrecked her son's beautiful new home and almost offed her.

A puff of wind stirred the cold air, and the trees waved at her eerily as her hair lifted from her neck. She lurched into motion and headed back inside the rambling, two-story farmhouse where she and Grayson had raised their family. It reminded her of a well-worn sofa, overdue for new upholstery or a trip to the dump, but it was comfortable, and it was home.

Her knees felt weak all of a sudden, and her hands shook as the aftermath rolled over her, flattening her in its wake. She was too old for this crap. Moreover, she was supposed to be finished with all of it.

She was just starting to set aside the constant tension, the cautionary room searches, the roving gaze, the twitchy reflexes. But here it all was, roaring back, ripping away the gauze of normalcy with which she'd bandaged her tired soul, exposing the raw nerves of a killer once more.

One last double check of the twin deadbolts in the steel reinforced door with its impact-resistant glass, and she was safe. At least as safe as she could make this place without turning it into a straight-up fortress.

Good grief, she didn't want to play this game anymore.

She folded her arms on the cold granite counter and buried her face in them. For just an instant, she gave in to despair. It was a luxury she hadn't afforded herself these past twenty years and more. It felt good to let go of all the discipline, all the tension, all the constant vigilance. Maybe she should just hang it up. Let whatever might come her way, come.

As soon as she gave in, even for an instant, she knew the indulgence for the mistake it was. Right now, her focus had to be on surviving. Not just for herself, but for her family. She had to figure out who'd tried to have her killed and take them out. Only then would her family be safe. Maybe then she could finally rest.

Of course, she knew what Yosef would say. She could rest when she was dead.

Tonight had been a close call.

She allowed that knowledge to pass through her. Became one with it. She'd gotten separated from her firearm. She'd left curtains open, lights on—made a stupidly easy target of herself. Worst of all, she'd gotten complacent. Let herself be distracted by her family. Heck, she'd allowed emotions in.

Brick by brick, she rebuilt the emotional wall around herself that she'd been working so hard to tear down. She locked away the budding feelings, put away her hopes for restoring her marriage and relationships with her kids.

Maybe someday, she silently promised her husband and children. But not yet.

First, sleep. Then a serious conversation with her former CIA handler. He had better come up with the names of those assailants, and fast. She was not on the company payroll anymore, and she had no compunction about going on her own to mete out a little jungle justice.

She needed to know who'd ordered the attack on her. And why. What did he or she want? What would make them go away? Could a settlement be negotiated, or was this going down old-school—spy on spy, assassin on assassin, until there was only one man—or woman—left standing?

She shoved all the stuff from her purse into a plastic grocery bag. Plucking the spare ammo clip from the detritus of her attempt at normal life, she limped to the stairs. It felt as if the bottoms of her feet were cut up from running around barefoot on the shards of glass and splintered wood littering Peter and Li's house. Muscles all over her body were sore from the violent activity, and her upper arm was hurting again. A medic at the scene had insisted on taking a look at it, and even bandaged it, but she'd lied through her teeth when he'd asked her if it hurt.

She checked the security panel by the front door one last time—*Hello, paranoia, my old friend. I've come to talk with you again*—and trudged upstairs in her ruined stockings, bloody bootlets dangling from her left hand, pistol dangling from her right.

Into the master bedroom. Solid wood door locked. Steel painted to look like wood plantation shutters closed. She exhaled in relief as her cocoon of safety locked down around her. She wouldn't let down her guard tonight, not entirely, not scant hours after someone had tried to kill her in the most emphatic possible way. But she could breathe in here.

Stripping off the ruined sweater, she dropped it on the floor. Slacks, unzipped. She shimmied out of them and left them where they lay. Tomorrow was soon enough to throw out the bloody garments. The shredded stockings went in the trash with a certain satisfaction, and, standing in her underwear, she stared at herself in the mirror.

Her body showed the wear of bearing three children and fifty-five years of life, much of it lived on the edge of danger. Some sun

damage around her throat and on her arms, a few wrinkles creeping in around her eyes and mouth. Gravity was having its due
here and there in the form of loose skin, but she was still lean and
hard underneath. And she wasn't dead—yet—by God.

Her bun had given up the ghost at her first dive for cover, and
her hair straggled around her face. Once naturally blond, she'd
faded to a dishwater color somewhere between blond, brown,
and gray. Which meant she got peroxide help now from a hair-
dresser in northwest DC. She'd been looking forward to growing
it out ever since she'd cut it all off twenty years ago. In her line of
work, she couldn't afford to have it get in her eyes at exactly the
wrong moment. A mistake like that could get her killed. But even
growing out her hair would have to wait, apparently.

Craning her chin to the left, she peeled back the bandage from
her arm.

The bloody stripe where the bullet had creased her was covered with a clear salve that had numbed the skin along with providing antibacterial coverage. The cut was more of a scoop than a
slice, the length of her finger and shallow. Darn it, she'd been so
looking forward to being a sissy in her old age and not having to
deal with wounds like this.

She replaced the large, square bandage over the wound. It
would scab over and heal soon enough. Probably would leave a
scar, but it wasn't like she didn't have any of those. She took note
of the thin one on her side where she'd nearly been gutted a
decade back. Without seeing it, she knew there was a round bullet
scar under her right shoulder blade, and various small nicks and
marks from other close calls over the years.

She called them her teachable moments. Each scar held a valuable lesson for her. And so would this one: Never let down her
guard. Ever.

As she headed for the bedroom, ominous little aches announced
themselves in her hamstrings and back, and both shoulders already pained her. She wasn't cut out for tonight's gymnastics anymore and was definitely feeling her age. She winced in dread of
tomorrow's stiffness.

She took one of Grayson's big T-shirts out of his drawer, pulled it over her head, and crawled into their cold, empty bed. She reached for his pillow and hugged it close. Almost all the smell of his aftershave had faded from it. Would it be weird to buy a bottle of it and dump it on his pillow?

He was somewhere in the Amazon jungle right now, crawling around on his hands and knees, looking for a new species of poison dart frog he'd gotten a lead on. Knowing him, he was as happy as a pig in mud. He loved his work as a naturalist fully as much as she'd loved hers. Past tense, damn it.

She lay in the dark, staring up at the ceiling, replaying the events of the evening in excruciating detail, analyzing and parsing her performance, which, on the whole, had been pitiful.

No doubt about it. She was out of practice.

At the end of the day, she faced a cold choice. She could roll over passively and wait for the next attack to finish her off. Or, she could pick her sorry derriere up off the ground and fight back.

As much as she hated what she had to do, it wasn't much of a choice. If nothing else, she needed to stay alive if she was ever going to make up to her family for the past two decades.

Her gaze narrowed in the dark. Somebody was going to pay for making Gray and the kids wait. That, and they'd scared her grand-dog half to death.